To: George [...] [...]ville Good luck wi[...] [...]dard! It [...] see you again after all thes[...] [...]! [signature] Anderson

THE CZECH FILES

Ryan Anderson

ISBN: 978-1-4303-1201-7

I dedicate this novel to my parents. Miles away, you are right beside me. Daddy….keep writing.

Everything in life, in everyone's life, happens for a reason. Think about it. Take the most profound moment in your life, and then look at what brought you to it, and also what all it set into motion...

CHAPTER ONE

As quietly as she possibly could, Anna held her breath and stepped over the bodies of her mother, father and her two younger brothers, towards the small ray of light shining in from the bottom of the bloody door. She hadn't heard any movements or voices for a long time, and desperately hoped that they had left her for dead. When she had woken on the floor an hour ago, she panicked and ripped the rope from her neck, flinging it on the floor, without thinking about the noise her actions would make. Her throat had been numb, but now, as she slowly limped toward the small light, she tried hard not to sob out loud. The burning in her throat made it impossible to swallow, and the burning between her legs made it difficult to walk. Her body was covered in blood, and her clothes had been ripped and cut open, leaving nothing covered.

She knew that she had been raped and strangled in front of her brothers, just like her mother had been; and she knew that her brothers had been shot, just like her father had been. Although the details were a little hazy of how the events had taken place before the attack and slaughter of her family, Anna remembered most of what happened. She remembered waking up in her canopy bed, hearing a loud crash downstairs, listening to her mother scream, and being dragged by the hair into her parents' bedroom by a man with a beard. The first thing they did after her entire family had been assembled in the room was shoot her father in the face. In her horror and shock, she had tried to cover her brothers' eyes and her own when the men began ripping the clothes off of her screaming mother. She only got to hold her brothers for a second before the bearded man had shaken her loose and repeated the same assault on her body as his partner was inflicting upon her mother. The rope had been tight and unmerciful, and Anna could do nothing but cry, bleed, choke, and die. But she had woken up. She hadn't died. Now, alone in the dark, in shock, and in searing pain, Anna went to the light.

She wasn't thinking about what she would do when she got to the door. In fact, nothing was entering her mind at all. It was her animal instinct approach to freedom. Light meant salvation. It meant something good. It meant exit. It meant the way. She didn't even realize that she was singing. The door wasn't heavy, but it seemed to Anna that it weighed fifty pounds. When she leaned on it to push it open, she fell hard onto the hallway floor, banging her head on the wall. In shock, she lay with her back against the floor and bathed her face in the light of the hallway for about ten minutes before she remembered what she had set out to do. The phone was in the living room, only two doors down. Still singing, the child rolled over to her stomach and raised herself on all fours, and slowly crawled across the carpet towards the living room. The pain held her back from rushing, making each movement slow and deliberate. A couple of times along the way, Anna stopped to catch her breath, still unaware that she was singing, resuming her song each time she started to crawl again. By the time she reached the doorway to the room that held the phone, her body gave out and she could no longer control her legs anymore. Urine seeped from her wounded vagina, and she lay in it unknowingly for quite sometime.

Finally, she gathered enough strength to pull on the phone cord until the receiver was in her hand, and with tiny bloody fingers she pressed the three familiar numbers that all children are taught from birth. She sang her song to the dispatcher, unaware of the questions she was being asked, until she had no more energy left. Then as all pain gave away to numbness, darkness took over, and Anna slipped into a deep sleep.

CHAPTER TWO

God damn it, the phone. Third ring. Fourth ring. *I am not answering that stupid phone*. Fifth ring.

"Hello?" He said quickly to the caller, trying to beat the answering machine. "Hi, you've reached Hank Jor--" Hank shot his other arm out to turn off the answering machine, knocking off the scotch and water that he didn't finish from the night before, found the button with his balled up fist and Bam! "Hello???"

"Hey, Hank, sorry, it's me, Hill…"

"*I know!* Hold on a minute." Hank sat all the way up, swung his legs out of bed and slammed them to the floor. He threw the phone onto the pillow and stomped into the bathroom in search for a towel to clean his spilled drink. The wet stain from the scotch looked like urine on the white carpet, and Hank cussed all the way back into the bedroom. After throwing the towel down over the soaked spot and stepping on it a little bit, Hank grabbed the phone from the pillow, sucked in a long breath and said, "Hillary, sorry, I was asleep, and when I answered the phone, the answering machine came on, and well, I tried to turn it off, and shit, whatever. It's 3:30 in the morning. What's going on? Something bad?"

"Yeah, it's pretty bad, Hank. And I don't think you would have appreciated it very much if I had called someone else, even if you *are* off tomorrow! I can hang up right now if you want and call Ja--"

"Cut the bullshit, Hillary. What happened?"

"Sorry, Hank. It's just that, well, it's as bad as it gets. Multiple homicide, 5 victims, 2 adults, 3 children."

"You gotta be kidding me!" Silence. "Hill, tell me it didn't happen here. Please tell me that Foley or Mobile PD called and requested extra men."

"Nope, unfortunately, it happened right down the road from you, at 313 Park Drive in Orange Beach."

"Oh my God! I'll be there in 15 minutes." Click. Hank threw the phone back down on the pillow and raced to the bathroom again. He plunged his face into the sink and splashed himself with cold water and soap. The razor fell into the sink, and when he hurriedly grabbed it, the blade sliced his finger open, causing him to curse until soap seeped into his open mouth. This day, as early as it could be started, was not going well. He spat the soap out, drank some tap water, dressed himself, grabbed his gun and badge and ran out of the door towards his car. By the time he reached Snapper's Lounge, one block from Park Drive, all hell had broken loose. There were lights everywhere, sirens screaming, and neighbors running around trying to see inside the house to confirm the rumors of what had happened. The house had already been taped off, and several policemen were standing around trying to keep the peace with themselves and with the crowd. The anxious looks on their faces spoke volumes to Hank as he pulled up to the scene. Nothing had ever happened like this in his little town, and obviously not wherever the other officers were originally from either. Searching the crowd he spotted Hillary. She was standing by the mailbox with one hand over her eyes and the other across her belly. She looked up at Hank and motioned him over as he began walking towards the house. Hank put a hand on Hillary's back.

"You ok?" he asked. Hillary looked as if she had seen a ghost.

"No, probably not. Neither will you be when you see what has happened in there."

Hank sighed and stared at the house. "Well, prep me before we walk in."

"Its not going to take away the shock, but I will. Like I said, two adults and two children DOA, and another child victim getting ready to be taken out. It's a little girl. She made the 911 call. She was raped and strangled, but lived." She paused for a moment to suck in a breath. "What has God wrought on this island? Nothing like this should happen anywhere, especially not here. Orange Beach is just too good for this. Hank, it's a bloody mess in there."

"Well, you ready to go back in? If you're not, that's fine. I will come back to get you in a few." Hank had never seen Hillary shaken up like this before.

Hillary shook her head and straightened up. "No, I am fine. Let's go, but I am telling you, prepare yourself."

They walked toward the front porch steps, stepped over the smeared blood and entered the front door together. Several policemen stood just inside the entrance talking to each other about what had happened, grumbling in their redneck ways.

"By God, that son of a bitch is gonna pay for this shit!" one blasted.

"I'm gon' tell you that piece a shit is gonna get what's comin' to him," another grumbled.

Detective Hank Jordan kindly asked them to exit and keep watch over the front porch to make sure no one got a peek inside. They did what they were told, feeling important and big, with chests bowed out and arms flexed. Orange Beach PD has good cops, but when something big happens, it turns most of them a deeper shade of red than normal. This isn't always necessarily a bad thing, especially when you are in the South. When people become a 'deeper shade of red', it usually means that problems are fixed quicker, crimes are solved faster. People are more focused, angrier, but also more determined to resolve the situation, as long as Jack Daniels, Jim Beam and their buddy Jose don't lend helping hands. Then things tend to get a little messy down in Margaritaville. That's why Hank preferred scotch, and for the most part, didn't mess around with the other three.

Hillary pointed the way to the stairs, and up they walked, following the voices ahead and struggling to steer clear of the blood on the hand rails, even though it was everywhere. They walked down the hallway and passed a living room on the left which now housed all the people assigned to Anna; they were tucking her away on a stretcher that was headed for the local hospital in Foley, the nearest city across the bridges to the mainland of Alabama. The second door down was the target destination, Hank assumed, from all of the blood on the doors and carpet, and the guarding officer perched at the entrance. He assumed correctly, as Hillary stood to the right to let him pass through what looked like to Hank, the gates of hell. The bodies had not been moved yet, or even covered, as the medical examiner and investigators were still collecting evidence. The young boys' mouths were gaping open, as if to spit out the rest of the brain matter that wasn't already blown out the backs of their tiny heads. The top parts of their heads were gone, splattered all over the floor and walls around them, as was their father, who was slumped, face down behind them. The mother's body was still on the bed, naked and strangled by the rope wound

5

around her neck. The killer had choked her with so much force that her neck had broken; the rope had cut deep into her skin, almost decapitating her. Her legs were splayed open in unnatural positions, only possible from the dead, with blood covering her thighs and what was left of her vagina.

Looking at the boys was horrible, but bearable, because they didn't look human anymore, and the father lay face was down, so that wasn't intolerable either. But Hank felt bile rise from his stomach to his throat the instant he laid eyes on the female victim. He immediately averted his face and shut his eyes, breathing deeply so he could manage to swallow the vomit that so desperately wanted out of his stomach. He had never seen anything like this, except in pictures, nor had anyone else in the room. Yes, there had been rape victims, and murder victims, but never ones that left behind the cruel and evil scenery as he was witnessing tonight. He let the nausea pass and allowed the sorrow and heartache to wash over him as he continued to close his eyes. It gripped him with severe force as he struggled with emotions he had never felt before; Hank knew the victims. Before now, he hadn't realized that they lived here, but now he knew. He went to Church with this family. He had graduated from Foley High School with the dead parents before there was even a school on the island. John, Tammy, Anna, and the twins Jeremy and Jacob; they were the Morrisons. Hank took a moment to think of them, and then followed Hillary back downstairs to ask questions. Hank was born and raised in Orange Beach, Alabama, which he now felt, as he stood in the Morrison's house, was being cast down into the pits of hell right along with places like Bourbon Street and the dark alleys of New York. He knew one thing and one thing only. No redneck from Orange Beach, no matter how bad, had done this kind of work; that he was sure of. Someone had been extremely pissed off, committing crimes to the Morrisons that Southern folk from his neck of the woods just weren't capable of doing. He kept his thoughts to himself for the moment and began taking notes.

CHAPTER THREE

Orange Beach, Alabama had always been a safe place to live, and a safe place to raise children. Many of the houses on the island were never locked. Keys were left in cars parked in driveways with the windows rolled down. Security systems weren't a popular installation with many of the permanent residents because it was considered an unnecessary bill each month. Things were just so easy and peaceful, even during the tourist season. The majority of the residents live on the bay side, while tourists vacation on the gulf side.

The Gulf Coast is to some, a heaven on Earth vacation spot, with its sugar white sands and blue waters, excellent salt water fishing, and golf courses that will take your breath away. It is to others, the Redneck Riviera, a place where you can hang out in bars on the beach and get drunk listening to Jimmy Buffett over and over and over again. Still to some, it is simply home. Off the coast of Alabama, there is a 32 mile long island that hosts 2 different towns: Gulf Shores, permanent resident population 5,044 and Orange Beach, permanent resident population 3,784. During the tourist season the island hosts anywhere from 300,000 to 400,000 beachgoers each year. This is when all the money is made on the island. The golf courses are packed, the restaurants are filled, the beaches are swamped with families, and the fishing charters are booked solid. Its popularity as a vacation spot has steadily grown over the years at a healthy pace, creating more and more jobs. There is a large population of immigrants from Brazil, Czech Republic and Mexico, who come over to work in the condos and restaurants during the busy season. These immigrants, mostly Czech, are able to make more money from one summer season on the island, than they are able to make in five years in their homelands.

The island connects to both Alabama's and Florida's mainland with only three bridges, one being a toll bridge. This made it extremely difficult for the hurricane clean up process in 2004 after Hurricane Ivan ripped though Haiti, skirted around Jamaica, and finally bulldozed into the Gulf Coast, with the eye passing right over Gulf Shores. Orange Beach and Gulf Shores were ripped apart by the winds and drowned by the water and waves. The clean up process is still unfinished; the effects of the hurricane are still very visible in some of the condos waiting to be torn down and rebuilt ten stories higher and twenty times tackier. Gone are the days where the ocean is visible for long stretches of the road. Gone are the days when college students preferred 'not' to come here for Spring Break because of the 'family atmosphere'. Goodbye easy going Orange Beach; hello, greedy loudmouthed politicians waiting to line their pockets. Hello to the real estate machines who demolish the quaint old summer houses on stilts and build in their places high rise condominiums that block out the view of the beach in their places.

To some, Hurricane Ivan was the Devil. To others, it is considered Saint Ivan, bringing along a serious rise in property value, high insurance pay outs and more construction jobs. To residents like Hank Jordan, Ivan was devastating because of the damage of what the reconstruction will ultimately bring to the island itself, eventually turning it into a tourist trap labeled 'the next Panama City'. But, on the other hand, residents also knew that no one, no matter what would be rebuilt to replace what was damaged, could ever take away the smell of the salty air, the feel of that soft sand through your toes, or the thrill of a big Spanish mackerel running away with your line on the end of the state pier. So, as difficult as it always is after a hurricane, people, still happy to be one of the 3,784 permanent residents of Orange Beach, had carried on, cleaned up the mess and rebuilt their homes on their safe little island.

Overnight, the murder of the Morrison family turned this safe little town upside down and inside out, transforming it into a place where evil things can happen, a concept none of the residents had ever known before. An act of God was one thing; hurricanes, floods, fires... but this wasn't like that at all and the residents were not prepared for it. Something evil had blown through Orange Beach, down Park Drive, and into the house numbered 313. Orange Beach, Alabama, would never be the same.

Straight out of high school, John Morrison had followed his father's footsteps and gone into the real estate business, which was booming now more than ever on the island because of Hurricane Ivan. He had gotten his license, worked for his father's firm, and then, after a couple of years, began buying and selling property on the side. Three years after graduation John had married Tammy, his high school sweetheart, who Hank had always had a crush on in school. Tammy then quit her job as a waitress at Doc's Seafood and talked her husband into renting some of his properties instead of selling all of them. They currently owned thirty rental units on the island, and Tammy handled all of them by herself, while John stayed in the real estate business with his father. Most of the properties were small, one and two bedrooms; the majority of them were rented to immigrants who worked on the island. She never had many problems with collecting rent payments. Occasionally, one of her Mexican tenants would pay late, but always in full. Usually, when this happened, a sealed envelope containing a money order or cash, because they usually didn't have a checking account, would arrive on her doorstep along with some Mexican food of some sort as an 'apology/thank you for understanding' gift. In addition to renting to Mexican immigrants, Tammy had also rented property to a large number of workers brought in from the Czech Republic and Brazil. Their rent money almost always came very controlled and always on time in the form of a business check from the companies that outsourced them. Business had been good, and Tammy had always been a fair and understanding landlord.

Anna and the twins had attended Orange Beach schools, which were in walking distance from their house only a short two blocks away, and they had, in fact, walked to school; many of the children walked to school on this island because it was safe. After they walked home from school, they were allowed to play outside unattended for the remainder of the day, building forts, playing house, riding bikes, or whatever else their imagination had allowed them to do.

Like many other families in Orange Beach, life had been perfect for John, Tammy, Anna and the twins, even after Hurricane Ivan. Not anymore. The sleepy little fishing village and summer vacation destination of Orange Beach, Alabama, had lost its innocence.

CHAPTER FOUR

Fortunately, Suzanna woke up to an empty bed at 9:30 am. Today was her off day, and she decided that some sun at the beach would do some good healthy repair work on the dark circled bags that continued to grow underneath her eyes. She had tried Mary Kay's products from her neighbor Amy, using them exactly how she was shown at the "makeover" last week, but the circles were still there, causing her to look 10 years older, in spite of her youthful appearance. Usually when young women have dark bags under their eyes, it is generally caused from stress or lack of sleep. However, Suzanna slept well, ate well, and her job was just about as stress and worry-free as they come. She worked in a little hut on the beach, selling vacation trinkets and souvenirs, like funky sunglasses and brightly colored towels, to tourists. The only work related stress she had to endure was during Spring Break when all of the families from Louisiana, mostly the New Orleans/Metairie area showed up; they were always loud and obnoxious and always demanding discounts. She made good money, paid her bills on time, and got a great tan in the process. The season was almost over, and things were winding down, allowing her to work four days a week instead of six.

No, the stress wasn't from a career source. It was from her dead beat Czech husband; he was the reason for the ugly bags under her eyes. No one really knew the extent of the physical and emotional abuse that she lived with. Suzanna would rather suffer in silence than to admit to someone else her mistake in choosing a mate for life. The very idea of divorce made her sick to her stomach; especially after all she had done for him. It made her feel like a failure in marriage. So, instead of reaching out to someone for help, she allowed him to control her life and abuse her on a daily basis.

In 1998 she started working as a waitress at a local beach bar. She was the only one of ten employees who spoke fluent English. The rest were from various different countries, mostly the Czech Republic.

They did all the dirty work that no one else wanted to do. They shucked oysters, prepped the restaurant in the morning, cleaned up vomit in the bathrooms from the drunks the night before, and anything else the managers barked at them to do. They were, for the most part, abused in their work environments, but didn't really care. It was the first time in their lives that they were actually able to make any kind of money. They didn't know or care about worker's compensation, or employee's rights. They just showed up for work always on time in their companies' vans, clocked in, worked their fingers to the bone, clocked out, and either went to their local hangout or someone's apartment from their homeland and drank unheard of liquor for the rest of the night. They occasionally got out of hand in bars, even though the ones who had been here the longest watched out for the new ones, stopping them from fighting and giving them rides home. Everyone on the island knew, except for Suzanna at the time, that liquor made Czechs fight. Liquor made the Brazilians dance. Liquor made the Mexicans sleepy.

The worst trait of Suzanna's personality was that she always saw, or tried to see, the good in everyone else. She ignored the bad, and believed that she could always change someone by helping them. Her personality was one of a caregiver. She needed to take care of people in order to feel good about herself; therefore, someone in need was always a project for her. After working at the restaurant for a couple of weeks, she decided that every Czech that she worked with was her new project. She picked up bits and pieces of their language and started teaching them English, holding classes in her apartment a couple of days a week. That's when she met her husband, Yuraslav. She never liked his name, and always called him Yuri instead. He had been different from the rest, very shy, always so appreciative, and willing to learn and practice English all the time. He dove into the language head first, and within weeks, could carry on a comprehensible conversation with anyone.

One day, soon after they had met, Yuraslav told her about his living situation, where ten people were made to live in a two bedroom house. He also told her about the company who brought him to the United States and about the abuse that the Czechs had to endure from them. He complained just enough to make Suzanna pity him. She offered her apartment to him in exchange for a small amount of rent, and to personally find him a cash paying job so he could cut his ties to the company. Thus, they became roommates, friends, lovers, and he asked her to marry him by Christmas, the following year. She said yes, believing that she truly loved him, and that he loved her.

Suzanna had met several men and women who lived on the island, who had married someone from Czech Republic or Brazil, and they were still waiting for interview time slots at the immigration office in Atlanta, and they were all light years, it seemed, from obtaining green cards. So, Yuri and Suzanna decided to get married in his homeland, to speed up the immigration process. Any U.S. Embassy has the same powers of any immigration office in the United States, which were bogged down indefinitely with too much paperwork to process anything quickly. So, it was decided to be much easier to get married in Prague and file all the necessary paperwork at the US Embassy there. Suzanna sold her car, saved money, quit her job and moved to Prague with Yuri for a year. It was the worst and best year of her life. She had lived in a small town in Alabama all of her life and known no one who had gone to Europe, not to mention anyone who had actually lived there; she jumped at the chance for change. Prague had been beautiful and full of opportunity for her, especially since she spoke English. Soon after they moved there, she accumulated over a hundred students whom she taught English too, and she learned the Czech language well enough to land a couple of translation jobs here and there. The money and experience had been outstanding.

However, as soon as the marriage vows were exchanged, the ownership took place and the beatings began. Yuri became the dog who bites the hand that feeds him. He became physically and emotionally abusive overnight and the abrupt change in his personality and behavior left Suzanna actually wondering if it had been her fault; maybe she had caused him to transform into the worst husband anyone could ever have. Embarrassment and shame made it impossible for her to tell anyone what was going on between them, so she kept her mouth shut and just lived with it.

Now, years later, as she got out of bed, she pushed her husband from her mind and focused on what she would do with her day off; from her limited options, hanging out on the beach was the best idea. As soon as Suzanna had stripped from her clothes to take a shower, her cell phone began ringing in the living room of her small apartment.

She grabbed a towel and ran to the table, flipping the phone open. The caller id read 'Mom'.

"Hey, Mom." All she heard was crying. Mom! *What's wrong?*"

"Suzanna, oh my God, I am glad you are awake," she said between sobs. "Have you heard the news?" Her mom had the same tone of voice that she did when she had called to wake Suzanna to watch the terrorist events of 9-11 unfold live on the news; Suzanna's heart raced with fear that something really bad had happened.

"Are you ok, Mom? What happened?"

"The Morrisons, the ones Julie baby-sits for, they were murdered last night and…"

"*What?* Mom, hold on..." Suzanna ran to the bathroom, cut the shower off and ran back to the table, dropping the too tiny phone before she could make its way back to her ear. "I'm back, Mom. What in the world are you talking about? Who was murdered?"

"The Morrison's, the ones…"

"Yeah I got that much, but are you serious? Murdered? Why? How?"

"I don't know everything about it yet, I just know they were murdered and that Tammy was raped…" she trailed off from the heavy sobs that wracked her being. A moment later she continued, "…and so was little Anna. Julie is devastated and, oh my God, Suzanna, I have never heard of anything like this before except on television. She was scheduled to baby-sit for them tonight! The phone call came from one of her friends this morning while she was getting ready for school."

Julie, Suzanna's younger sister, had babysat for the Morrison's for five years, since the twins' birth. Suzanna couldn't say anything; she was shocked. Why in the hell would anyone do something like this? "Mom, calm down. This is horrible, but I can't make out everything you are saying. Mom…"

"Suzanna, let me call you back, someone is beeping in…." Click.

She stood there, not knowing what to feel. She wasn't emotionally attached to the Morrisons, like Julie and her mom were. Yes, she knew who they were; everyone on the island either knew everyone else personally or knew who they were. She had met them on several occasions, out in bars or restaurants, and the couple of times when she had dropped Julie off to baby-sit. She didn't cry for them, but she felt something in the pit of her stomach that made her sick. Someone raped

13

and murdered a whole family? And here? In Orange Beach? She thought about calling Yuri at work and telling him the bad news, but why? She didn't want to talk to him, and besides, he wouldn't care anyway. She started to get in the shower, but stopped and picked up the phone and decided to call him anyway. She figured that if she didn't call him, he would be angry at her later when he found out from someone else. The phone rang twice and was picked up by the maid service's secretary, who was also Czech. Yuri cleaned condos for a living.

"Top Notch Cleaning, how can I help you?"

"Hey Svetla, its Suzanna. Can you page Yuri for me and have him call me back?" Employees of Top Notch were not allowed to carry their cell phones with them on a cleaning job.

"He didn't come to work dis morning, Susanna, and you can tell him dat Mister Tim said he cannot come back here for da work any-more. His check for pay is going in to the mail today." Svetla rudely hung up the phone without saying goodbye. Six months prior she had married a local Gulf Shores man and soon after, like most of the Czech immigrants who had married islanders, she had adopted a snooty atti-tude.

Yuri had not shown up for work a couple of times over the past two months. He had stayed out late drinking with his friends, usually pass-ing out at one of their apartments. Suzanna had started locking the doors when he did this so he couldn't come in and beat on her when he was drunk. Last month was the last time she had locked the door after he broke into the apartment and did it anyway, at four o'clock in the morning. The most hurtful part about the abuse to Suzanna was not the fact that he beat her, but that he did it where it wouldn't bruise, so that no one would know. He never hit her face, apart from the one time when she lived with him in Prague. It hadn't mattered then because there was no one over there to see the black eye or care. At the time, she had contemplated going to the Embassy, but thought better of it. From her experience there, she learned enough about it to know that it's not a refuge like in the movies. She had been scared of what Yuri would do to her anyway, and left it alone. Bruises go away.

Yuri had not come home last night, and Suzanna had not made the mistake of locking the door either. She figured that if he wanted in, he would find a way, and either pass out on the couch or crawl into bed while she was asleep. With the season coming to an end, his job loss wasn't that big of a blow; most of their money had already been made for the year. However, it didn't make her feel good either. She put the phone down, rolled her eyes in disgust, and walked back into the bathroom to take her shower. She would have sat down and turned on the local news, which broadcasts from Mobile, Alabama, but she figured that what had happened to the Morrison's wouldn't be very detailed, due to the fact that it happened on the island. Not that a lot of bad things happen on the island, but the bad things that do happen don't often make big news time. The politicians are always so successful with tucking away problems or downsizing crimes that happen in or near the island, so that the tourists who feed it every year don't stop vacationing.

Suzanna stepped into the hot shower, and thought about all of the places Yuraslav could be. The more she thought about him, the less nauseating the idea of divorce became. If she could just muster up enough guts to tell her family what he had been doing to her over the years they had been married, then surely, she thought, she could go someplace, hide from him for a while, and then file for a divorce. Or maybe, she thought, she could just call the Immigration and Naturalization Service, INS, and complain. The whole idea of being married to him just depressed her. Yuraslav was bad enough to make anyone have dark circles under their eyes.

CHAPTER FIVE

All morning long, little Anna floated in and out of consciousness in her hospital bed. Her pediatrician, Dr. Judith Esther, had either canceled her appointments for the day or had given them to other colleagues. She had examined and treated Anna throughout the morning and now sat beside her bed waiting for her to wake up. Besides being the Morrison's pediatrician, Judith and Anna's mother Tammy had been very good friends for the last five years. She had treated several cases of the flu, a broken arm from one of the twins, Anna's tonsillectomy and various other ailments that befell the children over the years.

Tearing up until she couldn't keep it in for another minute, Judith had cried for most of the morning, letting the sorrow that she felt for her friend roll out of her uncontrollably until she was able to catch her breath again. In any other town, she would have been dismissed from the case immediately, but people who knew her knew that crying and becoming emotionally attached to her patients didn't hinder her professional judgment; it only made her stronger and wiser of a person and of a doctor who made a living taking care of sick children. Being a pediatrician can be a very difficult and emotionally straining job at times; there is nothing worse than being surrounded by sick children, especially when there is nothing you can really do to help them. However, over the years, Judith had mastered the ability to separate her emotions well enough to get the job done.

Judith had moved to Gulf Shores six years prior from North Myrtle Beach, South Carolina, where she grew up. After practicing there for several years, she decided to move somewhere new and smaller, but somewhere that had the same laid back beach atmosphere as her home, so she looked into the Gulf Coast. She found Gulf Shores, moved, and successfully opened her practice within two months of her move. She had met Tammy Morrison one year later when the twins were brought in for a checkup. An immediate friendship blossomed, and they had become instant friends. For the past year, she and Tammy had met for

16

drinks once a month on Wednesday night, ladies night, at the Flora-Bama Lounge. Just like its name states, the FloraBama lounge is located right on the border of Florida and Alabama, and it is, by all accounts, a honky tonk, but one of the best bars in the whole world. They would meet there, sometimes with other friends as well, have a drink or two, and listen to bands pipe out the tunes from the Almond Brothers or various country songs that are fun and depressing at the same time.

Now, Judith sat by Anna's bed and thought of the last time that she and Tammy had met there which was only two weeks ago. She remembered that Tammy had been in great spirits because she had just accepted a year's contract on ten different properties that had gone without renters for almost a year. The properties had been vacation rentals in the past, but in light of the hurricane, Tammy had finally switched them to permanent leases. She had been relieved because the renters were individual Czechs and a company who outsourced Czech workers; they were notorious for being good renters, always on time, and respectful of property. The kids had all been doing great, and her husband John was making a killing with his father from the effects of the storm the year before. Companies were lined up left and right to buy properties from people who had had enough of hurricanes for one lifetime, and John and Tammy Morrison were raking in the cash. Judith remembered how she had marveled at how property values on the island shot up after the hurricane, and that people were practically buying and selling property sight unseen over the phone. According to Tammy, life had been great for the Morrisons, and she and Judith had parted ways after drinking their free drink. Judith had driven away from the FloraBama Lounge that night feeling a small dose of healthy envy of her friend's good fortune in life. She remembered thinking on the way home that night, *One day...I will have a loving husband and children, too.*

As she sat in the hospital room thinking about the last time she saw Tammy, she heard something that brought her back to reality. It was Anna. She wasn't exactly awake, but she was humming a song, pieces of it anyway. Judith couldn't make out the song, so she just sat and listened, waiting for her to wake up. She raised her hand and stroked Anna's hair, until the child stopped humming and fell back into whatever dark abyss the men who had wrecked her little body had thrown her into last night. Not wanting to disturb her, Judith quietly slipped out of the room to return a phone call to Detective Hank Jordan. He had phoned earlier that morning and left a message for her to call him as soon as the child woke up. She hadn't woke up yet, but Judith decided to call and tell him what they were able to find out by examining Anna's body, and to discuss the series of events that took place last night.

CHAPTER SIX

Detective Hank Jordan sat back in the chair so hard that it whined and creaked as if ready to splinter into a million pieces. He rubbed his eyes with vigor that to some people it might seem as if he was trying to rub his eyeballs right out of his head. His eyes did hurt from lack of sleep, but on a subconscious level, he was, in fact, trying to rub what he had seen at the Morrison house right out of his head. He continued to rub, thinking over every detail of the crime scene, trying to put together some sort of assembly to the horror and chaos of what had happened. The atrocities that had occurred in that family's home were almost incomprehensible. Hank wondered why anyone would want them dead, especially with such levels of malice and cruelty. He looked down at the crime scene photos that Hillary had spread out all over his desk, searching for any clues that would give him a lead. The gruesome displays of the children's corpses stared back at him like lost souls waiting to be avenged, when his cell phone rang. He didn't recognize the number on the caller id screen. "Detective Jordan here."

"Hi Detective, this is Doctor Judith Esther. I am returning your call from earlier this morning to discuss Anna Morrison's case."

Hank shot straight up in the chair, completely focused on what he was about to hear. "Yes, thank you Dr. Esther. Did she wake up?"

"No, not yet. I know your message said to call you when she woke up, but I wanted to discuss her examination with you."

"Alright. Go ahead." Hank reached over his desk and picked up a pen, ready to take notes.

"As you know from talking with the medical examiner, she was vaginally raped and strangled with a rope. There was semen found inside her as well as some sort of peach liquor. They have not finished with the tests as of yet to establish DNA but..."

"Yeah, I'm waitin' on them too. They found so many finger prints, hair samples under the mother's and daughter's fingernails, well, it's a mess, and..."

Judith cringed at hearing that, although she had already been told. "You can address them by their first names with me if you want. I would appreciate that. Tammy was one of my best friends. In fact, we met for a drink only two weeks ago. She had been so excited about her recent lease agreements with new Czech tenants. Anyway, you don't have to start sparing any details; I can handle it." She paused briefly. "I guess what I am trying to say is that you don't have to sugar coat it now that you know I was close to them."

"Ok, I won't." Hank didn't want to carry on this conversation over the phone. He had always been a face to face kind of man. He glanced up at the clock on the wall to check the time. "Uh, I tell you what, Doctor Esther, let's meet for lunch and discuss this. If you were good friends with Tammy, I would like to meet you face to face and ask you a couple of questions. Do you have a time?"

"That's fine, but you will have to come to the hospital cafeteria because there is no way I am leaving until she wakes up. And, anytime is fine with me. I cancelled all of my other appointments for the day. I am all Anna's."

"Sounds fine, Dr. Esther. I will meet you there in half an hour." They both hung up, and Hank looked around the office. He had one thing to do before he left for the hospital in Foley, and he was cringing at the thought of it. The mayor of Orange Beach had held a town meeting earlier that morning to assure everyone that he, personally, had his best men on top of the situation. There was no need for panic, and certainly no need to run to the local news spreading rumors; what happened on this island, stayed on this island, and there was no one out there better fit to deal with their problems than their own police. In his thick Southern drawl, the mayor had assured everyone that he was there to take care of them and that everything would be ok. Hank had suffered through ten grueling meetings on the murders and finally left after he was introduced as the lead detective. He hadn't wanted to listen to the mayor go on and on about how he personally will take care of the citizens in their time of need with no help from any outsiders.

Hank's task at hand now was to call the mayor and personally plead with him for permission to talk at length with seasoned investigators in Mobile. He also wanted to alert the local news with full details so that the public could perhaps help with any leads while they were waiting on DNA tests and possible finger print matches to any known criminals. Gritting his teeth and crossing his fingers, he dialed the private cell number. Mayor Fred Michaels answered quickly, "Yep, Fred here. Whatcha got for me, Hank?"

"Hi Fred. Uh, sorry about skipping out in a hurry like that this morning, but I had so much to get caught up on. I hope you understand."

"Aw, that's fine, Hank, I just needed to reassure the masses of this fine community. Any new info, Hank? I got people calling me every two minutes about this god damn mess."

Hank rolled his eyes. "Yeah, I know the feeling, but, no, I don't have any new news yet, and that's why I'm calling you. Fred, something's gotta give on your part about the media. This isn't your run o' the mill drug bust or fishing accident we're talking about here. This is something that's never happened here before, something of the worst nature, and well, the media will get in on it if they want to, and I assure you they will, once they get a whiff of how horrible the murders were. You might as well throw them a bone and see what they can offer any help. It's not going to hurt the tourism, Fred, the season's almost over." Hank held his breathe.

"I know, Hank, you're right, and the whole time we were in that meeting this morning, I knew you were gonna tell me this, and I agree with you. I have given it a lot of thought this morning and, well, go ahead and answer their questions and see if there is anyone out there that knows anything about it. And don't leave me in the dark about anything! You call me every time and anytime when you get new info. I want these assholes pulled out of whatever hidin' hole they've made for themselves and brought to justice."

Hank released a deep breath of relief. "Ok, thanks, Fred. I am on my way to meet with the doctor who did Anna Morrison's examination this morning and I'll call you when I'm done."

They hung up and Hank rubbed his eyes again. That conversation could have been horrible, but Fred had pulled through for him, and didn't act like the stubborn redneck that he was adored and admired for being by most. He grabbed his keys and quickly headed for the door. On the way to the hospital, he thought about the 911 call that Anna had made at three-twelve in the morning. After he and Hillary had left the crime scene, they had listened to it over and over again at the station.

"911."

Silence.

"911, can I help you?"

Silence.

"If this is an emergency and you can't speak, please press a number."

Nothing.

"If this is a prank call, we will trace it and press charges."

Someone began crying, not loudly, but audibly, then humming a song, more silence ... then ...

"Passion, I want your passion, Passion, just give me passion."

It was the voice of a small child, female, singing some song about passion.

"We are sending an officer over right away, please stay on the line. Are you okay? Did something bad happen?"

Silence, then click, the call went dead.

The dispatcher had retrieved the address of the phone number and sent out a rookie officer on graveyard shift to check out the residence. The young cop in training had almost passed out relaying the details over the radio of what he had found when he opened the front door that had been left ajar.

Passion? Hank had never heard of a song with those lyrics, but that didn't mean it didn't exist. He made a mental note to Google the words that the child had sung to the 911 operator. It might mean something, but yet again, it might just be the words of a popular song stuck in the head of an eight year old child in severe shock, trying to make contact with someone who would help her.

CHAPTER SEVEN

Judith was reluctant to leave Anna's room. She walked around the bed, making sure she was tucked in, and checked the monitors to make sure everything was as it should be. One of the emergency room nurses on break had volunteered to sit with her while Judith was away. Glancing down one more time at the girl's swollen face, she thanked the nurse, and quietly slipped out the door and down the hallway towards the cafeteria. She had seen Detective Jordan at the FloraBama a couple of times, but had never met him. Nevertheless, she knew who he was, and knew that he was respected in town as a good detective and a good man. As she rounded the corner to the cafeteria entrance, she spotted him standing beside a table, talking on his cell phone. He had on blue jeans and a fishing tee shirt, pressed, but nonetheless a tee shirt, which made her wonder if he took his job seriously or not; then, she checked herself. She had momentarily forgotten that she had moved to Alabama.

Hank looked up at the woman walking towards him and closed his cell phone, placing it back on his belt. He recognized her, even though he had never met her. A single attractive woman can't live in Orange Beach very long without being noticed; even though Judith was unaware, she was very much known to most single men, or married for that matter. The single men who lived on the island who were actually looking for more out of a relationship than to have anonymous sex with a tourist took notice when a female stayed more than two weeks on the island. Attractive successful single women didn't come to the island every day, at least not to stay. As she approached his table, he momentarily looked down to erase her prettiness from his mind, immediately feeling guilty for even noticing such things at a time like this. He waited until she came to him, extended his hand and said, "Hello, Doctor Esther, good to meet you. Wish it was under different circumstances."

Judith shook his hand and nodded, looking straight into Hank's eyes. He then noticed the puffiness of her face and instantly knew that she had been crying that deep kind of cry that only women are capable of; the kind that burst forth with so much emotion, whether it be real or hormonally induced, that it breaks blood vessels around the nose and eyes. He allowed her to sit first, and then he took a seat opposite her and placed his hands on the table.

"Detective Jo…"

Hank interrupted her with a smile. "You can call me Hank."

Judith nodded. "Alright, Hank, you wanted to ask me some questions? Tammy and I were very…"

Apologetically, Hank interrupted her again so he could open his notebook. When he was ready to take notes, he asked, "Doctor, why don't we start with Anna's report? I will ask you a couple of questions later, but for right now, I am more interested in the child's health and anything you might add to help the case along. Has she woken up since we talked?"

"No, she hasn't, but I left strict instructions with the attending nurse to page me immediately when she does. She is still out of it, going in out and out of consciousness. Her throat will heal quickly, as most wounds do with children. There was no severe damage from the rope, thank God, but the other wound is… well, it's pretty bad, there's no way to get around it." Judith looked down at the table for a minute, trying to stop the tears from flowing again. Hank let her pause, without interrupting. "Of course, I can't say for sure because of her age, but due to the severe damage to her vagina, inside and out, and the actual lacking of skin between her vagina and anus, well, it might be difficult for her to heal appropriately and give birth naturally when she becomes a woman. That is about as plain as I can put it, without going into a bunch of medical garbage that you wouldn't understand, or maybe you would, but I would rather speak plainly if you don't mind."

"That's fine with me. I think I understand and quite frankly, don't want to go into too many details of that right now unless you have something to add that would give me a clue as to who would do something like this."

"No, I wish to God I did, but that's it. I'm sorry; I guess we will have to wait until she wakes up." Judith stared at Hank, waiting for him to say something, but he didn't. He continued to sit there and wait for anything else she had to say. Finally she broke the silence. "So, any leads yet?"

Hank cleared his throat, broke his stare, and responded, "Well, no, we are still waiting to hear about the DNA as you know, and the fingerprints. The boys are canvassing the neighborhood, asking questions, interviewing neighbors and people who worked with John, but so far, no one has been able to offer anything as of yet; but it has only been eight hours since the 911 call, which we haven't been able to get anything from that either."

"Well, do you have any more questions for me now, because I really want to go back to her room? If she wakes up, I want her to see someone she knows. She has been through enough already. I don't want her to wake up in a white hospital room with strangers trying to talk to her all at once. Emergency room nurses are notorious for treating children like adults, and hell, I can't blame them. When you live your life around trauma, you become numb to people's emotions." She realized she was rambling but kept on. "I don't know. The whole thing is just horrible, what they or he or she, whatever, did to them. The only thing that Anna has done since she has been placed here is groan, sob in her sleep from the nightmare that she has been cast into, and sing this weird song that I don't know, well, not really singing, but humming, and I…"

Hank's head jerked up to attention, not that he wasn't listening, but hearing that the girl was singing in the hospital room made his heart skip beats. Anna had been singing a song to the 911 operator, something about passion. That had to be important. Judith had stopped talking the second she saw the change in his expression when she mentioned her singing.

"Doctor, are you sure she wasn't singing words?"

"No, I don't think so. I believe I have only heard her humming, or trying to hum at least, why?"

Hank told her about the 911 call, the words of the song, and asked her to listen for the word passion. Judith said she would call him immediately if she heard her say or sing anything else, and rose from the table to leave.

They shook hands and went their separate ways in fast paces; Judith hurrying back to Anna, and Hank hurrying back to his office so he could Google *I want your passion*. He forgot to ask her about her relationship with Tammy and made a mental note to remind her that he needed to interview her along with everyone else who the family was close to. Hank thought hard. *Passion. Was it a Britney Spears type song, popular on the charts, or did it mean something?* He couldn't place the words in any song that he knew. Highway 59, the road from Foley to Gulf Shores, was packed with tourists trying to get to the beach, so, he put his lights on and cruised on by. He turned on the radio to a popular hip hop station that was notorious for playing the top ten songs over and over again, just in case he heard the words to Anna's song. He never heard them; instead, he got an earful of lyrics that were disgusting and outrageously pornographic, and wondered why parents let their children listen to the radio anymore. He made a silent promise to himself to pay more attention to what flows over the pop charts before he married and had children of his own. Hank had never been a big Internet user, but for once in his life, he couldn't wait to get online back in his office and run a search.

CHAPTER EIGHT

Freshly showered, Suzanna sat on the couch in her apartment and debated on whether or not to go to the beach. She didn't really feel like sunbathing anymore, in light of the news of the Morrisons and Yuraslav's loss of employment, but she knew that she couldn't stay in the apartment all day long feeling sorry for herself either. Sitting around depressed, watching television and eating ice cream had never been her forte, and although crawling up in the down comforter of her bed to a good book sounded like a good idea, Suzanna couldn't shake the desire to get up and go somewhere. She tried to call Yuri's cell phone again, only to find out that it was still turned off. *Bastard...she thought to herself....he's probably passed out somewhere...* She decided to stop trying to get him on the phone, and allowed herself to appreciate an entire morning without having to deal with him in it. Thinking of her situation this way made her feel a little bit better, and out the door she went. Maybe, she thought to herself, she would just take a drive down to Fort Morgan Beach, the west end of the island on the bay side. And then, maybe she would pick her mother and Julie up and take them to lunch at the Cracker Barrel in Foley to get them off the island for a while and lighten their moods. She was trying to plan her day when she pulled up to the ATM machine at the bank, and slipped in her bank card. While punching in the security code, and selecting one hundred dollars for withdrawal, Suzanna noticed her friend, Ann Marie, waving at her through the teller window. She waved back, but then realized that Ann Marie was motioning for her to come inside the bank and not just waving. At that exact moment, the ATM's screen was warning her that she had insufficient funds in her checking account.

Suzanna thought, *hmm, that's really weird, maybe the machine is down and Ann Marie is trying to tell me to withdraw from the inside of the bank.*

Retrieving her card from the feed slot, Suzanna parked her car and walked into the bank. All it took for her to realize the seriousness of the situation at hand was the look on her friend Ann Marie's face as she walked through the doors of the bank. If some one had actually punched her in the gut, it wouldn't have felt half as bad as what she felt the second she knew what had happened. Ann Marie rushed to her friend, and confirmed what she already guessed. He had taken it all. Yuraslav had entered the bank earlier that morning at nine o'clock and withdrawn $22,874 dollars from their checking account and $5,000 dollars from their savings account. He had successfully and completely wiped them out financially.

Furious, Suzanna demanded, "Why in the hell didn't you call me? Ann Marie that was my money too, damnit!" Not wanting to further cause a scene, Ann Marie pulled her into one of the empty loan offices and quickly shut the door. Suzanna threw her purse down onto the floor, causing the contents to spill out in every direction, and then slumped into a chair, feeling as if she would automatically fall through the cracks of the floor if the chair failed to support her. Ann Marie was silent for a moment, letting the news settle in her friends head, then knelt down beside her and took her hand.

"Suzanna, honey, I didn't have a choice, I am so sorry. He came in and withdrew everything, stating that y'all were moving back to Prague for a while. I knew something was up, but I couldn't do anything. The accounts are in his name. I swear I was gonna call you, but my manager told me not to get involved. I was gonna wait until I got off work and call you if you hadn't already found out about it."

"But, Ann Marie, you don't understand! He lost his job today, and that's all the money we have, and I don't know what I'm gonna do now, and the rent is coming, is coming..." stuttering and unable to finish the sentence, Suzanna broke down into tears.

"Excuse me for a minute, honey, just hold on, I'll be right back." Ann Marie quickly walked towards the door where her manager was now standing. They conversed back and forth in hushed tones, and finally, Ann Marie came back into the room. She once again knelt down on the floor beside the chair and offered tissues to her friend. "Suzanna, maybe you should call the police and explain the situation to them. Maybe they can find him and figure out where all the money is and why he took it all. You wanna use the phone?"

She abruptly stopped crying, blew her nose, and looked up at Ann Marie who was now standing with phone in hand. Her sadness had just evolved into something far worse; Ann Marie noticed the glare in her eyes and the sharp inhalation of breath. Her friend was enraged with fury over what Yuri had done to her.

"Hell yes, I wanna press charges! This is it, I have had it! No fucking more!" Suzanna grabbed the phone. She didn't dial 911; she punched 911.

As Suzanna waited to explain her dilemma to an officer, she was mentally making a list of all the places she knew of that Yuri could be: The Crawfish Bar, where most of the Czechs hang out and drink, The Keg Bar and Restaurant, another one of his favorite places to get smashed, and a number of different houses and apartments, all belonging to either Czech workers or the Russian owned outsourcing company that he used to work for. He had become good friends with the Russians after he and Suzanna married, even though before he couldn't stand them. In Suzanna's opinion, they were all thugs, scamming and cheating their workers as well as the United States government. It was an extremely hush-hush thing on the island. Many people suspected the Russian outsourcing companies of illegal business, but no one would talk about it, at least not anyone of importance. The people who were important were the people who owned the tourist businesses, restaurants, hotels, and the rental properties. Without the foreigners here to work, they wouldn't have enough employees to keep their businesses running or rent their houses.

When the officer finally came on the line, Suzanna exploded on him with so much information and with such verbal force that he interrupted her in mid-sentence.

"Ma'am, you're talkin' way too fast! Perhaps you might wanna come down to the station and speak with an officer in person, and possibly make a formal report and complaint, depending on how serious the situation is."

"Fine, I will!" Being interrupted infuriated Suzanna even more, and she slammed the phone down, ignoring Ann Marie and the stares of people standing in line waiting for the tellers. Shaking uncontrollably, she gathered the spilled contents of her purse from the floor, violently threw them back in her purse, and stomped out of the bank towards her car. When she got inside and turned the car on, her elbow hit the radio power button and music started blaring. Enraging her even further, Suzanna hit the off button to the radio and screamed, "Yes,

29

Yuri, you stole all of our money, lost your job, turned your cell phone off, and what do you leave me with? A fucking David Hasselhoff cd playing in the cd player, turned up as loud as it can go! Who in the hell listens to this shit? Bastard!"

Suzanna threw the car in reverse and made a mad dash down the street towards the police station. Yuri had never done anything quite this extreme with their money before. Occasionally, he would dip into the account and take out far more than what was needed, but never had he wiped it totally clean. As far as Suzanna was concerned, it was the straw that broke the camel's back. As strange as it may sound to some people, the stolen money was the fire that fueled her anger and the acceptance of the prospect of leaving him; yes, he could beat her, yes, he could curse her and belittle her, but no way in hell was he taking her money and leaving her destitute! Keeping one hand on the wheel, she used the other to dig through her purse until she felt her cell phone. She flipped it open and speed dialed her mother.

When her mother answered, Suzanna screamed violently into the phone, "Mom! You are not going to believe what Yuraslav did to me!" She was crying uncontrollably and almost wrecked in between holding the steering wheel, juggling the cell phone, and wiping her nose so that she could talk into receiver. The phone slipped from her hand and fell to the floorboard as she struggled to gain control of the wheel. She could hear her mother screaming from the floorboard as she pulled her car into the parking lot of the police station. Screeching to a halt, she parked her car in the first space available, grabbed her purse from the passenger seat and leaned down to pick up the cell phone. Still crying, she sobbed to her mother, "Mom, I have to call you back."

CHAPTER NINE

"Passion. I want your passion. Passion. Just give me passion..."
Hank read the lyrics on the computer screen, truly puzzled by the fact
that it wasn't Brittany Spears, N'Sync, or any of the other popular teen
bands that would attract the attention of an eight year old child. The
lyrics he had found belonged to a singer named David Hasselhoff. He
Googled his name to make sure that this singer was the same David
Hasselhoff from Baywatch, and yes, it was the same person. Then he
cross referenced his name with a current weekly top twenty count
down and found nothing but old ratings in Europe. So, he thought,
maybe John and Tammy were Hasselhoff fans. Hank hadn't really
hung out with John much, not since high school, but as he listened to
the song play on the website, he just couldn't imagine the Morrison's
rocking out to Hasselhoff. Actually, he couldn't imagine why anyone
would want to. The music was horrible. But, he guessed, stranger
things could happen. Still, he put it on a back burner in his mind, in
case anything came up in the future, that would link this to a clue in
the case. As he read more about Hasselhoff's music career, the dispatcher rang in and asked him if he had time to take a complaint.

"No, I don't have time right now, unless it pertains to the Morrison
case. Put someone else on it."

"Sorry, Detective Jordan, but there is no one else here. Everyone is
out on the Morrison case, the phone is ringing off the wall, and a
woman is here waiting outside in the lobby, demanding to speak to
someone."

Hank looked at his watch and said, "Fine, send her back." Thirty
seconds later, in walked Suzanna, fuming and red-faced. He recognized her from the souvenir stand on the public beach and from a
booth at the Shrimp Festival every year, but didn't know her name.
She was definitely angry about something.

"Uh, yeah, how can I help you? What's your name?"

"Suzanna Novacek."

"Ok, Mrs. Novacek, I'm Detective Hank Jordan. Please have a seat." Hank hurried to cover up the crime scene photos that were plastered all over his desk. "What can I do for you? The dispatcher told me you needed to make a complaint."

"You're damn right I do! My piece of shit husband--"

Hank abruptly interrupted, "Whoa! Slow down with the potty mouth, Mrs. Novacek. That talk isn't gonna get you anywhere in here." Even though she was clearly not a child, Hank gave her a stern fatherly look and couldn't help but think of the vulgar music that he had heard on the radio station on his way back to the precinct. "Start over. You said something about your husband?"

Suzanna flushed with embarrassment, causing her face to redden even further. "I am sorry officer. I just, I am so angry. Anyway, I want to make a complaint against my husband. He left, well, I think he did anyway. This morning he didn't show up for work, which isn't unusual, but then he went to the bank and stole all of our money. I haven't seen him since yesterday afternoon. He didn't come home last night, and I have no idea where he is."

Hank interrupted again, "What do you mean stole? Are you legally married?"

"Yes, unfortunately."

Hank shook his head; he had better things to do. "Okay, then, well, he didn't steal the money. Were both your names on the account?"

Suzanna blushed again in embarrassment for her stupidity. Yuraslav had demanded that the account be in his name only at the time they opened it; he told her it would help his green card situation if he had an account in his name.

"No, only his name was on it." She paused, and then said loudly, "But it was my money, too! He can't just take it out!"

"Have you spoken with him? Is it possible that this is all just a misunderstanding that can be resolved face to face? Have y'all two been in a fight recently?"

"No, we haven't, he didn't come home last night, see, he's Czech, and he always staying out late and getting shitfaced, oops, sorry, drunk and I figured he just passed out somewhere. When I called his work this morning to tell him the awful news about the Morrison murders, Svetla, the receptionist told me he hadn't shown up for work and that he was fired. I tried to call him on his cell phone, but he has turned it off."

"Ok, Mrs. Novacek, why don't you give me his number, and I will see if I can get in touch with him and have him call you." Hank rolled his eyes as he turned around to grab a notepad to write the number down. "Do you have anything you want me to tell him? I think you should try to work this out without making a formal complaint on paper."

"Yeah, you can tell him that when he does come home, he can find his clothes, his pictures, his movies, and his stupid David Hasselhoff cd's in the bags on the..."

Hank almost jumped out of his seat. "Whoa, what did you just say?"

Suzanna thought she had cursed again and was about to apologize for it when he asked her, "Did you just say David Hasselhoff?"

Suzanna nodded slowly, unsure of why that would be of any interest to him. "Yes sir, all of the cd's are in my car. He left one playing in the cd player and when I turned the power to the radio on this morning, it was up all the way, scared the crap out of me for a second...hey, where are you going?"

Hank had suddenly bolted out of the chair, stopped abruptly at the doorway, and turned back towards Suzanna. "What is your husband's full name?"

"Yuri, I mean Yuraslav Novacek. Czech's don't have middle names. Why?" Suzanna gave him a baffled look and then frowned. "Is he in jail? Did he get a DUI last night or something?"

"Stay here, and don't move!" Hank disappeared down the hallway of the police station.

Puzzled, Suzanna watch the cop race down to dispatch. She didn't move an inch. She sat there and waited for him to return, wondering what in the hell was going on. From the way the officer was acting, she assumed that her loser husband was in a holding cell, and actually smiled at the prospect. Whatever he had done, he surely deserved to be arrested, especially since he wiped her savings out.

Hank Jordan felt like he couldn't get to dispatch office fast enough. He quickly rounded the corner to where Lisa Dubeaux sat, taking a call from a 911 caller about a break in on a charter boat. She ended the call by telling the caller to wait there for an officer, and looked up at

33

Detective Jordan's face; from the look on his face, she knew something important was about to happen. Lisa had worked as a dispatcher for the Orange Beach police department for nearly six years. She loved her job, as most dispatchers do. It gave her a sense of authority, much like the power that police officers feel when a big high profile case comes along, and they are there to witness and solve it. Her job even made her a little bitchy at times, turning her into the ultimate 'woman with a whistle'. She wouldn't hesitate for a second to speak her mind and tell any of the officers exactly what she thought and felt about them. The officers knew of her bitchy attitude, but didn't mind; she rarely made mistakes and was always bringing home-cooked meals to the precinct, so the officers put up with her attitude for the most part. The only officer whom she never talked back to or cross in any way was Hank Jordan. She'd had a crush on him since the first day of her employment. She also had a lot of respect for him, even though she knew that he wasn't interested in her like she was with him. No one knew she secretly liked him for a damn good reason; Lisa was married, and had been for nearly fifteen years. So, she kept her crush to herself, and figured that if Ben, her husband, ever filed for divorce or died, and Hank Jordan was still a single available bachelor, then she would make her move. Until then, she would just keep her feelings on the down low.

"Lisa, get on the radio right now, and alert all units to find a Czech resident named Yuraslav Novacek. I need everyone on this and tell them when they find him, bring him in immediately for questioning on the Morrison case. Run his name through the computer and get his description and see if he has a record. Tell everyone to check all the local Czech hotspots and hangouts, but tell them also to be careful. I know a lot of them are here illegally, and probably won't give any information as to where he might be. Tell them, under no circumstances are they to threaten any of them with the INS…got it?"

Lisa had already begun to search his name in the database. "Yes, sir, I got it." She began rattling off all the information and instructions into her headset as quickly and factually as she could while Hank bolted back down to his office where Suzanna was waiting for him with big eyes. He had left his radio on in his office, and she had just heard what the dispatcher had said. Something between liberation and joy washed over her body and mind like a big cup of warm relief that she hadn't expected, but right behind it was a surging wave of fear. Was her husband in anyway connected with the Morrison's murder? She knew he was violent, God knows she had dealt with her share of it for years now, but rape and murder? She thought of little Anna and her two precious twin brothers, and she couldn't shake the graphic visual of their murders out of her head. Surely to God, she hadn't married a man that was capable of committing such a horrible and evil crime. Suzanna became light headed and nauseas, and Hank walked in the office just in time to see her face go completely white. She stood quickly to say something to him but lost her balance and passed out on the floor at his feet.

She came to about fifteen seconds later, still white as a ghost, and mortified. Hank picked her up and held her steady until she could breathe normally.

"Mrs. Novacek, do you want some water?"

Suzanna responded shakily. "Yes, and please don't call me that anymore. I heard the dispatcher on your radio. If my husband had anything to do with that stuff, I don't ever want to be called by that name again. Just please, call me Suzanna." Her voice was shaky and barely audible. Hank walked over to the water cooler and returned with a small Dixie cup of water. She took it, and sipped a little bit, then returned it to his desk and took a deep breath.

"Suzanna, do you know your husband to be violent in any way? To you, or anyone else? If you don't want to answer any of these questions I am about to ask you, I understand. You are not obligated to in any way."

"Yes, I understand, and yes, I will answer any questions you have. I don't love him; actually, I think I hate him." Suzanna looked at the floor in shame before she spoke again. After a couple of seconds, she slowly raised her head to look back at Detective Jordan. "Yes, he's violent. He has beat me since the day we got married, but I never told anyone, and he always gets into fights at the Czech bar when he gets drunk. He is a very mean person. I should have never married him, but I didn't know. He didn't act like this before we got married. But for everything he has done to me, I can't imagine him being capable of raping or killing a child."

"Is he violent when he's not drunk?"

"Yeah, but it's much worse when he is. He is just an asshole all around. Sorry."

"That's alright; you can cuss all you want to now. Suzanna, what does your husband usually drink--beer, liquor, wine?" Hank remembered what Dr. Esther had mentioned to him earlier that day at lunch about the peach liquor found on Anna's body.

"He usually drinks Jim Beam straight, but sometimes he drinks vodka, especially when the Russians come down from Atlanta to pick up checks and do paperwork."

This sent Hank's mind reeling, and he grabbed a pen to jot down notes. Russians? Checks? What paperwork is she talking about? "What kind of vodka does he drink? And tell me, if you can, a little bit about the Russian people that you just spoke of."

"He likes some Czech shit made from peaches, hell, I don't know what the name of it is…I can't drink it, it makes me crazy drunk and it tastes like bad moonshine out of an old Seven Up bottle. As for the Russians, they scare the shit out of me. I have met them twice before, and I know why they are here and I know what they do. A lot of people know what they do, but no one talks about it. The whole thing is fake and illegal, every bit of it, and all the locals that hire them know it, but they don't care. They don't ask any questions as long as the Czechs have proper documentation and work visas."

"So, if they have the correct paperwork, then what are you trying to tell me?"

"What I am trying to tell you is that the Russians own the small Czech outsourcing companies, and they supply real and fake paperwork to all of the people who come over here to work, in exchange for a cut of the money they all make. When the Russians come down here to collect their cut, all the Czechs kiss their asses until they leave, always aspiring to get in their good graces so they can leave the Czech companies and go to work for the Russians for better money. Only a few of them have ever been truly been trusted by the Russians. It's all a big mess. All of them want to be gangsters in the Russian Mafia, including Yuraslav. They think it's cool. When I lived in Prague, that's how so many Czechs made money, because good jobs are so hard to find over there. They work for the Russian and Polish Mafias." Suzanna rolled her eyes and stared at Hank for a second. "You mean you don't know any of this already, or you think I'm full of shit?"

Hank sat there almost openmouthed. He knew that all the immigrant work here on the island wasn't always on the up and up, but had no idea it was this crooked. Since she was being so cooperative and answering all of his questions, he jumped at the opportunity to ask her for more information. "Suzanna, would you be willing to say all of this for a recorder? And also be willing to get me a sample of your husbands' DNA?"

Suzanna bit her lip, and tried not to cry. She realized for the first time that the general public didn't really know a damn thing about all the crooked business she knew of; she guessed that the only reason she knew was because her dumb ass husband told her stuff about it all the time and that she had married into it. She knew she had said too much to turn back and wondered how dangerous the water that she was now swimming in would eventually become. Then, she thought of her money. She had to pay rent and utilities, and survive until the next season started. "Yes, what do I need to do?"

"Where do you live?"

"Summer View Apartments."

"I will escort you home to make sure he isn't there. Then I need you to go into your bathroom and get me his hairbrush."

"Okay." Suzanna sighed and wiped a tear from her eye before it made a track down her cheek.

Hank eyed Suzanna. "Are you alright to stand up? Maybe we should wait a couple of minutes before we go. You still look a little pale."

CHAPTER TEN

It was 5:15 in the afternoon when Anna Morrison finally woke up from her nightmare. She felt someone's hand holding hers, and for a moment, she thought it belonged to her mother. But when she opened her eyes, she saw Dr. Judy smiling at her and remembered what had happened to her mother. Anna did not return the smile. She just stared blankly into her doctor's eyes, knowing that what happened was not a dream; it was real. She opened her mouth to speak but nothing came out. Her throat was too sore from the rope burns. Judith quickly leaned down to smooth her hair from her face and said, "Shhh. Anna, everything is going to be ok, just lie here for a moment and take a deep breath. I am not going anywhere, I am right here." She looked down at the child and bit her lip, trying not to cry. "Sweetie, I am going to ask you some questions and I don't want you to try to talk right now, ok? All I need you to do, if you can, is shake your head yes or no when I ask you some questions. Ok? Can you do that for me?"

Anna shook her head yes.

"Ok, good girl. Do you hurt?"

Anna nodded.

"Do you know the person who hurt you?"

Anna shook her head no.

"Do you remember what happened last night?" Judith continued to stroke her hair.

Anna blinked for a moment, and started silently crying. This was a good sign to Judith; if Anna was crying, it meant that she was not in such severe shock anymore, or at least for the time being. Judy gave her time to cry and didn't interrupt her. Finally after a few minutes, Anna looked up at her and nodded.

"Do you remember everything?"

She nodded again.

"Okay, Anna. I want you to just lie here and relax and listen to me for a few more minutes. Okay?" Anna nodded once more, and then looked away. "I am so sorry that this happened to you and your family, but I promise you that I will protect you, and no one is going to hurt you anymore. When you feel better, and your throat stops hurting, then we can talk about anything you want to. But for right now, I want you to rest as best you can, and I promise that I won't leave your side, and if I do, it's because I absolutely have to, and I won't be gone long, ok? Everyone here, all of the doctors and nurses that work here, are my friends, and we are all working together to protect and help you." Anna looked back at Judith and nodded again. Judith thought that the child's haunted eyes looked like they belonged to a dead woman instead of an eight year old girl. They were dark, and hollow, as if they had never seen the light of day. Then, Anna closed them, shutting her and the world around her out.

Making sure she was asleep again, she stepped out of the room and alerted the nurses of what had just taken place. Then, she quickly dialed Detective Hank Jordan's cell phone to tell him that she had woken up. He picked up on the first ring. "Detective Jordan."

"Hi, it's Dr. Esther. Anna woke up about ten minutes ago, tried to speak, but couldn't, so I asked her a couple of questions and let her nod yes or no. She nodded yes to remembering everything, and then she cried. That is a wonderful sign, Detective. It means she's not in shock like she was when she was found."

"Is she awake now?"

"No, she communicated with me for about ten minutes, and then fell back asleep. I didn't pressure her with many questions, especially about the song. I was afraid it would lead to too much anxiety, and the last thing she needs is a panic attack; the child is exhausted. I will be with her when she wakes up again. I am moving into the room with her for the time being."

"Alright, thanks so much for calling me. Let me know when she wakes up, and listen, all hell has just broken loose down here…had a girl come in earlier to complain about her husband stealing money from her account. Turns out that he's Czech, didn't come home last night, likes to drink peach vodka, and loves to listen to David Hasselhoff in his spare time. You know that song we were trying to figure out? It's on one of his cd's, that just so happened to be in the cd player of the car that he and his wife share. His wife said he has a violent history to boot. We have everyone down here looking for him, but so far haven't found him anywhere. Oh, and his name is Yuraslav Novacek. Ever heard of him?

"No. Does he have brown hair too? Anna had brown hair under her nails."

"Yes, he sure does Doctor…"

"Please call me Judith."

"Yes, Judith, he does. That's four strikes against him so far, and I am waiting on DNA tests. His wife gave me his hairbrush, and I had it rushed over to the lab in Foley. Hopefully we will hear something from them soon, before the sun goes down. I need to go for right now, but please call me when she wakes back up."

"I will. Bye, Detective." Judith closed the phone and walked back into the room. For the time being, Anna looked almost peaceful; her cheeks showing a little more color, but Judith could only imagine the horror of the nightmares that the child was running through in her sleep. She closed her eyes and prayed to God for Anna's peace of mind, even if it only lasted for a couple of hours.

CHAPTER ELEVEN

Down the hole of insanity Yuraslav Novacek fell, lost in the after-math of the fantasy of what he had accomplished only eight hours ago. He and his partner Mirek had entered the house quietly, done what had been asked of them to do, and left quietly on their way to a new life. Gone were the days that he had to put up with his pathetic wife who was of now, no more use to him. He had used her wisely over the years, gaining from others the kind of respect that comes only with a green card, and now had the admiration of those who were higher up. Only six years ago he was considered the lowest of the low, working minimum wage jobs earning less than minimum wage paychecks, kiss-ing the asses of the Russians who controlled his every move. Then, he had met Suzanna, his wife. He had wooed her, courted her, and relied on the charm of the heart of Europe to entice her into his life as his wife. She had fallen for it, like a true bimbo American, like David Hasselhoff's beach babes. She had rushed in to save him, and he had taken advantage of it, milking her for everything she was worth. Now, he could sit back and relax, work for the Russians as a top man, and live the life that he always dreamed of. He could visualize himself in New York, or perhaps California, perched somewhere in a VIP booth in a dark night club with beautiful lusting women hanging all over him.

He was proud of himself, and never gave one single remorseful thought to what he and his friend had done to the Morrisons. As far as he was concerned, they deserved what they got from him, and he made sure that they suffered. He didn't really know exactly what they had done, but if the boss was angry with them and ordered their murders, then surely they deserved it. He had been ordered to kill them, and to rape the woman if he so desired, but the little girl…that had been his idea, just a little something he had added at the last minute. He had raped her, not only because he wanted to, but because he thought it might impress the boss and further his chances of becoming one of the few respected Czechs in the Russian Mafia world. He wanted it so bad, he could taste it.

When he was growing up, he, like other aspiring thugs in his neighborhood, use to run errands for the Polish Mafia in Prague. Several times he had raped, once on orders and twice just because he wanted to. It had always been his little secret. Rape had always been the subject of many of his sexual fantasies, since before he could remember having them. But, up until now, he had never raped a child. Children didn't really turn him on.

The very thought of being a pedophile was beneath him; he considered himself much classier and suave than that. He only did it to impress others, hoping that his act of brutal violence would shout 'Hey, I am the man you need! You can trust me to do the job, whatever it takes.' Still, he had enjoyed it. The only thing he hadn't enjoyed was washing the blood and brain matter from his body. The job had been messy; his experience with murder of that volume had been limited. Mirek's experience had been even less.

The father had been an easy kill. When they had pointed their guns at him, he had been willing to do anything that they asked him to do. Yuraslav had laughed at his cowardice. He knew that if anyone had rushed his family like that in the middle of the night, he would have fought them to the death, earning their respect in the last seconds of his life. He had always hated American men because he thought they were all spineless; they never fought back, never took up for themselves, but most importantly, never tried to gain the respect of others. To Yuraslav, American men lived in their own little worlds; driving their children to school in their Volvo station wagons, going to grocery stores to buy food that their wives were too lazy to shop for, and helping their children with their homework at night after school. To him, they took on the role of a woman, and he had always hated that. Mr. Morrison had proved his little theory correct when he began crying for mercy, and allowing them to man handle his wife and children into the room to meet their deaths.

The wife, on the other hand, had not been so easy for them to put down. She had screamed and kicked and fought the entire process, which only made it worse for her in the end. After he finished raping her, he watched Mirek put the rope around her neck. He had struggled for several minutes before he had a good hold on it, then finally, he had to use all of his strength to tighten it. The woman had made him so angry that he nearly separated her head from her neck.

Looking back on what they had done, Yuraslav was confident that he and his partner had done the job well.

CHAPTER TWELVE

Driving through Atlanta will make anyone panicky, especially if you are on the run from the police. The traffic is horrible, let alone the road rage that it infects you with. The best drivers in the world will be the worst as soon as they hit the high traffic in Atlanta. Yuraslav, Mirek, and Petra sat silently while the honking cars raced past them. They were nervous, and nervous people tend to drive really fast, or really slow. Petra didn't know what had happened the night before, nor did she want to know, but she knew it was bad when they showed up at her house covered in blood. They had showered, cleaned everything up, and given her a packet of instructions written in Czech; she was given only four hours to complete the instructions before burning them. Then they left her alone to do what she had to do, telling her to be ready when they came for her. She always knew that something really bad would eventually happen the entire time she had worked for the company. Everyone that was connected to the business was crooked. She had never wanted to take the job, but it beat working in the restaurants for pennies. Working in the office for the Russians gave her privacy, more money, and a house that wasn't stuffed with roommates. She just hoped that she could have all the money that she had saved sent safely to her family before she was caught and deported.

From the backseat Mirek asked her in Czech, "Petra, are you sure that you have everything?"

"Yes, I am positive. I have all the record books from 1998 until now; I have all the documentation and all of the passports and socials."

"And you burned the instruction packet?"

"Yes, I made a fire in the barbecue pit and placed the documents inside."

"Do you like your new hair?" Mirek laughed at her.

Petra ignored his question and focused on the road ahead and thought, "*Skudce.*" The pride and joy in her life had always been one of vanity, her hair. It had always been long, full, blonde, and perfectly straight, which made her a very popular prostitute growing up in Pardubice, a smaller city north of Prague. She became of age when Baywatch hit the screen in Czech Republic. The fever that show caused in her country practically reduced men to their knees in reverence to David Hasselhoff, while Pamela Anderson and friends became the leading characters of every dream and sexual fantasy that a Czech male could have. She shook her head and laughed to herself as she thought of how much she had learned about Americans while living in the United States. She laughed because Czechs in general thought that all of America was like Baywatch, that is, until they come over. People here were as normal as they could possibly be, in all shapes and sizes. She looked more like a Baywatch beach babe than most of the women who lived on the island, or, at least she did a couple of hours ago. Now her hair was gone, cut short and dyed black, making her look like an albino with a bad wig.

She knew that her hair would eventually grow back; that she could deal with. But what she couldn't cope with was the prospect of getting into serious trouble with the United States government, being deported, and losing all of the money that she had managed to scrape together and save over the years. Her family needed that money, and that had been the sole reason that she had decided to come to work in Orange Beach. Over the years she had sent money to her mother, to help her family along, but she saved the rest for when she would return. Thinking of her family, Petra made no sound as one tear slipped from her eye, down her check, and onto her bare shoulder, a shoulder that should have been covered with blonde hair. She stared at Mirek in the rearview mirror.

"Mirek, are you going to tell me where our final destination is, or do I just keep driving to nowhere?"

Mirek glared at her. "We are going to Myrtle Beach to the other office. Someone at the office there is doing the same thing you did this morning. Then we will pick up more instructions and go from there. Don't ask me anymore questions, if you need to talk, talk to Yuraslav."

Yuraslav shot him the finger from the front passenger seat with one hand and stroked his face where his beard had been earlier with his other hand. He was thinking about last night with pride and contentment, and wondered what blessings and grace the boss would bestow upon him for doing such a wonderful and thorough job. Although he was no stranger to violence, he had never gone that far with anything before. He didn't regret anything, except perhaps how much vodka he drank before they went over there. He wasn't even sure if he ejaculated or not; his instructions had been explicitly not to if he chose to rape the mother and child. He was also supposed to wear a condom, which he hadn't. He kept this information to himself as they continued through Atlanta. Thinking about last night, and glancing over at Petra's legs turned him on, and he accepted the fact that the crimes he had committed last night had unleashed a monster inside him that he wasn't necessarily willing to silence just yet. He liked it, and wanted to do it again. Maybe to Petra. He closed his eyes and began to relive it. He never once thought about forgetting the computer; that had been the most important task that the Russians had given him. He had been so wrapped up in his sexual perversions that he had left the most damning piece of evidence behind.

CHAPTER THIRTEEN

Hank and Hillary were on the phones talking with the state police and the FBI. The mayor had given him the go ahead to speak to whomever he needed to get the ball rolling, but Hank was sure the shit would hit the fan when he found out the FBI had been contacted. There was now a statewide manhunt for Yuraslav Novacek, with his picture plastered all over the news. The picture supplied by INS was from five years ago, when Yuraslav had been clean shaven as he was now. He had worn a beard for the last three years, and most people knew him with hair on his face. News always travels fast in a small town, as everyone knows; you can't pee behind the A&P without everyone knowing about it by the end of the day.

Telephone calls had been pouring in all day long from people who had worked with Yuraslav, people who drank with him, people who knew Suzanna...Hank had let Lisa handle most of it, and while she was a great dispatcher, even she had had enough of the callers. It seemed like everyone in town thought they knew him, or if they didn't, they would call anyway, being nosy, trying to get information about the case.

His cell phone rang again, and Hank flipped it open. "Detective Jordan here."

"Hey Hank, it's Paul, from the lab, we got a DNA match and a fingerprint match to your man o' the hour Yuraslav. You better catch him quick, before he stinks up another household." Paul was known for his inappropriate sarcasm.

"Damn, Paul, you got a crude sense of humor. Thanks for rushing this, I owe you. Gotta go." Hank flipped the phone off, looked at Hillary and yelled, "We got a match! The bastard was there and only his semen was found on the girl. Call the FBI back, work the phones, and tell the news stations in Alabama, Mississippi, Tennessee, Florida, and Georgia to show his picture all day and all night. If this guy is running, I want every gas station, every store in every mall, every

Tom, Dick, and Harry in all five states to know his picture like they know their own brothers! I want him found as soon as possible if not sooner! I am going to back to the Morrison's house to see if I can find anything else. Call me immediately if you hear anything or if you need me."

"You got it!" Hillary picked up the phone and Hank ran out of the police station. He pulled into the Morrison's driveway in a hurry and walked under the tape, nodding to the patrolman posted outside. All of the information he had come across today was tangled in his mind, weaving in an out, trying to form some sense. As he was walking up the front porch steps, he heard a car pull in the driveway behind him. Hank recognized the black Mercedes SUV with the real estate sign on the side. It belonged to Ed Morrison, John's father. Hank turned from the house and walked to greet him. Ed, the most jovial and fun loving guy whom Hank and most people on the island had ever known, looked like a dead man walking across the lawn towards the house. Over the years, Ed had never really aged, except for his jet black hair growing gray. He had never grown a gut like most men usually do in their later years, his shoulders never slumped, and he never lost the youthful twinkle in his eyes, until now. The man Hank knew to be in his sixties now looked every bit of eighty. There were wrinkles that had never been there before around his eyes and mouth and his face was swollen and red from all the tears that he had shed in the past twenty-four hours. His hands shook violently, even by his side, and Hank thought for a second that he detected a slight limp. When he reached Ed, he realized immediately that it wasn't a limp. It was the effects of alcohol that makes someone swagger a little bit, even if they aren't legally drunk. Hank held out a hand to Ed, but Ed didn't take it, so he stepped forward and put his arms around him, feeling him shudder and shake. Ed didn't move away. He allowed Hank to hold him while he sobbed for at least two minutes. Finally, the crying subsided and Hank took a step back from him, allowing the grieving father to collect himself and catch his breath.

Hank spoke softly to the sobbing man. "Ed, I don't think you need to come inside yet. The investigation hasn't been finished yet, and the house needs to be cleaned. You really don't wanna go in there."

"I need to, Hank. I need to go in there right now, for my own peace of mind. I need to see what was left behind, even if it's bloody, I don't care. It's my son's, my family's blood, and it's the only way for me to begin to deal with this. You gotta understand. Please let me go in with you. I have to do this."

Taking one look into the eyes of Ed Morrison made Hank's mind up for him. He might have to answer for this later, but there was no way in hell that he was going to cross this man's wishes or second guess what he needed to be able to cope with what had been done to his family. Hank could only imagine, not that he dared, what depths of hell this man was going through at the moment. "Alright, Ed, you can come in with me, but you gotta listen to me for a second."

"I'm listenin'." Ed wiped the tears from his cheeks.

"Right now I gotta go in there and see what, if anything, I can dig up that they haven't already found to help the case. I am particularly interested in Tammy's office and the contracts that she kept on the rental properties. I know they rent to a lot of Czechs, and as you know, we have a manhunt going on for a Czech as we speak."

Ed's expression changed from hopeless to fuming angry in less than a second. "Yeah, I've seen him on TV already, the foreign son of a bitch, if he's the one that…"

Hank put his hand up in the air. The last thing he needed at the moment was a drunk and angry father walking into the house and losing his cool. If any evidence was still in the house, Hank needed to make sure it was brought out safely and not ruined in a fit of anger. "Ed, stop. We don't know for sure if he did it or not, and I'm not in a position to talk to you about it either. So, don't start pressing me for details. But if you're set on going in there, you gotta stay with me the whole time. You can't touch anything, and I mean nothing, ok?"

Ed nodded. "Yeah, I understand."

"Now, do you know anything about Tammy's office? Where she keeps everything, mainly the files or papers on her rental properties?"

His face lit up a bit at the prospect of helping in any way. "Yeah, I sure do. John and I set it up for her, and taught her how to process all the rental agreements. She takes care of it by herself, and does a damn, uh, did…Christ!" Ed looked down at the ground and cursed himself bitterly. "Yeah, I know where everything is at. C'mon, I'll show you."

With that, they climbed the front porch steps and entered the house. It had already begun to stink, even with the air conditioning still running. Clean up was scheduled for the next morning, and by the end of the day, the blood and brain matter of John, Tammy and the twins would be erased from the house forever. Ignoring the stairs that led the way to the remains of the crime scene, they walked straight to Tammy's office on the first floor off of the kitchen. Ed opened a file drawer and pointed to the lease contracts, and stepped aside. "She kept the current contracts in the top drawer, and the old ones in John's office at work. If you need 'em, I'll go get them for you when we leave."

"Yeah, I might need them, for what I don't know yet, but yeah, you can go get them. I'll follow you over there." Hank reached down into the drawer and began pulling the files out and placing them onto the computer desk. As each one was pulled from the drawer, they were opened to make sure they weren't empty. The sixth one that Hank pulled out was bare.

Hank closed the empty file folder and read the name of the property at the top. "Ed, do you know if this property on Flamingo Avenue is being rented? The file is empty."

"I have no idea, like I said, Tammy always did everything, and so, if it's empty, I would say no, the property's probably not being rented."

Hank kept pulling and checking. Finally, he finished, counting sixteen file folders that were empty out of the thirty properties that were on Tammy's rental list. He remembered what Dr. Esther had said to him on the phone earlier about meeting Tammy at the bar two weeks ago. She had been excited about properties she had recently rented to Czechs, but he couldn't remember how many. He would call the doctor as soon as he left. He picked up the file folders and placed them in an empty box, and was turning around towards the door when he spotted a Post-it note to the side of the computer. There were many of them stuck everywhere, on the computer, the table, the file cabinet. Tammy liked Post-its. But this one, however, stuck out. It read: *264 Marina Road, Cerny. Deceased?* Hank placed the box back down on the desk and flipped through the files until he found 264 Marina Road. The file was empty. Saying nothing to Ed, who was preoccupied with a photo of his dead family that Tammy had hung on the wall, he grabbed the Post-it and placed it in the empty file. There were several other Post-it notes as well, with last names and the words deceased. He found the corresponding files and did the same with them as he did with the first, counting ten in all.

"Ed, do you mind helping me with the computer? I'm gonna go ahead and take it down to the station, just in case we come across anything. And one more question. Did Tammy usually run a routine background and credit check on her renters?"

Ed placed the picture back on the wall, wiped his face with the back of his hand, and turned to help. "No, not usually. Everyone knows everyone here. And as far as the Czechs go, they ain't got any history, apart from their reputations as good renters. Hell, I know several people that rent to them, and they always pay on time. And Hank, I changed my mind. I don't wanna go up there. I can smell it from down here, and I don't wanna see it anymore." Hank nodded in agreement. They unplugged the laptop, grabbed the box of files, and walked outside.

CHAPTER FOURTEEN

Thirty minutes later, Hank was back in his office with the new files, the old files from Ed's office, and Tammy's computer. Lisa, the dispatcher, met him in the hallway with a look that made Hank pause to make sure she wasn't pointing a weapon at him. She was frazzled, to say the least. "The phones have not stopped ringing all day! No one has anything useful to say, just questions."

"Just keep answering them, Lisa, until Meagan gets here." Lisa immediately returned to her desk and answered the phone. She knew enough about Detective Jordan that what he had just said was his polite way of saying, "Back off, shut up and do your job." She also took a second to laugh at the visual of Meagan, the new girl, dealing with the volume of calls tonight by herself. It wasn't a mean laugh, but a laugh nonetheless.

While plugging in Tammy's computer and resting the file box on his desk, Hank speed dialed Paul at the crime lab. The lab technician answered immediately.

"Hey, Hank."

"Hey, Paul, I know you faxed me everything earlier, but I have a quick question for you."

"Okay, shoot."

"Were Mr. Novacek's fingerprints found in the office of the Morrison house?"

"Yep. They were pretty much all over the house, even on the refrigerator. He must have been hungry during the..."

Hank cut him off. "Thanks, gotta go." He wasn't trying to be rude, but if there was a reason why Yuraslav had been in Tammy's office, then he needed to quickly dive head first into those files and find out why.

While Tammy's computer was booting up, Hank took out all of the empty file folders that he had retrieved from her office and placed them on his desk. One by one, he organized them so that he could glance down and see each tab with the address of the property listed. The computer finished booting up by the time he had the files organized. Tammy's computer screen was a family photo taken at the beach. In the photo, the wind was blowing Tammy's hair in her mouth. John's face was sunburnt but smiling. Anna was proudly posing beside her sand castle, and the twins were making stupid faces with their fingers up their noses at whoever was taking the picture.

What a damn shame...Hank thought. He shook his head for a second to let the emotion pass, and then studied the screen. There were ten different icons. He searched for any sign of the rental properties, and was rewarded. There was a file saved to the desk top labeled, current rentals. He looked at Tammy's face in the picture and thanked her softly. Then he logged onto the internet and clicked on her history, hoping he would see what he thought he would see. Emeril's kitchen, Gulf Coast Lawn Care, Doc's Seafood menu.... he scrolled down until he hit pay dirt. Equifax. Underneath that was Google: Cerny. He read on, seeing Equifax repeated, and more names Googled. Excitingly, Hank grabbed the file folder for Marina Road, and scrolled back up to where Tammy had Googled the name Cerny, pointed the cursor and clicked. An obituary appeared from Myrtle Beach, South Carolina. It stated that a man named Pavel Cerny, citizen of the Czech Republic, employee of the Yachtsman in Myrtle Beach, perished in 1997 in a car accident. Other details were given, but that was all that Hank needed to know at the moment. He quickly minimized the screen and clicked on the current rental file from the desk top and found the folder for Marina Road.

It was an application for a man named Pavel Cerny, dated almost one month ago in September. His last known address had been given as 26375 Willow Way, Myrtle Beach, South Carolina.

Hank sat back in his chair and let his mind digest the information that he had just read. *Something had spooked her. What? Ed had said that she usually didn't run background checks, especially not on the Czechs, but something definitely made her run background checks on these renters. In doing so, she found out that they were dead. What did she do after she found out? Did she attempt to call them? Did she notify anyone about the dead people who supposedly wanted to rent from her?* Hank opened his eyes and snapped back to his surroundings. He picked up the phone and called Hillary.

"Yeah, Hank?"

"Did anyone get phone records from the Morrison household?"

"Yes, they are on my desk. Why? You got a lead?"

"I found something, to what degree, I don't know, but I'm tellin'
you, it stinks bad. Worse than a six pack of ass. Where are you?"

"I just dropped Suzanna off at her parents. I sat with her during the
recording in Mobile, and then I took her home to get some of her
things. She is scared shitless, keeps talking about the Russians coming
to kill her.

She may have a point, too. I was talking with a field agent in the
Atlanta FBI office today, and he said they can get pretty ugly when it
comes to retaliation."

"Well, then, do us all a favor. Turn back around and go get Suzanna
and her parents and put them in a hotel room somewhere on the strip.
Use your credit card, and I'll reimburse you later. Get them there as
quickly as possible and get back here. Don't tell anyone where she is. I
won't be here; I'm going to the hospital. I'll leave you some instructions on my desk. If you can get started, I'll be back in a while to help
you. I don't have time to tell you everything right now, but you'll get it
when you see what's on my desk."

"Okay…be there in a few."

Hank ended the call, dialed the hospital, and asked for Anna's
room. The receptionist started to inform him of the hospital's phone
hours in the pediatric ward, but Hank interrupted her and told her who
he was. She apologized and connected him. Judith jumped in her seat
when the phone rang. Her watch read eight-thirty pm. *My God…how
long was I out? She thought.* She quickly grabbed up the receiver,
afraid the noise would wake Anna. "Hello?"

"Judith? Hi, it's Hank Jordan. Glad you're still there. I am on my
way, and we need to talk…how is she? Is she awake?"

"No, she's still asleep. I gave her a light sedative hours ago, hoping
it would help her sleep better. I was watching the news earlier, but
nodded off. Did they find him?"

"No, not yet. I am about ten minutes away. We need to talk privately, and I know you don't want to leave her room, so I will meet
you there. Just let them know at the desk that I am coming."

"Ok, see you in a few." She replaced the phone back to the bedside
table and studied Anna's face. She still seemed peaceful, no twitching,

no murmurs, no muscle jerks or facial expressions. Judith stared at her a moment longer, and walked to the bathroom mirror. Her face was red on one side, with an indentation of the button from the cuff of her sleeve on her cheek from napping in the chair. The rest of her face was swollen from crying. She rolled her eyes in disgust at her reflection and splashed cold water on her face to revive it a little bit. Then she noticed how flat her hair was and began brushing through it with her fingers. Suddenly, she realized that she was primping. *Huh? Why am I doing this?* she thought. But as soon as she asked herself that question, she knew the answer. Hank was cute. Well, no not really cute, but something. Yeah, ok, he was cute, but there was something else she couldn't quite put her finger on. She rolled her eyes at herself again for being so melodramatic. *This is not the time nor the place, Judith, get your shit together, and stop thinking about it,* she told herself. The cold water felt good as she doused her face one more time. She looked at herself in the mirror again, pulled her hair back in a ponytail, and walked out of the bathroom, just in time too see him open the door and walk in.

Hank tiptoed towards the bed, looked down at Anna, then up at Judith. He whispered, "You mind stepping outside for a second? I don't want to wake her up."

"Yeah we can talk outside the room by the window, that way I can keep and eye on her. Oh, did you have any trouble? I forgot to tell them you were coming." *Because my dumb ass was in the bathroom too long. God, how long was I in the bathroom?* Judith rolled her eyes at herself again, but only in her head.

"No, it was no problem." He turned towards the door and escorted her out of the room to the opposite side of the window. "I found some interesting things in Tammy's office. I shouldn't tell you any of this yet, but I trust you, and, well, you knew her, so I thought maybe you could help. I need to trust that you won't repeat any of this."

Judith nodded quickly. "You can trust me. And I will help in any way possible. What did you find in Tammy's office?"

"Do you remember talking to me today about the last time you saw Tammy at the FloraBama? You mentioned something about her being excited about some new rental contracts...how many did you say there were?"

Judith paused to remember the conversation. "I didn't, I don't think, but I am pretty sure that Tammy said she had ten new contracts with Czech people, and she was extremely happy about them. Why?"

"Do you know if they had already moved in?"

"Uh, well, hmm, now that you mentioned it, I do remember her saying that they were all coming down from Myrtle Beach to help with the hurricane reconstruction crews this fall and winter, but that they wouldn't be here until the first of November which is the end of the tourist season up there. You know, I'm from North Myrtle Beach, and that's why I remember her telling me that. But she also said that all ten properties had been paid for in advance. How much? I don't know, but she was happy for the money."

"You are from North Myrtle?"

"Yep, born and raised. Ever been there?"

"No, but I have a feeling I will be soon." Hank thought about this for a moment, then asked, "Do a lot of Czech people work up there like they do down here?"

"Yeah, alongside people from every other country you can think of. But yes, there are a lot of Czechs there, come to think of it. They have been coming there to work for a long time."

Simultaneously, they looked up at the window at the noise they had just heard. Anna was sitting in the bed looking at them. Judith rushed into the room and placed her hands on Anna's face, while Hank stood still outside the room.

"Anna, honey, it's me, Doctor Judy. Do you know where you are?"

In a feeble and pained voice she forced out the words. "Yes, ma'am. I need to go to the bathroom." Anna had been catheterized but still felt the need to urinate. "Okay, sweetheart. You can pee-pee, but there is a special way you have to do it, okay? There is a plastic tube that takes your pee-pee out of your body for you so you don't have to walk to the bathroom, so when you feel like you need to go, you don't have to worry, and the tube will do it for you. Just lay back and relax, and let your pee-pee come out, ok?"

"Okay." she whispered.

"Do you want some Jell-O? I have some for you. You can have cherry, strawberry, or lime...or red, pink, or green, however you want it."

"Pink."

"Okay, Anna, I will be right back. My friend works here, too. She is a nurse and her name is Angela. Do you mind if she sits with you while I get you some pink Jell-O?"

Barely audible, Anna asked, "Will you be right back?"

"Yes, I will be right back." Judith leaned down to page the nurse. She smiled at Anna and squeezed her hand. The child did not smile back. She rose from her chair as Nurse Angela walked in, and left the room to get pink Jell-O, and to tell Hank that she would have to get back with him later; he was already gone. She watched him disappear into the elevator, and turned in the opposite direction toward the refrigerator that held the Jell-O.

CHAPTER FIFTEEN

Petra was nervous, tired of driving and wanted to listen to the radio so badly. Mirek told her that if she turned any music on, he would wait until she pulled off at an exit to get gas and beat her ass. So, she drove the interstate in silence. She knew the way to North Myrtle Beach by heart from all the times they made her come to visit the bosses. "Visit" was a nice way to put it. She was a whore in Pardubice, and she was still a whore in the United States. Her visits meant that she was to show up with money at a certain time in a designated spot, smile, take her clothes off, and pretty much do whatever the hell they wanted her to do. She had been raped plenty of times in her life by plenty of different men. The Czechs were quick. The Germans were slow and always stunk. The Polish were sloppy. But the Russians…they were just down right brutal. They liked gang rapes, the type where she was passed around and beaten. That's where she was headed tonight, to the Russians. She had been saving some pain pills from a prescription she had filled when she had a kidney infection last year, and before she left Orange Beach she had thrown them into her purse at the last minute. She made a mental note to remind herself to take them once they reached their destination. If the Russians were going to abuse her body tonight, then she would need all the help that she could get.

Mirek's cell phone rang in the backseat. He checked the caller id and answered in Czech, "Ano? *Yes?*" Mirek was silent as he listened to the man scream at him through the phone. Petra's butt muscles clenched tightly in her seat as she strained to understand what was being said from whoever had called. She understood nothing, but from the mirror she watched Mirek's face turn as white as a ghost while he listened to the caller. Petra slapped Yuraslav awake and held a finger to her mouth to warn him to stay quiet. He snapped to attention and wheeled around to look at Mirek. Mirek's face was the shade of milk, and Yuraslav took that as a really bad sign. Mirek rarely, if ever, lost his cool. Even as Yuraslav was raping the woman and child from last

58

night, Mirek's facial expression never changed, not even when he pulled the trigger on the man and two boys. Now, as he was apparently getting his ass chewed out on the phone, Mirek reminded him of a small frightened child, about to be whipped with a switch.

Mirek finally spoke back to the caller. "Yes, ok, we have everything you asked for. Yuraslav put everything in the trunk under the spare tire, yes, everything…but, we need gas, we will have to stop soon…ok, she will…yes, she cut it and dyed it black…What? What have they said?" Mirek received no answer, only a click in his ear. As he put his phone down on the seat, his face transformed itself from a ghostly pale white to a flaming angry red as he glared at Yuraslav.

"You dumb fucking idiot!" Mirek screamed at the top of his lungs. "Your face is on every news channel from here to New York! They know your name! They know your face! Your fingerprints were found on the scene! And to make everything worse, you piece of shit, you didn't kill the girl! She's alive! She's at the fucking hospital in Foley!" Yuraslav didn't dare utter a word. He just sat there, scared shitless, knowing that he would have a bullet in his head before dawn. "God only knows what else they know that they aren't telling the media. You are a fuck up, you know that? I always knew you were a fuck up! If you believe in a maker, you better make your fucking peace with him right now. That was Vladimir on the phone! He told me to give you his regards. Petra, pull off the next exit and get gas. You will pay with cash and you will make eye contact with no one, do you understand?"

A petrified Petra, answered, "Ano." She hadn't known exactly what had happened the night before, but when she had seen all of the blood, she assumed that they had either killed someone, or gotten in a very ugly fight. Now she knew that they had attempted to kill a girl, but failed. And to make matters worse, she was driving the car that they were hiding in.

"We will not be going to Myrtle Beach. There has been a change of plans. After you get gas, drive to Charlotte, North Carolina. Do not utter a word, not one breath to me or to the dead piece of shit you are sitting next to. Just fucking drive."

Petra parked at the pump and entered the gas station. Yuraslav sat in the passenger seat, silently weeping over his failure. He finally found the guts to turn around in his seat to look at Mirek. He asked,

"Please, if you have any mercy, shoot me with the gun in your pocket."

Mirek thought for a moment, and then responded, "Fuck you. The only chance I have to live now is to deliver you alive. I am just as dead as you are." But as he spoke, Mirek was already forming a plan. Maybe Vladimir could kill Yuraslav, but he couldn't kill them both, until he had access to the paperwork and computer that Yuraslav had placed in the duffel bag in the trunk. He had to find a way to hide the bag before they arrived in Charlotte.

CHAPTER SIXTEEN

Suzanna Novacek and her parents did not want to leave the security of their own home. They had already notified other family members and all of their neighbors of what was going on, and they argued with Hillary that they would be safer if they were allowed to stay at their house. To prove his point, Suzanna's father had even produced a loaded shotgun to show Hillary that he was well prepared to blast away anyone who stepped within thirty feet of his property. Hillary almost panicked when he began waving it around the room while he talked. She managed to calm him down before he shot a hole in the ceiling and talked him into putting the gun away for the moment. Grudgingly, he placed it back into his closet and returned to the family room. When everyone had calmed down, Hillary pleaded with them to allow her to take them in safe hiding, at least for the night.

At first, Suzanna had been just as reluctant as her parents were to leave, but Hillary pulled her aside and repeated the conversation to her that she had earlier with the FBI agent from Atlanta. After hearing how vindictive and vengeful the Russians are known to be, she didn't want to risk anyone else's life. Suzanna said that she was willing to go with her. She and her parents packed overnight bags, made sure that the neighbors knew they were leaving for the night, and slid into the backseat of Hillary's cruiser. On the way to the hotel, Hillary stopped at her house and changed cars to make sure that no one would suspect anything if she pulled into a hotel and dropped three people off in a cruiser.

Approximately thirty minutes after Hillary had convinced Suzanna and her family to pack up and leave for the Holiday Inn, two men wearing all black silently snuck onto Suzanna's property and broke into the house. The neighbors, who had promised to watch the house until they returned, never saw the two thugs entering or leaving. They went from room to room, just like they had done in Suzanna's apartment in Gulf Shores only minutes before. Finding nothing, they quickly exited the house, retraced their steps to where they had hidden their car and made a phone call to their superior. One of the men in black listened as the call was placed and accepted.

In Czech, the man in black spoke into the phone, "She isn't here either. We have checked both places, but no sign of her. There are three cars in the driveway, one belonging to Suzanna and the others, I assume, belong to her parents."

"Keep an eye on the house and the apartment until I can call you back. The police may have her hidden somewhere." Click. The men in black backed out of the trees and began to slowly case the neighborhood. Eventually, they pulled out onto the main road and drove towards the Summer View Apartments in Gulf Shores to make sure a light wasn't on in Suzanna's apartment.

The two Czech men in black had been recommended to the boss by Mirek, if something were to go wrong with the murders. Something had definitely gone wrong with the murders as Yuraslav's face was shown on every local news station. They had no idea what they were getting themselves into, and if they had, they wouldn't have been so excited at the prospect of helping, and wouldn't have eagerly waited on the phone call that would send them on their mission. They had even put on all their gold chains for the special event before they left their houses to hunt down Suzanna. They wanted to be thugs, gangsters, just like in the movies. They knew very little, only that Mirek had messed up and that they were now receiving phone calls and directions to find Suzanna from a Russian named Vladimir. They were to locate her, kidnap her, and take her unharmed to an unknown destination. When their mission was accomplished, they had been promised that they would both be greatly rewarded by Vladimir himself.

CHAPTER SEVENTEEN

As soon as she dropped Suzanna and her parents off at the Holiday Inn, Hillary quickly returned to the station to find out what Hank had been so excited about. She bolted through the doors, rushed into Hank's office and began studying his desk. It didn't take long to read the instructions and notes that Hank had left for her; she understood immediately what he was thinking, and dove head first into Tammy's computer and phone records. Going back a month prior in the history of the computer, she printed every page that Tammy had visited that mentioned Equifax and any of the names that she had Googled. Astonishingly, Tammy Morrison had successfully found out that all ten names that she had been given on the applications were names of Czech citizens who, according to their obituaries and other references from newspapers and articles, were deceased. Three of the people had died in Myrtle Beach, four in Atlanta, two in New Orleans, and one in Biloxi, Mississippi. Next, Hillary cross referenced the names with the ones found in the current rentals folder to find out which names belonged to which properties, and placed the printed sheets into the corresponding empty file folders that Hank had organized on his desk. She found information for ten different properties in all.

After she finished what Hank had started with the file folders, she opened the phone records, and began taking notes. Tammy used a separate phone line from the household line to conduct business, which made Hillary's life at the moment much easier. She read both anyway, but didn't come up with anything from the main line. Tammy's office line, however, proved interesting, to say the least. Two days prior to the murder, the phone records showed phone calls to all four cities that Tammy had come across during her research on the rental applications. There were numbers to each citie's police departments and to county and parish records. Hillary assumed that Tammy had been calling to first verify the information of the deceased, and also to report identity theft to the authorities. Then, she found phone numbers belonging to several different companies in Myrtle Beach and a couple more to private cell phone numbers, also with a Myrtle Beach area code. Hillary circled each number in red ink, and then typed them on a separate sheet of paper. She wanted to call the numbers, but decided to call Hank instead, to let him know that she had hit the jackpot.

Surely everything can't be this simple and sad, Hillary thought to herself. If it was this simple, then Tammy had told the police about what she had found out concerning the people who had supposedly rented from her, then called the companies to tell them that she would not be renting them her properties. The companies got angry, the police got involved, and somewhere along the way, someone had ordered Yuraslav to go to her house in the middle of the night, rape her and her daughter and then murder her entire family. Anna had somehow escaped their little party of death.

She flipped her phone open and speed dialed Hank, who was on his way back from the hospital. "What did you find, Hill?"

"Exactly what you thought I would find."

"How did you know what I was thinking?"

"Because I know you…Tammy had been talking to authorities from four different cities about ten different deceased Czech citizens, who supposedly wanted to rent her properties. She also had been talking to the outsourcing companies who were probably the ones that paid her for the rentals. I also found several calls to private cell phone parties in Myrtle Beach, who are most likely the individuals who gave her the rental applications. They knew what she had done. She told them. And the rest, well, I guess you already know that. Someone obviously called Yuraslav and ordered the hit. You know, I was just sitting here thinking to myself before I called you that if it really is all this simple, then who in the hell would think that five murders is justifiable punishment for being busted on listing a couple of dead guys names on rental applications?"

"I don't know the answer to that question, but what I do know is that she was paid up front for ten different properties, every one of them for a years lease. Do the math. Even if they were only five hundred dollars a month, the total amount she would have received would have been sixty thousand dollars. That is not exactly pocket change. What is the usual reason behind a murder? Money. I will be there in less than five minutes. I'm coming over the bridge right now. Have you called any of the numbers?"

"Alright, see ya in a few, and no, I haven't. I figured you'd wanna do it yourself." They hung up, and Hillary went to check on Meagan, the new dispatcher. She felt sorry for her, with the volume of calls pouring in. In a small town like this, she quickly found out that a lot of people don't always use 911 for emergency calls only. Sometimes they, especially the elderly, used it like a hotline or a gossip line, trying to figure out the details and the progress of any crime or accident committed on the island; at times people even call to ask questions about crimes that happened in Foley and Mobile. On the island, if someone wanted to find out if anyone died in the car accident that happened on Highway 59, they just picked up the phone and dialed 911 and asked. Sometimes the dispatcher on duty would give them small bits of information to stop them from calling back, and sometimes they wouldn't tell them anything at all. Meagan looked up at Hillary and shook her head, wild-eyed and weary. "These people are crazy!"

Hillary just laughed and said, "It'll die down soon enough, people will be going to bed here shortly."

"I have answered so many calls tonight for no reason at all. These people just want to talk. Occasionally, someone will call with some decent questions, like, who is the lead detective on the case? Can you please describe Yuraslav's car so we can look for it? And, have the police placed Yuraslav's wife in protective custody? And this one woman keeps..."

Hillary's face frowned as she interrupted Meagan, "What did you just say about Yuraslav's wife?" Meagan's face went blank for a second, then said, "Oh, someone wanted to know if we had placed her in protective custody."

That gave Hillary an uneasy feeling and she thought to herself, *Why would someone want to know that?* "Meagan, do you remember if that caller had any kind of accent or not?"

"Well, yeah, maybe a little bit. He sure didn't sound like anybody I grew up with. I figured he was a reporter or something."

Oh, no! They are looking for Suzanna! Damnit! "Ok, Meagan, listen to me. Don't answer anyone else's questions, and under no circumstances are you to even respond to any questions about Yuraslav's wife, okay?"

Meagan looked a little upset, thinking maybe she had done something wrong. "Ok, I won't, but I told them I didn't know, because, well, I don't. But I assume, now, that she is in protective custody, right?"

Hillary was already gone. She ran out to the parking lot just as Hank was pulling in. Breathless, she caught up to the car as he was parking and hurriedly motioned for him to roll down the window. Hank saw her mouth moving, but couldn't understand, so he rolled the window down, just in time to hear her say, "Hank, don't turn the car off! Go to the Holiday Inn and check on Suzanna! I think they are looking for her. Someone called earlier and asked dispatch if she had been placed in protective custody. She's in room 212. I will call the room while you are in route." Then she ran back into the station to grab her phone. She stopped at Meagan's station and asked quickly, "What time did that call take place? Just give me an estimate."

"Uh, probably about an hour ago."

Damnit! They have an hour on us; God I hope they haven't found her, she thought to herself as she dialed the number to the Holiday Inn.

In a thick Czech accent the receptionist answered, "Thank you for calling de Holiday Inn, Gulf Shores, Alabama. Dis is Ivana speaking. How may I direct your call?"

"Ivana, this is Detective Hillary Thompson with the Orange Beach Police Department. Will you please ring room 212 for me?"

"Yes, one moment, uh, 212, you wanna talk to Suzanna?"

Hillarie's heart sped up. "Ivana, do you know Suzanna?"

"Oh, yes, I cannot believe what her husband did to dos people! I feel so sorry for her. My friend used to work wit him. Dey were always drinking together."

Hillary's heart beat raced. "Ivana, did you tell anyone that Suzanna was staying at the hotel?"

Ivana was silent. The tone of the officer's question let her know that she had messed up. Her silence spoke volumes and nearly crushed Hillary's hope that no one had found her yet. Ivana quickly patched her through to Suzanna's room, and when no one picked up, Hillary began to panic.

CHAPTER EIGHTEEN

Suzanna had been placed in room 212 and her parents in 213. As Hank walked through the hallway toward the rooms, he felt his heart beat quicken when he saw the hotel manager, a young woman, and an older couple standing in front of an open hotel door with the numbers 212. All four people became suddenly silent as Hank ran up to them. "Is Suzanna here? I am Detective Hank Jordan," he said as he pulled out his badge. The older woman began to cry and her angry husband started hurling questions at Hank and the hotel manager. The young woman said nothing as the manager and the older man began to argue. Hank put his hand up in the air and whistled, grabbing all of their attention again. "Hey, calm down! I asked if she was here."

The older man introduced himself as Suzanna's father and said, "Hell no, she's not here! You guys were supposed to watch us! All of her stuff is still here! We went to bed an hour ago and never heard her leave. Where the hell is she? Did y'all move her without telling us?" The man's nostrils were flaring with anger. He hadn't wanted to leave his house in the first place.

"No, sir, we didn't move her." He asked the parents to step aside, and he walked through the open doorway of Suzanna's hotel room. Nothing looked out of place and there was no sign of any struggle. Her clothes were still packed in a suitcase, a wet towel hung on the bathroom door from where she had taken a shower, and her purse still lay on the dresser. He reached down inside it to make sure that her wallet was still there, and found it; it still held a little cash, credit cards, and her driver's license. Hank grabbed his radio and called all available units to the hotel, then looked at the manager. "I want every one of your employees, including yourself, in the front office now. No one is to go anywhere until I say so, is that clear? I need to know if anyone saw her leave!"

"Yes, sir, Detective." The manager quickly turned to escort the young woman who had been standing next to him back down to the office. Hank noticed that her name tag read 'Ivana'. Her name didn't sound like the usual American name on the island so he stopped them before they could disappear around the corner toward the office. "Hey, hold on a second. Your name is Ivana? Are you Czech?"

Ivana slowly turned around to answer Hank. Her face was enflamed with embarrassment and guilt. "Yes, sir. I just spoke wit another Detective, a woman, about Suzanna. She asked me if I told anyone she was here. I never answered her and she hung up da phone." She began to cry. "I am so sorry! I did tell people she was here. I told my friends. We all want to help, and I told dem she was staying here so her husband couldn't find her. I didn't know dat I was making mistake. I am so sorry."

Hank was furious. "I need a list of all the people who you talked to about Suzanna. I need their names and phone numbers, on paper, now!"

The manager apologized again and turned to escort Ivana to the office to gather the rest of the employees for questioning. Hank and Suzanna's sobbing parents followed.

CHAPTER NINTEEN

Thirty minutes before Hank found Suzanna's room empty, the two Czech men in black had been sitting in their car behind some trees that marked the entrance to a wooded bike trail, waiting to make their next move. They were across the street and down a couple of houses from Suzanna's parent's house. They were listening to a local radio station about the details of what Yuraslav had done to the Morrison's when one of their cell phones rang. One of the men checked his caller id, and saw that his girlfriend, Ivana, was calling from work. He rolled his eyes to his partner and answered the phone.

He spoke to her in Czech, "Ano, Ivana, what do want? I am busy."

Ivana was proud of herself for learning English so quickly and preferred to converse in English over Czech. "Good to hear you, too! Listen, you know dat piece of shit dat you used to work wit, Yuraslav? Da one everybody is looking for?"

That caught his attention. "Ano, what about him?"

"Well, his wife is hiding from him here, at da hotel. I saw her in da parking lot when her parents came to check in."

He tried very hard to suppress his excitement over his good luck; his partner noticed it and leaned in to listen to the conversation. He still spoke in Czech. "Hmmm. Well, I hope they catch him! I can't believe what he did to those people! Are her parents staying there too?"

"Yes, I felt so sorry for dem, so I gave dem two suites for regular price."

He thought about this for a moment, trying to figure out how to ask her what rooms they were staying in without making her suspicious. What he said next had rolled right off of his tongue, as if he had been born to be the greatest liar in the world. "Oh, yeah, I remember when I worked in house keeping there last year. It sucked! The suites are difficult to clean because they are bigger. Which ones are they in?"

Ivana continued in English. "I never knew dat you worked here! You never told me."

"Oh, well, it was only for two weeks, before they could find me a better job." He paused for a minute then asked, "I remember cleaning the ones in the back, and they were pretty."

"No, those aren't da good ones; they are away from da beach. I put her in 212 and her parents next door in 213, so dey could have a waterfront view. Do you remember those? Dey are much nicer."

Yes! Oh, Ivana, thank you. "Oh, well, Ivana, I need to go now, I was watching something on TV. I will call you back later, ok?"

Ivana sighed at the lack of interest that her boyfriend was showing. "Okay, call me back."

They hung up. He looked over at his partner and grinned from ear to ear. Thanks to Ivana's stupidity, they would really show the Russians that they could handle business. They found the girl by themselves, and would deliver her with no help at all. Surely that would get them more money, not to mention the trust and respect of the Russians in Atlanta. They started the car and headed to the Gulf Shores beach strip. They parked next door behind a closed souvenir shop, walked up the beach to the back entrance of the Holiday Inn and hoped that the privacy gate did not require a key card to gain entrance. It didn't. Quietly, they snuck in through the indoor pool entrance and found the elevator to the second floor. Within a minute, they were at her door with a soft knock. Ivana's boyfriend stated softly, in his best English accent, that he was sent to check on her from the front office, to make sure everything was ok. Suzanna wearily got out of the bed and went to the door, opened it, and before she could even look at her attacker's faces, they rushed in with their hands, clamping them over her mouth and eyes, and forced her to the floor. Ivana's boyfriend quickly blind folded her, taped her mouth shut, and her hands together. He leaned toward her ear and whispered, "Suzanna, I will kill you if you try to get away from me. Don't fight me; just walk where I lead you. Nod your head if you understand."

Suzanna nodded limply at her Czech kidnapper. *This is it,* she thought. *Now, I am going to die. Yuri's not going to kill me, some other stupid Czech is. Oh my god, I hope they don't have my parents!* Scared, confused but submissive, Suzanna allowed them to lift her from the floor and walk her to the exit stairs, past the pool, down the beach and into the trunk of their vehicle. She didn't stop crying until the car started moving. *I can't believe this shit, she thought as she listened to the music coming from the front seat.* Not only was she hog tied and taped up in the trunk of a car, on the way to her probable death, but they were making her listen to David Hasselhoff on the way there. *What is it with Czechs and Hasselhoff?* She shook her head, and started to think of all the bad things she had ever done in her life; some were things that she hadn't thought of in years. She carefully called upon God in prayer and asked for forgiveness and thought, *How easy it is to recall all of your mistakes and wrongdoings when you feel like your time is up.* She made her peace and waited.

CHAPTER TWENTY

When they were fifteen miles outside of Charlotte traveling Interstate 85 North, Mirek phoned Vladimir to let him know where they were.

"Take the first airport exit, park in the back of the parking lot by the dumpster of the Days Inn and wait until someone shows up for you. He will park in front of you, flash his lights, and then you are to follow him. Before you go, put Yuraslav in the car with him." Vladimir said to him. "Oh, and you can tell Yuraslav that I have his wife."

Mirek smiled to himself as he hung up. They would spare him and kill Yuraslav, just like he had hoped. On the way to Charlotte, he had decided that when they stopped for gas again, he would hide the contents of the trunk and use them as a bargaining chip later. He put his plan into action, and repeated the instructions that Vladimir had just given him to Petra, although tweaking them just a little to fit into his plan.

"Petra, we are to take the airport exit and park in the back of the parking lot of the Days Inn. But, stop at a gas station first, I'm thirsty."

"Do you want me to stop now at a gas station or wait until we take the exit?"

"No, stop now."

Petra looked up at an exit sign that read McAdenville, a quarter of a mile ahead. She pulled into the far right lane and took the exit ramp.

"Take a left to that gas station."

Petra turned left and pulled into a CITGO gas station and tire repair shop.

"I suggest that you both use the bathroom now. I have no idea when you will be able to go again. He didn't tell me where we are going. I will stay in the car until you both get back. And by the way, Yuri, Vladimir asked me to tell you that he has your wife. I wonder what he will do with her." Mirek belted out a long dramatic laugh at his partner.

Yuraslav and Petra looked at each other, shrugged and left the car. The possibility that Suzanna might die a horrible death at the hands of Vladimir didn't really bother Yuraslav; but thinking about her being with another man sexually bothered him greatly, and he knew Vladimir would rape her. It made him jealous; after all, she was his property. He fumed at the thought as he stomped toward the bathroom door.

While they were gone, Mirek quickly popped the trunk and removed the spare tire. At first, everything looked normal, but as he began to remove the paperwork, he realized that the dead woman's computer wasn't there. Where was the laptop that Yuraslav had taken from the house? He threw the spare tire on the ground and started violently searching through the contents of the trunk. It wasn't there! *The son of a bitch put it somewhere else!* He thought to himself. Mirek laughed. *Maybe the stupid son of a bitch wasn't so stupid after all. He must have hid the computer to ensure his life, the same thing I'm trying to do right now! He is smarter than I thought he was. Alright then, we both live. You have the computer, and I have the paperwork.* He removed all the papers and folders to make sure they weren't just garbage replaced by Yuraslav; satisfied, he put them back in the black bag, and scanned the grounds of the gas station for a good hiding spot. On the side of the tire repair shop that was connected to the gas station, he spied a huge pile of old rotting tires. The tires were surrounded by a collection of trash and tall weeds growing all around them; it appeared that they had been there for quite some time and in no apparent immediate threat of being disposed of. Looking around to make sure that there were no better hiding places, Mirek made a mad dash towards the tires with the duffel bag. He had to hurry before they got back to the car.

Petra exited the bathroom just in time to see Mirek run for the tires with all the paperwork she had given them. From a window in the gas station, she watched him bend down at the pile of tires. She immediately figured out what he was doing, and rushed back into the bathroom to gather her thoughts before he saw her at the window. This was her chance! If he was hiding the documents, then the documents were very valuable to him. His life depended on it maybe? If his life depended on it, then hers did too, and if she played her cards right, then she would rat him out, leaving herself at the top; a true Darwinian,

73

survival of the fittest. She waited five minutes before exiting the bathroom again, and nonchalantly crossed the parking lot in the direction of the car. Yuraslav had already returned. He was just sliding into the passenger seat when Mirek yelled at Petra to return to the store and purchase him a soda.

She went back into the store and bought him a Mountain Dew. While standing at the counter, she saw a stack of business cards by the cash register from the tire repair shop and slipped one of them into her pocket. She didn't want to forget the exit, and, if she decided to rat out Mirek, she would have proof that they stopped here on the way. On second thought, maybe, if she could find a way to run from them, she would slip back here and use one of the passports to get somewhere else. There were many of them in the duffel bag, along with matching work visas and social security cards. Sneaking away from these men might be impossible, but she would keep that idea on the back burner in case she didn't have to drop the dime on Mirek in order to live.

She brought the drink to Mirek, who sat casually in the backseat with a slightly smug look on his face, and returned to the interstate towards the airport exit. *Ha-ha-ha,* she laughed to herself, *you're not as smart as think you are, you piece of shit.*

CHAPTER TWENTY-ONE

Ivana handed Detective Hank Jordan the list of people that he had asked for, but had purposefully left off her boyfriend's name and made no mention that she had even talked to him; she did not suspect him of anything, but his visa had run out six months ago, and she didn't want him to get in trouble. After the detective interviewed all of the employees and left the Holiday Inn, she tried to call her boyfriend several times, but he wouldn't answer his cell phone. She figured that he was still engrossed in whatever television show that he had been watching earlier, probably Baywatch. Her boss had raked her over the coals. He had warned her that she probably wouldn't be there much longer after he got in touch with her placement company, but that she would have to work the rest of the night because there was no one else available to come in. She wasn't worried about getting another job. No Czech ever went without a job for very long. If she was fired, there would most likely be new employment available for her as soon as she woke up the next morning.

Ivana had a good heart, and felt terrible about what she had done, although she didn't feel that it was her fault that Suzanna was missing. She knew everyone she had told very well, and none of them could ever do something as bad as kidnapping someone. Still, she couldn't shake the uneasy feeling that had consumed her since the Detective showed up. She should have written her boyfriends name on the list. Perhaps, she would call the detective in the morning and explain to him why she had left his name off the list, and ask that he turn a blind eye to his expired a visa. Americans were known for their sympathy, and the thought of coming clean with Detective Jordan in the morning actually made her feel a little bit better. Ivana returned to her duty answering phones.

The disappearance of Suzanna was a terrible blow to the case, and Hank was devastated and exhausted. He had personally gone to several of the homes of the people on the list that Ivana had given him, while

Hillary had visited the rest. No one admitted to knowing anything about Suzanna's disappearance, much less the whereabouts of Yuraslav. They were all very cooperative, mostly because they didn't want the police digging into their work history and visa information. The general consensus had been the same from all of them; no one had a nice thing to say about Yuraslav Novacek. He was well known for his belligerent and aggressive attitude, and most people stayed away from him, especially when he was drinking in thc local hangouts.

On the way back to the station, Hank decided to call Judith to check in with her about Anna's status. Remembering that she had called his cell phone earlier, the best idea would be to scroll through and find her number instead of calling the hospital room this late at night; but then again, she would be in the room, so it would be the same. Either way, he wanted to talk to her, so he found her number and programmed it under her name so he would have it in his saved directory. She answered on the first ring.

"Hi, Detective."

"Hey there. You know, earlier you asked me to call you Judith, so you can do the same by calling me Hank."

"Absolutely! Hank it is. How is everything?"

"Well, it's about as bad as it can get. We placed Yuraslav's wife and parents in protective custody today, and now, well, she is missing. Either someone took her, or she ran, and my guess is that she was kidnapped. Her purse and clothes are still at the hotel, being poured over at the moment for any clues. I doubt if there will be any. Yuraslav is still missing, and there hasn't been one single report of anyone seeing him. How is Anna?"

"I am so sorry, Hank." Judith sighed into the phone. "She was awake for about two hours after you left, answering questions and taking me through what happened to her last night. It was so painful to listen to her talk about it. I cried, she cried, hell, we all cried. But, the whole time she talked, I kept thinking about how amazingly brave this child is. She knows that her family is dead, and she knows what happened to her, even though she doesn't understand it really. She wants to help. She wants to tell everything she can remember so they will be caught. Those were her words. Amazing! I can't believe she is not still in serious shock."

"Are you staying at the hospital tonight?"

"Yes, I am. I had a friend bring over some personal items for me earlier tonight, and I will be with her for at least a couple of days, until she feels comfortable enough with the nursing staff for me to leave her with them for any extended period of time."

"Ok, well, I will probably drop by there in the morning before I go to the station. Please call me if you need anything, or if Anna needs anything, and goodnight, Judith."

"Goodnight, Hank, and thank you." She caught herself smiling and wiped it from her face. *This is not the time for this, Judy,* she thought to herself. *How could I be the least bit happy about this man calling me at a time like this?* She pulled her hospital bed closer to Anna's, laid down and fell asleep.

Hank stopped by the station, met with the officers on duty about the recent course of events, returned a couple of phone calls to the feds and to a few media people in Mobile, and then made his way home. It was two in the morning by the time his head hit the pillow. Five minutes later, he was snoring. The last thing he thought of as he drifted to sleep was Doctor Esther. *She is so pretty...*

CHAPTER TWENTY-TWO

"We have the girl. Where do we need to take her?" He asked when his Russian boss answered his phone call.

Taken completely by surprise, Vladimir cleared his throat, and said pleasantly, "Excellent! I am not even going to ask you how you found her, but I trust that no one saw you do it?"

"No, no one saw anything."

"Gas up, and drive to Atlanta. Call me when you are fifteen miles outside the city, or if something goes wrong, but otherwise do not call me. Where is she now?"

"In the trunk."

"Take her out. Cut her hair off and make her wear a hat, but do not harm her. I am sure that her face will be everywhere, right alongside her husband's in a short time. Threaten her with death if she tries to run, and tell her that her parents have been kidnapped as well. Do not stop unless you have to get gas, and make sure you drive the speed limit. If you fail to get her here within seven hours, I will kill you, do you understand?"

"We understand. And don't worry; we will have her there on time. How much are you going to pay us?" His question went unanswered; Vladimir had already hung up. The two men drove until they reached Foley, and then stopped at a gas station. Ivana's boyfriend walked into the gas station and bought sodas, a couple of bags of potato ships, and a pair of scissors, while his partner pumped the gas. After the gas was paid for, they drove for about a mile and then pulled into the back parking lot of another gas station on the outskirts of town. Suzanna was pulled from the trunk and quickly thrown into the backseat. They removed her blindfold, so she could see them, but they kept her taped up so she couldn't scream while they relayed Vladimir's message to her. After they finished telling her what would happen if she did anything stupid, she was asked if she understood. Suzanna nodded and the tape was removed from her mouth and hands. She recognized the one who had been talking to her but couldn't remember his name. She thought to herself while trying to remember his name. *He used to work at Sea Ray's Restaurant, and his girlfriend's name is Ivana.* Occasionally, she saw them at the bar together. The other man who was driving the vehicle was a complete stranger, but she knew he was Czech just by looking at him. They both wore black Nike jumpsuits, accessorized by at least twenty gold chains and bracelets between the two of them.

She took the scissors as she was told and cut all of her hair off, watching the locks fall onto the seat beside her. It was painful for her to watch her hair fall down, and she knew immediately what it must have felt like for the Jews when their hair was cut off before they were gassed in the chambers. She quickly dismissed the thought, and decided to think about better things, as if she had anything better to do; she sat silently in the backseat as they took off down Highway 59 towards Interstate 65. They hadn't told her where they were going; just that they would kill her if she tried to get away. It didn't matter, she told herself. After the Russians find out what she had told the police, there would be nothing to hope for; she was dead already.

CHAPTER TWENTY-THREE

Petra found her way to the hotel that Vladimir instructed them to stop at and parked beside the dumpster in the back just like he had told them to. All three of them sat in silence, waiting for the next move. Finally, they spotted the SUV that Vladimir had promised them. It drove straight towards them, stopped, and flashed the headlights on and off several times. That was Yuraslav's signal to change vehicles. Submitting, he shakily exited Petra's car and got into the one that was waiting for him. Petra and Mirek watched as he disappeared behind the heavily tinted windows, and then followed the SUV back out onto the interstate. They drove up I-85, for about thirty minutes, past Charlotte, and exited again. Petra continued to follow the SUV from the exit and drove for another thirty minutes until they turned again. Several turns later in the middle of what felt like nowhere, the leading SUV pulled into a long driveway that led to a large house. There were no neighbors on either side of the house, just a couple of other cars with South Carolina tags parked in the driveway. Worrying about what would happen to them next, Petra was so nervous that she could hear her own heart beat. As she parked her car behind the other ones, she debated on whether to take the pain pills now, or wait until later. She guessed that she could at least wait until she found out who was in the house and what they were planning to do; she didn't want to waste the pills by taking them too early.

Three men appeared on the front porch, and waited for the four of them to walk to the house. The driver of the SUV pointed a gun to Yuraslav's back and motioned him to the trunk of Petra's car to retrieve the paperwork and computer, while Petra and Mirek watched in silence. Suddenly, Yuraslav winced, remembering for the first time that he had forgotten to grab the computer from the house. He had been so preoccupied with what he was going to get to do to the woman and girl that he had totally forgotten about the computer. He had grabbed the files, but walked right out of Tammy's office without her

80

laptop. As he slowly opened the trunk and removed the spare tire, shock left him speechless and motionless. The trunk underneath the spare tire, where earlier that day he had placed the duffel bag and all of its contents, was now an empty cavity, holding nothing but a tire wrench. Openmouthed but unable to actually speak at first, Yuraslav spun around and looked questioningly at the driver who still had a gun pointed at him, then turned his attention to his partner, Mirek. "It's not here! I put it here. You fucking stole it! Where is it? They will kill you, you bastard!"

The driver hit Yuraslav in the back of his head with the gun, knocking him out cold on the gravel. His head hit hard with a thump, and for the time being, was ignored. Mirek looked at the three men on the porch and said quickly, "Yes, I placed it somewhere safe because I didn't trust him! When I looked in the trunk to make sure it was all there, I noticed the computer missing. He never put it in the trunk like he was supposed to. I will only tell Vladimir where the papers are when I see him. As for the computer, you will have to ask Yuraslav when he wakes up. He hid it somewhere, I'm sure."

One of the Russians slapped him hard across the face, and told the driver to take Yuraslav and Petra into the house. "You know, Vladimir will kill you for this. You are a very stupid man, you know?"

Defiantly, Mirek stared back at the man who slapped him and said very slowly as he licked the blood from the corner of his mouth, "Vladimir might kill me, this is true, but you can't because you don't have the papers yet, so I guess I will take my chances when I see him."

The Russians looked at each other and then exploded in laughter, "He thinks he is a funny man?"

"Yes, he thinks he is a smart and funny guy." More laughter. They patted him hard on the back and invited him to join them inside the house, suddenly pretending that they were his best friends in the whole world. They poured him a glass of vodka and called Vladimir to tell him what had transpired.

"He did what!" Vladimir screamed into the phone. "Tie him up, Yuraslav too! Tie them up and beat them until they tell you where everything is. But do not mark their faces and do not kill them. I have to have those files and computer. As for Petra, she may know something that she is not telling. Do whatever you want to her. I don't care.

She is nothing more than a dead whore anyway. I will leave for Charlotte in the morning."

As the Czechs were being tied up, Petra saw the three Russians staring at her; she knew what was about to happen. She slowly lowered her hand into her purse, popped the top off the bottle and quickly palmed five Lortabs. That would be more than enough for her frame of ninety five pounds, maybe ninety now that her hair was gone. She popped them all into her mouth at the same time and began swallowing them as fast as she could while the Russians finished their jobs. Then, they came for her. She was picked up and thrown into a bedroom, her body sliding across the hard wood floor and slamming into the foot of the bed. The pills would take a couple of minutes to work, and she screamed in pain as her hip bone met the metal frame. The door slammed shut, and she was left alone on the floor. Twenty minutes later, they came for her again. Her clothes were ripped off, her breasts were roughly groped by squeezing hands, and then her face was smashed into the groins of the Russians. Six hands were on her at the same time, beating her, pulling her, and slapping her. The drugs had taken effect by the time the real abuse started, and Petra couldn't even cry. She just let them bounce her around like a rag doll, penetrating her in every orifice she had, raping her until they were spent and exhausted. Then she and her clothes were gathered up, taken outside to the backyard and thrown on the floor in the closet of a locked utility shed. She laid there in her own blood, and finally fell into a drug induced sleep.

CHAPTER TWENTY-FOUR

While Petra was falling asleep, Suzanna Novacek was wide awake in the back seat of the car traveling to what ever hell lay waiting for her at the hands of the Russians in Atlanta. She had begged and pleaded with the two Czechs off and on throughout the trip to let her go. She offered them sex, money, anything she could think of, but they just laughed at her and told her to shut up. When she realized that nothing would make them have any kind of compassion for her whatsoever, Suzanna began to think of ways to kill herself before the Russians got to her. She wished that she had slit her wrists earlier with the scissors from the gas station but now there was nothing in the backseat but her hair in a plastic bag on the floorboard.

When they were fifteen minutes from Atlanta, The Czech man in the passenger seat made a phone call to Vladimir.

"We are passing Peach Tree City right now, where do we go from here?"

Vladimir gave him directions to a house in Buckhead, which he repeated to the driver. The phone call ended, and Suzanna began to recite over and over in her head the address of the house in Buckhead; she committed it to memory in case she found a way out of the mess that her husband had gotten her into. *4591 Hillshire Road. 4591 Hillshire Road. Remember, please remember. Buckhead, Hillshire Road, 4591.*

Earlier, when they had kidnapped her from her room at the Holiday Inn, she had recognized one of the Czechs who now sat in the passenger seat but couldn't remember his name. Now, she knew it. The driver had spoken his name, Jan, and Jan had spoken Vladimir's name. She still didn't know the driver's name; he hadn't been much of a talker. At this point, the only information she was equipped with was the address of their destination, one of the kidnapper's names, and the Russian boss' name. She repeated all of the known facts and details in her head until they arrived at Hillshire Road. *Vladimir, the Russian boss' name is Vladimir. Ivana's boyfriend's name is Jan. We are going to 4591 Hillshire Road.* When they finally pulled into the driveway of the house, her stomach leaped into her throat, and she strained to suppress the urge to vomit. All of the lights in the house were off making Jan doubt they had come to the right house. Just as he was about to call Vladimir again to make sure that they had the right address, the garage door began to open for them, allowing them to park alongside a black suburban.

Vladimir stood smiling in the doorway with a glass of wine in his hand, motioning for them to come in, as if they were guests arriving at his birthday party. His strange mannerisms and attitude made everyone in the car, not just Suzanna, nervous. He was a thug, but he was also the boss of many other thugs. In light of the situation, Suzanna thought that he was behaving a little too politely and pleasantly for her comfort; when a mafia boss behaves this way at an inappropriate time, it usually means someone is going to die soon or be seriously injured. And this was definitely an inappropriate time for him to be leisurely sipping a glass of wine in an unlit house, beckoning them with warm hand gestures into the pitch black garage. The two Czechs nervously glanced at each other as they slowly parked the car alongside the Suburban. When the car doors opened and the two kidnappers emerged, Suzanna heard Vladimir say in a joyous voice, "Welcome!" Seconds before they turned around to release Suzanna from her backseat prison, two men leapt like lions from the corner of the unlit garage. They grabbed Jan and his partner, placed bags over their heads, and quickly shoved them to the concrete floor of the garage. Each man received a swift bullet in their temples.

Speechless, Suzanna watched in horror as the two Russian thugs picked up the dead Czechs and quickly began cleaning up the mess they had created on the garage floor. She couldn't scream, breathe or move, even as Vladimir opened her door, grabbed her arm and pulled her into the house. The shock of what she had just witnessed made it impossible to defend herself or fight off Vladimir's grip. As soon as he got her into the kitchen, he taped her mouth shut, drove a syringe filled with liquid Rohypnol into her arm, and patiently waited until the drug took effect; it didn't take long. The drug swam through her veins quickly, like a fire through a vineyard. After Suzanna groaned and slumped over, he picked her up and carried her into a bedroom, where she was tucked in tightly and handcuffed to the bed post. Then he walked to another bedroom and laid down to catch a couple of hours of sleep before he left in the morning for Charlotte. He hadn't expected her to be so pretty in person, and he fell asleep thinking about what he would do to her when the time came. Instead of counting sheep, he counted the bruises and cuts that would eventually cover her body; Vladimir slept like a baby.

CHAPTER TWENTY-FIVE

The alarm clock buzzed loudly at precisely five-forty five. Groaning and pleading with time to allow just five more minutes of sleep, Hank finally shut off the alarm and rolled out of bed. He felt like a dump truck had run over him, then backed up and unloaded a couple pounds of concrete into his mouth while he slept. He slowly walked to the bathroom where he proceeded to complete three "S" tasks of the morning, and was dressed and ready for work in thirty minutes. The first task of the day was a visit to the hospital to check on little Anna and talk with Judith. On the way to the hospital, he phoned Hillary, who was already at the station, making phone calls, and preparing the brief for the morning meeting.

"Good morning Hill. How is everything? Tell me something good."

"Hey Hank. Well, umm, I am going to wait until after the meeting to work on the phone numbers from Tammy's phone records. I would like for you to be here, so you can talk with them also. Something really bad is happening here, Hank. This island is going to be a lot different in a couple of hours. The press will be all over this place like stink on shit when we expose what I think is going on here. Would you ever have imagined? The Russian Mafia, here, on this island? Think of all the business owners who depend solely on these workers? God, what a mess!"

"Yeah I know. Have you talked to the mayor yet about all of this?"

"No, but he is supposed to be here any minute, for the meeting. Why?"

"Well then, maybe you ought to pull him aside and prep him a little bit, before all hell breaks loose. He gave me the go ahead to get others involved, but I haven't exactly told him every step we have taken so far. The FBI is going to be there, along with the INS, and they are going to be investigating, pretty much, everyone who has a business on this island."

"Oh! Thanks, Hank! I really owe you one for entrusting me to the job of prepping Fearless Fred. In fact, I am so excited about it, that I will hang up now because I can't wait to talk to him!"

Hank laughed at the sarcasm which always flowed so naturally from Hillary's mouth. It was one of the reasons he loved working with her so much. Hillary was a Class A, bona fide smart ass, who would say anything to anybody, regardless of who they were. She had the verbal skills to be able to say something sarcastic to someone and immediately walk away, leaving them wondering if she was being nice or a brutal bitch. Hank had always admired that about her, and often joked with her about teaching a Mouthy101 class at the local junior college instead of being a police officer. "Alright, call me if you need me. I am on the way to the hospital right now. I thought I would stop by before coming in."

They hung up with each other as he pulled into the hospital parking lot. Hank had always hated hospitals. The smell of antiseptic, the fluorescent lights, and that occasional light headed feeling that he got from the high oxygen levels had always disturbed him. When he approached the window of Anna's room, he paused for a moment to watch Judith sitting next to Anna; she was reading a book about Sponge Bob Squarepants. He noticed once again how beautiful the doctor was, especially for almost seven o'clock in the morning, with no makeup, and her hair pulled back in a ponytail. There was another woman in the room with them. She looked familiar, but Hank couldn't quite place her. He hated to interrupt the story, but the meeting back at the station was scheduled for eight o'clock; he tapped lightly at the door and walked in. Judith smiled and glanced at the other woman who was already standing to shake his hand.

"Hey, Hank. It's been a long time. Judith said you were coming. I don't know if you remember me...I'm Gwen, Tammy's sister." She spoke Tammy's name very softly and looked down at the hospital floor as she held a hand out to Hank.

Now, he remembered. Gwen was about five years older than Tammy, and had left the island for college after graduation when Hank, John and Tammy had been in junior high school together. She had married an attorney from Biloxi, and now lived in Tupelo. He guessed that she and her husband would now be the parents of Anna.

Her took her hand and said, "Hey Gwen. Yes, it has been a long time. I am so sorry about everything. Is there anything that I can do?"

"Just find them, Hank." she whispered and turned from Anna so she wouldn't see her tears. Hank nodded and hugged her, allowing her a couple of minutes to calm herself before he spoke to Judith.

She wiped her face, and looked back at Hank. "Gary, my husband, and I are staying with Daddy. As soon as Tammy's house is cleaned, we will be going through everything and placing it in storage, and getting Anna ready for her new life with us in Tupelo. I am in charge of all of the funeral arrangements, because, well, Daddy and Mama just can't deal with it. It's just horrible. I, uh, just want to thank you for all that you are doing. We appreciate everything." Then, she looked at Anna, who was engrossed in Spongebob, and asked, "Sweetie, do you mind if I read to you for a little while so that Doctor Judy can talk to her friend?"

"Aunt Gwen, will you read me the next one too?" Anna asked sweetly. Gwen let go of Hank's hand and sat down beside her niece.

Checking his watch, Hank slipped quietly out of the room to wait for Judith. She followed him to the waiting room, and they sat down together on a brightly covered couch, chosen especially for the pediatric ward.

"Good morning, Hank." she said. "Want some coffee? One of the nurses just made a fresh pot. I can get you a cup if you want."

"No thanks, I gotta get to the station. We are meeting with just about everybody and their dog this morning. We gotta get a lead on this thing quick before all the trails get cold. I feel like Suzanna's missing is entirely my fault. We have to find her."

Judith nodded in agreement and saw Hank checking his watch. "Did you have something to tell me? You said you wanted to stop by here, and I didn't know what about. I guess I was so tired when you phoned last night that I forgot to ask."

Hank's face turned red. He thought to himself, *Why did I come here?* He knew. He cleared his throat and shifted his weight and said, "Uh, I, uh, just wanted to check on Anna, to make sure she was feeling better."

Judith smiled at him, swallowed, and responded after an awkward silence, "And to see me?"

He let his breath out slowly and looked at her. His poker face sucked. "Yes, I did want to see you."

"Ok, good, because I wanted to see you too." She reached over and patted his hand with hers, and stood up to say goodbye. "You are going to be late."

Hank looked down at his watch, nodded and lunged forward to stand up. "Ok, well, I will call you later, or call me if you need anything."

"Be careful."

He turned and walked towards the elevator, extremely unimpressed with himself, shaking his head and thinking, *That was real smooth, Hank.*

Smiling the whole time, Judith watched him disappear into the elevator. She really liked this guy, and now, he knew it. Relieved that Gwen had arrived, she sat back down on the couch and drank some coffee, relaxing a little before she had to return to the sad little broken being of what used to be a precious innocent little girl. The timing was worse than terrible, but she was glad that she had met Hank. Seeing him walk into the room moments before, somehow, just made her feel and safe and at peace.

CHAPTER TWENTY-SIX

Mayor Fred Michaels, or as Hillary liked to refer to him, Fearless Fred, stood at the conference table and greeted each person who sat down with a smile that didn't necessarily constitute a display of happiness. He was grateful for the all the help and dedication to the case, but not for the attention that came along with it. Nausea had hit him earlier, when Hillary prepped him for the meeting; the feeling still lingered as he thought about all the damage that the situation had and would cause to the island. Not only was almost an entire family of a very close friend of his murdered, but the entire town of Orange Beach, that he personally was in charge of looking after, was now under serious investigation. He had already turned his cell phone off, tired of fielding calls from business owners and friends who had been contacted by the FBI and INS for hiring illegal immigrants. Hell, almost every member in the Chamber of Commerce had at least one Czech, Brazilian, or Mexican working for them. His own housekeeper was from the Czech Republic. She didn't speak a lick of English, but she cleaned the hell out of a dirty house. For eight months, Fred had written her wages in the form of a check made out to the company, Top Notch Cleaning,

who outsourced her. The checks were mailed to a PO Box in Foley. In the back of his mind, like everyone else who had employees through these companies, he figured that everything wasn't truly as it should be. But everyone else was doing it, and business on the island carried on smoother than it had before Hurricane Ivan hit; merchandise sales were high in the tourists shops, the restaurants were packed, and the hotels were clean and running smoothly. No questions were ever asked; if no questions were asked, then no one would have to know anything. As far as everyone was concerned, it was just another matter of dealing with normal contract labor. While Fred waited for everyone to walk into the conference room, he silently cursed himself for being so blind to the situation, or rather being unwilling to acknowledge the serious repercussions of allowing this large of an illegal labor problem to grow in his community. He nodded at Hank as the he entered the room and settled in for the meeting.

"Good morning, everyone." He looked around at all of the people stuffed inside the small conference room. "I am Chief Investigator Hank Jordan. My partner on the right here is Hillary Thompson, and the man sitting to my left is the Mayor of Orange Beach, Fred Michaels. As you all know, Suzanna Novacek, Yuraslav Novacek's wife, disappeared last night after being placed in protective custody at the local Holiday Inn. We believe that she has been kidnapped by either Czechs affiliated with her husband, or members of the Russian Mafia, who we believe currently own most, if not all, of the outsourcing companies that provide many of the workers on this island. That being said, I will allow Officer Thompson to speak to everyone about where this case currently stands." Everyone nodded and glanced at their personal notes as she began to speak. She was the only female in the room with any clout, and it was obvious that it made some of the men uncomfortable.

Hillary stood proudly as she spoke to the sea of male officers. "Good morning, gentlemen. We have learned that John and Tammy Morrison owned thirty different rental properties here on the island. Tammy Morrison handled all of them by herself. Although she, like most people here, did not rent her properties based on credit checks, somewhere along the way she decided to do some research on ten different applications that were submitted to her a month ago. We don't know why she chose to check up on these, but something evidently spooked her. When her office was investigated after the murders, the contents of the files that she kept on these ten properties were missing. However, her computer was confiscated and brought in as evidence, and when we searched through her saved history, we learned that Tammy had come across the obituaries and other articles stating the deaths of each one of the ten applicators via a search run through the Internet. The deceased were all Czech immigrants, residing and working in various states. I have provided each of you with a file, containing all of this information." She paused as another officer began passing out the files. "All in all, we believe that Tammy reported her findings to the corresponding local authorities the day before she and her family were murdered. We also believe that she contacted the company or companies who sent her the applications, to tell them what she had done. DNA and fingerprints, as you know, place Yuraslav Novacek at the crime scene, but Detective Jordan and I do not think he is acted alone. We believe that these outsourcing companies are owned, for the most part, by the Russian Mafia, who under the circumstances, benefit quite nicely from the Czech workers here on this island and the other states mentioned in the file. We also believe that Yuraslav was either ordered or hired by these Russians to murder the Morrison family, because of what Tammy had found out. At the end of this meeting I will be contacting the numbers of the different police stations we found in Tammy's phone records, to see who Tammy spoke with, and about what. As you all know, the murder itself was quite a shock to this small community. However, the loss of employees and the scandal that will be sure to follow will be an even further blow to the business owners. We have estimated that between Gulf Shores and Orange Beach, there are approximately one thousand five hundred Czechs employed, not to mention the Brazilians and Mexicans."

"Are all of these people illegal?" Someone asked.

"No, but we have to ask ourselves, 'How many of them are legally here under false identification and how many of them are just still here under an expired visa status? It's more complicated than most would think. There are many people that are working here under totally false names, unbeknownst to their employers. We believe that the Russian Mafia basically owns these people and provides them with whatever documents they need to continue working here in the United States." The last folder was passed out and Hillary sat back down next to Hank.

Hank took over from there, discussing with the FBI what measures were being taken to locate Suzanna and Yuraslav. There were a couple of arguments here and there, since there were so many people stuffed into the small room, but finally, after an hour, everyone knew where everyone else stood on the case. Hank stood to end the meeting, "Due to the volume of work and people dedicated to this case, we will be, effective immediately, using the courthouse for meetings throughout the remainder of the case. The FBI has already set up research tables and phone lines there, and a number of people from the community have volunteered to answer tip lines on the whereabouts of Mrs. Novacek and Yuraslav. We will be meeting there every morning at eight o'clock instead of here. This place is just too small. The courthouse is just across the street for those who don't know the area. Thanks for coming, and welcome to Orange Beach, Alabama."

Everyone scattered in a million different directions, and Hank walked out of the conference room to Hillary's desk. She was already seated and making phone calls to the numbers she had circled; she gave Hank the thumbs up as he walked through the office. Holding one hand over the receiver so the caller couldn't hear her, she whispered to Hank, "Did you think anyone noticed when I adjusted my balls back there in the room?" Hank laughed and walked outside to get some air.

CHAPTER TWENTY-SEVEN

They were racing up I-85 towards Charlotte, North Carolina, when the cell phone rang. Glancing down, Vladimir noticed that the caller was from one of the offices in Myrtle Beach, South Carolina. He grabbed the cell phone up from the console and flipped it open it a hurry.

"What is it?" he yelled into the phone.

A very scared Czech girl whined into the phone, "Vladimir, I am so sorry to bother you like dis, but a police officer, she was a woman, from Orange Beach just called here asking questions about Tammy Morrison."

"What?" At the sound of Vladimir's outburst, the driver jumped in his seat and almost swerved into a car passing on the left.

Nervously, the caller said, "I didn't tell her anything, Vladimir. I swear it! I just told her dat someone would have to call her back. What was I suppose to say? Is that alright?"

Vladimir glared across at his driver, who was concentrating more on the conversation that he was on the road, and thought for a moment. The driver immediately turned his full attention back to the road. Vladimir changed his tone and calmly spoke to the caller. "Yes, ok, that was fine. Listen, here is what you do now, ok? Clean the office out right now. Take everything, the files, the books, and the computer; take everything out. Wipe down everything! Leave nothing behind. Then go to a hotel room and pay cash. Call me when you get there." Fuming, he hung up and dialed a number from speed dial. "Ivan, get on the phones right now! Call everyone, and I mean everyone! Tell them to clean their offices, take everything with them and get to a hotel room. Then you call someone to clean the offices. Everything needs to be wiped down! I want every office gutted immediately. A police officer is calling around asking questions. How the fuck they know anything is beyond me. Go, do it now!"

Vladimir ended the call with a quick snap of his cell phone and pounded his fist on the dashboard, making his driver jump again. Thankfully this time, no one was in the other lane. Vladimir shot his eyes over to him quickly and yelled, "If you can't drive worth a shit, then tell me, why in the hell are you my driver? Hmm? Pay attention to the goddamned road!" His driver sat up as straight as he possibly could in the driver's seat and nodded his head quickly.

Vladimir sat still in his seat, raging with anger and wondered, *"How in the hell did they find out about this? Could they have found where Yuraslav and Mirek hid the papers and computer? Surely, they didn't hide them on the island! Surely, they aren't that stupid. Maybe the police are just following up from phone records. They obviously don't know who they are fucking with. But they will. They will soon enough. No one messes with Vladimir.* He thought about the contract labor business that he had single handedly created over the past eight years. He had started in Atlanta, and eventually branched out into Myrtle Beach, South Carolina, New Orleans, Biloxi, and his personal favorites, Orange Beach and Gulf Shores, Alabama. The little island in Alabama turned out to be a gold mine that he himself just happened to find on a golf trip six years ago. It had been so easy to bring workers to the island. The locals there were laid back, carefree, and in need of good workers. They didn't ask any questions, minded their own business, and always had jobs open for him to fill. Czech workers had been the answer. Not only did they work hard at their jobs, but they were so damn easy to control as well. Russian workers were more difficult, smarter, always wanting to branch out on their own. Even the Polish workers were quick to think of ways in which they could profit more. But the Czechs? They were content to do what they were told and basically kiss his ass when he wanted it kissed. It had been perfect, until Tammy Morrison became involved. He regretted so much the day that he had ordered those applications for her rental properties to be faxed to her office. The properties had been cheap, managed by a woman, and was supposed to be a sure and easy bet for future Czech housing. How was he supposed to know that she would actually research the names on the applications? Other people that he knew had rented property from her, and she had never checked before. Now, because of her, he was being forced to shut his offices down while he tried to clear the mess up. He knew he could always move to another area under a different name and start over; but thinking about all of the hard work he had put into this, all of the contacts, all of the people he had at his beck and call, not to mention the money pouring in...he punched the dashboard one more time. His driver quickly announced that they were only forty five minutes from Charlotte.

Hearing this, Vladimir calmed down some and started to feel a little bit better just by thinking about all the things he could and would do to the two Czechs waiting for him at the house. He would torture them before he killed them, and enjoy every minute of it. Thinking about it turned him on, and he wished that he had had sex with Suzanna earlier that morning before he left for Charlotte. He had checked on her and injected her again before he left her in the care of his two friends who had shot her Czech kidnappers last night. They were ordered to keep her sedated and untouched until further notice which, he was sure, pissed them off. She was hotter than a match, and knowing his friends, they would be drunk from vodka shortly after noon. As he thought about Suzanna, he suddenly remembered Petra, who was also waiting at the house in Charlotte along with the two idiots Yuraslav and Mirek. He hoped that his men hadn't roughed her up too bad. It wasn't that Vladimir didn't like bruises and cuts; he just preferred to inflict them himself. He knew that doing her wouldn't be half as good as doing Suzanna, since he had raped Petra before; but a little bit of her wouldn't be bad after he finished with Yuraslav and Mirek. As his driver drove closer to Charlotte, Vladimir closed his eyes and fantasized.

CHAPTER TWENTY-EIGHT

"Myrtle Beach Police Department, how may I help you?"

"Yes, this is Detective Hillary Thompson with the Orange Beach, Alabama, Police Department. I need to speak with the officer on duty four days ago. I am calling in regards to a phone call and possible complaint made by a Mrs. Tammy Morrison. It's in connection with a murder investigation involving the murder of Mrs. Morrison and her family. Do you know who could have taken that call?"

"Okay, looking...hold on a sec, okay, uh, Detective Thompson, that would be Officer Dell Myers. Can you hold a sec, and I will patch him through to ya?"

"Absolutely." Hillary tapped her nails across a picture of Suzanna that was lying on her desk while elevator music piped through the receiver.

"Officer Myers here, what can I do for you Detective Thompson?"

"Hi, well, I guess you may have seen on the news all the mess that's happening down here with the murder case. I am investigating the Morrison murders, and I found this number on Tammy Morrison's, one of the murder victims, phone records. Your dispatcher told me she had talked to you."

"Yeah, as a matter of fact, I have heard some of what is going on down there, and now that you mention it, I did talk to someone named Tammy Morrison the other day. I'll be damned! She called to make a complaint about some identity theft and fraud. Said she was a real estate agent down there and that someone had used a dead person's identity on an application, and that the dead person was supposedly from Myrtle Beach."

"And you took her statement?"

"Yeah, well, if that's what you want to call it. I told her that there was nothing I could do because she didn't really know who sent the application to her. Said she talked to them by phone, but never met in person. She told me that she had accepted the application and some money for rent. Then, as an afterthought, she submitted the name to Equifax and Googled it, only to find out that he was dead. The office that sent her the application is here in town. I called them but got no answer. I am thankful that you called this to my attention, because otherwise, I may not have put two and two together. The call only lasted a couple of minutes, and like I said, there wasn't really much that I could do for her. When I didn't hear anything back from her, I figured that it was just an honest mistake or something."

"Okay, thank you Officer Myers. Can you do me a favor?"

"Definitely! What do you need?"

"Can you have an officer go to that office and check things out and give me a call back? We have found out that Mrs. Morrison made a number of phone calls to different cities, making the same complaint. Something stinks really bad, and I think what's going on on this island right now is happening in your city as well." She filled him in on the details of the case and by the time she was finished, Officer Myers wasn't just merely interested, he was overwhelmed with the picture she had painted for him.

"Ok, let me get this straight. So what you are saying is that basically there is a Russian Mafia type ring running a large scale illegal job outsourcing business throughout the entire South East, and we are right in the middle of it? I will do better than just poke around that office. I will go and talk to my superiors and get back with you in a few minutes."

"Thanks. And commit Yuraslav and Suzanna Novacek's picture to memory. The way things are looking, they may be in your town." They hung up, and Hillary continued the calls until everyone on the list was alerted and notified of the situation. Just like she had suspected, Tammy had complained to every jurisdiction that she found deaths in. And how strange, she thought, that none of the outsourcing offices, except for one in Myrtle Beach, had even answered their phones; and even that one had clammed up, telling her that someone would have to call her back.

CHAPTER TWENTY-NINE

Suzanna Novacek woke up to the happy cheers of the game show contestants on television screaming, "WHEEL OF FORTUNE!" Unable to move or open her mouth, she had no other option but to just lie there looking around the room in the dark. She allowed her eyes to adjust to the dark room, while Pat Sajak and Vanna White amused her drunken Russian babysitters in the next room. She strained to listen to their conversation, praying for a little English or Czech, but they just rambled back and forth to each other in Russian. *At least I am alive*, she thought. That brought her a little comfort until she remembered that she was handcuffed and tied to a bed. She knew she had been drugged but had no idea for how long. All she knew for a fact was that the two Czechs who had kidnapped her were on their way to another life, and hopefully to one that was eternally on fire. As the drug slowly wore off, she remembered the details of their murders. Everything had happened so fast that neither of the two men had had a chance to defend themselves in any way. She recalled how quickly her life had passed before her eyes when she saw the two gunmen shoot them; at the time, she thought she was going to be next. There had been no time to even be scared. But when a bullet didn't enter her head like her kidnappers', the fear had spread over her like a wildfire, especially when Vladimir had walked her into the house. His eyes had gleamed with a light that couldn't have come from anywhere other than the Devil himself; the smile he had given her when he drove the syringe into her arm had been no less evil. A shudder came over Suzanna's body as she remembered the way he had looked at her.

Her eyes had almost fully adjusted to the dark, and she silently cursed herself for wasting precious lucid time on remembering Vladimir's face. She wanted to search the room for any signs of help before she was drugged again, or whatever else happened to her next. The room was pitch black except for the small ray of light shining in from the bottom of the door. There was a book shelf, a closet, and an armoire to the left of the bed; that was all that she could see. Suddenly, an alarm clock began ringing loudly from the next room. One of the Russian men jerked open the door to check on her, and he saw that her eyes were open before she had time to shut them. He quickly walked over to the bedside table and prepared another syringe while Suzanna fought to squirm even an inch away from him. Her efforts were of no use, and he laughed at her futile attempt to escape.

"Goodnight bitch." He said.

Goodnight, asshole, she said to herself as she felt the needle pierce her arm. Two minutes later, she was out cold again. As he reached down to make sure she was asleep, he noticed the wet spot growing around her on the bed sheets. He laughed and shut the door, leaving her to simmer in her own urine.

CHAPTER THIRTY

Doctor Judith Esther made sure, one more time, that it was alright with Anna and Gwen that she go home for a while. After they both assured her that it was ok, Judith bent down to hug them.

"Really, Judith, it's fine. I will be here until she is released, and I can take her home with me. Go home and get some rest. And thank you, so very much, for everything." Gwen hugged her back with genuine gratitude.

"Ok, then, if you are ok with it, I will pack my bag and go home. I need to do some laundry and make a few phone calls, and then I will be back later this afternoon to check on her."

Gwen cocked her head slightly and smiled gently, trying to figure out the best way to say what she needed Judith to understand. Finally, when she could think of no ways to give her hints, she decided to just say it out right.

She motioned Judith towards the doorway and spoke softly, "There is something I need to say before you go. Let's walk out into the hall for a second." Judith gave her a puzzled look and followed her out. "You know, Judith, you really should take a break. You know I appreciate everything you have done for Anna, but I think that maybe we, me and Anna, need some bonding time, you know? I saw the children often enough on visits and family stuff, but this, as you know, has been as traumatic as it gets for her, for all of us. I am her mother now, and she needs to feel comfortable around me. You understand, don't you?"

Judith's face turned red with embarrassment. She hadn't even thought about that. She had been so wrapped up in taking care of Anna since Tammy's death, and trying to hide her own grief over the loss of her friend, that she hadn't thought about Gwen's role now as the child's mother. She shook her head in agreement and placed her hands in Gwen's. "You, know what, Gwen, you are absolutely right! I haven't even thought about that until now. It's just that, well, I have been so wrapped up in all of this, trying to do the right thing by Tammy, I just never thought of it. I am so sorry!"

"How could you even apologize, Judith? I needed you here just as much as Anna did. And I know Tammy would have wanted you here. But now, I just need some time alone with Anna, and she needs it with me."

Judith leaned over and hugged Tammy, and they both choked on swallowed tears. Smiling she said, "Ok, but call me if you need anything, and I mean it. I only live about twenty minutes from here, and I will have my cell phone on me at all times, and you have my home phone number, right?"

Gwen nodded. "Yes, I have everything. Now, please go home and get some rest, and I promise I will call you if I need to." They hugged again and Judith left.

She was exhausted, having been at the hospital since Anna was admitted. The entire time she had been there, she hadn't even walked outside to get some fresh air. When the breeze blew across her face in the parking lot, she realized that she couldn't wait to get home. The twenty minute drive wasn't bad. Traffic had begun to slow down rapidly since the ending of the season. During summer time, it sometimes took an hour to get home from the hospital, and during Spring Break, it could take even longer. The drive was nice, and the sun felt wonderful shining through the windows. Her exhaustion had been real when she left the hospital but as she pulled into her drive way, it really kicked in. It felt like she hadn't been home in a month.

Judith lived on the beach in what used to be a vacation rental. It was older, and a little run down in appearance, but she figured that it was fine with her if it was able to take on Hurricane Ivan without being condemned. It was a two bedroom cottage on stilts with a porch that looked out over the coast. There used to be a little wooden walk way down to the water, but Ivan managed to claim that. The walk wasn't bad anyway, as long as she didn't wear her shoes. That was one of the things that she loved about the Gulf Coast, was the sand. The sand was like soft powdered sugar, white and shiny, not like the gritty brownish-green sand that she grew up with in North Myrtle Beach. Walking on the hard compact sand of the Grand Strand beaches of the Carolinas was quite different than walking the beaches of the Gulf Coast. The water was different here too. Sometimes, on a really good day when the currents and winds weren't carrying all the mud from Mobile Bay, the water was almost as clear and blue as the Florida Keys or the Caribbean. Judith loved to sit on her porch on those days and watch the schools of fish swim by. The porpoise shows were beautiful as well. Sometimes, late in the afternoon, there would be anywhere from ten to twenty porpoises, jumping and playing right in front of her house.

She looked out into the water through her binoculars, and sighed, thankful to finally be home. *Nope, today is not one of those days* she thought to herself. The water was dingy, and the clouds were coming in. In the middle of hurricane season, everyone on the island had been sitting on the edge of their seats for two months, keeping one eye on the weather channel and the other on the birds' and animals' behaviors. Another hurricane like Ivan would be worse than devastating, it might be permanently crippling for most of the residents. Judith put her binoculars back into their case and placed them onto a shelf in the living room. Looking around her little cottage, she toyed with the idea of calling Hank, but then decided not to. He knew she liked him, so if he wanted to call, then he would; besides, she didn't want to interrupt the case. So, she adjourned to the bathroom, ran a scalding hot bath, and fell asleep in the tub after soaking for only five minutes. She didn't even dream; she just slept.

CHAPTER THIRTY-ONE

Hank had been working the phones with Hillary all day long, taking calls from people she had spoken to that morning and other people assigned to the case. The case was growing bigger and bigger by the minute, now involving the police in New Orleans, Biloxi, Atlanta, and Myrtle Beach. FBI agents and police officers from all over the South East had been talking with business owners who had Czech employees, trying to figure out the names of the people who supplied them with the workers. They had come up with so many names that Hank was ready to pull his hair out. Not only was it difficult to get people to talk, but it was also difficult to access information they could actually use because the INS was getting so heavily involved. They were walking into businesses left and right, questioning the Czech workers. Some of the employees were found to be legitimate, and not all of the outsourcing companies were owned by the Russians. Hank also figured that some of the Russians were probably running legitimate contract labor businesses as well, but from the volume of names pouring in, it would take forever to find out which ones were real and which ones were illegal. Faxes were pouring in by the second, and Hank and Hillary were trying their best to organize them all. Breaking for lunch had not been an option, and around two o'clock in the afternoon, Hillary tapped Hank on the shoulder. "Umm, I think I found a common denominator here in all of this crap. Before I say mine, do you have one?"

"No, not really, I just got off the phone with Officer Myers in Myrtle Beach, and I haven't been reading the faxes for the last thirty minutes. Why, whatcha got?"

"Well, in the beginning, about six years ago, it seems that the first places around here to hire Czechs remember talking to a guy named Vladimir, but reported that they never saw him again. Some of them say they talked to him on the phone after the Czechs started working, but only a few times. They have talked with a number of other people over the years, but none of them reported that they had anymore contact with the man named Vladimir. Some said he was Russian, others said he was Czech. But all the people who reported that they had met him when this business first came to town said he was 'something', something other than American." Hillary looked up at Hank after she said that and placed the loser sign on her forehead. "Well, now that was a stupid comment, wasn't it? Uh, I guess I am a loser. Just because you have an accent doesn't mean you can't be American." Hillary sat in silence for a moment, checking herself, and then looked over at Hank who was laughing back at her.

"You are not a loser, Hill. Just stupid is all." Hillary slapped his arm. "Ok, seriously. Vladimir. I always thought that name was Russian, could be Czech though. Does this Vladimir guy have a last name?"

"No, not as of yet. I thought you might be interested in talking to the people who mentioned him again, to see what they remember about him. As for the rest of the names, I placed them all on a list for you. Some have last names, and others don't. None of them sound normal; they're all like Vladimir, Bratislav...you know? There are a lot of 'Slav' names. I looked up it in a dictionary online, ya know what I found?"

"What?"

"*Slav* is Latin for *slave*. Go figure. Some of the reports that are filtering through about how these Czech people are treated are pretty bad. A lot of the business owners around here let them work over time and give them extra cash because they suspect that they don't always receiver all their pay from their company. Some of the employers even said that they don't always report all of their hours, and just give them the difference in cash. I had no idea. I mean, I have seen them around town. Everyone has seen them, but I have never met one, except for a couple here and there arrested for DUIs and fights. I do know they like to drink and fight. Oh yeah, what did Officer Myers in Myrtle Beach find out? Didn't you say you took a call from him earlier?"

What Hillary had just told him about the reports of abuse had reminded him briefly of how Suzanna Novacek had described initially meeting her husband. She had sat right where he was sitting a couple of days ago, and poured her heart out to him, telling him everything, including some of the mistreatment that the Czechs had to endure. His thoughts were interrupted by the mentioning of Officer Dell Myers. "Hill, I am sorry, what did you just ask me?"

"Earth to Hank! Officer Myers? What did he say on the phone? About the office?"

Hank snapped back to attention. "Oh, yeah. He said that the place is empty, not even a roll of toilet paper in the bathroom. He said that they have been combing the place all day and haven't even found one single finger print. The office is located in a strip mall of other offices, and he said that the other people who have offices there hadn't seen or noticed anything, except for an employer of a vacuum cleaner store. The man there said that he saw two men and a woman moving stuff out earlier, but that he didn't pay much attention and couldn't give any details about them or any vehicles. My guess is that they have all been cleaned out, every damn one of them, in all states. I mean, we have been trying to call them all day long, and not one of them has answered; not even a voicemail picked up. What kind of office conducts business like that?"

Hillary tapped her pen up and down on the desk. "I know, Hank. I had already thought about that. Well, it doesn't surprise me. Along with the names that have been reported, I also have a growing list of P.O. Box's that all the Czech's checks were sent to...now how many times have you ever heard that one? The Czech's checks. Anyway, earlier I put in a couple of calls to the places that rent the boxes, but one of the FBI agents, the cute one, over at the courthouse is taking care of that. What's his name?"

"Huh? Who?"

"The cute FBI agent with blonde hair?"

With his hand on his hip, Hank gave her a look with one eyebrow raised and answered with a feminine lisp, "Oh, yeth, that one. Mmm, mmm, mmm, he ith cute, ithn't he. I think hith name ith Thteven." Hillary laughed as Hank rolled his eyes, shook his head and started for the door. On his way out, he stopped at her desk and grabbed the list of business owners who recalled talking to a Vladimir "Doe".

Hillary slapped her thigh as she laughed. "Well, Hank, *Steven* is taking care of that, the P.O. boxes I mean, and congratulations, you have just successfully finished your Mouthy101 class. Please pick up your schedule for class 102 at the door on your way out."

"I'll be on my cell if you need me," he called out as he reached the exit.

The sun hit him square in the face. The rays were brutal, but felt so damn good. In another minute they would be gone, hiding behind the clouds of October, so he paused for a second to let them shine down on him before sliding into the driver seat of his car. He wished so much that he was on the Alabama State fishing pier, waiting for a King or a Spanish mackerel to pounce on the menhaden swimming from the end of his line. He missed the pier; Hurricane Ivan had destroyed it, and the State of Alabama had not yet rebuilt it. Then he remembered that it was Redfish season, and changed his wish. He didn't care what it was really. It was the fishing part that he wished for, the feel of a taunt line being dragged out to sea, the sound of the ripples in the water, and the sweet stink of shiny fish scales cooking on the concrete of the pier. It had been a while since he had found the time to go, and now that the Morrison case had started, he figured that he wouldn't be going again until next spring. So, he gave up thinking about fishing, and started to think about Judith, which he had done off and on since he left the hospital earlier that morning. Keenly aware of his interest in her, she had out right busted him in the hallway of the hospital wing, but gently enough that it made him want to see her again. He decided that he would call her after he finished talking to the people on the list that Hillary had made for him. His mind skipped back to the list.

Number one on the list was the local coffee shop, Beautiful Beans. A local named Dorris Madden had owned it for twenty years. It had miraculously survived Ivan with nothing but some scratches and bruises, which she and her husband had fixed within two days of being allowed back on the island. They reopened for business a week after the storm, selling coffee and snacks to the FEMA agents, insurance adjustors, construction workers, and everyone else that came crawling to see the damage. Dorris had been one of only a few people open for business during that time. Hank suspected that during the clean up process, she gave away more coffee than she had sold. Dorris was a good woman who had always run a good business. For years she ran Beautiful Beans all by herself, until six years ago when she had a heart attack. That was right around the time when the Czechs started showing up for work on the island.

Hank pulled into the parking lot of Beautiful Beans and walked up the ramp towards the entrance. The smell coming from the shop was heavenly and relaxing. He didn't know what coffee Dorris had chosen to brew for the daily special, but he knew he would be having a cup before he left. When he walked in, he was greeted with a smile and a hug from Dorris, who was cleaning the menu mats and stacking them by the door.

"Hank! I haven't seen you in a coon's age!" Dorris proclaimed with excitement at first, but then quickly frowned. "But, I guess I'd be happier if you were comin in here under different circumstances." She glanced at the kitchen door. "I know why you're here. You wanna know about the girls I got and then take 'em away from me and send 'em back to that horrible poor country they come from."

Hank chuckled at Dorris. "Actually, Dorris, you will be pleased to know that I did not come for them. And I am not taking them anywhere, unless they know something about the Morrison murders or where Yuraslav and Suzanna Novacek are."

Dorris shook her head at Hank. "You can ask them yourself if you want, but we been sitting in here talkin' about it for two days now, and they don't know nothing. Hell, every time the door opens, they run to the back and start washing stuff that don't need to be washed. They are scared to death! Sweet girls, too. They'll do anything you ask 'em too, and they always do a good job. I've been through a couple of different ones over the years since my heart attack, but the two I have now are the best ones ever. Sweet as they can be. You wanna cup of coffee on the house? I'll make it myself." She put the menu mats down and hobbled around the corner of the bar towards her daily brew.

"Absolutely."

"You want the special? It's Jamaican Blue Mountain, best there is."

"I wondered what it was. You can smell it from Foley…smells damn good. Oh, and nothing extra, just black."

"Alright, Hank, just have a seat at the bar. You need to talk to the girls or just me?"

"Just you for right now, and then maybe I will ask them a few questions before I go. I won't be here long. You are the first one on the list out of many."

Dorris placed the cup of coffee on the bar in front of Hank and leaned into him from the other side. "Whatcha wanna know? I've already talked to the officers who came by earlier, so I can't imagine I'd have too much more to say. I done told 'em everything I know about this Czech stuff."

"Well, you can start by telling me what you can remember about Vladimir, the guy who came around about the Czech workers in the first place. That would be a big help. What do you remember about him?"

"Well not much really. He was cute and nice, and his English was real good. Said he was from Atlanta, and that he ran a business outsourcing college kids from different countries looking for summer jobs in the United States. He come around right after I had my heart attack, and to tell you the truth, my husband and I thought he was the answer to our prayers. There was no way in hell I could have run this shop by myself anymore. He said that if we was interested, that all we had to do was give him the go ahead, and they would be here immediately. I said yes on the spot. Hell, I would have rather hired some local teens, but you know how they are these days--they don't wanna work, and their parents don't make them either. So I said yes, and the next week, I had two full time Czech employees. One was a girl and one was a boy. I didn't like the boy too much. He had an attitude and tried to boss me around like this was his shop, so I called Vladimir back after a couple of days. The boy, I can't even remember his name, left and another girl showed up. Like I said, I have been through several of them over the years, but anytime I had to talk to the company about any of them, it was always someone else who answered the phone. I never talked to him again."

"Do you remember Vladimir's last name?"

"No, but I might have one of his old business cards at the house. My husband won't be home for another couple of hours. I already tried calling him. I wish he would let me buy him a damn cell phone. I have been trying to talk him into it for a couple of years now, but he won't have anything to do with 'em. Calls 'em an invasion of privacy and says it's just another way for the government to keep tabs on folks." She rolled her eyes up to Heaven, as if praying for the sanity of her husband, then looked back at Hank with a grin and a wink.

Hank chuckled at Dorris. "Ok, Dorris, here is my card. Will you call me straight away if you find his card or if you remember anything else about him?"

"Yeah, sure, Hank, just don't let 'em take my girls. That's all I ask."

"Can I talk to your employees, now?"

Dorris called out to her "girls" who were hiding in the back. They appeared at the kitchen door with big frightened eyes, looking as if they were ready to bolt out of the back door at any time. Dorris looked at them in pure sympathy and said very slowly and loudly, "He is a good man. No INS, I promise." She looked back at Hank and said, "They speak English well enough, but sometimes they don't understand everything you say. You gotta talk slow to them."

Hank suppressed a laugh and gave a serious nod to Dorris. He suspected that they understood more than she thought they did. "Hi. My name is Detective Hank Jordan. I need both of you to think really hard about the question I am going to ask you, and remember, whatever you say will not get you into trouble, ok? I am not here to deport you, understand?"

"Yes," the girls said in unison, heads quickly bobbing up and down.

"There is a man named Vladimir, who is in charge of finding Czech people jobs. Do either one of you know anyone in your company named Vladimir?"

They looked at each other fearfully; the one on the right spoke, "Yes, but I have never met him. He is da boss. He doesn't work, he just takes money now. No one ever meets him unless they are in some troubles."

"What kind of trouble? Do you know someone who has met him because they were in trouble?"

"No, but I hear stories about people who met him." The girl on the left said something to her in Czech, and they started arguing. Whatever the girl had told Hank had worried the other one.

"What kind of stories?"

The girl who had been talking to Hank just looked at the floor and shrugged her shoulders.

"Ok, listen to me. What kind of stories have you heard? You need to answer my questions. It's very important that I find Vladimir. I promise I won't tell anyone that you told me."

The girl on the left stomped back into the kitchen, leaving the other girl to answer the question by herself. Her voice was shaky, and she was on the verge of crying when she spoke. "If you do something bad, you have to go work somewhere else. Sometimes they beat you up and take your money. Sometimes, they find your family and take their things from them, steal from their houses. And there are stories about people who die."

"Who are they? Who beats people up and takes their money?"

"Vladimir's people. The Russians. The ones who pay us our money. I have only seen dem maybe two times. Please don't tell them dat I told you." She started crying and walked back into the kitchen. Hank could hear the other girl scolding her in rapid Czech, while the other girl sobbed. Dorris shook her head and said, "See what I mean? Hank, I hope you find this guy. I really do. John Morrison used to come in all the time for coffee, and it's just a damn shame what they did to him and his family. But I feel sorry for them girls back there. They are so scared, and I'll do whatever I can to keep them here, whatever's within the law anyway."

"Dorris, thank you for the coffee, and please call me if you find that card or if you can think of anything else about Vladimir."

"You're welcome. You wanna to-go cup?" Hank accepted the cup from Dorris and went to the next name on the list. For three hours he listened to people say the same things about Vladimir. No one knew his last name. Some of the Czech workers had repeated what the Beautiful Beans girl had said, and a couple said that they would look through old business cards to see if they had kept one from him when he first showed up. Everywhere he went people gave him coffee, sodas, food, and desserts, and before he got back to the station, Hank had to stop at a gas station for a pack of Rolaids. Hillary was gone by the time he arrived back at his office. She had left a note for him on his desk, along with a folder she had put together, detailing everything she had accomplished that day. He made some phone calls to a couple of the out of state officers with whom he had spoken to earlier. Then he grabbed up Hillary's folder, said goodbye to the officers on duty and Lisa in dispatch, and headed home.

CHAPTER THIRTY-TWO

From the moment that Vladimir had arrived at the house in Charlotte, he and the two other Russians had taken turns beating and torturing Yuraslav and Mirek, trying everything to get information from them. One of their favorite implements of torture was whacking them across the face and head with the large Charlotte area Yellow page directory. Between the two of them, there were several broken ribs, lacerations, and dozens of purplish-black bruises. The bones in Mirek's left foot had been crushed by the boots of Vladimir, and Yuraslav's left hand was missing two digits. Through all of the pain that they had endured they kept their mouths shut. They couldn't rat each other out because neither one of them knew what the other one had done with the missing documents and computer. Mirek had also changed his mind about telling Vladimir where he had hidden the documents. Before, when he had placed them in the rotting tires off the exit, he thought he could use them as a bartering chip with Vladimir; but when the beating and torture had started, he knew that telling him would not keep him alive. Only keeping the truth from them would ensure his life, for now anyway. Yuraslav also had the same feeling that Mirek did about his life. The only difference was that he let the Russians keep thinking he hid the computer, instead of forgetting it. The pain was excruciating for both of them, but not bad enough to break the silence.

Vladimir stood over the two bound men and yelled at them over and over again. "What is it going to take to make you tell me what I want to know? Hmmm? I can be fair, even though you have not been very fair to me, no? I trusted you both to do a very serious job. I always thought you were smart and able to handle a job like this. People told me, 'No, Vladimir, you cannot trust a Czech', but I ignored them! I gave you both a chance to better yourselves, to make more money, earn respect from people! But you shit on me, and everything I have done for you. Why? Have I not been good to you? Did I not make it

112

possible for you to come to the United States and better your lives?" Vladimir paused for a moment, letting his words sink in. He hoped that one of them would crack under the pressure. "I am not sure you understand what will happen to me if you don't tell me where my stuff is. I will lose everything that I have worked for in this country. I will have to start over, do everything all over again. If you had brought me the stuff like I asked you to do, and something else had gone wrong, I would have taken you with me when I started over. I would have given you opportunities that you never dreamed of. I still might do that, if one of you would be so kind as to tell me where the things are. I will give you both a couple of minutes to think about what I have said. Then, I will place a gun into one of your mouths and pull the trigger. I don't know which one of you it will be yet, but I can assure you that I will make up my mind in the time I have given you to make your minds up."

Yuraslav knew that he was about to take a bullet. He had no information to give that would help his situation. So, he closed his eyes and thought about his family. His mother and father would never know what had happened to him, because there would be no one to tell. He never once thought about his wife. He never loved her; he had just used her for his green card. Now, his life was over, and being an atheist, he wasn't concerned about where he was going when he ate that bullet. He took a deep breath and exhaled, as he felt the barrel of a gun pry his mouth back open. That was the last thing he felt.

Mirek began screaming and pleading for his life, promising to take Vladimir to the place where the duffel bag was hidden, but refused to speak openly about it. His last hope was to somehow run from them when they got to the gas station. He cried and sobbed, staring at what was left of Yuraslav's head.

Finally, amused by his cries for mercy, Vladimir gently patted him on the head like he was comforting a small child and spoke, "Mirek, you are exhausting me. Why don't you just tell me where you hid it? Then, maybe we can just put an end to all of this. Hmm?"

Mirek tried to speak plainly, but his sobbing was so violent that he could hardly catch his breath. "I don't want to die and if I tell you now, then you will kill me."

Vladimir sighed heavily. "Yes, you are right, I would kill you. You are not as stupid as I thought you were. Ok, have it your way. I will be back in here shortly, and we can all take a road trip, how does that sound?" All of the pain and blood he had just witnessed had excited him, and he could not stop thinking about Petra. He stood up and walked towards the utility shed in the backyard of the house where he had been told Petra was still locked up in the closet. He and his friends had been so consumed with the two Czechs that he hadn't even checked on her. The dirty part of his business, when things went wrong and he was forced to beat and torture and kill, of course made him nervous and angry, but it also aroused him. He would have sex with Petra, and then leave with Mirek and the other three Russians to retrieve his belongings and what was taken from the Morrison house. On the way across the lawn he noticed blood on the grass and the door of the shed, which was not a good sign. Petra would be useless to him if she was bloody. Bruises and a little bit of blood wasn't bad, but a lot of blood and sex just didn't go together. If he saw blood on the grass and door, then chances were, Petra had bled enough to make him not want her, and he cursed himself for not asking them earlier what they had done to her last night. Thinking about the possibility of being unable to relieve himself infuriated him as he stomped to the door of the shed. He placed a key in the lock, but the doorknob turned before he could slide it all the way in. *Idiots! They forgot to lock the shed,* he said to himself. He knew that they had locked the closet though, because they had told him last night. But his heart started to race and his head began to pound when he entered the shed and looked at the closet door. It was wide open, and nothing lay beyond it but cleaning chemicals and a ripped open bag of old clothes. Petra was gone. She had woken up, picked the lock, and found some old clothes stashed in the shed. Vladimir noticed the work sink to his right. There were strips of bloody cloth, a bar of Lever soap and a container of Clorox in the bowl of the sink where she had bathed and bleached her hair before escaping. Vladimir punched the mirror above the sink with his fist, shattering it and sending shards of glass everywhere. His rage made him breathless, turning his face from red to purple. His friends heard the mirror explode and came running and shouting to the shed, but when they looked inside and took in the scene, they didn't utter a word. She was gone, and it was their fault.

Vladimir and his thugs ran back into the house where they had left Mirek to contemplate his fate. He was still bound and bleeding, and when he saw the men return to the room, he screamed pitiful pleas of mercy to them as Vladimir grabbed his hair and ripped his head backwards.

"You, my friend, are at the end of your rope! You tell me where my fucking shit is now! Or I will begin to inflict so much pain on you that you will wish you were already dead! Petra is gone! Does she know where you hid it? Tell me now!" Vladimir screamed at him, spraying spit all over his face.

"She doesn't know anything, I swear!" he screamed back. One of the thugs began ripping his pants down to his ankles, pointing the gun at his penis. "Okay! Okay! I hid it at a gas station! Oh, God... I can take you there, oh, please! It's on the interstate, south, in some tires, oh my God..." Mirek gulped at the air for any breath he could find, making wretched gurgling sounds in the process.

Vladimir's rage continued, and when he saw Mirek desperately trying to breathe in air, he yanked his head back even further almost to the point of snapping his neck. "What exit?" he roared into Mirek's ear.

"Mc..." his face was turning purple and couldn't get the words out, so Vladimir eased up just enough for Mirek to complete his sentence. "McAdenville! McAdenville!"

CHAPTER THIRTY-THREE

Petra had found her way to a gas station just by sheer luck. Her strange appearance stuck out like a sore thumb, so during her escape she had tried to stay off the roads as much as possible. Whenever a car had passed by, she had scrambled into the shallow ditch that followed parallel to the road until it was gone. When she finally reached the gas station, she asked the attendant to call a cab for her. She tried to smile at him as he stared at her for a few minutes. Because of her appearance, he was not sure whether to call a cab or the police. Finally, she had told him that she had been in a car wreck that morning, and that was why she was all bruised up. Reluctantly, he picked up the phone and dialed a number. Ten minutes later, a taxi pulled up in front of the station, and Petra calmly walked to the window with her head hanging low. The only money that she had in her pocket was the change from the soda that she had bought Mirek yesterday from the gas station where the documents were hidden. She bent low down into the window, so that no one could see her from the road and said to the driver, "Look, sir. I am in trouble. My boyfriend is trying to find me, he beat me up last night, and I understand if you don't want to take me. But I only have eight dollars and some change, and I need to go here." Through the window she handed him the business card of the tire repair shop that she been smart enough to pick up the day before.

The driver looked down at the card and said, "Lady, that's at least a forty five dollar ride. What the hell am I suppose to do with eight dollars?"

"Please, sir, I will do anything you want me to do, anything! If you will please take me to this place. I am begging you."

The driver looked at her bruised and swollen face, and against his better judgment, told her to get in. "Look lady, I'll take you, and I don't want anything more from you either. Looks to me like somebody has already taken everything you got to give. I don't know what kind of trouble you got yourself into, and I don't wanna know either, so don't tell me."

"Thank you so much." She slid into the backseat and laid down low so that no one could see her.

The driver anxiously glanced around him and in the mirror, to see if there was anyone out there watching. It was apparent that she was hiding from somebody, and it made him nervous. He thought about changing his mind, but something told him that if he didn't leave now, he might not have a mind to change later. He pulled out onto the road drove towards I-85.

He watched her from the rearview mirror. She was shaking uncontrollably. "Where are you from, lady? Somewhere in Europe?"

"Czech Republic. I am from Czech Republic." She coughed and cleared her throat. The pain pills that she had taken the night before had made her so thirsty, that when she tried to lick her lips, her tongue slid across them like sandpaper. Before she escaped, she drank the nasty water from the sink in the utility shed when she had bathed, but it had not been enough to carry her through three miles of running through the woods and ditches on the side of the road.

"Hey, isn't that guy on the news, the one they're looking for in Alabama, from Czech Republic?"

She quickly said, "I don't know. I haven't been watching the television lately." Immediately she regretted telling him where she was from.

"Yeah, well, he is a very bad man. Raped and killed a whole family, except for a little girl. He raped her but she didn't die. He tried to choke her to death. They got a man hunt out for him all over the South. Him and his wife. His wife's American--went missing yesterday after she was put into protective custody."

So, that's what they did. Petra thought to herself. *That's what they were running from, but why did I have to clean out the office and leave town with them?* "I haven't heard anything about it, sorry." *Something is missing and I have figure it out. I just hope I get to the tire repair exit before they do.*

"Well, we will be at that exit in about thirty minutes, alright? You okay back there, lady?" The taxi driver stared at her pitiful hunched over frame through the rear view mirror and shook his head in pity.

"Yes, thank you, I'm fine." She was far better riding in the back-seat of a taxi cab than locked up in the closet on the floor, but she was far from fine. Even if she did get out of this alive, there was no way she could send the money that she had saved back to her parents. Her purse and pocketbook that held her fake id and social security card were still in the house that she had escaped from, and even though she had an extra check card at home, she knew she could never go back there to get it. Someone would be waiting for her, waiting to kill her. All of the time that she had spent working in Orange Beach was now for nothing. She was angry. Angry at Vladimir and angry at herself for living her life the way she had. She had thrown it all away. Thirty years, and nothing to show for it, but a bruised and battered body that could probably never bear children, and a broken heart that could never be healed. If getting to these documents before the Russians gave her a second chance at life, she swore to herself in the backseat of that taxi that she would change and live a better life. She closed her eyes and tried to relax a little.

Meanwhile, Vladimir was getting into the passenger seat of a black Mercedes SUV. He swore to himself that when he found Petra, she would die a slow and painful death worse than anyone he had ever killed before, and that Mirek would follow in her footsteps. Although he suspected that Petra knew where the duffel bag was, he didn't know for a fact if she had seen Mirek hide it; Mirek swore she didn't know a thing. It didn't matter; he would kill her anyway. After all, she had been hired to run the Orange Beach office, and that's where he had kept most of the paperwork. She knew too much. He wasn't particularly concerned with anyone identifying Petra. The way the businesses were set up, no one in the offices dealt with local Czechs' employment in their area. The Orange Beach office only dealt with employees and employers in Biloxi. New Orleans dealt with the ones in Atlanta. The Myrtle Beach offices dealt with Orange Beach Czechs, and the Biloxi office dealt with Myrtle Beach. *But,* he thought, *if she saw Mirek hiding my stuff at that gas station, then that's where she's going, and if she gets there before I do, then she can literally disappear from the map, using any one of hundreds of name and identities.* "Drive!" he screamed. He couldn't afford to lose those documents. It had taken years of theft and forgery to obtain them, and losing them would probably mean the end of his career in the United States. It would just take too much time to get more, and it would be ten times more diffi-cult to do so since 9-11. One of the Russians punched the gas and slid out onto the road headed for I-85, smashing Mirek's face into the win-dow of the door in the process. He was still tied up, and struggled to get upright again when Vladimir's elbow came crashing down over the passenger seat into his left ear. Mirek blacked out and sank to the floor of the SUV.

CHAPTER THIRTY-FOUR

Petra's cab driver saw the exit ahead. "Uh, ma'am, the McAdenville exit is just up ahead. Where do I go from there?"

Still lying down in the back seat, she answered in a frail voice, "It's the first gas station off the exit, the one with the tire business. Can you pull up to the right side of it where the tires are lying on the ground?" She was desperately trying to speak perfect English.

"Yeah, no problem. Hey, are you sure you don't need to call the police or something? You are scared shitless. I mean, your boyfriend ain't gonna be sitting here waiting on you, will he? I don't wanna be in any trouble."

Petra had been thinking of the possibility of Vladimir being there the whole time she had been running from the house. She figured that if he was, she would just start screaming, drawing attention from everyone at the gas station. She knew enough about Americans to know that they don't put up with men who beat on their girlfriends or wives, not like Europeans, who often pretend like they don't even see it happening. And with the way she currently looked, bruised from head to toe, it would not take much effort to draw a strong band of American male sympathizers from the tire repair shop, ready and willing to defend her. "No, he will not be there," she answered, "And, no, I don't want to call police. It isn't necessary; it will only bring me more troubles. Just please take me to the tires."

When Vladimir had called her the morning before to give her directions for what she should bring from the office, her list had included all of the office files, all of the passports, visas, and social security cards. There were also dozens of American driver's licenses, pay checks waiting to be mailed, cell phones, phone cards, some petty cash and various other important papers. It suddenly dawned on her what Vladimir was trying to do. He was closing the office in Orange Beach. Something big was going on, but she didn't know what. Did Vladimir tell Mirek and Yuraslav to murder those people, and if he did, then why?" Petra wished that she knew more, but she only dealt with the businesses and the Czech people working in Biloxi. She did, however, work in the office that posed the biggest threat to Vladimir's entire business if exposed for what it was. It was in her office that Vladimir kept the bulk of the fake and stolen documents. She prayed that he wouldn't be at the gas station as the driver took the ramp. Nervously checking through the back window for any signs of anyone following, Petra spoke again to the driver. "Listen, I have to pick something up. I will have more cash for you, and then will you take me somewhere else, maybe to a hotel?"

The driver sighed, watching her look through the rearview mirror. "Yeah, I can do that. How much cash will you have?"

"Well, didn't you say that the price of this ride was forty five dollars?"

The cab driver felt sorry for her, knowing that she didn't have very much money. "Well, ma'am, just give me twenty dollars and we will call it even." He pulled into the gas station and parked on the right side as she had requested.

Petra took a deep breath and slowly slid out of the car, checking all around the gas station and parking lot for any signs of Vladimir or his Russian thug employees. It would take only one second to know if someone was a Russian thug; they would most assuredly be wearing gold chains and a greasy mullet hair style. Not seeing anyone who would fit the profile, Petra took a deep breath, and walked quickly across the blacktop, past the gas pumps toward the tire repair shop. She kept her head low until she reached the rotting tires on the side of the building, then knelt in the weeds at the tire Mirek had chosen. The black duffle bag was barely poking out where it had been stuffed down into the old rubber, and it took a couple of minutes to lift it out of its hiding place. Petra unzipped the bag and quickly glanced inside to make sure it wasn't stuffed with garbage, and sighed in relief when she saw that it still contained the contents from the office. Darting her eyes quickly from left to right to make sure no one was watching her, she stood up slowly, and made her way back to the taxi, so as not to draw any unwanted attention to herself from the tire repair workers. Some of them had noticed her, but when they saw her bruises and a duffle bag, they assumed she was homeless or a runaway, and went back to their work. When she got closer to the taxi cab, her slow movements sped up and adrenalin kicked in. Petra threw the duffle bag onto the seat, slid in beside it, and slammed the door shut. She had been successful. She was now at least one step ahead of Vladimir and his thugs.

"Okay, thank you, please take me to a hotel, now. I don't care which one, but please, on the next exit." She opened the duffle bag again and fumbled around for the bank deposit bag that carried the petty cash from her office. She didn't remember how much was there, and was pleasantly surprised when she saw some one hundred dollar bills and twenty's. She would count them later in her hotel room, but for the time being, she took out a twenty and shakily handed it to the driver.

He accepted her payment and slid the bill into his pocket as he turned the cab around toward the road that led back to the interstate. "You got it, ma'am. If my memory serves me correctly, then I believe there is a Holiday Inn going north at the second exit up in Belmont. That okay with you?"

"Yes, that is fine, thank you." She almost cried from the relief of her good luck. Yesterday, she had pretty much resolved herself to the fact that she was going to die. Today, now, in the backseat of the taxi, she thanked God for the first time in her life, and remembered what she had promised herself earlier if she got out of all of this alive.

Five minutes later, she was dropped off at the entrance of the Holiday Inn. The driver had told her good luck, and drove off, leaving her standing at the doorway to the lobby by herself. Petra knew she looked worse than just rough. Both of her lips were busted, her hair was slightly green from the hurried bleach job in the utility closet, and one of her eyes was almost swollen shut. She walked with a slight limp caused from the pain of being thrown on the floor into the metal bed frame the night before. The stares from the desk attendants only made it worse, so as she pulled out her bank deposit bag, she explained to them that she had had an awful car accident the day before, and had just been released from the hospital, with no permanent injuries. The attendants seem to ease a little at this explanation and began the process of booking her into a room. A young snooty girl with a name tag that read Missy started to type away at the computer, checking availability.

"Ok, ma'am, what kind of room would you like?" she asked condescendingly.

Trying to hide her accent as best she could, Petra said, "Umm, the cheapest one please, uh, my parents are on their way to get me."

The attendant raised her eyebrow and stopped typing to look at Petra again. She had noticed her accent. "Where are you from?"

Petra paused only for a second before her lie rolled genuinely off of her tongue. "Uh, Yugoslavia. I am a student."

"Oh, ok, that explains the accent. Did you say your parents are coming to get you? Are they coming all the way from Yugoslavia?" Missy smiled at Petra and attempted to cover up her sheer nosiness with interest and concern.

Shit! Petra thought to herself. She hadn't taken the time to figure out this lie she was beginning to tell, and didn't want to raise suspicions, nor did she want to tell anyone that she was from Czech Republic, especially now that Yuraslav's face was all over the news. "Umm, well, no, they are not. I have an adopted family here, while I am in school. My adopted parents are coming to get me." She held her breath and waited for her lie to backfire on her and raise the alarm of the prying employee.

Petra answer must have made sense because Missy smiled and returned to her typing. "Oh, ok. Hold on a sec, and I will see what I can do for you." She punched a couple more keys, then walked into the back and rounded a corner, out of Petra's sight. She could hear her talking to a man, explaining her situation to him. After a couple of minutes, a man wearing a manager's name tag stepped up to the counter, smiled at Petra and said, "Wow that must have been some wreck! You are lucky you didn't get seriously hurt." He began typing on the computer while the attendant stood behind him with a fake smile on her face. "Ok, let's see, we can give you a discounted room, two twin beds for forty nine dollars. It's got a mini fridge, and of course, HBO. Does that sound ok?"

"Yes, that's fine." Petra smiled back. "Thank you so much."

"Absolutely! Is there anything else we can do for you?"

"No, that's fine, I will just rest some and wait for my adopted parents to pick me up," Petra repeated to him.

The manager gave her a quick little nod and clapped his hands together to signal that his job was done. "Okay then, Missy will take care of you from here and welcome to the Holiday Inn."

Missy stepped back up to the desk and began typing on the computer again. "Okay, ma'am, I need your driver's license and payment for your room, and you will be all set to go."

Petra hadn't thought about the id part. As much as she loathed giving her a fake one, she didn't have the guts to tell her that she didn't have one. She knelt down where Missy couldn't see into the bag and quickly fumbled through the driver's licenses until she found one for a girl around her own age. The name was Katerina Dolezal. Petra couldn't help but to laugh a little to herself at the irony. 'Dolezal' is a surname derived from the Czech phrase 'to lie'. It was a most appropriate name to have at the moment, and she handed it and the cash over to Missy, who typed in the information and printed a copy of the receipt.

"Okay, Miss Dolezal" pronouncing it as 'doll-is-all'. "Here is your license back, receipt, and room key. Your room is down to hall to the left, near the Coke machine. If you need anything, just call me."

"Thank you." Petra lifted the duffle bag and quickly walked towards her room. By the time her head hit the pillow, she was already asleep.

CHAPTER THIRTY-FIVE

The Russian driver hadn't even parked the SUV when Vladimir opened the door to jump out. On the way to the gas station, Mirek had woken up, and given him exact details and precise location of where the duffel bag was hidden. Vladimir ignored the tire repair shop entrance and approached the rotting tires. A couple of workers craned their necks and watched as the tall man in the black leather jacket knelt down where Petra had just been, to search for the black bag. One of the tire repairmen was unable to ignore the coincidence; he walked across the parking lot and asked, "Uh, excuse me sir, can I help you?"

Vladimir slowly turned around and smiled at the man, shaking his head, "Oh, no thank you, I was just looking for something." He continued to smile at the man, pretending that nothing was wrong or out of the ordinary about the situation, and that it was perfectly fine for a grown man to be on his hands and knees, searching through rotting tires in the middle of the day.

"Well," the worker said while he gave Vladimir a suspicious look, "If you're searching for salvageable tires, you ain't gonna find them here. These ones have been sitting here rotting for years now."

"Oh, ok, sir, thank you for letting me know that." Vladimir chuckled in a good friendly gesture. "But actually, I was looking for something that my friend left here by mistake yesterday. You see, he had been waiting for a ride, and left his bag, or thinks he did anyway, and I told him I would look for it for him."

The man thought about the bruised homeless girl that had just been here and debated on whether or not to say anything. "Was it a big black one? Like a duffel bag?"

Vladimir's lips twitched in anger as he forced himself to continue to smile. "Why, yes it was," he said slowly, trying to hide his rage.

"Oh, well, somebody already came and got it. Was a girl earlier, she came in a taxi, so you can tell your friend that she already found it."

"Oh, ok, that's nice, maybe it was his girlfriend. Did she have short hair?" Vladimir was visibly shaking now, with sweat dripping down his neck. His smile no longer looked like a smile. He was so angry that his lips were peeled back from his teeth, showing his gums, making him look like a crouching rabid dog waiting to pounce and attack the man who stood in front of him. Fortunately, the worker was wiping the sweat from his own forehead with a dingy oiled cloth while looking back at the tire repair shop, ignoring Vladimir's appearance.

"Yep, she's the one. Didn't talk to her though, we just saw her come over here and get the bag and leave in the taxi." He turned and walked back toward the tire repair shop and yelled back at him, "Have a good one, man."

Vladimir rose to his feet, took a deep breath and stared at the window of the backseat where Mirek was sitting. He couldn't see him through the tinted windows, but he knew Mirek was staring back at him. He could smell his fear from across the parking lot, and Vladimir couldn't wait to kill him. He got back into the passenger seat and calmly told the driver to go to Atlanta. The driver paused for a second and asked, "Did you find the stuff?"

Vladimir screamed at the top of his lungs, "No, you fucking idiot! She has already been here and taken it! Drive me to Atlanta, now!" For the time being, Mirek was ignored. Vladimir let his fear fester from the silent treatment.

Three hours later, the group arrived in Atlanta at the residence on Hillshire where Suzanna was being kept, and where the bodies of the two Czech kidnappers were rotting in garbage bags behind the tree line in the back yard. Vladimir had to get Suzanna out of the house and leave Atlanta as soon as possible. If Petra had gotten to the duffel bag and turned over the contents to the police, then it was just a matter of time before they raided his house and his friends' houses.

Vladimir ran into the house and barked at the driver to help him load Suzanna into the SUV. She was still passed out, and when they opened the door to her room the smell almost took their breath away. Vladimir shouted and cursed at the Russians who had been watching and drugging her. Throughout the entire time that Vladimir had been in Charlotte, they allowed her to lie unconscious in her own urine and feces, and the smell was horrendous. Vladimir watched as the thugs picked her up from the bed. "Clean her off, now! Put some new clothes on her and get her to the SUV you pieces of shit!" He cursed and slammed the door on his way out.

New worries popped into his head as he stomped through the house. He fought off as much anger as he could so that he could begin to form a plan. His next destination was South Carolina; that he was sure of. He couldn't risk going to the safety deposit box at his local bank to get new identification, and he wasn't even going to think about going to his own house down the road. The closest place that he could go to get new identities and papers was Myrtle Beach. He would drop Suzanna off at a Russian house there, have her killed, and leave everything and everyone behind. Vladimir wasn't even going to try to save his businesses anymore. He would just simply disappear and start over.

CHAPTER THIRTY-SIX

Water violently splashed all around her as Judith woke up with a jerk when the phone rang. She didn't know how long she had been sleeping in the bathtub, and quickly shook her head to gather herself and clear her mind. Her cell phone was in the living room, and by the time she got to it, it had stopped ringing. Cursing herself, she flipped the phone over to see who had called. The last thing she wanted to do was miss a call about little Anna. The caller id showed Hank's number and the time. According to the phone, she had only been asleep for thirty minutes, but it seemed to Judith like a couple of hours. She pressed the call back button and listened to the rings as she dried herself off. Hank answered on the fourth ring, "Hello?"

Judith felt a surprising little tingle in the middle of her belly when she heard his voice, and unconsciously dropped the towel on the floor so that she could run her fingers through her wet hair. "Hey there Hank. Sorry about that, I couldn't get to the phone on time. How are you?"

"I'm fine. Frustrated, but fine. Just wanted to give you a call back like I said I would. How is Anna?"

"Well, actually, I am not at the hospital anymore. I am home. Gwen politely asked me to step aside and allow her to take care of Anna for a while, let her get used to her being there. So, I came home. It was the right thing to do, even though I didn't want to leave her. But, she was doing fine when I left. I guess that was about an hour or so ago."

"Yeah, you're probably right. I guess they do need time together." Hank paused, not knowing what to say next. He rolled his eyes at himself and felt stupid; he was relieved when Judith finally came to his rescue.

Judith bent over and fumbled for her towel on the floor. "Well, do you have dinner plans? You could come over here and have dinner, talk about the case? I am a great cook."

Hank was still full from all of the food that he had been served all day long, but didn't tell her that. "Sure, I can do that. Sounds great! What are you cooking?"

"Well, I don't know yet, what do you like?"

"Anything is fine by me, really. I am not picky."

Judith laughed to herself and said merrily, "Ok, sounds great! Then I will make liver and onions. How does that sound?"

Hank's gag reflex took over and made his stomach lurch. He cupped his hand over the receiver, while he made a gross face, as if she could hear him make the face.

Judith laughed at his silence and said, "Hank, I am kidding. I have never met a man in my life that liked liver and onions." She laughed again. "How about some steaks? I am a great griller!"

Hank laughed back and said, "Uh, yeah, that sounds a lot better! Tell you what. You tell me what to get, and I will go to the grocery store. You like wine?"

"Yeah, I do, and I really need a glass or two right now. Umm, ok, pick up a couple of filets, a Caesar salad in a bag, and a couple of bottles of Luna de Luna, the red bottles. I already have a couple of baking potatoes, so I will go ahead and throw them in the oven. Sound good?"

"Yep, sounds like heaven. I need to go home first, but I will be there in about an hour." Hank said, smiling. It had been so long since he had been excited about seeing a woman, much less having dinner with her. Judith gave him directions to her house, and they hung up. He headed home to take a shower, and an hour later, he was knocking at her door with a grocery bag in one hand, and a bouquet of flowers in the other. He hadn't been sure if the flowers were a good idea when he purchased them at the grocery store, but the look on her face when she saw them assured him that it had been a fine idea after all. The bouquet held a dozen white lilies with a white ribbon tied around the stems. At the grocery's floral department, there had been roses of all colors, carnations, sunflowers, and other exotic flowers to choose from, but Hank thought they were either too colorful or too serious. The lilies had struck him as soft and subtle, and he thought they would be more appropriate for a first date. Judith placed them in a crystal vase, and smiled from ear to ear as she admired them on the kitchen counter.

"Thank you so much. It's been years since someone gave me flowers." She hugged him in appreciation and took the grocery bag. "How about I put the groceries up and marinate the steaks while you open up one of these bottles and pour us a glass?" she said as she handed him a wine bottle from the bag. "The glasses are on the shelf above the stove. They might be a little dusty, so you might have to rinse them off first."

"No problem." Hank said. He couldn't help himself as she bent over to put the food in the refrigerator, and stared openly at her rear end. He cleared his throat and mentally reminded himself how to open a bottle of wine; not that he didn't know how, but for a second, Judith's butt had taken over his mental capability of processing normal behavior and thought. Stealing one more look at her before she stood up again, he shook it off and screwed the opener into the cork. "Do you want a half glass or a full one?"

"Umm, thinking back on the last forty eight hours of my life, I am gonna have to go with a very full one, please, and if a little spills on the counter from being so full, then I might just bend over and lick it up. That's how full I want it." Judith giggled and concentrated on opening the steaks, not even looking at him as she spoke. It was a good thing that she didn't or she would have seen Hank almost drop the bottle on the carpet. Not only had he been sidetracked by her butt, but he now had to complete the task of pouring the glasses with a mental image of her licking up spilt red wine off the counter with her tongue. It was almost impossible, but he finally managed to pour them and hand her a glass. "Hmmm…" Judith said as she gulped down her first sip. "That's more like it. How is yours?"

Trying not to stare at her Hank took a sip, smiled, and said, "Yeah, that's good. I have never had this before, not really much of a wine drinker."

Judith hadn't even thought of whether or not he drank wine. "Oh my God, I am sorry! What do you drink, I didn't even ask?"

Hank laughed and took another sip of his wine. "Oh, don't worry about it. Wine is always good with steaks, and this stuff is pretty good. But, since you asked, I am a scotch man."

"Well, good, then. I have some Dewar's. So, you can switch at any time. Just let me know."

"Alright, thanks, but this is perfect for now." Hank glanced around the open area of her house. It was very open, with the kitchen, dining area, and living room being basically all one room that looked out over the Gulf through the sliding glass doors. Everything was neat and placed thoughtfully in each spot, making the room very cozy and inviting. There were family pictures on the stand around the television and a couple of canvases depicting beach scenes on the walls of the living area.

Judith noticed him looking around at everything and said, "It will take me a couple of minutes to get these steaks ready. Just make yourself comfortable. I have a hell of a view from the porch, and you're more than welcome to take a seat out there. That's where I'm headed as soon as I am done in here. Oh, and there are some binoculars over there in that case, just in case you want to use them. The porpoises should be playing right about now, if they show up." She pointed to the binoculars and gave Hank a smile.

"Sounds good. I'll grab the wine and meet you out there." He grabbed the open bottle, but then put it back down so he could open the other bottle. He figured that the first bottle wouldn't last long, so he would give the other one a chance to breathe a little before they drank it. Then he grabbed his glass and the wine bottle again and headed for the door.

She was right; it was a hell of a view. He slid open the sliding glass door and stepped out onto the porch, letting the tangy smell of the salt water wash over him. It was a breath of fresh air that he needed desperately at the moment. Watching Judith had turned him on. He sat at the table and looked out over the water while he thought about kissing her. Moments later, she arrived outside with the binoculars. He watched her as she looked through them, searching for the porpoises or anything else swimming in the water.

"Nope," she said as she continued to gaze through the lenses. "Doesn't look like they are going to play for me today. You know, sometimes I see sharks out there too, big ones. It gives me the creeps. I hate sharks. Last week I saw a hammerhead swimming right on the shoreline in about two feet of water. He was at least seven feet long. It gave me the willies."

Hank laughed. "Well, I fish a lot. I use to see them all the time down off the state pier. I don't like them much either, but the small ones are fun to catch sometimes. You can't legally fish for them, but every once in a while, they get hooked up on the live bait, and you have to reel them in to get them off the line. They are mean; they'll bite your hand in a second if you give them a chance."

Judith placed the binoculars on the table. "I love to fish! Even though it's been a while since I went. I guess the last time I did fish was down in the Keys last year. My family took a trip down to Islamorada. There were twelve of us, and we rented two fishing boats for a couple of days. I caught the biggest fish, a thirty eight pound bull dolphin. I had to have some help bringing him in, mind you, but I did catch him. I was quite proud of myself."

"I imagine you were! That's a damn fine catch. Got any pictures?"

"Yeah, remind me to show them to you when we go back inside. I will have to go through them and find some good ones. You know, I have never fished off the pier here. Is it good fishing?"

"It can be, well, it was until Hurricane Ivan blew it away. I have caught some damn good ones off that pier over the years. The most fun I ever had though was the day I caught a sailfish about five years ago. It was a big one, especially for a sailfish off the pier. Forty three pounds. It was beautiful. If you like to fish then we ought to go together to the pier in Pensacola sometime. I was actually thinking about it today before I called you. I haven't been in a while."

"I would love that, Hank," Judith stood up to light the gas grill. "Are you hungry yet?"

"Starving," Hank lied, still feeling the food rumble around in his gut from earlier.

"The potatoes are done, so I will go ahead and throw the streaks on. It's nice out so I figured we could just eat out here. Is that ok with you?"

"Yeah, that's perfect. You need any help?" He rose half way to help her, but Judith motioned for him to sit back down.

"No, absolutely not, just sit down and enjoy the view. I will be back in a second." Judith went to the kitchen, grabbed the steaks and returned to the grill, placing them side by side. Then she returned to the kitchen to toss the salad. She watched the back of Hanks head while she prepared the food, and thought about him with a smile on her face. She could tell it had been a while since he had been with a female. He was a little nervous, in a good way; the kind of way that makes a

woman feel like she is doing her job. She knew that he had been looking at her butt when she had bent down in front of the refrigerator earlier, and had lingered a few seconds in that position so that he could
look at her longer. It had made her feel sexy to tease him those few
seconds. As she stared at the back of his head, she wondered if he was
going to make a move on her tonight, or if she was going to make a
move on him. That was the question. After she was finished tossing
the salad, she decided that if he didn't make a move on her, she would
let it be, and not throw herself at him. Then, on second thought, when
she began to unwrap the potatoes, she decided that it would depend on
the wine and how much she drank. She made a mental note to slow
down, since she was already feeling the effects of it. Grabbing silverware, napkins, the potatoes and salad, Judith walked back to the porch
to flip the steaks. When she leaned down to place the items on the table, she felt Hanks hand on her arm. As she turned to look at him, he
was smiling and no longer seemed nervous. Apparently, the wine had
begun to affect him too. "Thanks for inviting me over tonight, Judith. I
was very much looking forward to seeing you."

Judith placed her hand in his and squeezed, "Thanks for coming
over. I was looking forward to seeing you too, Hank." Their lips met
slowly. Hank slid his arm around her waist and cupped her face in his
other hand while he kissed her. The feeling of his tongue sliding into
her mouth made Judith's knees weak, and she let him hold her tightly.
He finished kissing her mouth, then kissed her nose and her forehead
and gave her a hug as he let go of her waist.

"Would you like for me to grab the steaks?"

She had forgotten about the food entirely. "Uh, yes, you can do
that. I'll set the table." She looked up at him and stammered, "Wow,
that was nice. Thank you."

He winked at her and said, "Your welcome. I am not finished
though. So, if you are finished, then just let me know. Otherwise, I had
planned on eating your meal, finishing off that other open bottle of
wine, and then kissing you again."

Judith giggled and blushed. "No, I am not finished."

They ate the meal as the sun disappeared into the water, flirting
back and forth until neither one of them could stand the wait any
longer. Then they walked together though the sliding glass door and
kissed each other the whole way to the bedroom door. Their lips didn't

part until they started removing each other's clothes. Hank laid her down gently on the bed and worked his tongue from her lips, to her ears, to her breasts, and down to her open thighs. He tasted her for thirty minutes, launching Judith into a string of orgasms that left her wondering if she had really ever had sex correctly before. Then he slowly stretched her legs open and entered her all the way. The orgasms were long and powerful, gripping Hank and truly testing his restraint. Then, when he was sure that he had pleased her enough, he whispered into her ear that he was going to explode, giving her the option of what to do. She pressed his body further into hers, allowing him to orgasm inside of her. He did, so deep that he picked her up off the bed in the process, sending her into another tidal wave of orgasms. He stayed in her for a good while, kissing and holding her, until they both came down from their high; then he got up to grab a towel from the bathroom. He cleaned her first, then himself, and finally lay down beside her, exhausted. Breathing hard, Judith laid there, in open wonderment. "When I say this to you, I want you to understand that I am being dead serious."

"I'm listening."

"No one has ever made me feel that good before. No one. You made me feel like I have never even had sex before this." She paused to catch her breath. "Thank you."

Hank smiled at her and placed his hand over her belly. "You're welcome, but I wasn't finished." They both laughed. "I just needed to take a small break. Were you finished?"

Judith smiled, placed her hand over her mouth in embarrassment, and giggled while she shook her head. "No, I wasn't finished." Hank watched as she disappeared beneath the covers. Then, he closed his eyes and allowed her to take him where he had taken her moments before. They made love off and on for hours. Finally, Judith said to him, "Hank, don't go home, stay with me tonight."

So, he did, and they fell asleep in each others arms, holding on to each other as naturally as if they had been together for twenty years. The contentment Hank felt from the comfortableness as they fell asleep together was enjoyed just as much as the orgasms she had given him. He thought about that as he fell asleep and wondered if she felt the same way. She did. It was exactly the same thing Judith was thinking as she fell asleep; everything was just so comfortable. The next morning proved them right. They made love again, showered and sat down on the porch and had breakfast. There were no awkward moments, no pauses. They talked a little about the case, both agreeing that it was nice that it wasn't mentioned the night before. When Hank got up to leave for work, he noticed the gulf and pointed.

"Your porpoises are playing."

Judith excitingly looked through the binoculars and smiled. "Yes, they are aren't they?"

He bent down to kiss her as she watched them swim. "I will give you a call later."

"I will answer the phone," she giggled back at him as she watched him walk through the house and exit the door. If she had been a teenager at the moment the door shut behind him, she would have gotten up and done one of those stupid little excited dances that only teenage girls do in private after they have been kissed by the cutest guy in school. That's what she felt like doing. But instead, she watched the dolphins and relived what all he had done to her in the bed the night before and only an hour ago when they had woken up in each other's arms.

"Wow!" she said out loud to herself.

CHAPTER THIRTY-SEVEN

Hillary noticed that Hank walked into the office at seven o'clock with an unusual spring in his step. With great interest, she watched him walk through the station until he sat at his desk.

"Good morning, Hillary!" Hank said cheerfully.

Hillary laughed, "Uh, good morning, Detective Did You Get Laid Last Night, or, maybe, is it Detective Did You Catch A Bad Guy And Didn't Tell Anybody Last Night? My guess is the former."

"And, maybe, you will keep guessing Officer Very Intuitive But Nosy." Hank laughed.

"Whew, Hank, that was a good one! You're getting the hang of it. You will be graduating in no time at all." She laughed and handed him the report for the meeting. "We have an hour to catch up and talk before the meeting."

"What is there to talk about? Anything new?"

"Not much. There are no leads whatsoever on Yuraslav, Suzanna, or this Vladimir guy. And we are still waiting to hear back from the other police officers assigned to the case in the other states. This whole thing is a damn mess. None of the Czechs anywhere are really coming out with any information worth using. They are all scared to death."

"Well, then, we ought to start cracking down and shipping them out, especially if they won't cooperate."

Hillary sighed. "Yeah, I agree, but then who will shuck our oysters? I don't know if I can handle living here anymore without fresh shucked oysters."

Hank laughed and shook his head. His cell phone rang. "Detective Jordan speaking."

"Hi, Detective, this is the manager at the Holiday Inn. You left me your card if anything should surface about Mrs. Novacek."

"Uh, yes," Hank stumbled across the room to his desk, pointing at Hillary, letting her know that something may be important. "Do you have anything?"

"Well, I tell you one thing I do have. I have a very scared employee who is crying in my office. You remember Ivana, from the front desk?"

"The one who gave me the list of everyone she talked to?"

"Yes, that one. It seems that she hasn't seen or talked to her boyfriend since she left work that night. And what's bad about that, or could be bad, is that she left his name off of the list that she gave you. She told him about Suzanna being here the night she went missing."

That sent Hank reeling. "Uh, could you hold on for just a second?"

"Sure."

Hank placed a hand over the receiver. "Hillary, get dispatch to send units over to the Holiday Inn immediately! I want them to take Ivana, I don't know her last name, into custody and bring her here. I want the phone records for the front desk of the Holiday Inn pulled, from the time Mrs. Novacek was checked in until now. This might just be our first lead." Hank switched from Hillary back to his cell phone, "Yes, sir, thanks for holding. There are some units on the way to pick up Ivana. Please see to it that she is still in your office by the time they get there. And thank you very much. One question, was it her idea or yours to call me?"

"Well, she told me about it ten minutes ago, and I thought it best to call you. In fact, she doesn't even know that I have called you."

"Alright, thank you." Hank ended the call. Within ten minutes, Ivana was led into the police station by two officers and seated at a table in an interview room. They allowed her to wait alone in silence for about ten minutes to get her good and ready to spill her guts. When the officers had walked into the office of the Holiday Inn to place her into custody, Ivana had started screaming and kicking. She had thought her manager had gone to get her tissues because she had been crying so hard when she told him about her boyfriend Jan. After Suzanna had gone missing, she had gone to his apartment, called his cell phone, and to his places of work. But no one had seen him, talked to him, or knew anything about where he had been. Nor had anyone seen his best friend, Luda, who was usually with him all the time. She thought she knew Jan well enough to believe that he could never be involved with anything like what Yuraslav had done to the Morrisons, much less the kidnapping of his wife, an American. But, it was also not like him to just disappear and not call her. She had been hesitant to alert the police because Jan's visa had expired a year ago, and she didn't want him to be deported. So, she had turned to her employer, and told him of her fears.

Subconsciously, she had known that her boss would eventually call the police, but she would never have told him had she known they would arrest her. Her visa was expired also, and for six months she had been using fake documents and id's given to her from the Russians. The last thing she wanted was to be sent back to her country. There was no money to be made there, unless she wanted to prostitute her body to the Germans who frequently traveled across the border in search of kinky sex. She was originally from Terezin, Czech Republic, which is on the border of Germany. Many of her friends had resorted to prostitution there because the Germans were notorious for coming across the border to find a cheap date for the night. She had always managed to stay away from that life, even though the money was so much better than anything else she had done. That's why she had come to the United States, to answer the promise of a decent job, great pay, and possible university education, something her parents never could afford for her in the Czech Republic. That had been such a joke she thought to herself, as she sat in the empty room at the police station. She never should have come to the United States. She never should have trusted the Russians who came to her town seeking young talented people such as herself. Since she had arrived, she had done nothing to better herself. The only thing she had accomplished, besides learning to speak English, was accumulating a debt to the Russians that she could never repay.

When Ivana had first arrived in the United States at the airport in Pensacola, Florida, two men had been waiting for her, to take her to her new apartment. When she had agreed to work in Orange Beach, she had been promised a temporary place to stay until she was given a job. After that, she had been told that she would be given one month to save up enough money to be able to pay her own part of the rent, from wherever she chose to live. The spiel that the Russians had given her and her parents was like a dream come true. They had made them believe that Orange Beach was a thriving community in which Czechs and Americans happily lived together, forming their own community, while helping the economy by supplying the Americans of the small island extra hands to help during the busy tourist season. There was supposed to be thousands of dollars just waiting for Ivana to earn, and she would be helped by the Russian company to save her money and send it safely back home to her family. In the process, she would be taught English by other Czechs who had been sent there for that purpose only. All she had been told to do to get there was to acquire a visa and pay for her own plane ticket, and after that it was smooth sailing, easy and legal.

All of it had been a lie. She was trapped. The men who had been waiting for her at the airport had taken her bags, placed them in the trunk of a car, and then demanded five thousand dollars from her. There she had stood, empty handed, broke, and unable to communicate with anyone since she hadn't known any English at the time. She had only twenty American dollars, which was all her family could give her after purchasing her plane ticket. She remembered telling the men that she didn't have the five thousand dollars, nor was she told that she had to give them any money. They had reassured her by telling her that it was no problem; they would just take it out of her pay until she had paid it off. In the meantime, they took her to two bedroom apartment that housed ten different Czechs in the same position that she was in.

That was how she had been welcomed into her new community, and it had gone down hill from there. The Russians had given her the option of paying her debt with sex, and she had accepted it for a while. But, then she got a job, and started to pay them in cash instead of giving them her body. Living in Orange Beach had been the worst experience of her life. Now, as she sat in the interrogation room, waiting for someone to come in, she decided that this might be an answer to a prayer instead of a punishment. Deportation didn't sound half as bad as what she had gone through here, even though she knew she could never come back. She knew that she could have reported the abuse while she was legally here, and that the authorities would have looked kindly upon her, allowing her to possibly come back one day. But that option had passed when she decided to stay in Orange Beach when her visa had expired. She had taken up the Russians offer for fake documents, paid them, and accepted her new job at the Holiday Inn. She figured that she would be on the next flight home after this thing was over, and so she stopped crying and thought about her mother. At least she could be with her family again.

After watching her marinate in fear, Hank finally walked into the room. He sat across from Ivana and placed a notebook, pencil and tape recorder in front of her. He didn't say anything for a second; he just watched her squirm in her seat with embarrassment and guilt. He pressed the recorder on and said "You know, Ivana, you could have told me the truth the other night about who you talked to on the phone, and then maybe the INS would have looked more kindly on your situation. And maybe, God forbid if anything bad has happened to her, you could have helped us locate Suzanna after her kidnapping took place. Because of you, we now have no idea where to even look for her, much less your boyfriend. If he is responsible for her kidnapping, then they have a full two day lead on us, unfortunately placing them anywhere in the United States. The United States is a big place, Ivana. Do you have anything to say about any of this?"

Ivana looked up at Hank with eyes blurred by the tears falling. "I am so sorry for dis. I had thought I knew my boyfriend. He is very nice person, you know? He never did anything bad to me or any other person." She continued to sob while she spoke. "You think I am bad person too, and I am not. I have tried to work very hard here, and everything is always so bad."

"You say that your boyfriend has never done anything bad to anyone. Did you know him before you came to Orange Beach?"

"No."

"Have you ever known your boyfriend to do any jobs for the Russians?"

"Well, yes, we all do. They are da people who give us our jobs."

"No, Ivana, I am not talking about normal employment. I am talking about other jobs. Mafia jobs."

Ivana shook her head. "No, he always just works at his normal job."

"How long has he been here, and how long have you been here?" Hank studied her body language and eyes. Her tears stopped, and she immediately became nervous and fidgety.

"He was here one year before I come to Orange Beach."

140

"Is your visa expired? And is your real name on your employment file at the Holiday Inn?"

Ivana hesitated for a second before she spoke. Her voice was unsteady, and her English skills seem to go down the toilet the more she spoke. "Yes, it is expired, no dats not really my name from Holiday Inn. Da Russians, dey gave me new papers so I can work."

"Ok, Ivana, do you know a Russian named Vladimir?"

"I know many Russians wif dat name. Which one?"

"He is the one that owns the companies that you work for. Do you know him?" He noticed the terrified look that spread across her face as he told her which Vladimir he was inquiring about. Ivana didn't respond, and Hank knew that she knew him. "Listen, Ivana, you have to tell me the truth about him. You know him, don't you? Tell me what you know about him. We know that he is a very bad man, and he probably has something to do with Suzanna's disappearance. You have to tell me what you know."

"Can I have water?" she asked. Her face was as white as a ghost as she remembered what he had done to her one night after she had agreed to pay for her debt with sex. He had visited the island one night to meet with one of the men who had met her at the airport. He told Vladimir that she was available for the night, and he had come for her after her work shift was over. It had been the worst night of her life, and afterwards, she swore to herself that she had had sex with the Devil himself.

Hank stood up and walked out of the room to the water cooler. On his way, he spoke with the others who were watching and listening through the interrogation window. The morning meeting was supposed to have been at eight o'clock at the court house. However, in lieu of Ivana's confession, everyone who was supposed to be present at the meeting was crammed into the viewing room, some spilling out into the hallway, craning their necks to listen. After he secured their attention, he returned to the room and gave Ivana some water and spoke slowly. "Ok, Ivana, I am listening. Please help me by telling me who Vladimir is."

Ivana took a deep breath and wiped the sweat from her brow before she spoke. "He is da boss. He is very mean man. He raped me when I got here because I owed money to da company." She began to tell Hank her story of survival. After finishing her story, she looked up to

Hank in embarrassment and asked, "Do you think I am bad person now?"

Hank had listened to her tell her story through sobs and spasms of painful crying. His heart broke as she told him everything she and all of the other Czechs she knew had endured, especially the rapes, since their arrival to the United States. He knew it was bad, but had no idea of what all it entailed until now. He spoke softly to her. "No, Ivana, I do not think you are a bad person. I know that you are scared, and I think you are very brave for telling me these things. I will do whatever I can to help you with the INS. But I can't promise you anything, ok?"

"Yes, ok." Ivana shook her head that was buried in her hands.

"Ivana, I have one more question for you, and then you will have to talk to other people today. Do you remember Vladimir's last name?"

She slowly lifted her head in thought, looking across the room, as if she would find the answer written on the wall. Finally, she cleared her throat, and wiped her eyes with the back of her hand. She slowly spoke the name. "Bereovsky. Vladimir Bereovsky. I have been to his house, too. He lives in Atlanta, Georgia."

Excitement ripped through the police department like a tidal wave. Hank bent closer to her. "Ivana, do you know his address?"

She shook her head. "No. I don't remember. I just remember it was in Atlanta, and it was very big. I went to there six months ago."

Hank bolted from the chair, ran through the doorway to the other side of the window where everyone was standing, and began barking out orders. "Alright guys, this may be it…Someone get in there and see if she can remember the address for a Mister Vladimir Bereovsky in Atlanta. If she can't remember, ask her about landmarks or a specific area. She said the house is big. It's probably nice and in a prestigious part of town. Folks, we need to find that house! Also, find out what Jan and Juda's last names are. Get their pictures from INS and start pumping their information on television. We need this lead really bad. They are probably either the men who kidnapped Suzanna, or they know who did. And everyone, treat her kindly! Granted, she has possibly messed this case up pretty bad, but right now we don't exactly have Czechs banging our door down with information, so as long as she is willing to cooperate, I see no reason to treat her bad in anyway. That means no yelling, no cursing, and get some female officers in there! Let's go people! "

Everyone scattered in different directions, to the phones, dispatch, and back and forth to Ivana. For the first time since the Morrisons were found slaughtered in their home, the Orange Beach police department had stumbled on the first possible real lead in finding Suzanna and putting an end to the horror of what had happened on their island.

CHAPTER THIRTY-EIGHT

Petra woke up in her hotel bed, swollen and bruised, but clear headed. She checked the window to make sure no one was waiting for her in the parking lot. When she was sure that she had not been followed, she gathered her duffle bag from the floor and spilled its contents onto the bed. As she looked through the files and felt sorry for herself about what the men had done to her before dumping her in the utility shed, a sudden thought occurred to her. She remembered Mirek telling Yuraslav at the gas station that Vladimir had Yuraslav's wife, Suzanna. She had met Suzanna only a couple of times at several Czech Christmas parties and twice at a local bar. Suzanna had seemed nice enough, although Petra hadn't taken the time to really talk to her. She knew that Yuraslav abused her, but then, most Czech men that she knew abuse their wives or girlfriends.

Strangely, the thought of this girl in the possession of thugs such as Vladimir and his Russian friends bothered Ivana greatly. Her new found appreciation for life and determination to live it more wisely, coupled with her hatred for Vladimir, made her hungry to help her. For the first time, she flipped on the television to listen to the news. It seemed that every local station was covering the story. As she watched and listened, she saw the familiar faces of Yuraslav, Suzanna, Mirek, and two other Czechs, Jan and Luda, who were suspected of kidnapping Suzanna from the Holiday Inn in Gulf Shores. Vladimir's face was not shown because they had yet to find a picture, but his name appeared, adding him to the list of people the police were searching for.

Petra wanted to help, beyond all things, but the thought of calling the police made her want to vomit. She had been raised in a culture that didn't trust the police who were usually on the take, and didn't have much respect for females either. Pondering her next move, Petra began to separate and organize all of the contents of the bag that were spread across the bed. She grouped all of the various forms of ids and papers together, and looked through each file. It was so tempting to just grab a couple of new identities from the pile, and go on the run. Perhaps, she thought, she would eventually do that, but for right now, she had made up her mind to help Suzanna. She would somehow have to leak information to the press or the authorities, in hopes that they would save her, if she wasn't already dead. Either way, Petra wanted Vladimir to fall, to suffer, and to be destroyed in the United States.

First, she had to leave the hotel and find a store that could help her change her appearance once again. She located the address of the hotel on a notepad, and then opened the phone book to find stores near the hotel; she needed hair dye or a wig and new clothes. Finding what she was looking for, she dialed a taxi company, and requested to be picked up in thirty minutes. The money from petty cash totaled five hundred and fifty dollars, plenty for what she needed it for. The taxi arrived, and Petra asked him to take her to the Westview shopping plaza, which hosted a Cato's clothing store, a Sally's Beauty product store, and Kinko's. At Sally's, she bought makeup to conceal her bruises, auburn hair dye, and snap on hair extensions. Then she walked into Cato's and purchased a couple of cheap outfits, and a pair of shoes. Her last stop was to Kinko's. There she made copies of all the files and paperwork that detailed even the smallest information about Vladimir's businesses. After she finished making the copies, the taxi returned her to the hotel. The shower was intoxicating, and two hours later, Petra had completely transformed herself into someone else. The heavy makeup had easily covered most of the bruising, leaving her looking like she really could be recovering from a car wreck that could have happened two weeks ago. Her hair was now auburn and to her shoulders, thanks to the extensions, and the clothes were feminine and basic, covering the bruises on her arms and legs. She thought to herself, *Okay, this is it. I am going send the information to the police, and then I will run like hell, as fast as I can.* Carrying all of her belongings in the duffel bag, the new Petra slipped quietly from the back entrance of the hotel, and crossed the street to a gas station where another taxi picked her up. Moments later, in a UPS store, the copied paperwork was first faxed directly to the Orange Beach Police Station, and then mailed. After the fax and package was completed and paid for, Petra walked outside and dialed the number of the police station from one of the cell phones in the duffel bag.

"Orange Beach Police Department, can I help you?"

Petra's hands were shaking, right along with her voice, making it difficult to speak. Finally, she caught her breath and spoke as clearly as she could. Her nervousness killed her perfect English and she stammered her words into the phone. "Umm, yes, I cannot tell you my name. I am sorry for dis. People are want to kill me. I am faxing you information about Vladimir Bereovsky. I think he is keeping Suzanna Novacek in his house. Please help her." After turning the phone off, she closed it, returned it to the duffel bag, hopped in the taxi and asked to be taken to a Greyhound Bus Station. Doing the right thing by trying to help Suzanna did not ease her tension and anxiety, and she fidgeted quietly in her seat until the ride to the bus station was over. She had decided that her next stop would be Myrtle Beach. She had friends there who would help her hide out for a couple of days until she could think clearly, heal, and make new plans.

CHAPTER THIRTY-NINE

Lisa, the dispatcher, had answered the call from Petra. When she was sure the caller had hung up, she slammed the phone down and ran into the hallway to wave down the first person she could find.

"Is Hank still here?" she asked the officer who was walking towards her.

"Yeah, I think so. You need him?" the officer asked.

"Yeah, get him in here now! I just got an anonymous call from someone who is faxing us information about Mr. Vladimir Bereovsky. If he isn't here, send Hillary in."

The officer hurried off to find them, and Lisa ran to the fax machine to make sure something was coming in. Sure enough, the information the caller had promised was coming through, page after page. There were fifty two pages in all, and by the time they were all in the tray, both Hank and Hillary were there to retrieve them. They had spent most of the day trying to get an address and picture on Vladimir, but had come up with nothing. Between the two of them, they hurriedly poured over each page for his address, and Hillary finally found it first on page five. Vladimir Bereovsky, 4306 Hillshire Road, Atlanta, Georgia.

"Hillary, can you take care of this? I need to talk to Lisa for a second about the caller."

"You got it." She ran from the dispatch office to the meeting room where everyone had been working the case all day and quickly told them what had just happened. The FBI office and police department in Atlanta were phoned immediately. Within minutes, their agents were putting together a task force to raid Vladimir's residence. Their suspicions told them all that Vladimir was smarter than to keep Suzanna there. They hoped that if she wasn't there, that they would at least find something or someone in the house that would lead them to her. While Hillary worked with authorities in Atlanta over the phone, Hank questioned Lisa about the anonymous phone conversation. "Lisa, try and tell me word for word what the caller said to you."

"Not much, the phone call lasted for about fifteen seconds. It was a female with an accent, and her voice was very shaky, but I understood everything. She said that someone wanted to kill her so she couldn't give her name, she was faxing us information, and that she thinks Suzanna is being kept at Vladimir's house. Then, she just hung up. I would have tried to keep her on the phone, but she didn't give me a chance. The call registered as a private number. "

"That's alright, Lisa, you did really well. I am going in the room with the others. Just make sure that if she calls again, alert me or someone else immediately, and go ahead and set the phone up for trace. I want it to be ready if she calls again."

Hank quickly left dispatch and walked back to the meeting room. Phones were ringing everywhere, and people were running back and forth across the room. Hillary had already made one copy of the faxed information before she faxed it to Atlanta. She placed it on the table for everyone to view, and then returned to the copy machine with the original to make more copies. When she returned to the room, she began handing out copies to everyone. Hank poured over the information. Most of what Petra had faxed them were contact sheets, information on Vladimir's various offices, and the basic set up of each one. The contact sheets listed dozens of Russian names with phone numbers and addresses, several different law firms in Atlanta and Myrtle Beach, and many other various names, addresses, and numbers. Hank hoped that they were not too late in getting this information. As he studied the sheets of paper, another address on Hillshire Road popped up. 4591 Hillshire Road. A neighbor of Vladimir's. Hank called the task force in Atlanta and told them that there was another residence on the same road. It was added to the list of raids which grew larger by the second. Thirty minutes after Petra had made her anonymous phone call to Lisa, many Russian and some American homes were being staked out in New Orleans, Biloxi, Atlanta, Orange Beach, and Myrtle Beach.

Vladimir's house proved to be empty and clean. There were several things taken from it, including a safe, which had not yet been opened. The other house on Hillshire, however, which was raided second, held more than enough evidence to suggest that someone had been kept against their will. When the Atlanta agents and officers broke into the house, they found the room in which Suzanna had been kept. They took pictures of the handcuffs, dirty sheets, and empty syringes that were left on the bedside table. After about fifteen minutes into the raid, cadaver dogs were brought in. They immediately alerted officers to the tree line in the back yard. Barking furiously, the dogs sniffed out the body bags of Jan and Luda which were hidden under a pile of dead leaves. When Hank got the call about the bodies, he knew in his heart that they were the bodies of Ivana's missing boyfriend Jan and his best friend, Luda. He said nothing of this to Ivana, who was still being held and interviewed, mostly by the FBI.

The Orange Beach Police Department's phone lines were ringing off the hook. Some of the homes being raided proved empty, while others housed many of the people on the contact lists. Mostly Russian, they were all arrested and detained at their local police stations, awaiting interviews and questions about their relationships with Vladimir. Every one of them had lawyered up and kept their smug mouths shut. Not one single person on the list was in the United States illegally, and many have them denied even knowing Vladimir. Hank decided to take a break and get some fresh air. He phoned Judith, to tell her about the leads, but her voicemail came on. Seconds later, his cell phone rang, showing her number on the call id. Hank answered her call. "Hello?"

"Hey you. Sorry about that. I am at the hospital visiting with Anna, and I didn't want to talk in front of everyone. By the time I stepped out into the hallway, the phone had stopped ringing."

"That's quite alright. How is she doing?"

"She is doing so much better. She was happy to see me; she gave me a big smile. At least she has the color back in her face, although after what she has been through, I don't know how. You know, children amaze me all the time. They are so much more resilient than adults. Speaking of adults, how are you doing? I was watching the news earlier and I saw the new people and names. Can you talk about it?"

"Yeah, I can talk, but I am afraid that I don't have much more to tell you other than what you are seeing on TV. Atlanta police and FBI just raided the house of the Russian guy who we think is responsible for all of this. We were all hoping that Suzanna would be there, but she wasn't, and we have no idea where they could have taken her. I am about fed up with this case." Hank was trying not to sound depressed but couldn't help it. He didn't want to talk anymore about the case so he let Judith say something next.

"Well, how about we meet at my house later on about six? I will grab take out from the Chinese place on the strip. Is that alright with you?"

"Yeah, make it seven though; it's gonna be a long day here." They hung up, and Hank was headed for the door when his cell phone rang again. Hillary was on the caller id. "Yeah, Hank here."

"Yeah, it's Hill. Uh, one of the houses on the list was just raided right outside of Charlotte, North Carolina. They found Yuraslav's body, and some other things. You might wanna come back in and take a look at this."

The body count was rising, and Hank felt himself drifting further and further away from finding Suzanna and Vladimir, not because he wasn't confident, but because things weren't happening on his turf. Things weren't even happening in his state anymore, not that he particularly wanted anymore destruction on the island. He felt a certain sense of duty to put an end to this, to give closure to Anna, the remainder of her family, and Judith. There were so many people involved now, so much information, so many leads, and so many dead ends. As he walked through the hallway toward his office, he thought about Suzanna. He had to find her, dead or alive.

Hillary was talking to an FBI agent when he arrived at her desk. When she saw Hank approaching she gave Hank a somber look. "Hank, the house in Charlotte is being poured over at the moment. In addition to finding Yuraslav's body with a bullet in his brain, the authorities there think they may have found some clues about our anonymous caller. The information that we received earlier was faxed from a UPS store right outside of Charlotte in the small town of Belmont. Apparently, there was a female who was recently at the residence, according to some identification in a wallet left inside a car behind the residence. Her name is Petra Svoboda, and she is from Orange Beach. The car is also registered in her name. They didn't find her body, but they did find a female's blood all over a bedroom and inside a utility shed were they think she was kept. If it is our girl, it looks like she might have escaped to make contact with us. The techs seem to agree since the blood isn't very fresh. The house belongs to another Russian, go figure."

"Petra Svoboda, huh? Well, any idea who she is, really? Do we know where she works?"

"Not yet, but I sent some people over to question Ivana about her. My guess is that since Yuraslav was there, and Petra was there, then she was the one who drove Yuraslav out of Alabama after the murders."

"Yeah, that makes sense. Anything else?"

"No, not yet, but we are getting ready to put her name and picture on the news along with everyone else's. This is turning into a nightmare. Too many names and too many faces, and no one is coming forward."

"Ok, I am gonna be on the phone for a while. Keep me posted. And actually, hold off on sending her picture to the news. I don't want to send her into hiding. If she wants to help, we will help her help us."

Hillary left the room while Hank returned calls. He wanted to call Judith again, but stopped himself. Instead, he thought about Suzanna, and took out a notebook. *Time to brainstorm,* he thought. He glanced down at one of the faxed sheets and was immediately drawn to an Orange Beach address. He read a little more and finally realized what he was reading. He had just discovered where the Russians kept their Orange Beach office. No time to brainstorm now. Hank put his pen down, grabbed the sheet of paper and bolted out the door.

CHAPTER FORTY

On the way out of the police station, he caught up with Hillary. "Hey!"

Hillary whirled around to look at Hank who was practically running down the hallway to catch up with her. She excused herself from the conversation she was having with another officer and answered, "Yeah? Whatcha got?"

Hank reached her and pulled out the piece of paper with the address on it. "You are never going to believe what I think I just found! I was looking at the faxes that this girl Petra sent, and boom! I found this Orange Beach address. It is an address for the local office. Before now, we haven't been able to find it. I am going to look at it right now. Wanna come with?"

Hillary took the sheet of paper from Hank's hand and nodded quickly. "Absolutely! Give me a second to drop this stuff off at my desk. I will be right back."

She was back in less than five minutes. "Alright, let's go."

They left the station and drove to the address on the paper. They were expecting it to be in a small strip mall or office complex of some sort, but what they found instead was an old beat up singlewide trailer set back off of a residential street on the far end of the island. From the outside, it looked as if no one had been there in years, except for the wear and tear in the gravel in the driveway. There were other trailers on the lots next to it, and they looked even worse. Hank looked at Hillary from inside the car and said, "Well, so much for asking neighbors if anything suspicious or out of the ordinary was going on here."

Hillary nodded in agreement and opened the passenger seat door to get out. Hank followed, and soon they found themselves at the front door. Both had their hands on the guns when Hillary knocked twice on the door. Waiting and listening, neither one of them could hear a single sound coming from within the trailer. Finally, after a couple of minutes of waiting and knocking, Hillary reached out to try the door. It was unlocked. She almost turned the doorknob to open the door, when Hank stopped her. "Let's go around back and look through the windows first."

Hillary jerked her hand from the doorknob as if it was on fire. "This trailer gives me the willies for some reason. Go ahead, I will follow you."

Hank chuckled at his partner, "Are you scared? Say you're scared if you scared. If you can't run with the big dogs, you might as well stay on the porch."

Hillary rolled her eyes as she followed him around the trailer to the back yard. She replied in a hushed tone, "No, ass, I am not scared. But I will have you know that I don't mind staying on the porch. I don't wanna run with the big dogs. The porch is much nicer and it provides shade; I hate to sweat." Hank laughed and shook his head.

They reached the backyard and walked up the steps to the back door of the trailer. From there, Hank leaned into the window and searched the main room, seeing nothing. Hillary lost interest in what he was doing and ventured out into the backyard towards a barbecue pit, while Hank popped his head up to every available window. As she neared the pit, she could smell the burnt charcoal, and figured it had been used recently. Over her shoulder, she called out to Hank, "Hey, there is a barbecue pit out here, and someone has used it recently."

"What's in it?" Hank yelled back, too preoccupied with the interior of the trailer to look around at her.

Hillary reached the pit and gasped. Someone had definitely used the pit recently, as in a couple of days ago at the most. Apparently, the fire had not burned everything like it was supposed to. From within the pit, Hillary saw articles of partially burnt clothing covered with blood, and pieces of burnt paper. She could also make out a couple of burnt floppy disks in the bottom as well. "Hank, I think you may want to take a look at this!"

The tone of her voice was what made Hank leave his windows. He dropped down from a railing that he was standing on and ran over to the pit. Sure enough, there laid enough evidence in his mind to convince him that this was the place that Yuraslav had come to after the murders. There were men's clothing, partially burned, still covered with dried blood.

Hillary drew her gun and ran to the side of the trailer, while Hank called for back up. Then they both broke down the front door to the trailer. It was completely empty. Every room was bare, and the only indication that anyone had been inside recently was the smell of a household cleaner that had been used to wash it down. No finger prints, no garbage of any kind, no clues as to who had ever been inside the trailer.

Back up arrived shortly and the contents of the pit were taken as evidence. Of course, the DNA testing would take a while, but everyone at the scene knew in their hearts that the blood on the clothes belonged to the various members of the late Morrison family. Hank and Hillary sat on the front porch steps of the trailer for a moment before they returned to the office. They quietly contemplated the case and added another dead end to the list.

"Well," Hank said as he rose to walk to the car, "At least we found out where the damn office was. That in itself was driving me crazy."

Hillary nodded and slid into the passenger seat, "Yeah, it was bothering me too."

They rode back to the station, totally let down, and tired from the sudden burst of adrenalin.

CHAPTER FORTY-ONE

Suzanna woke up in the backseat on Vladimir's SUV hogtied and gagged with something covering her face and body. She thought it was a blanket, but was too weak to try and figure it out. She gurgled and made noises, alerting the men in the car that she had woken. Vladimir turned around from the front seat and took the blanket off of Suzanna so she could look around at her surroundings. The first thing she saw was Mirek's face, and it made her gag. Of all the Czech people she hated, she hated Mirek the most. More off than on, he had been a fair weather friend of Yuraslav's over the past five years. His treatment of Yuraslav was not what made her hate him; it was his personality and the way he treated other people. In her mind, he was a punk trying to be a big league thug. Mirek had always wanted to run with the big boys in Atlanta, and made himself out to be a gangster, even though he was as dumb as a rock.

When Yuraslav had first come to Orange Beach to work, before the Russian businesses were finely tuned, Mirek had been in charge of collecting money from Czech people who owed more to Vladimir than they could make. He had been perfect for the job since his nature was one of a bully. He used to come around to the crowded Czech apartments and bang on the doors. When they let him in, he would sit for hours, eating all of the food in the refrigerator, and beating up people if they didn't have the money that he came to collect. Sometimes, he just beat people for the hell of it, especially the women. Mirek had always been on the take too. Suzanna figured that for every dollar he had taken from his fellow Czechs, he kept ten cents for himself.

Mirek and Yuraslav had never gotten along until Suzanna married him. Then, people came out the woodwork to be Yuraslav's friends, including Mirek, because he had a green card. One day, shortly after they had returned from Prague to the States, Mirek and some of his Russian cronies had shown up on her doorstep to congratulate Yuraslav. They had taken him out to the bars that night and gotten him so drunk that he couldn't even fight with her when he returned. Actually, as she looked back on that night, she silently thanked Mirek for plying her husband with that much alcohol, or she surely would have gotten beaten. She remembered Yuraslav being so proud of himself that night, like he had really accomplished something important in life.

She shook her head in disgust and glared at Mirek. Mirek would have glared back at her if he had been able to open his eyes all the way; they were so swollen from the beatings that he had taken from the telephone books, that it was too painful. He didn't utter a word as he sat next to her in the back seat. Vladimir noticed the hatred in her eyes and laughed. "What, you no like your backseat buddy? He doesn't do it for you?" He laughed again as he watched Suzanna refocus her hatred on him. "I am going to take that gag from your mouth, so you can drink some water. I want you to be able to talk back to me when I ask you some questions, no?" He leaned over and removed her gag. Suzanna gasped for air and licked her numb lips which were cracked and bleeding. She tried to gulp down all of the water that Vladimir was feeding her, but she spilled more than she drank. He thought this was funny too, and laughed at her as she strained to get the liquid down her throat. "Now, then, that's better, hmmm? So, Mrs. Novacek, you are now a widow. Congratulations."

Suzanna let the word widow sink in for a second before she tried to speak. It made her feel neither sad nor happy, but it was strange nonetheless. She had always thought that she would die before him, at his hands of course. She licked her parched lips again, and whispered, "Thank you."

This sent Vladimir into hysterics. He laughed so hard that the driver felt compelled to chime in. "This one, she is funny. She has humor. I like that in a woman!" He reached over and gave her more water. "Okay, Suzanna. Now, I want you to listen to me very carefully. Your husband did a very bad thing to me, and because he was your husband, now you have to pay the consequences. Because of his actions, I will lose everything. I have to disappear. People are looking for me everywhere I go, so I cannot afford to try and make it on my own, so you will be my hostage. Yes, and I will use you to get what I want. If I don't get what I want, then I will kill you. It is very simple. Do you understand, Mrs. Novacek?"

156

Suzanna wanted to spit in his face, but didn't have the strength or the spit to spare on him, so she just nodded her head.

He shook his head at her. "When I ask you a question, Mrs. Novacek, you speak to me. You don't swing your head at me. I will ask you again. Do you understand?" Vladimir smiled at her with sinister eyes.

"Yes." Suzanna defiantly held his stare as long as she could, and then looked away to the window to watch the cars pass them by. She would have cried but she didn't have any tears left. "Where are we going?" she whispered, barely audible. Her throat was on fire, and it hurt so badly to speak. The water had done nothing but inflame it, causing the numbness to fade away. When she had first woken to the sight of Mirek, she had been numb all over. But now, as the water trickled down her raw throat into her empty stomach, she began to feel pain and hunger. Suzanna had no idea how long she had been out, and didn't know when the last time she had eaten anything. "And can I please have something to eat?"

"We are going to Myrtle Beach. Here." Vladimir flung a candy bar at her face and it bounced off her forehead and fell into her lap. She was still tied up and couldn't reach it. He laughed at her again from the front seat, then snaked his arm back to her lap. He picked up the candy bar and began sliding up and down the inside of her legs, prying them open. "How bad do you want this candy bar?"

Moments before, Suzanna had thought that she didn't have any tears, but as she felt him violate her thighs with a Payday, tears fell down her burning cheeks. "Please stop. If you want me to help you, I have to eat something, please."

Vladimir stopped rubbing the candy on her and sighed. He took off the wrapper and fed it to her, making sure that he smeared the melting chocolate all over her face in the process. He gave her more water until she ate the last bite, and then turned back to the road ahead.

Suzanna cried in silence as she listened to the driver and her kidnappers speak in Russian. With chocolate smeared all over her face and no way to wipe it off, she felt hopeless and humiliated, bound by rope and sitting next to a Czech whom she had always despised. It would be a matter of minutes before they reached Myrtle Beach, so she passed the time by dreaming of ways to escape. The candy bar had done nothing to nourish her body. It had made her nauseous, and the cars flying by made her dizzy. All of a sudden, Suzanna lurched forward and projectile vomited. Half of her vomit hit the side of Vladimir's face, and the rest hit the back of the driver's head and the floorboard. She gagged again, and her body threw itself into series of uncontrollable dry heaves that became more and more violent. The only thing that stopped the dry heaving was when she felt Vladimir's hand come down on the side of her face while the driver almost wrecked when he pulled over on the side of the highway. The sudden stop of the SUV threw Suzanna to the floorboard, pinning her face in between Mirek's bloody boot and the center console, which was now bathed in vomit. Grumbling something hateful under his breath Mirek feebly managed to kick her face away in disgust. For about ten seconds Suzanna passed out; she came to when she felt the cool breeze flowing in through the open passenger door. She coughed violently and tried to spit out the rest of the candy bar that was lodged in her throat and nose. Everything in the car was quickly wiped down with the blanket that had been covering her, and they were back on the road within five minutes. Vladimir strapped Suzanna in with a seat belt, and no one spoke for the remainder of the trip.

As bad as everything was for her, Suzanna still managed to find within herself a little humor. An undigested regurgitated piece of chocolate covered peanut was still stuck on the back of Vladimir's ear, despite his thorough efforts to clean himself.

CHAPTER FORTY-TWO

The day was winding down for Hank, but not for the station. It was still very much alive and busy, with people running everywhere. In Orange Beach and Gulf Shores, there hadn't been a single arrest pertaining to the Morrison case since the murders. Hank guessed that most of the residents were hunkered down in their homes watching television, wondering what the outcome of all of this would be and steering clear of driving drunk on the busy roads due to all of the law enforcement that was in town. Over the last couple of days the FBI and INS had created quite a stir by rounding up immigrants whose visas had lapsed and arresting them for deportation. Several mom and pop stores had been forced to close for a couple of days while they looked for new employees, and some of the bars and restaurants were severely short staffed at night. Even though the season was close to ending, there were still quite a number of vacationers still coming in to get the last of the fishing and sunshine. Complaints from business owners were flooding in constantly, concerned about how the media coverage had affected their customers. Many restaurants had already pulled their Czech employees from any kind of face to face customer service because of the way they were being treated. Customers were staring at them suspiciously, not tipping them, and demanding an American server instead.

Earlier, Hank had phoned Suzanna's parents to update them on everything. They were just preparing to do a press conference with the media to plea with Suzanna's kidnappers for her safe return when he phoned. Hank told them that Yuraslav's body had been found dead from to a gunshot wound to the head. That information had given them a little happiness, until they started worrying if Suzanna had met the same fate. He had reassured them that Suzanna would be found alive, and ended the call. He had not told them that the raid in one of the houses in Atlanta had proved that a female, probably Suzanna, had been held there for some time. He figured that until DNA testing was done and they were sure that it was Suzanna, it would probably be an unnecessary image to put inside their heads. They hadn't thanked him for the call, nor had he expected them to. They were still angry at the police for placing her in protective hiding, then losing her. Suzanna's father had already been tooting his lawsuit horn all over the local news stations for the last couple of days, citing that it was the Orange Beach police department's fault for her kidnapping. In truth, it actually was, and Hank knew it.

While looking at the pictures of the dead bodies and details of the raids from all over the South East, Judith had popped in and out of Hank's head all day long. The smell and feel of her body from last night were still fresh in his mind, and she had become in the last couple of days, the only thing that calmed him. Thinking of her and the wonderful night that they had spent together, he suddenly remembered their Chinese dinner date. He glanced down at his watch to check the time. If he left the station now, he had about thirty minutes to spare before meeting her at her house at seven o'clock. Then he realized that he hadn't eaten all day long, and a hunger pain hit him in the gut like he had been punched. He gathered up his paperwork and notes and headed home to change.

Thirty minutes later, Judith answered his knock and invited him in. The takeout food was already prepared on the table, and they sat down to eat. They flirted back and forth in silence, both amazed that the silence wasn't at all awkward, and after dinner, they ventured out onto the deck to watch the sunset. Hank was thinking about Suzanna when Judith interrupted his thoughts. "So, how are you? Not the case, I mean how are *you* doing?"

Gazing out over the rippling water, Hank sighed and absentmindedly tapped his finger on the table. "Well, I'm ok, just can't help thinking about her being out there. I really don't want to be the one to have to call her parents to inform them that she is dead, you know, especially since we are the reason that she was kidnapped. There have been so many leads, and today, hell, we could have been close to rescuing her. I just hope we can get to her and Vladimir before anything bad happens."

"I know you do." Judith kept her comment simple because she knew that there was nothing she could say to make him feel better. She smiled softly at him and held his hand. "At least we don't have to worry about Yuraslav Novacek anymore."

Hank nodded his head at her. "This is true; one less psychopath on the loose in this country."

They continued to watch the sun go down and finally, when the last bit of orange light disappeared into the waves, Suzanna stood up behind Hank, and pressed her chest into the back of his head. She held his shoulders for a moment and then whispered in his ear, "I want to make you feel better." They went inside to her bedroom and made love. With a deliberate tenderness and passion, it was just as good if not better than the night before.

After they both showered and dressed again, Hank said, "You know, meeting you in the middle of all of this chaos sure has been wonderful. I don't know what to make of it, but I hope when this all blows over, we still have whatever we got now. Does that make sense?" He laughed at himself for trying to put what he felt for her into words.

She kissed him and said, "Oh, I think we will. I am not worried about it. Everything happens for a reason, the good and the bad."

"Hmm." He reflected on what she just said. "Yeah, I guess you are right." He didn't want to say goodnight, but she hadn't asked him to stay either, so he hugged her, thanked her again for dinner, and said that he would call her in the morning.

"Not staying?" Judith asked, wondering if he didn't want to.

"Do you want me to?"

"Do you want to?" They both started laughing. The game they were playing was so juvenile, but it fit the moment. Judith broke up the laughter.

"Alright, how about we have a drink, watch some TV, and if you stay, you stay, if you don't, you don't."

"Sounds like a plan." Hank put his car keys back down on the counter and headed for the couch. He had waited to see her all day long, and he wanted nothing more than to just lie beside her and feel fortunate for having found her.

CHAPTER FORTY-THREE

"911 Myrtle Beach, can I assist you?"

"Uh, yes, ma'am. I, uh, think I just saw that Russian guy from the news, you know, the one in connection with that girl's kidnapping?"

"Sir, do you know this man? His name is Vladimir Bereovsky. The media has not yet released a picture of him."

"Yes, ma'am, I know, but I am at a gas station, and I heard him speaking what I think is Russian, and he had a girl in the car that kind of looks like the girl on the news, the one that is married to the Czech guy, the one that was kidnapped. She was beat up, and had short hair but it kind of looked like her. He is driving a black SUV."

"Sir, can you please tell me your location, and do you still have him in your sight?"

"I am at the Shell Station on Highway 17, the one across from the mall. He is already gone, heading north on the highway."

"Sir, did you get his license plate number?"

"No, ma'am, I didn't. Actually, it dawned on me as I was pumping gas that it could be them, but by the time I got to my phone, they were already pulling off. There were two men in the front seat, and a woman and, I think, another man in the backseat. The driver's door was only opened for a second so I couldn't really tell, and the windows were tinted too dark to see inside."

"Thank you, sir, can you hold please?" The dispatcher sent out the tip over the radio and came back on the line. "Thank you, sir. An officer will be there shortly to speak with you, and did you say he was traveling north on Highway 17?"

"Yes, ma'am, in a black Mercedes SUV. He pulled out about five minutes ago."

"Thank you, sir. Please stand by for the officer." The dispatcher sent Officer Dell Myers, who had spoken at length with Hillary and other officers over the past couple of days about the Morrison case. When he arrived at the gas station, several other units were dispatched to the area north of the gas station to look for the SUV. He thanked the man for phoning in and took notes from him, including a description of the Russian who had been pumping the gas. Then he walked into the gas station to inquire if they had a video recorder set up for the pumps outside. Unfortunately, the only recorder was the one above the register, and the Russian had paid with a credit card outside at the pump. Officer Myers had them run a credit card report on the last twenty transactions of the pump, and asked the 911 caller to come down to the station and work with a sketch artist. Apparently, Dell thought, along with the officers who had raided Vladimir's house, Vladimir was not fond of photographs. Not one single photograph of him had turned up, so maybe the sketch artist could come up with an idea of what he looked like so the public could keep an eye out for him. Little did he know, the 911 caller had actually seen the Russian driver who looked nothing like Vladimir who had been sitting in the passenger seat. Before Dell left the gas station, he called dispatch and told them to contact the Orange Beach Police Department to inform them of a possible sighting of Suzanna and Vladimir. Then he escorted the caller to the police station to make a full report. Meanwhile, the units that were dispatched to locate the Mercedes SUV searched Highway 17 in vain. Several black Mercedes SUVs had been pulled over, but none of the passengers were Russians or females resembling Suzanna. With more units responding, the search continued all over Myrtle Beach, and the media was alerted so that the public could keep an eye out. The FBI flew in to help with the search, and all hell broke loose in Myrtle Beach.

Vladimir's phone rang. One of his hoodlums, Ivan, who had been responsible for making sure that all of Vladimir's offices were closed and stripped, had been listening to the police scanner, and heard that he was possibly spotted in Myrtle Beach at a gas station. He had called to warn them. Listening carefully, Vladimir repeated what was being said to his driver in Russian, and told him to stay calm. The driver was not calm. He chewed his lip and cursed in his native tongue while he took back roads through residential areas to stay off the main streets. Vladimir spoke at length with the caller, telling him where they were and with what kind of car he needed to switch to. Since the police were now looking for their SUV, he asked Ivan to find them a blue sedan, or something that was boring which wouldn't even come close to looking like an SUV. Ivan assured him that he would personally find them another car; then gave them directions to a house that they could hide out at until he could find another vehicle. Vladimir hung up and looked at the nervous driver.

"Take a left there," he spoke in Russian and pointed to the next street. "Take the next two rights and pull into the garage on the second house on the left."

His driver nodded and drove them to an ugly small green house that had seen some seriously better days. The paint was chipping everywhere, and two of the brown shutters were hanging on by one hinge each. The grass had been consumed by weeds long ago, and the fallen mailbox had been propped up with rocks. As they pulled into the garage Vladimir rolled his eyes in disgust and wondered if there was anywhere nastier that he could have been sent to. He made a mental note to yell at Ivan later, but for the moment, he was just relieved to be off the main road where the cops were busy looking for him. The garage door slowly moaned and groaned behind them, and finally sealed them into a musty damp garage that looked like no one had parked in it for twenty years. A door to the house opened, and two frightened young Czech men peered out into the dark garage at them. Ivan had called them only seconds ago to inform them that the boss was coming to their house. In the two years the young men had worked in Myrtle Beach, they had paid a lot of money to the boss but never met him. Ivan had not told them why he was coming, and they thought the worst. As they watched the passengers unload from the SUV, they suddenly figured it out. They recognized Suzanna from the television, and knew that they were about to be in some seriouse trouble. Vladimir yelled at them to go inside and prepare him something to eat while the driver hoisted Suzanna out of the car and carried her kicking and screaming into the house. When he put his hand over her mouth to control her screams, she bit his finger so hard that it broke the skin. Cursing, he threw her down onto the cheap linoleum floor, and was about to kick her when Vladimir stopped him. "No, there will be enough time for that later. Get Mirek out of the car and take him to a room somewhere. We should have taken care of him before we got here." He turned back toward the garage and watched as Mirek was taken out of the car and led into the house.

One of the young Czechs carried a warm plate from the kitchen into the dining area, and carefully set it onto the table for Vladimir. "It is Svickova with dumplings. My girlfriend made it."His voice was full of fear.

Vladimir didn't even thank him. He just sat at the table, stabbing a piece of the Czech food with a fork while staring at Suzanna on the floor. Ivan had told him that it wouldn't be a problem to get the car to him, but that it might take a while, anywhere from an hour to all day long; he had to make sure that the windows were tinted, and that the registration and plates weren't suspicious in any way. Ivan had also promised him that he would plan a safe way for him to leave Myrtle Beach, possibly to New York, where other Russians were already waiting for him.

The longer he stared at Suzanna, the angrier he became at himself. How could he have gotten himself into such a mess as this? Had he not worked so hard over the last years to accomplish so much? He thought of all the money he had made, all of the contacts, everything that he owned, the houses, the cars, for what? Now nothing. It reminded him of when he was sixteen and living in his mother's apartment while running small time errands for the local gangs, selling drugs, and pimping his sisters out for extra money. Both his mother and his sisters had been prostitutes, sharing men, and whoring themselves out to anyone who would give them something. He grew up watching things that no child should ever know about, much less see. Born out of prostitution, he didn't have a father. At the young age of sixteen, he had been heartless and ruthless, doing jobs that not many other grown adults would do. He raped, pillaged, murdered, stole; he never turned down a job, and always came through. He had been sneaky too; he was never arrested by authorities. When it came time for him to broaden his evil horizons by moving to the United States, it had been smooth sailing. He had obtained a visa fairly easily, moved to New York, and started working for the Russian mob there. He had quickly earned respect early on from the gangsters who he worked for, and was eventually given a territory of his own in Atlanta. That's where he had come up with the brilliant outsourcing idea. The business had been slow to grow at first, but as soon as he had the trust of the locals in the areas that he pursued, his business grew like wildfire.

Myrtle Beach had been his first conquest. Orange Beach, Gulf Shores and the others had followed soon after.

As he thought about his life and all of the effort that he had put into his companies over the years, his anger grew until he had no appetite. He could no longer eat, and decided that he would just sit for a while and watch Suzanna squirm around on the floor. She was pathetic, he thought. Maybe the Czech guys who lived here could wash her up and make her ready for him; he had every intention of raping her before he killed her. As long as Ivan was successful in getting a car to him in decent time, he would no longer need her as a bargaining chip. At least he would enjoy her before she died.

CHAPTER FORTY-FOUR

Hillary answered her cell phone immediately when she saw Officer Dell Myer's number on the caller id. She had spoken to him several times over the course of the investigation, and knew that he wouldn't be calling her late in the evening if it wasn't important. She listened as he told her about the 911 caller, and what was transpiring in Myrtle Beach. Of course, they weren't sure that the man seen was Vladimir, but the fact that the caller had been suspicious of him and a woman who resembled a beaten Suzanna raised the stakes and made it a definite possibility. He informed her that his precinct was on the phone with hers at the moment, but that he wanted to tell her personally since she was already gone for the day. She thanked him and told him that she would be calling Detective Jordan to alert him and hung up.

Law and Order Special Victim's Unit, Judith's favorite television show, had just begun when Hank's cell phone rang. Since very few people outside of his job called his cell phone at night, Hank was quick to jump from the couch and answer. Hoping that there was news of Suzanna's or Vladimir's whereabouts, he quickly opened the cell phone. He got what he hoped for as he listened to Hillary on the other line.

"Hank, do you remember me talking to you about an Officer Dell Myers in Myrtle Beach? I have spoken to him several times. He is the one who went over to check on the local Czech/Russian office in Myrtle Beach and found it empty."

"Yeah, I remember, what's up?"

"Well, apparently he is at his police station talking to someone who called in a possible sighting of Vladimir."

"Wait a minute, how does he know what he looks like? We don't even know what he looks like yet."

"Well, Officer Myers said that the man who called 911 told them that a man was pumping gas into a black Mercedes SUV and speaking Russian and for a brief couple of seconds, when the door was opened, he saw a female in the backseat that looked like Suzanna, only that she was beaten up. The whole city is looking for the SUV right now."

Hank's heart began to race, and Judith noticed from the look on his face that something big was happening. She turned the television off and stood next to him as he continued his conversation.

"Are you going in to the station?" Hank asked Hillary.

"Yes, when I hang up with you, I am going down there. Officer Myers said that his station was talking to ours right now. I suspect your cell phone will be ringing any moment now."

Just as she said that, Hanks call waiting began to beep. "Yeah, Hill, that's the station right now, I will meet you there." They hung up and Hank took the call, informing them that he already knew what was happening, and that he was on his way over. Hank looked at Judith who was patiently waiting to hear the news. "Well, congratulations! Looks like the first possible sighting of Suzanna and Vladimir has occurred right in your hometown. I am going to go down to the station for a while, but I will be on the phone. Watch the news, and see what they say."

"I will. Call me if you get a chance."

Hank grabbed his keys, kissed Judith quickly and barreled down the stairs to his car. Moments later he was walking through the doors of the station, where everything had suddenly turned into a madhouse. Everyone was excited of course, hoping that tonight was the night to save Suzanna and lock up the criminals who were responsible for the horrendous murders of the Morrison family. Ten minutes later Hillary walked in the office, and Hank motioned her over to his desk so she could listen to the phone conference that he was on with Officer Myers.

"We have damn near every unit out there right now looking for the vehicle, but it's black and its getting dark outside. Hopefully, someone else will spot it and call it in. We have had about fifteen calls already about Mercedes SUVs, but none of them have panned out so far. We nearly gave one woman a heart attack about fifteen minutes ago. Pulled her over with lights. She was about eighty years old. Scared her to death."

"Do you have any hunches about where they would be going in Myrtle Beach?" Hank asked the Officer.

"Hell, there are so many places they could be. My guess is that they are hiding out in a friend's house. They are so many Czechs and Russians here. Could be hundreds of possibilities."

"Hmmm, ok, well, is there anything we can do?"

"Well, not really, but if you would like to come up and help, I would appreciate it. You have been working this case from day one, and I know how bad you must want to find Mrs. Novacek. I have already cleared you if you are interested."

Hank had secretly hoped for the invitation, but down played his excitement as much as he could. "Well, now that you mention it, that's probably a good idea. I could probably get a flight in from a buddy that works at the local hangar. Let me make a couple of calls and get back with you." The call was ended. Hank looked at Hillary who was already scrolling through her rolodex to find Sammy Perdue's number. Sammy was local pilot and small aircraft mechanic at the Jack Edwards airport in Gulf Shores until he retired last year. These days, he made pocket change by making quick private pick up flights in his single engine Cessna.

"You looking up Sam's number?"

"Yep, I knew that's were you were headed. Here it is. Better you than me. There is no way in hell that you could get my land loving butt up in one of those little things." She handed him the card and sat at her desk to take a phone call from a federal agent that was on hold.

Hank wasn't particularly fond of flying either, especially in a small plane like Sam's. But he had been up with him a couple of times, and had known Sam since he was a child. Sam was an excellent pilot who spent every day of his retirement tinkering with his Cessna to make sure it was always in perfect condition, and Hank trusted him. He called Sam and told him what was going on. After explaining the situation, he asked him what the price would be; he had already decided that he would pay for it out of his own pocket.

"Hank, there ain't no charge, son. I've been friends with Ed Morrison since I was knee high to a grasshopper, and there ain't no damn way I am charging anybody anything if it pertains to helping find the pieces of shits who killed his son and family. Hell, I'd pay you just to be able to help. When you wanna go, son?"

"Actually, right now, Sam, if not sooner. I just got off the phone with the officer who asked me to help. I've got to call him back with an answer."

Excited with his role in the investigation, Sam said, "Meet me at the hangar as soon as you can. It will take me a couple of minutes to prep her, but we can be in the sky in thirty minutes from now, oh and Hank?"

"Yeah?"

"We won't be flying in the Cessna."

Hank was confused. "Huh? What are we flying in?"

"I'm flying your ass up to Myrtle in style, son! I got a buddy over on Ono Island who's got his Lear 35A parked in the hangar. He knows Ed from way back too, and he won't have one bit of a problem with me flying us in it. We'd be there in an hour."

Hank smiled at that little bit of information and good luck; from a Cessna to a Lear. Not bad! "I will be there! Thanks Sam." Flipping the phone closed, Hank looked at Hillary and said, "Well, call me if you need me. But not for about an hour. I will be in the air on board a private jet."

"What? I thought Sammy had a Cessna." Hillary said.

"He does, but we are taking his friend's Lear instead, at no charge. Nice, huh? Does your butt still love the land?"

Hillary rolled her eyes at him and laughed. "Yes, it does! It's still a small plane, and in my mind, bigger is better, in all forms of life, especially when it pertains to planes, guns and men."

Hank laughed on the way out of the office. "I will call you when we land. You're in charge while I am gone!" He quickly informed everyone about his plans, grabbed a copy of Petra's fax and the files that he had put together on the Morrison case, and then headed toward his car. On the way to his vehicle he thought of Judith and wondered if she would be interested in going. After all, she was from Myrtle Beach, and it certainly would be a great time to impress her. He immediately felt guilty for worrying about impressing her while he was worried about finding Suzanna before the Russians killed her; but it didn't stop him from phoning her anyway. "Judith, I am going to Myrtle Beach in about fifteen minutes. You want to go with me?"

"Uh, yeah," she stammered, "But it's a long drive from here and pretty short notice. Fifteen minutes? What's going on? Have they found Suzanna?"

As he hurriedly stuffed his piles of paper into the passenger seat, he talked hands free with the phone cradled between his head shoulder and ear. "Well, first of all we are not driving, we are flying, and second, I know it's short notice, but if you want to come with me, I can arrange to have you driven to your parents house when we get there if you want; and third, no, they haven't found her yet. I have been asked to come up and help with the investigation there."

Judith was already up and in her bedroom packing. As she hastily stuffed her suitcase with clothes and toiletries, she asked, "Ok, where do I go?"

"I would pick you up but I don't have time. I have to go home and grab a change of clothes, so just meet me at the hangar at Jack Edwards airport."

"Got it," Judith said hurriedly, "I'm on my way." She finished packing in less than five minutes, and then made a list on a sheet of paper of who she needed to call on her way to the airport. It wouldn't be a problem to find someone to take care of her patients in the morning, but it would be the second time in a week that she had done it. She knew it didn't matter, because everyone on the island and thirty miles inland knew what was going on with the Morrisons. And those who worked with her knew that she had been best friends with Tammy for several years. She had been reassured at the hospital that her patients would be taken care of at a moment's notice, and she had few appointments scheduled for the office, all of which could be canceled. Nonetheless, she felt guilty for rescheduling and farming her patients out twice in one week, but not guilty enough, however, to stop her from going. Several reasons pushed her to pack and go to Myrtle Beach. Hank, of course, was one of them. She had been so happy for the last couple of days that she had been with him. She had felt things that she had never felt before, and an excitement that she hadn't felt in a very long time. Just the way he looked at her made her knees shake like a fifteen year old girl in love with the high school quarterback. She wanted to go with him because she liked being with him. But she also wanted to go with him because she felt like she owed it to Tammy and Anna. If she could have one chance to play a part in finding

Vladimir and Suzanna, then she would take it, even if it meant flying to Myrtle Beach and staying at her parent's house for a few days while Hank searched for them. She grabbed her suitcase and ran through the house checking windows and doors to make sure everything was locked. Glancing down at her watch made her walk faster towards the door; since she only had eight minutes before Hank's plane left.

On the way to the hangar, Judith phoned her parents to tell them everything so they would be expecting her. They were more than happy to hear that she was on her way home, and told her not to worry about Hank staying anywhere else but at their house. The mere fact that Judith was bringing a guest made her mother, Marie, happy. Marie had always strived to be the greatest hostess. Over the years Judith had often referred to her mother in loving jest as Martha Esther, instead of Marie.

She arrived at the airport in less than seven minutes and parked quickly beside Hank's car. The Lear that stood open on the tarmac took her totally by surprise. She had thought that they would be flying in something smaller and less grand, definitely not a customized private Lear jet. Hank noticed the surprise in her face when her eyes lit up as she saw the plane. He had already told Sammy that she was coming, and he walked over to Judith to introduce them to each other. After the introduction was made between the two, the suitcases were boarded, and they were in the air on their way to Myrtle Beach.

Sammy yelled back at them from the cockpit, "Well, folks, we got this baby until we don't need her anymore, courtesy of another fellow Orange Beacher that would like to see them Russians strung up and gutted like the pigs that they are, so we're not on a deadline to get back. I got a brother who lives up this way, and I'll have my cell on in case you need me. The owner's got Cokes and snacks in the fridge back there, if you want something. Make yourselves comfortable, we'll be there in a little over an hour. I hope that's not too much time to lose them Russian sons of bitches."

Hank and Judith looked at each other and suppressed a little laugh.

Sammy Perdue had gotten that redneck fever that most men from the South get from time to time when they feel important, especially when they are out to get the 'bad guys'. Hank leaned over and whispered to Judith, "You gotta love the South."

CHAPTER FORTY-FIVE

Back at the little ugly green house, Vladimir, his driver, Suzanna, Mirek and the two young Czechs who lived there sat nervously in different parts of the house, watching the local news talk about them. Vladimir waited for the phone call that would tell them what to do next. It was the first time that Vladimir had had a chance to watch the news since he had gone on the run. They had his name, sure enough, but they still didn't have a picture of him. He seethed in his chair as he watched and listened to the smug reporters talk about how Yuraslav had killed the Morrison family, but failed to kill the little girl. They gave him all of the credit for the murders and only mentioned Vladimir as being someone in connection with Suzanna's disappearance. Part of him wanted everyone in the world to know that he was responsible for everything, not stupid, pathetic Yuraslav Novacek! He wanted the respect, but not enough, of course, to trade it for the rest of his life in prison.

Vladimir had called Ivan several times since they had arrived at the house to yell at him for the long wait and for sending him to such a nasty hideout; he felt that it was beneath him to stay there with two low life Czechs. Each time he called, Ivan had tried to explain to him that it would take some time to figure everything out and make the car safe enough, but Vladimir yelled at him anyway. Usually, he had more patience than this, and thought out problems diligently in a more sophisticated manner. But right now, faced with the possibility of being arrested, he was very much like a wild animal trapped in a corner trying desperately to escape. During their last conversation, Ivan had suggested that Vladimir take a shower to calm down; it had enraged him to hear someone else telling him what to do. But now, as he sat alone in the small dining room watching Suzanna on the floor, he thought that a shower might do him some good.

He handed a gun to one of the young Czechs in the kitchen and ordered them both to watch Suzanna while he bathed. Welcoming his departure from the room, the Czechs had anxiously agreed and took the gun. Moments later, he was soaking under a hot stream of water in the shower. With both hands pressed on the shower walls, Vladimir hung his head low to his chin to let the water scald his back while he urinated down the shower drain. The water did feel good, but it didn't relax him. It made him horny. Vladimir was the type of guy that liked for his sexual tension to build up and lead into an explosion. He always preferred violence and sex together, rather than just straight sex. *Maybe,* he thought as he fingered his gold chains in the hot water, *after my shower, I will take Suzanna into the bedroom that Mirek is in and make her watch while I finish him off. He is no good to me anymore, and should have died in North Carolina. This will be a good time to get rid of him.* The more he thought about his little plan, the hornier he became. He just wished that he knew when Ivan would call so he could time everything just right. Since this would be the only time he had left to do it, it would ruin everything if Ivan called before he had time to finish Mirek and have Suzanna. He had planned to use Suzanna as a hostage and then kill her after he escaped, but if Ivan pulled through with the car and an escape plan, then he wouldn't have to worry about keeping her alive. He would have a new driver's license, a new social security card, and a new life, enabling him to go wherever in hell that he damn well pleased. He would leave Mirek's and Suzanna's death in the hands of his driver who thoroughly enjoyed killing just as much as he did.

His thoughts were suddenly interrupted by the sudden worry over where Petra had disappeared to. In his attempt to get somewhere and hide from the Myrtle Beach police, he had totally forgotten about her. Petra was no fool; that he had always been sure of. That was precisely why he had chosen her to run the Orange Beach office. She did what she was told and kept her mouth shut. In his line of business, people like that were valuable, especially if they were Czech. There were so many of them in Orange Beach now, that it would've been strange to place a Russian in charge of the office. From the time Petra had shown up to work in Orange Beach, Vladimir and his thugs had used fear to manipulate and mold her into what he wanted her to be. In his opinion, most of the Czechs, especially the women, were too stupid to be trusted to work for him at that level. But, there had always been something special about Petra. Maybe it was her willingness to work her debt off with sex that caught Vladimir's attention. In his eyes, she had always been a true whore. Of course, Vladimir knew that Petra hated him, but she was good in bed. When he had sex with her, she actually pretended that she liked it, even when it was rough. She had always showed up to work everyday like she was suppose to, made her money and pretty much kept to herself. All of the other Czechs quickly made friends and hung out in the local Czech bar every night, drinking their sorrows away. Oh, but not his Petra. No, she kept to herself, and saved every penny that she could.

Finally, when she had realized the cold hearted truth that she was, in fact, unable to pay her debt off entirely, Petra had stopped showing up for work. Not wanting to lose her, Vladimir called her one day and offered her a special job. He had offered her the job of running the local office, which up until that point, hadn't really existed. She had readily accepted, and the rest fell into place. Not once while Petra ran the office, did things go wrong. That, in itself, had been extremely valuable to Vladimir.

He stood in the shower and wondered where she could have hidden. As far as he knew, she had never made any real friends in the States.

CHAPTER FORTY-SIX

Petra had slept on and off during the entire bus ride to Myrtle Beach. Even if she had been awake, there were no televisions on the bus, nor did she have a radio to keep her up to date on the news. She had no way of knowing that the search for Vladimir and Suzanna had found its way to Myrtle Beach, or else she wouldn't have gone there. The ride had been long, and the bus had smelled bad. The passenger seated next to her was a severely overweight man who snored loudly the entire time. Petra wouldn't have slept at all if she hadn't made homemade earplugs by wadding up pieces of paper napkins and stuffing them in her ear canals. Because of her good deed of faxing the documents to the Orange Beach police department, her conscience allowed her to sleep peacefully, in spite of everything that had happened; the only times she had woken up were when the bus stopped for gas and once to use the restroom. When the bus finally arrived at the terminal in Myrtle Beach, Petra sighed in relief as she grabbed her duffel bag and headed for the gate. She reached into the bag for a cell phone and recalled from memory a phone number to a friend named Lanka. Petra had worked with her briefly when she first came to Orange Beach, and had kept in touch with her on and off after Lanka was moved to Myrtle Beach to clean condos. Even though they had remained good friends, Petra had already decided not to tell the truth about her visit to Myrtle Beach. She felt like she couldn't trust anyone anymore.

Lanka answered the phone and was quite surprised to hear from her friend. It had been a while since they last spoke, and almost one year had passed since they had seen one another. Making small talk and exchanging pleasantries in Czech, they conversed back and forth on the phone. Finally, Petra told her that she was in town and asked her if she could stay the night at her house. Lanka happily agreed and gave her the directions to her house. Nervously, Petra hailed a taxi. Fortunately, the driver was from Nigeria and had absolutely no interest in his passenger. Within ten minutes, she and Lanka were reunited, and Petra felt a blast of relief as she sat down to a warm Czech dinner that was already prepared for her on the dinner table.

Lanka was pouring wine in a decanter and talking in fast Czech about her new boyfriend, when suddenly, she looked over at Petra and exclaimed, "Oh my God! I am sitting here talking about my boyfriend, and I wasn't even thinking about all the stuff going on in Orange Beach. What in the hell is happening down there? Do you know any of those people? I have tried to remember their faces but I don't. Did I know any of them?"

Petra looked down at her food and tried not to make eye contact with Lanka for fear of giving away her real reason for coming. "Yeah, I heard about it, but I don't know them."

"Yeah, well, me and my friends have all been talking for the last couple of days, and we don't know how long all of this is going to last. I mean, they are looking for the boss, and you know what that means. It's deportation time, at least, for me, anyway. My visa has been up for a long time." Lanka paused to let Petra respond, but when she didn't, she kept the conversation going by adding, "Well, it's probably going to all end up here anyway. I know they have a lot of places to hide, but if they do find them here, then they will go around yanking all of us up and putting us on the next flight out. A few, not many, have…" Petra almost choked on her food as she tried to swallow the bite down. The information Lanka had just given her took her totally by surprise. "Are you okay Petra?" Lanka watched as her friend tried to catch her breath.

Red-faced and coughing, Petra asked, "What do you mean catch them here?"

"What, you don't know? There is a huge manhunt going on all over the city for the boss and some American woman from Orange Beach who was married to that Czech guy, Yuraslav… the one who killed that family. Somebody called the police and said that they saw them in a black SUV today at a gas station right here in Myrtle Beach. Where have you been? It's been all over the news! The police and FBI are everywhere, I mean, they have been everywhere before today too. They have been questioning every Czech worker they can find for a couple of days now. It's a real mess…Petra, are you ok?"

Petra's face was white as a sheet. She sat limply in her chair as her friend talked. She couldn't believe what she was hearing. Why would

Vladimir come here? Had he followed her somehow? Or did he have another stash of documents hidden here somewhere that he could use to escape. She had been told that hers was the sole office that kept everything important, but she had never really believed them.

"Petra, are you sick? What's wrong?" Then, suddenly Lanka gasped and threw her hand up to cover her own mouth. She openly stared in horror at her friend, who now looked as though she was going to pass out at the dinner table. For the first time since she had walked into her house, Lanka noticed the bruises showing through Petra's makeup. She had been so preoccupied with getting dinner ready and talking about her boyfriend that she had failed to see the bruises or notice that Petra's beloved and beautiful long blonde hair was now chopped off and dyed auburn. As she studied her friends face, it suddenly occurred to her. "Oh my God, Petra! You are involved in this, aren't you? What have they done to you, what have they done to your hair?" Lanka nervously sat down next to her silent friend and took her hand. "You are running from them, aren't you? Petra, please speak to me. I will help you, you can trust me! No one knows you are here but me, right? I don't even have a roommate." Silence. "Petra, please." Lanka stroked her hair and coaxed her to look up and answer.

Finally, Petra looked into her friend's eyes and tried to hold back the tears, but they came rushing out anyway. She wanted so badly to trust her friend. She just wanted to talk to someone, to tell them everything, but she was so scared of what would happen to her and her friend if she did.

"Lanka," she said between sobs, "You don't want to know everything. If they are looking for me, then they will be looking for you too if I tell you what happened." She paused to wipe her face. "Vladimir is a very bad person. I don't want him to hurt you. Maybe I shouldn't have come here. I am so sorry."

Holding her friends face to her shoulder, Lanka gave Petra plenty of time to cry. Finally, when she caught her breath and stopped sobbing, Lanka looked into her friends' eyes and said, "Listen to me, Petra. You know me! I am not afraid of them! I am not afraid of anyone! I promise you, you can trust me. Let me help you find a way out of this safely. If they deport me, it's ok. I miss home anyway, and I have been thinking of going back for quite some time now."

Petra studied her friend and thought about the pros and cons. At last, through sobs and tears, she said, "Ok, I will tell you. But can I please just take a shower first and calm myself. I will tell you everything when I finish."

Lanka nodded quickly and took her friends shaking hands in hers. "Of course, of course! Would you like to shower or soak in a hot bath?"

"Bath." Petra's hot tears had made tracks and streaks through her thick makeup, and Lanka could see the bruising more clearly now.

"Okay. Finish your meal while I run your water for you. Oh my God, Petra, I am so sorry this is happening to you. I will be right back. Do you need anything else?"

"No, and thank you so much." Still sobbing, Petra picked her fork up and forced the food down her own throat. Even though her friend was an excellent cook she couldn't taste a thing. Her mind was elsewhere, running as fast as it could go through fields of countless fears and anxieties that now grew in her mind. If Vladimir followed her here, then her hours, not even days, were numbered. He would kill her without even thinking twice about it, especially since the duffel bag was here with her. Maybe after she took her bath, if Vladimir hadn't shown up at Lanka's house yet, she would talk her friend into staying with her at a local hotel that didn't employ Czechs. She would pay for it; after all, she did have plenty of Vladimir's cash in the bag. Petra might not feel comfortable going to a hotel, but she would feel safer if her friend was with her; she wouldn't want her to be alone here in case Vladimir showed up. As she put the last bite of food into her mouth and swallowed, she decided that she would indeed ask her friend to leave with her, now, and not later. Her bath could certainly wait until they were safely checked into a hotel room.

When she walked into the bathroom, Lanka was bent over the bathtub checking the water's temperature. Without making a sound, Petra reached out and touched her friends shoulder, causing her to scream at the top of her lungs and almost fall into the bathtub. As serious as the situation was, it still didn't stop Petra from letting out a small laugh. She hadn't intended to scare her, but she knew that she should have at least thought twice about sneaking up on her, especially right after what had just taken place at the dinner table. Lanka whirled around, half mad, half laughing and embarrassed to be frightened in such a way.

"Lanka, I am so sorry!" Petra said between laughs, "I didn't mean to scare you!"

Lanka laughed it off and shook her head, "That was a good one, whew!" She paused to wipe off the water that had splashed onto her face from the tub. "Almost ready. You feeling better?"

Petra's demeanor became somber again, and she took in a deep breath before she spoke. "Lanka, you said you want to help me. Well, if you want to help me, then I suggest that we leave right now and go to a safe hotel, one that doesn't hire Czech people. If Vladimir followed me, then he will come here to get what is in my bag. I will explain everything to you, but for right now, I would feel better if we left. I will pay for the room, it's not a problem."

Lanka immediately turned the water off and pulled the drain. She didn't ask any questions or pause to think about the request. "Let's go. I know the perfect place." Petra followed her into her bedroom. While Lanka packed an overnight bag, Petra looked at pictures of her new boyfriend. He was cute, just like she said he was; an American with big blue eyes and jet black hair. She picked one up from the dresser and admired him; dressed in a wet suit, he was smiling and holding a surf board.

"Won't you miss him if you get deported?"

Stuffing clothes in a bag, Lanka sighed and said, "Yeah, he is really good in bed. No, seriously, I will, he is a great guy..." Suddenly, the door bell rang and the conversation came to an abrupt halt. The picture that Petra had been holding went crashing to the floor. The glass from the frame shattered everywhere and clothes flew in the air as Petra dove under the bed to hide. Lanka dropped to the floor as well and quickly crawled to the window to see who was at her door, but the bushes outside the window obstructed her view. Crawling back across the room to the doorway, she leaned her head to the floor and whispered, "Petra, hold on. I will be right back. I can't see from this window."

Petra watched in fear as her friend crawled across bedroom floor and closed the door quietly behind her. Pressing her stomach tightly to the wooden floor beneath the bed, she held her breath and listened for any kind of movement from the rest of the house. When she thought she would pass out from the lack of oxygen, the bedroom door slowly swung open and two pairs of feet appeared at the end of Lanka's bed. Her heart was beating so fast that she was afraid it would beat right out of her chest. She looked around the floor and spied a high heeled shoe. It was the only weapon she had.

"Its ok, Petra. You can come out. It's just Peter."

Peter? she thought. *Who is Peter? That's a Russian name!* With dread, Petra grabbed the shoe and quickly slid her body out from under the bed. She looked at Lanka with suspicion and asked, "Who is Peter?"

Lanka looked at her like she like she was going crazy. "Peter, my boyfriend, the one in the picture you were just looking at? And by the way, be careful, there is glass all over the floor." The man standing next to Lanka was indeed the same man that she saw holding a surf board in the picture. Petra gasped in relief and threw the shoe back on the floor as Lanka made the introduction. "Peter Esther, meet Petra. Petra, meet Peter." All three giggled at what Lanka had just struggled to say; the introduction had been a natural tongue twister.

Peter extended his hand to Petra and said, "It's nice to meet you. And if you don't mind me asking, why were you hiding under the bed with a shoe?"

Lanka immediately answered for her friend, "Oh, uhmm, she is hiding from her boyfriend; they got into a fight today."

Noticing the bruises that covered Petra, Peter shook his head in sympathy. "Yeah, looks like you need to stay away from him for good. Did he put those bruises on your face?"

Petra looked away, and absent mindedly checked to make sure that her sleeves were down to her wrists so that neither Peter nor her friend could see the rest of the bruises that the Russians had given her. Lanka noticed her friend's embarrassment and spoke for her again. "Umm, Peter, she is kind of shy, and she doesn't speak very good English. Why don't we go into the living room and talk for a second? I will meet you in there; give me a second, ok?" Peter smiled and walked out of the room while Lanka turned her attention back to her friend. "Hey, don't worry about him. I won't tell him a word, unless you want me to."

"No!" Petra quickly shook her head back and forth.

"Okay, okay, calm down, it will only take a minute. He said he just dropped by to say hey on the way home. Said something about his sister coming in from out of town tonight. Don't worry. I will be right back." Lanka returned to the living room to say goodnight to Peter, and promised that she would call him in the morning before he went surfing. He left, and within five minutes, both girls were packed and ready to go. Petra noticed a Czech sticker on the bumper of Lanka's car and opted for a taxi ride to the hotel instead. She called the same company that had dropped her off earlier, and then, they waited in darkness for the taxi to arrive.

CHAPTER FORTY-SEVEN

Hitting only a minimum amount of turbulence on the way to Myrtle Beach, the jet ride was quite relaxing. As she popped a can of soda open, Judith told Hank about her family. "I called my parents on the way to the airport to tell them that I am on my way home. They are so excited to see me, and my mother told me to tell you not to even think about staying anywhere else. It would hurt her feelings. They have been following the news, and, of course, they know about my friendship with Tammy. They are just devastated for her and her family, even though they only met her once several years ago. Mom is the hostess with the mostess, and if you decide to stay there with me, I can assure you, you won't regret it. There is a guest house in the backyard, and mom said she would have it ready for you by the time we get there. No pressure, of course, but it is nice, and you can come and go as you please without waking anyone up during the night. They are more than excited to accommodate you, but if you feel uncomfortable, I totally understand."

"No, not at all, that sounds great! As long as you are serious about the coming and going when I need to. I don't want to wake anyone, and I have no idea what's going to happen. So, if that's not an issue, then I really appreciate the hospitality. I probably will not be spending that much time with you while I am here, so I just want to make sure your family is not offended by that."

"No, of course not. I already explained to them why you are coming. They are just happy to provide somewhere for you to stay while you are here. I haven't even told them that we have been seeing each other, so as far as they know, we are just friends and nothing more."

"Ok, good. I just didn't want to feel obligated to hang around. As long as I am here, if it's within my power, I will find Suzanna and Vladimir. I just hope we can get to her before they kill her, if they haven't already."

"I'm with you, babe." Judith yawned and sipped her soda, hoping the caffeine would wake her up a little bit before they landed. "So, what are you going to do first when we land?"

"Well, I gotta go to the station with Officer Myers first. He is meeting us at the airport. I really don't know what will happen from there, but we will probably compare notes and ride around looking for the SUV."

"Ok, then I will not wait up for you. But I will make sure mom puts some dinner in the guest house for you in case you are hungry when you get back. I wrote down the address and directions for you." When she handed him the paper, he held onto her hand for a second, rubbing his fingers over hers, before letting it go.

"Thank you, Judith." They felt a slight dip, and the plane slowly began to descend through the clouds.

Sam yelled back to them from the cockpit, "You guys buckled in? We're gettin' ready to land." They buckled themselves in, and Judith unconsciously grabbed Hank's hand. She laughed at herself when she realized what she had done, and tried to pull away, but Hank held on to it anyway. Sammy had proven to be quite the skilled pilot. When they came to a stop on the tarmac, Hank looked at her and said, "You know, Sammy was in the military, and I bet you a hundred dollars that he was in the Air Force."

"Huh? Why do you say that? How do you know?" Judith was interested in this tidbit of information Hank was about to offer.

"Because of his landing." he revealed. "Most of the time you can tell if the pilot was trained in the Air Force or the Navy. Pilots who were trained in the Air Force land smoothly and easily. Pilots who were trained in the Navy land hard and choppy, stopping the plane faster."

"Why is that?"

"Because they are used to landing planes on ships, and if they don't, they might just go right over the edge."

Judith nodded thoughtfully as she visualized a plane skidding off the tarmac of a landing ship and slipping into the ocean. "Hmmm. Makes sense. Thanks for that fun fact."

Hank nodded and grinned at her, "Well, you are so welcome. Seriously, though, test it out. Next time you fly, judge the landing, and then ask the pilot to see if you are right."

Sam turned around to the couple and grinned. "So, how was the flight?"

Judith unbuckled her seatbelt and walked towards the cockpit. She glanced back quickly at Hank, and then back to Sam. "That was really great, Sam! Thank you so much! You know, Hank told me that you were in the military years ago. What branch?"

Sam turned the plane off. "Air Force! My God, I miss those years! Alright guys, go get the Russians! Call me if you need me!"

Hank winked at Judith. "I told ya!"

The door to the plane opened, and Hank and Judith exited onto the tarmac where several police officers where there to greet them. Officer Dell Myers walked over to Hank and introduced himself, "You must be Detective Jordan. It's nice to meet you in person, and thanks for coming up on such short notice. I am Officer Myers, but you can call me Dell."

Hank shook his hand. "Dell, good to meet you. You can call me Hank, and believe me, the pleasure is all mine. I just hope I am not too late."

CHAPTER FORTY-EIGHT

While Vladimir showered, Suzanna tried in vain to make eye contact with the young Czech who now carried the gun, but he refused to look into her eyes. She could tell that he was not like her husband or the other thugs who had kidnapped her and were now dead in garbage bags in Atlanta, Georgia. He appeared kind, and deeply upset that she was bound and gagged on his dining room floor. She watched him with pleading eyes as he paced back and forth across the room. He looked like he was going to cry at any given second. The gun seemed to weigh his arm down, and he carried it around the room like it was burning a hole in his hand. Each time that he stopped pacing, he looked at the gun and mumbled something inaudible under his breath. She assumed that his friend was still in the kitchen, probably crouched in a corner and wishing he was anywhere but here. She was about to give up trying to get the young man's attention when she noticed him in the doorway whispering to his friend in Czech. Obviously, the man didn't know that Suzanna knew the language, or he would have never spoken in front of her. Bound and gagged on the floor, she strained to hear their conversation.

In whispers, they argued back and forth in Czech. "We can go now! We can run while he is still in the shower!"

"No, you fool; do you know who that is? That is the boss! He will kill us!"

"No, he won't have time. I am telling you, we can make it! We can slip out the back while he is still in the shower."

"Listen to what you are saying! Where will we go? If he doesn't kill us, he will get his friends to do it. I am telling you the truth! You will be making a big mistake if you leave here. And what about the girl? You would leave her here? They will kill her!"

"I know, I know. But maybe we can call 911 and then sneak out the back."

186

Then the man with the gun slipped into the kitchen out of Suzanna's listening range. She cursed to herself and tried to inch her way closer to the door. The young man with the gun appeared again and she froze, trying not to alert him that she was moving. The men had stopped talking and the one with the gun began to pace back and forth across the room again. He walked to the hallway and listened to check if the water in the shower was still running. When he confirmed that it was, he sighed nervously and wiped the sweat that had collected across his brow. Then he made the mistake of looking at Suzanna. She pleaded to him with her eyes. *Please, please help me.*

Staring down at Suzanna, the man stood still for a moment, cocked his head in pure sympathy, and then checked again to see if the water was still running. He crouched low to her, and asked her not to say anything if he took her gag off. She shook her head furiously as he put the gun down on the floor. Just as he was about to remove the gag from her mouth, the Russian driver who had been watching Mirek opened the door at the end of the hallway. "What the fuck are you doing!!!!!" he yelled at the Czech.

The man jumped and quickly recovered the gun from the floor. Shaking with fear, he turned to face the Russian, and in English he stammered, "Uh, I, umm, was trying to fix de thing on her mouth. It was coming off, and I don't want her to scream."

The Russian driver stared at the Czech with piercing eyes. "If you tell da truth, then I say you did good thing. If you don't tell de truth, I tell you dat I will cut your dick off and put it in your mouth. You understand?"

Suzanna watched the Czech guy nod over and over again to the Russian. He was so scared that he looked like he would pass out right there beside her on the floor. The Russian pushed him out of the way and grabbed Suzanna's head by what little hair she had left and wrenched her face close to his. His rancid breath smelled like soured boiled eggs and vodka; it wafted slowly into her nostrils, toying with her gag reflex. She couldn't move her head away. All she could do to keep from vomiting was hold her own breath so she couldn't smell his.

The Russian spit on her face while he talked. "If you try to spit your gag out again, I will cut out your tongue. Understand?" He didn't let go of her hair; he wrapped his fingers through it to get a better grip and bounced the side of her head onto the linoleum floor. She cried out through her gag, but couldn't hear what he said next. Her ears were ringing so loudly from the impact that it rendered her momentarily deaf. The next thing she heard was the Russian laughing as he walked back into Mirek's room. She closed her eyes and waited for the ringing to stop. When she opened her eyes again, she saw no one in the room. The ringing for the most part had ceased, but she couldn't hear the two Czechs who were whispering again in the kitchen. All she could hear was the sound of her own heart beat, racing away to its own death, which she prayed would be soon and painless.

CHAPTER FORTY-NINE

The tarmac was lively as everyone shook hands and introduced themselves and chatted feverishly about the case and what a circus it had turned into. It didn't take long for things to wind down; each officer who was present was eager to get back on the road and search for the SUV.

"Do you need a ride to your parent's house, Dr. Esther?"

Judith turned to Officer Dell Myers and said, "No, that's quite alright. My brother should be waiting outside the terminal to pick me up. You guys go on. I will be fine." She looked at Hank and smiled. "Good luck, and call me if you need anything. The door to the guest house will be open when you get in and I will see you in the morning." She thought about kissing him goodbye, but figured it would be inappropriate. She noticed that he wasn't leaning over to her either, so taking the hint, she said goodbye to the officers whom she had met and walked away.

Outside the private terminal, she immediately spotted her brother's old beat up Volkswagen van. When she saw it, all she could do was laugh and shake her head. The van was covered in bumper stickers, peace signs and other graffiti painted on the windows. The steering wheel was incased in purple fur, and there was a collection of stuffed Grateful Dead Bears hanging from the rear view mirror. On top of the van were empty multicolored surf board racks with some kind of old party streamers attached to them that blew in the wind for decoration. Her brother was a new age hippy who spent most of his days, when he wasn't in culinary school, surfing and listening to the band Phish. Although most of his friends were deadbeats destined to be the next generation of beach bums and drunken bartenders, he made decent grades in college and had somehow managed to stay out of trouble for the most part. He was the exact opposite of her. Judith had always been a prude in high school, not in a nerdy way, but in a way that her life had always been predictable, regimented and solid. She had graduated high school with honors and completed college and medical school without a single hitch or deterrent. Her brother, on the other hand, had always been a free spirit with long black surfer hair and a natural tan year around. At the age of twenty four, he had successfully changed majors eight times and schools three times. His latest interest had been the world of culinary arts. So far, he had been enrolled for six months and was doing great. Judith and her family had been keeping their fingers crossed, and hoped that this would be a long term commitment for him; so far, he had proven himself to be genuinely dedicated.

She called out to him and saw his Rastafarian colored hat pop up from the driver's seat. He had been napping. Judith ran over to him as he slid out of the van and wrapped his arms around her in a big bear hug.

"Hey big sis! What's happening?" He grinned at her while he picked up her suitcase and tossed it in the back of the van.

Judith grinned back as she hopped into the passenger seat. She had not seen him in so long. "Well, a lot, really! How have you been, Peter? You are looking quite tan as usual. How is school?"

"Ah, school is very cool. Maybe I can cook something for you while you are here. I'm doing pretty good you know."

"Yeah, that's what I hear. I am so proud of you! Have you cooked for Mom and Dad yet?"

"No, I haven't, but I will. I haven't seen them much lately. I have been really busy, you know, my classes, and trying to get in some good surfing before the season is over. The last time I went home was a week ago when I got back from the Phish concert. Wow, what a wild time! Didn't want to leave, the concert, I mean. So, what's going on with you? Mom called about an hour and a half ago and asked me to pick you up. What's the occasion, kind of short notice?"

Judith looked at him as if he was crazy. Surely her mother had told him, and even if she hadn't, he could have at least wondered if it had anything to do with the Morrison case. It was all over the news. "She didn't tell you why?"

"No, I could barely hear her. My cell phone doesn't always work in my apartment. She finally said that you would tell me when you got here."

"Well, have you been watching the news about Orange Beach?" Judith wasn't entirely surprised at her brother's ignorance. He lived in his own little world most of time, going wherever the wind blew him.

"Yeah, I heard something about some murders, but you know I don't really pay attention to the negative stuff that goes on in this world. I try to concentrate on the positive stuff, you know, the good things about the world." Peter grinned at her as he flipped his long surfer hair out of his eyes with a sharp quick neck movement that only surfers and models can master.

Judith looked hurt, even though she knew that Peter didn't mean to offend her. He had no idea that Tammy had been her best friend. He had never met her, and had no reason to know the situation. "Peter, I guess Mom didn't tell you that the woman who was murdered, along with her husband and two of her children, was my one of my best friends. Her name is Tammy Morrison. I have been her children's pediatrician for five years, since I moved to Gulf Shores. I can't believe Mom didn't tell you."

Peter's face grew solemn as he pulled over to the side of the road. He put his van in park and looked over at his sister. "Oh my God, Sis, I didn't know. I am so sorry. Mom didn't tell me, and I have been gone so much the past couple of weeks. I am really sorry." He reached over and took her hand in his. "You know what? I will plan an extra special dinner for you for tomorrow night. I might have to get Dad to give me some money, but I will cook an awesome dinner for everyone. Maybe I will invite my new girlfriend over. She's pretty cool." Hoping that he had redeemed himself, he looked at Judith and was relieved to see her smiling back at him.

Judith gave his hand a little squeeze and shook her head. "That's alright, you didn't know. The dinner sounds wonderful. It's been a while since someone has cooked for me. And a new girlfriend? Wow, it's been a while since I heard you say that!"

"Yeah, she's way cool. I am still not totally into that exclusive dating thing, but she is cool, you know? You will like her."

Peter pulled back onto the road and drove to their parents' house. On the way, they discussed everything about the case and Hank. Judith told him all about little Anna Morrison and how she had survived the horror of it all. By the time they had reached the house, Peter had heard enough. He was sickened by what the man had done to the Morrison family, and was totally surprised by the fact that they were currently hunting them in Myrtle Beach. He was shocked at his lack of knowledge and began to rethink his passion for ignorance when it came to the world. Maybe, he thought to himself, he should listen to the news more often. He was so wrapped up in Judith's story about how Anna had survived, that not once, throughout the entire conversation, did he stop and think about the fact that his girlfriend Lanka was from the Czech Republic. Judith had told him everything about the investigations into the businesses, the arrests, and the deportations, but he had been so enveloped in the details of the murders that it didn't set off an alarm in his head. Besides, he and Lanka had only met a month ago and weren't very serious.

When they finally pulled into the driveway, Marie Esther was waiting at the front door in her bathrobe to greet them. Usually, she wouldn't have gone outside her house dressed the way she was, but it was late, and she couldn't contain her excitement long enough to change into something else. Peter hadn't even parked his van yet, and Marie was already running into the driveway with open arms to hug them both. Peter grabbed Judith's suitcase, and they all walked into the house together. For two hours, they sat around the kitchen table talking about the manhunt and watching the news. None of them could believe that it was actually occurring in their own town. After each family member exhausted their own opinions on what should be done to the Russians responsible for everything, they finally said goodnight to each other and went to bed. Judith fell asleep worrying about Hank. She struggled to keep herself awake and listen for his return, and she would have been able to if she had been in her house in Gulf Shores. But now that she was tucked into her old bed in her old bedroom, the completely satisfying comfortableness of being home and the familiar comforting smell of her parents' house shrouded her mind and lured her softly to sleep.

CHAPTER FIFTY

While Petra and Lanka safely checked into a small "mom and pop" motel that didn't have any Czech employees on staff, Hank and Dell combed the streets for the Mercedes SUV and discussed the details of the case. Earlier Dell had given Hank a file that contained the names of all the Russians and Czechs who had been arrested in Myrtle Beach for the past five years. Some had already been questioned by other officers and the FBI earlier that afternoon and night, and the rest on the list were scheduled to be contacted first thing in the morning. Except for the information that they had received from the local news, everyone who had been questioned denied knowing anything or anyone that had anything to do with the case.

After they drove around the city for a couple hours, Dell dropped Hank off at the Esther's residence, and agreed on a time to pick him back up in the morning. Hank was absolutely exhausted. Between working the Morrison case and making love to Judith for the past couple of days, his energy level had plummeted to an all time low. He easily found the guest house tucked neatly behind the garden of the Esther's backyard and quietly opened the door. The heavenly smell of a home cooked meal hit him square in the face. The food that Judith had promised him earlier had been placed in foiled hot plates in the oven. There was a large piece of pot roast with potatoes and carrots cooked into the gravy, green bean casserole, three chunks of buttered cornbread, and a big sloppy slice of homemade apple pie on the counter with a note attached to it that read 'vanilla ice cream in freezer- Marie Esther'. Hank sat down and ate like he hadn't had a meal in two weeks. Marie Esther proved herself to be quite a cook, just like Judith had said, and Hank all but licked his plate clean. He made sure that he washed his plates and utensils thoroughly, stacked them neatly on the counter, and then showered quickly before going to bed.

He laughed and shook his head when he entered the bedroom. Not only were his sheets turned down with an after dinner mint resting on top of the pillow, but there beside it lay a hand written note in a personalized monogrammed envelope that was scented with some kind of sweet perfume from Marie Esther, welcoming him into their home and wishing him sweet dreams. The hot shower was like taking a Valium. Coupled with the exhaustion from the long day that he had endured, Hank spiraled into the deepest corners of sleep that his mind could seek out before his head was even properly rested on the pillow. As much as he worried about finding Suzanna, he didn't even dream.

CHAPTER FIFTY-ONE

Petra paid for two nights at the hotel, but suspected that she would be hiding somewhere else the next night; she didn't want to stay in one place for very long. For two hours, she and Lanka went over the contents of the duffel bag and talked in their native language about what had transpired over the last couple of days. Because her job at the Orange Beach office had been a secret, not many people, including Lanka, had known where she had been working. Petra began her story with Yuraslav and Mirek showing up at the office in Orange Beach with instructions for her to close the office down and to take everything with her and drive them out of Orange Beach. Through tears and sobs, she relived what the Russians had done to her once they arrived at the house in Charlotte. From what she could remember before the pain pills had kicked in, she described the rape in full detail, showing Lanka the bruises and cuts all over her body that were now starting to heal. The girls cried together and held onto each other through the whole ordeal. When Petra was finished with her narrative, Lanka took her friend in her arms and hugged her for a long time. Then, she broke away and stared admiringly at her friend. "You are so brave, Petra! I can't believe you had the guts to escape! I probably would have been looking for ways to kill myself instead of ways to run away."

"Believe me, I was. I wanted to die. In some ways, I still do because if the police do not find him and Suzanna, I will either die of guilt for not helping her enough, or Vladimir will hunt me down like an animal and kill me in ways that I can't even imagine. Or, worse, he will kill my family. He knows where I come from. He has information sheets on everybody that comes over here to work." Petra dried her face with a hotel pillow, amazed at herself for having any tears left to shed. "Lanka, I just don't know what to do. I want to help her so badly. I can't bear the thought of them doing to her what they did to me, or killing her. I can't stop thinking about what her family must be going through. I have to help, but I just don't know how. I am so scared."

Lanka shook her head in thought and stared down at the comforter on the bed. "I don't really know either. But you know, I have been thinking, and don't get angry before you hear everything I have to say, ok? Promise?"

Petra slowly nodded at her friend, although a wary flicker of light gleamed in her eyes. "Ok, I am listening."

Lanka took a deep breath and prepared to convince her friend. "You know, Peter, my boyfriend, you met him tonight? Well, he is very smart, and I know he would protect you. He has a lot of friends, and he knows everybody! He could help hide you. Or maybe if we tell him what's going on, he will at least have some advice for you. If you ask me, we need the help of an American who doesn't have anything to do with hiring Czechs. I mean, if we go to a Czech person, then how would we know if we could really trust them? They are not going to stick their necks out to help us! Vladimir would be after them too, not to mention they might be deported after everything is said and done. Personally, I think we should tell Peter. It makes perfect sense. Even if he doesn't have any advice, he won't tell anyone, especially not the police. He is kind of a hippy, you know, and hippies don't do stuff like that." She paused to let Petra think about it. "It's worth a try. Think about it."

Chewing her bottom lip, Petra sat on the bed and pondered what her friend had just said. What she had proposed made perfect sense, but she wasn't sure if she was ready to take that step. She had never opened up to an American before, mainly because they were just different. They handled problems and dilemmas differently than Czechs. It seemed to her that all Americans loved the police, except for rappers and drug dealers. Anytime something bad happened, Americans were always so quick to run to the phone, dial 911, and rat out the person who did the crime; regardless of the repercussions of what could happen in revenge to them or their family. Where she was from, people just simply did not play those cards in life. To be considered a 'rat' by anyone was like the kiss of death, and either you or your family would eventually pay the consequences for being one. She was so deep in thought about what she should do that when she stood up from the bed to use the rest room, she fell flat on her ass to the floor; her legs were completely asleep from sitting in the Indian style position for so long on the bed. Thinking something was seriously wrong with her, Lanka shot up to help her friend and shouted as she lunged for her flailing body, "Oh my God, are you ok?" She grabbed Petra's arms.

Petra was laughing on the floor, "Yes! Yes! Both of my legs are asleep! I am ok." They both got the giggles then; the kind that people get in a classroom in junior high school when you just absolutely can't stop laughing, even when you try to think about something else. Ten minutes later, the laughter had run its course. Petra spoke gently to her friend. "Alright, I have had enough for one night. I am going to drink a glass of water, and then let's go to sleep. I will think about what you said and tell you how I feel about it in the morning. I am so tired right now."

"You are right. You need to get some rest. We can talk about it in the morning. Tomorrow is my day off, so we can spend the whole day deciding on what to do." They said goodnight. After she finished her glass of water, Petra curled up in the fetal position on the bed and immediately fell asleep. Lanka, on the other hand, stared at a flashing neon sign through the window and worried about their predicament.

CHAPTER FIFTY-TWO

Vladimir toweled off from his shower and rummaged through the Czechs' closets for clean clothes to wear. In the end, the hot water had managed to wash away some of the sexual tension that had built up inside of him, but did little to quench the anger and anxiety that fueled his thoughts and plans. He was in the shower for so long that he used all of the hot water; he had been so lost in thought that he didn't immediately notice the water becoming colder and colder. When he did, he turned the water off and waited for the hot water to build back up, then turned it on again. Finally, after being locked inside the bathroom for nearly two hours, Vladimir had emerged to call Ivan back. Although he had not forgotten about what he wanted to do to Suzanna, he was more interested in how he would escape and what was taking Ivan so long to arrange it. Inside a closet he found a black Nike jogging suit and a clean pair of socks. After he dressed and put his gold chains back around his neck, he stepped out into the hallway that led to the living room. Everything in the house was quiet. Too quiet. He quietly snuck into the living room and found the two Czech men dozing on and off on the couch and floor, taking turns glancing over at Suzanna.

His driver had also fallen asleep watching Mirek, who had passed out shortly after their arrival due to a kick in the head from his thug babysitter. Somehow, even Suzanna had managed to fall asleep on the linoleum, still bound and gagged. Picking up the gun that had absent-mindedly been left on the floor, Vladimir quietly raised his hand high in the air and slapped the Czech man who was asleep on the floor in front of the television. The Czech jumped up immediately and stammered backwards into the coffee table. Vladimir rolled his eyes in disgust, and then spat on the floor near Suzanna's head.

"Wake her up!" he yelled at the man. "Take her to the bathroom and clean her. After you are done, take her to the other bedroom and tie her up again." The Czech just looked back at Vladimir blankly, as if he didn't understand a word that had been spoken. But it wasn't con-

198

fusion that made him unable to move or speak; it was raw fear. He saw the gun in his hand, and knew he had made a huge mistake by leaving it on the floor as he dozed off. Vladimir yelled at him again, "Are you fucking deaf you piece of shit? I said move! Take her to the shower, clean her, and then tie her up again!"

With one eye watching Vladimir to make sure that he wouldn't shoot him in the back, the Czech moved slowly toward Suzanna. He bent down low to the floor and shook her gently to wake her. She would have immediately woken up from the commotion, but her ears were still ringing from the blow to her head. Vladimir laughed at his gentle attempt to stir her from sleep. He pushed him out of the way and kicked Suzanna hard in the ribs. She woke up coughing and twitching in pain, unaware for a second of where she was. "You want to play nice with her, no?" Vladimir laughed again at the sight of her flailing in agony across the cheap yellowed linoleum floor. "Are you a faggot? Hmmm? Is dat what you are, a little Czech faggot?"

The Czech shook his head violently and hoisted Suzanna to her feet as gently as he could under the circumstances. He certainly didn't want to take a bullet in the head for being too nice to her in front of Vladimir. When he finally got her to her feet, he realized that she couldn't stand on her own. Because of a concussion from the brutal kick to her head, and being tied up for so long, she was unable to control her neck muscles; her head bobbed up and down like a rag doll. Placing one of her arms over his shoulder and grabbing her by the waist, the Czech man slowly struggled down the hallway in the direction of the bathroom. In spite of Vladimir's anger, he made a conscious effort to be as gentle as he possibly could. Vladimir watched them disappear through the doorway, then picked up his cell phone and dialed Ivan's phone number.

After the young Czech was finally able to seat her on the toilet, he used a cup of water to moisten the edges of the gag. He removed it slowly and gently so that it wouldn't peel off the cracked and bleeding skin from her lips. When she attempted to speak, he quickly put his finger to his own mouth and whispered, "Shhh. Wait until de water is on." Propping her up with the left side of his body, he reached over to turn the water on in the bathtub and placed the plug in the drain. Then he turned his attention back to the girl. He started to speak, but stopped at the mere sight of her; his nose began to burn with oncoming tears.

The girl was pitiful. Her lips were swollen and bleeding, and her eyes were blackened. She had lacerations on her arms and legs that were decorated with dark sinister patches of blue and purple. He managed to swallow back his tears, but through her swollen eyes, Suzanna noticed where a couple had already made their way to the corners of his eyes.

"I am," he whispered weakly, "So sorry, for dis. I have to take…" he paused and looked away from her. To help fight off the tears, he stared at the sink and continued talking. "I have to take your clothes off." The young Czech was paralyzed with shame and humility and could not bear to look her in the eyes.

Suzanna was way past the point of any embarrassment or shame that she would have normally felt in the hands of a stranger undressing her. She understood, and weakly nodded to him. He took a deep breath and began to undress her. As he unbuttoned her shirt, the young Czech could not stop himself anymore; he cried in silence for her and for himself and wished that he could do something to stop this from happening. Although he tried to avert his eyes as much as possible, he noticed that her breasts were bruised like the rest of her body. With tears in her own eyes, she watched him. She cried for him because she sensed the almost unbearable pain that it caused him to do this to her. Finally, after every article of clothing was removed, the young man slowly picked up her battered body and gently laid her into the warm water. As she felt it cascading down over her head from a cup that he had used, she opened her mouth to let some of the water trickle down her throat.

He noticed what she was doing, moved quickly to get her a cold wet cloth from the sink, and held it tenderly to her cracked lips. Although the water stung her lips as she drank, she drank it anyway. After the water loosened her tongue from the roof of her mouth, Suzanna closed her eyes and allowed him to finish his task of bathing her. She smelled like death; a combination of stale urine, feces, vomit and sweat. As he bathed her, he fought the urge to gag.

Even though her throat and lips burned like lava, she mustered up enough energy to speak and turned her head to face him. She whispered, "Please. Please call the police. They are going to kill me and you too." She waited for him to respond, but he looked away and continued to bathe her. "Please. I know that he is going to rape me when you finish washing me. Wait until you hear him doing it, and then please call 911." She began to cry. "I don't want to die, please." Suzanna was unaware that her voice had slightly risen from a whisper during her pleas for help; her ears were still ringing.

Terrified that Vladimir would hear her, the man placed his hand over Suzanna's mouth and shook his head at her. "Please, ma'am, do not talk to me. He will hear you, and he will kill me." Suzanna gave up. She saw the terrified look in his eyes and knew that she was wasting her breath. Czechs were not like Americans when it came to relying on the law to protect you; that much she knew from being married to her husband. She closed her eyes again and prayed to God that whatever Vladimir did to her would be quick and as painless as possible. She asked forgiveness for every sin she had ever committed, one by one, and then prayed for her family. If she was supposed to die this way, then she would accept it and make her final peace.

The Czech listened to Suzanna pray to her god, and he knew what she was doing. She was accepting death. Growing up in Communism for most of his life had made his family atheists, except for his grandmother, who was still quite religious. He didn't believe in any God, and had never been inside of a church except for Catholic mass on Christmas Eve. Due to years of Communism, there were a lot of atheists in the Czech Republic. Strangely, even for someone who didn't believe in God, the tradition of going to Catholic mass on Christmas Eve had managed to survive in his country. He hadn't thought about how strange that was until now. Why did he go to church with his family on Christmas Eve if he didn't believe in God? He thought about this while he listened to Suzanna repent and ask God for forgiveness of her sins. Something about her words moved him, but he didn't know why. Whatever it was, it made him cry uncontrollably.

Meanwhile, Vladimir slammed the phone down on the kitchen table. Ivan had given him little information. He was still working on finding a car, and informed Vladimir that it would probably be tomorrow before he located one suitable enough for a getaway. Enraged, Vladimir had cursed and threatened him for a full ten minutes before finally hanging up. He stomped into the living room where the other Czech man was watching television, demanded that he move from the couch, and grabbed the remote control to watch the news. Nothing was new on any of the channels; the reporters rehashed the details of the 911 call from the gas station and flashed the same pictures of the all the people linked to the case. They spoke at length about Yuraslav and the condition of his body which had been found in North Carolina, and then did a special recap on the assault and murders of the Morrison family. One by one, Vladimir watched the pictures of the family members appear across the screen. He felt nothing for the victims except anger. If Yuraslav had killed them correctly and followed his instructions properly, then the entire country of the United States wouldn't be searching for him now. He saw Suzanna's picture flash across the screen, and suddenly realized that he had momentarily forgotten about her. When he craned his head toward the hallway, he could still hear running water, and assumed she was still being prepped for him by the young Czech. He wasn't worried. They weren't going anywhere. Czech people were easily intimidated and didn't usually have enough guts to cross him; besides, there wasn't any other way for them to escape from the bathroom except through the door, which he could clearly see down the hallway from his view on the couch. Glaring at the petrified Czech who sat on the floor opposite him, Vladimir settled into the couch and started flipping through the channels again. After a few minutes, the young Czech who had been bathing Suzanna appeared in the doorway. Vladimir asked him, "Is she ready?"

The man nodded his head and said, "She is toweling off right now. What do you want me to do with her?"

Vladimir waved him off and barked, "Tie her to the bed, like I said! Get me something to drink first!"

The man slowly walked into the kitchen to pour a glass of wine for Vladimir. He had been thinking about Suzanna and dreading what Vladimir would surely do to her once she was tied up in the bedroom. No matter how hard he tried not to think about it, he could not force the brutal images from of his head. As he picked up the wine bottle, a sudden thought occurred to him. He remembered that he had several Rohypnol pills that his mother had given him to help sleep off the jet lag when he had first arrived to the United States. Even though Rohypnol was illegal in the United States, he had decided to keep them for a rainy day. That rainy day had come. Maybe, he thought to himself, this decision would eventually cause his death, but at least it would spare Suzanna from what Vladimir had in store for her. He could easily use pills to send Vladimir into a deep sleep and save her. It was the only safe way he could think of to help her at the moment

202

without risking his throat being cut. Rohypnol is tasteless and odorless. He remembered that much from watching the warnings on the news about American men using Rohypnol pills as date rape drugs. He could slip one of the pills into the glass, and Vladimir would never know the difference. Not allowing himself any time to second guess his decision, he opened a cabinet above the sink and found the pills in an envelope. After crushing one as best he could between two metal spoons, he dropped it into the wine glass. Then he poured the wine on top of it and swirled it around with the spoon to melt the medicine. Just as he was about to walk out of the kitchen with the glass of drugged wine, he had one more idea. He quickly grabbed the other pills from the envelope and dropped them into the open wine bottle. He figured that he would eventually have to pour another glass for him, and if one pill wasn't enough to do the job, then the other two dissolving in the wine bottle would surely be.

Vladimir grew impatient and yelled, "What the fuck are you doing? What is taking so long?"

The Czech man jumped at the sound of his voice and spilled some of the wine on the counter. With shaky hands he quickly poured more wine to replenish what was lost. His pulse quickened to a severe state of alarm, and he had to physically force his own feet to walk himself into the living room with the wine glass. Amazingly, in spite of his shaky hands, he successfully handed the glass to Vladimir without spilling any more of the wine and without raising any suspicions. Then he nervously backed away in the direction of the bathroom to finish his job with Suzanna.

CHAPTER FIFTY-THREE

Marie Esther had set her alarm clock the night before for five-thirty a.m. When the alarm rang, she jumped to switch it off, and quickly got out of the bed to cook breakfast. When Judith had called last night to tell them she was coming, she had excitedly written down what to cook the next morning for breakfast, and had laid the ingredients neatly on the counter in preparation before she went to bed. The fact that Judith was coming home to visit was exciting, even under the sad circumstances. Marie was also excited that Judith had brought along her detective friend to visit as well; she couldn't wait to meet him! Because of the way her daughter spoke of him, she secretly wondered if he was more than just a friend to her daughter. Marie loved to cook, but enjoyed it most when she was able to play hostess to a group of people. Four hours of sleep wasn't much, but it was plenty for Marie to wake up completely refreshed and ready to serve.

When Judith woke up an hour later, she opened her eyes with a smile. It wasn't an alarm clock that had interrupted her sleep; it was the heavenly smell of Eggs Benedict, bacon, sausage, cinnamon toast, homemade pancakes, buttermilk biscuits and shrimp and cheese grits. The shrimp and cheese grits, Judith's favorite, was a traditional recipe that had been passed down from generation to generation in her mother's family, all of whom had been from Charleston, South Carolina. Energized from the smell of the food, she got out of bed, made the covers, and followed her nose to the kitchen. She laughed when she saw her mother perched at the kitchen bar. Marie was leisurely sipping a cup of decaffeinated coffee from her tiny Wedgwood coffee cup and reading a Good Housekeeping magazine, as if she had been up for hours doing nothing but just that. Tucked in the center of her mother's best china and silverware, the food had been neatly arranged on the kitchen table which, of course, had already been set for five guests.

Judith bent over to kiss her mother and exclaimed, "My God, Mom! How long have you been up? Did you even go to sleep last night? This must have taken hours to cook!"

Nonchalantly, Marie waved her daughter off with a slight hand movement and downplayed her breakfast spread by keeping her eyes pinned to the magazine in front of her. "Oh, for Heaven sakes, Judy Booty, I have only been up since six. It's not that big of a deal! It's just a little food. You act as if you have never eaten my breakfast before."

Judith rolled her eyes and bit her lip to suppress her laughter. She had expected nothing less than what was currently on the table, right down to the fresh roses that had most certainly been picked from the flower garden out back and arranged while everyone else in the house had been enjoying their sleep. She picked up a piece of cinnamon toast on the way to the bathroom. "Thanks, mom. Everything looks wonderful! I am going to freshen up a second, and then I will wake up Hank. I assume he got here ok last night. I didn't hear a thing. I wiped out as soon as my head hit the pillow."

"That's fine, dear. And, yes, he got home ok last night. I peeked through the bedroom window to make sure he was in the bed when I cut the roses earlier. Oh, and your father offered his car to Hank while he is here. The keys are on the counter. Speaking of him, while you're up, poke your head inside my bedroom door, and ask your father if he will be gracing us with his presence this morning. I will wake up Peter." Even though Marie had been pretending to read her magazine article on the many varied uses of Oxy Clean, she had been secretly darting her eyes around the room, checking to make sure that everything was aesthetically pleasing and arranged in its appropriate place. After she inspected each inch of the table and kitchen, she closed her magazine and went upstairs to wake her son.

Judith grabbed the keys from the counter and walked to the back door. Outside, Judith crossed the yard, walked through the garden and up the walkway to the guest house to wake Hank. He barely heard the soft knocking on his bedroom door, but sprung to attention when he felt Judith's warm body slip into the covers and snuggle up against his. He had been sleeping on his side when she snuck into the room, so she had decided to spoon him, holding him snug to her belly and chest. They lay there for a couple of minutes, enjoying the position, and then

Hank rolled over to face her. She closed her eyes and went in for a kiss but was interrupted when she felt him put a hand up to cover his mouth. He spoke through closed fingers. "That's not fair! You already brushed your teeth."

Judith laughed and poked him lightly in his belly. "Well, if I were you, I would wait until after breakfast to brush them, because you will just have to do it all over again. You should see what mom cooked. It's ridiculous there's so much food on the table." They both got out of the bed together, and Hank began making his way to the shower.

"Oh yeah? Well, hell, I'm still full from the dinner she left me in the oven from last night. That was one of the finest meals I have ever eaten in my life! Can you cook like that?" Hank raised an eyebrow at Judith and a smile spread across his face.

"Yeah, I can, it might take me all day long, but yes. Remind me to thank her later for setting me up for that one!" she smiled back at him. "Anyways, I hope you're hungry; you're in for a treat." She picked up the guest bathrobe and tossed it to him along with the keys to her father's car. "Dad is loaning you his car while you are here. I will meet you in the kitchen. Just walk through the back door and take a right, or better yet, just close your eyes and follow your nose." She giggled as she walked out the door and left him to his shower. Along the way, she stopped to smell her mother's flowers and think about Hank. She knew she was falling in love with him, and was pretty sure that her mother had noticed it last night when she was talking about him, although she hadn't said anything to her about it. She certainly wasn't trying to hide it from anyone, but at the same time, figured that this wasn't the best time to divulge her emotions, since Hank wasn't here to visit and really get to know her family. She was about to pick a flower for him when it dawned on her that she hadn't woken up her father like her mother had asked her to. Her brother had already woken up and was talking on the phone when she entered the house.

Peter saw the spread on the table, and shook his head at his mother before giving her a hug. "Wow, Mom. Maybe I should be taking classes from you. It's been so long since I have eaten over here that I forgot what a master chef you are!"

She swatted him lightly with the magazine as he walked by.

"Nonsense! Just keep going to class. But, Peter, you could come by more often. You act like you don't even remember where we live."

She gave him a stern look while pouring freshly brewed coffee into a silver carafe.

"Hey, Mom, would you mind if I called my girlfriend and invited her over for breakfast? She would really dig this."

Marie smiled with delight. "No, I don't mind at all! As long as she doesn't take too much time getting here; this food isn't going to stay hot forever. It's about time I met her!"

"Cool." Peter grabbed the phone and dialed Lanka's cell number. She answered the phone in a sleepy voice. "Hello?"

"Hey baby, it's me. You up?"

Lanka lazily scratched her head and glanced over at the alarm clock. Immediately, she noticed that Petra wasn't in the bed beside her and nervously sat up to look around the room. Then she heard the water from the shower in the bathroom and relaxed, turning her attention back to Peter. "Uh, yeah, Peter, I am awake. It's early. What's going on?"

"Well, my sister came into town last night, and I want you to meet her, and the rest of my family. We are having a huge breakfast, wanna come over?"

Lanka looked at the bathroom door and chewed her lip for a second before answering. Now, she thought, was the perfect time to get Petra the help that she needed. She remembered what Petra had said last night, and wondered if she had really thought about her proposal to meet with Peter. "Umm, well, can I call you back? My friend is over here still."

"Nope, you have to tell me now, and then come straight over." He laughed into the phone. "You don't know my mom. She might have a heart attack if the eggs are cold by the time someone puts them in their mouth. Seriously, just throw some clothes on and come over, and bring your friend too. Mom won't care." He figured that his mom really would care, but he personally always agreed with the concept "the more the merrier" and knew that his mother would eventually love the extra attention.

Lanka knew that she had to make the decision without asking Petra. She thought about it for a second then answered, "Yes, we will come. Where do I go?" Peter gave her directions and then they hung up. Not sure of what she would say exactly about where they were going, she anxiously crossed the bedroom to the bathroom door and took a deep breath before she opened it.

Petra heard the bathroom door open and popped her head out from behind the shower curtain. "Good morning," she said in Czech, shaking off the water from her face.

Lanka exhaled and cheerfully answered, "Good morning to you, too! Whew! I am starving, want to go get some breakfast?"

Petra shut the water off and grabbed a towel from the rack beside the shower. "Yes, I am hungry, too. Where can we go where we won't be noticed? Is there even a breakfast place around here that doesn't hire Czech people?"

Lanka smiled at her through the reflection in the mirror, brushed her hair into place and said, "Of course! I know the perfect place. But we have to hurry, its better when it's fresh and hot. It's buffet style." Behind her innocent smile, Lanka was hoping that her friend would take the bait without any suspicions.

Petra gave her a weird look, but then shrugged it off. "Ok, let me throw some clothes on, and I will be ready."

"Me too, but, umm, Petra, you might want to throw a little makeup on those bruises so you don't get any looks. They are pretty nasty." In the mirror they both stared at the purple and green marks all over her naked body, and then Lanka walked out so that her friend could have some privacy. Hurriedly, she used a mirror above the desk to freshen up, and then repacked everything they had brought to the motel. On the bed she placed an outfit for Petra to wear and used the phone to call a taxi. She wanted to make sure that they left in a hurry so that Petra did not have time to change her mind, and also so Peter's mother didn't have a heart attack at their expense. Ten minutes later, they were in a taxi en route to the Esther residence. Petra was still applying foundation to her face when the taxi pulled away from the motel. Peering into a compact mirror, she dabbed a little onto her cheek and began smoothing it across a bruise. She asked in Czech, "Lanka, where are we going? You never said where we are going to eat."

Lanka bit her lip and looked out of the window when she answered her friend. "Well, don't get mad at me when I tell you." Petra stopped fixing her face and slowly looked at Lanka who squirmed uncomfortably in her seat. "Peter called and invited us over for breakfast."

Petra was infuriated. "What! I never said ok to that, Lanka! I haven't even had time to think about what I should do next! Why did you do this?" Anger inflamed her face, and she slammed the compact into her purse. "Lanka, you don't understand what these Russian guys are! You don't know who you are messing with! If we tell the wrong people, they will kill us, and maybe even our family! Do you not understand that?"

Lanka cringed and thanked God for the window that separated the driver from them, just in case the driver could speak Czech. She turned to face Petra and said sternly, "Look! I do know what we are dealing with! I have heard the rumors of what these people can do. I see your face, and that is enough for me to understand! And besides, it's not as if I haven't been working here under their rule for the last couple of years of my life! But you need help, Petra, and this is the only way I know how to give it to you. I am not just going to let you walk away and disappear, leaving me worrying if you are alive or dead. It's your choice to talk to Peter. I won't say a word about anything you told me. I promise! All I am doing is giving you a chance to talk to someone besides illegal Czech people who can't give you any help or advice. We are going to eat breakfast with him and his family and that's it. You can make your own decisions from there. I am sorry that I wasn't totally honest with you about where we were going at first, but it's only because I know that you would have said no." Petra stared at the floorboard while Lanka scolded her. "And plus, there are other people to consider in this situation. You said so last night. Think about Yuraslav's wife! You might be the only chance she has to be found, and if they find her dead, then at least I will know for my own peace of mind that I did something, even if this is all, to help her. Don't you want that, too?" Lanka regretted raising her voice, but she had to make her friend understand why she had chosen to do this.

"Yes." Petra said softly. Even if she had disagreed with Lanka, it would have been too late. The car was pulling into the driveway of the Esther residence as she spoke, and Peter was waving at them from the front door.

CHAPTER FIFTY-FOUR

"Don't be scared. You don't have to talk to him if you don't want to, but I think you should. Oh, and your face looks fine. You can barely see anything." Lanka squeezed her friends hand and exited the taxi to pay the driver. With the duffel bag around her shoulder Petra reluctantly followed her down the driveway and up the stone walkway to where Peter was waiting for them. He smiled at them. "Hey, baby! Thanks for coming! Y'all hungry? I see that you have brought luggage with you. Plan on moving in?"

Lanka rolled her eyes at him while she gave him a quick peck on the cheek and said, "No, we went out last night and stayed at a hotel."

He opened the door and welcomed them in. "Cool, sounds like you guys had fun! Here, you can just set your stuff right inside the door here. It's Petra, right?"

Petra nodded but didn't make eye contact with him as she walked through the doorway. Her nerves were shot, and she wondered if she would able to eat anything at all. But when she walked through the door and entered the foyer, the smell of the all the food was enough to make a dead man hungry, and she felt her stomach rumble.

Lanka leaned into Peter and gave him another quick kiss before he led them into the kitchen. "Thanks for inviting us. I hope your mom doesn't mind at all. Smells great!" She looked at Petra in hopes that she would at least speak in approval with her, but all she received was a nervous nod before she looked away again. They followed Peter to the kitchen where his mother was busy taking out food from the oven where she had been keeping it warm. She had expected Peter to walk in with one girl, not two, and couldn't help looking disapprovingly at him before she could compose herself with an introduction. Peter ignored the look and smiled at his girlfriend. "Mom, this is Lanka. And this is her friend, Petra. Ladies, this is my mother, Marie."

Marie took her cooking gloves off and welcomed them to sit down at the table. "Very nice to meet you both! Umm, give me just a second while I fix another setting. Peter didn't tell me that two of you were coming, not that it matters, the more the merrier." She pointed at the chairs, "Please girls, have a seat. Coffee?" Both girls said yes, and Marie turned to Peter. "Go ahead and pour their coffees, son, so I can get another table setting for your friend." When she passed him, she pinched him on the arm and whispered, "Peter, you could have told me she was bringing a friend, and then I would have had her plate ready!" Peter stifled a giggle. He knew that his mother wasn't really put out by the two strangers being there; she was angry because she wasn't prepared properly, and she felt like it made her look bad. He poured three coffees for himself and the two girls and returned to the kitchen table to wait on everyone else to join them.

Meanwhile, in the formal dining room, as Marie bent over into the china cabinet to collect another setting for her unannounced guest, Judith and Hank snuck up behind her and surprised her with their presence. Smiling, she whirled around and hugged them both. Judith's father walked in and joined them, and they spent several minutes introducing themselves to Hank. He shook hands with Judith's father and thanked him for the use of his car. He also thanked them for the food, warm welcome, and wonderful hospitality. After all the formalities were finished, the four of them walked into the kitchen and repeated the process all over again with Peter and his two friends.

Peter stood up to shake Hank's hand and then turned to Lanka and Petra. "I would like for you all to meet my girlfriend, Lanka, and her friend Petra. Petra doesn't speak much English, so y'all go easy on her. They are both from the Czech Republic."

Simultaneously, Marie, Judith's father, Judith and Hank stared at the two girls sitting at the table. The overall jovial mood morphed quickly from pleasant to awkward in one quick second. In the uncomfortable silence the girls shifted nervously in their seats. They were fully aware that the origin of their birth was the cause for the uncomfortable pause, and Peter hurriedly jumped in to interrupt the momentary silence. "Anybody hungry?" When he spoke, everyone instantly became aware that they all were staring at the girls. They began talking at once, trying to change the subject and lighten the mood back to the jovial point that it had been before Peter had introduced them. Completely embarrassed, Judith immediately took a seat beside Lanka. "Hi, I am Judith, Peter's sister. Sorry about that. It's just with the case and all; it's quite a coincidence that you are from the Czech Republic. I hear it's a very nice country. I would love to visit Prague someday." Hoping that they were not offended by what just happened, she smiled at the girls.

Lanka smiled back and spoke first; she tried hard to keep her response short, sweet and to the point. "That's ok. Yes, we are from the Czech Republic, but we are not like those Czech people on the news. I hope they find them."

Petra nodded in agreement but said nothing. She relied on Peter's admission earlier that she couldn't speak English well enough to converse. Soon, everyone began passing food around and wondering how they were going to eat everything piled on their plates. After Judith finished preparing her plate, she turned to Lanka once more before taking her first bite. "You know, Lanka, I am from Orange Beach, well, I am sure Peter told you already, where those murders took place. And Hank over there is the lead detective on the case. He flew up here with me last night just to help with the search."

Petra literally choked on a bite of her food and instinctively brought her hand up to her throat while she tried to suck in air. Everyone stopped talking when they saw what was happening to her. Just as Judith was about to perform the Heimlich maneuver, Petra managed to swallow the piece of food and suck in a breath of air. With shaking hands she grabbed her glass of water and tried to drink the rest of the partially lodged food down her throat. She spilled most of the water in the process, drenching the table cloth around her plate. Marie brought a dish towel to the table and started dabbing up the spilled water while Judith made sure that Petra was ok. After a few minutes, everything was back to normal and people went back to their conversations. Petra on the other hand, was an absolute emotional wreck. How could a coincidence happen such as this? She was actually sitting at a breakfast table with five Americans, two of whom were from Orange Beach, Alabama, one of which was the lead detective in the Morrison case! Her instincts told her to bolt, to immediately get up from the table and run as fast as she could through the front door. But Lanka's hand was pressed firmly onto her leg underneath the table, and she knew that her friend was physically trying to stop her from leaving.

Lanka leaned over to her while everyone was busy talking and eating and in hushed tones spoke to her friend in Czech, "I swear, Petra, I didn't know any of this. Please, don't be mad at me. Just eat, and we will figure it out later." Lanka smiled at everyone at the table and said, "She is ok." Underneath the table she kept her hand pressed firmly on the top of Petra's leg, urging her to sit still and not make a move.

Hank noticed with much interest how pale Petra's face had become after Judith told her who he was, and what he was doing in Myrtle Beach. He also noticed, as he pretended to be involved in a conversation with Judith's father about sport fishing, the bruising under her painted face and knew she had gone to great lengths to cover them up before arriving at the Esther house that morning. Finally, he broke the conversation with Judith's father and mentioned the bruising to Judith, who was too busy eating and talking to have noticed on her own. She glanced over at Petra, and her eyes widened. Not only were they on her face, but peeking out from the bottoms of her sleeves were dark purple marks on her arms as well; these bruises were not covered with any makeup. Petra's silent and extremely tense behavior made Hank and Judith nervous. In light of everything that was happening, it was too much of a coincidence that they were from Czech Republic to ignore, and something about her just wasn't right. After breakfast was finished, Hank stood up to stretch, along with everyone else, and asked Peter if he could speak with him for a moment before he left to join Officer Myers on the road. Judith stayed at the table and made small talk with the two nervous Czech girls.

They walked into the living room and sat down on the couch in front of the television. Frowning and unsure how to begin, Hank pressed his fingers to his lips before he spoke. "Umm, Peter, it was really nice to meet you and your friends this morning. But I can't help but notice the way they are acting in there. Both of them are scared to death of something, especially Petra. Have you noticed the bruising all over her?"

Wondering why Hank had asked to speak with him, Peter had been looking at Hank with a confused expression when they first sat down on the couch together. "Yeah, I saw the bruises last night. Actually, I just met her last night. Lanka told me that her and her boyfriend had gotten into a fight. Why?"

Hank truly believed that it was just too much of a coincidence for Petra to be the same Petra whose wallet was found in a car that was raided in Charlotte. But, still, stranger things could happen. "I don't know. Something about it just doesn't feel right. How well do you know your girlfriend? And is Petra from here? I mean, I thought Petra was going to vomit right on the table when your sister mentioned that I was helping with the case here on loan from Orange Beach. Not to mention the fact that she almost choked to death on her food. Watching them in there made me feel like they were both going to bolt and run from this house at any given second."

Peter glanced back toward the kitchen and frowned. "Yeah, now that you mention it, Lanka has been acting strangely. Last night when I stopped by her house on the way to the airport, I saw her peeking out from the bottom of the blinds to see who it was at her door. Then when she answered it, the lights had all been turned off, and she looked both ways down the street before she let me in. I followed her to her bedroom and there was Petra, hiding under the bed. And there was glass all over the floor where she had dropped a picture frame when I knocked on the door. Apparently I scared the shit out of her. I didn't think anything of it because Lanka told me that she was hiding from her boyfriend." Peter paused and thought about the whole scenario. "But now that you mention it, it does seem really strange. Lanka isn't acting like herself."

Hank nodded at this and wondered what he should do next. He wanted to find out more about the girls, but Marie's breakfast had already made him a little late. "Ok, it's probably nothing, but do me a favor ok? I have to meet with Officer Myers at the local station; I am already a little late. Do you mind relaying all of this to your sister, and between the both of you try to figure out what the deal is with them? I will have my cell phone on the whole time. Call me if anything seems out of the ordinary."

Peter nodded. "Sure, man. No problem." They walked back into the kitchen where everyone else was chit chatting the morning away. Hank thanked Marie for the wonderful food and hospitality, and said goodbye to Judith. Before he left, he gave her a wink and pointed to Peter, who was already poised at her side to tell her what Hank had said to him. She waved good bye and turned her attention back to the girls, who were saying nothing and trying hard to make the least amount of eye contact possible. Peter cleared his throat and poked Judith in the back with his finger. He looked at Lanka and said, "Can you excuse us for a minute? I will be right back." Lanka nodded with a nervous smile and watched the two leave the kitchen. Petra had already stood up from the table, and was looking around for her exit. She shot past Marie who was washing the dishes, and stumbled into the hallway that led to the foyer. Lanka was close behind her, calling out a hurried thank you to Marie as she went running by. Judith and Peter heard the front door open and Lanka shouting at Petra, and they too ran towards the door.

The duffel bag was so heavy, and even if Petra had her full strength, it would have weighted her down too much to run far. She finally stopped in the middle of the road, and slumped over on her knees, trying to catch her breath. Peter caught up with her and stopped at her side to pick up the duffel bag from the concrete. She was blind from the sweat and hot tears in her eyes. He bent over with one hand on Petra's back and said gently, "Hey, slow down, it's ok. Take a deep breath." Lanka and Judith caught up with them and they stood around her forming a barricade so she couldn't run anywhere else. Finally, Petra caught her breath and stood up. Apparently, standing up too fast, coupled with a belly full of food and the hot morning sun, was just too much for Petra to deal with. She collapsed, and all three of them lunged forward to break her fall. They carried her and her duffel bag inside the house and laid her down on the couch. Her thick makeup had melted almost completely away from the heat outside, and her face was a shock to everyone who sat in the living room. After placing a cold towel on her forehead, Judith looked at Lanka and said, "Ok, tell us what is going on. Something isn't right. Why was she running?"

Lanka began to cry. She shook her head slowly and placed a hand on her friend's face to make sure she was not awake. Fearing that she too might pass out next to her friend, Lank slowly sat down beside Petra's head on the end of the couch and leaned onto the side for support. In a shaky voice she admitted, "I brought her here because I thought that maybe she would ask Peter for help. She is running from the Russians. The ones that Mr. Hank is looking for. We had no idea that Mr. Hank would be here, or we never would have come. It was just coincidence. The boss is going to kill her, and I have to help her. She is my friend." Even though she was relieved that everything would now finally be out in the open, she also felt shame for betraying her friend's trust; Lanka buried her face in her hands.

Judith placed her hand on Lanka's lap to reassure her that everything was ok. "Honey, take a deep breath. Everything is going to be alright." She stroked her leg, and Lanka begin to cry. "When you catch your breath, I need you to tell us everything, ok? You can trust us. We won't let anything bad happen to you. If you know anything about any of this, please tell us, because Hank desperately needs to find someone. It's Yuraslav's wife, Suzanna. She is…"

Lanka nodded her head and interrupted her through sobs, "I know about her. That is why I wanted to bring Petra here. So she could get help and maybe find a way to help Suzanna."

Worry clouded Judith's face as she watched the two girls. "Peter, stay here with her, make sure they are okay, and don't let them leave! I am going to call Hank." Peter took his sister's place beside the couch and began to comfort his girlfriend while Judith called Hank. He answered on the first ring. "Turn around, Hank, the girls know something! Petra is running from them. You have to get here quick!"

Hank dropped the cell phone on the floorboard to make a u-turn at the intersection. Finally, he regained his bearings and brought the phone back to his ear. "I knew something was up with those two! I will be there in a few minutes. Judith, hold on to her. Don't let anything happen. I will call Dell right now." They hung up and Hank dialed Dell's cell number.

CHAPTER FIFTY-FIVE

Dell answered his phone and said, "Hank, good to hear from you, I am..."

Hank shook his head and began rapidly speaking into the phone, "Dell, you are not going to believe this! I think that the girl who sent us the anonymous information, all the files and paperwork on Vladimir, is at Judith's parents' house right now! Don't ask any questions, just meet me there!" He spun off the address to the Esther house again to make sure Dell remembered where it was and snapped the phone shut. Moments later, he pulled back into the driveway of the Esther's and ran into the house where everyone was gathered around the two crying girls. Petra was awake, crying and shaking so uncontrollably that Judith wondered if she should call an ambulance to take her to the hospital. The sight of Hank walking through the door sent her into waves of spasms. Her fear knocked the breath out of her and turned her face into an angry mottled combination of dark purple and bright red. Judith wrapped her arms tightly around the girl and began to rock her soothingly. In times like these, she thought, the best medicine is the simple act of human contact to calm someone down; adults are no different children in a lot of ways. Hank understood the situation and quietly sat down on the chair next to the couch while Judith consoled Petra back into a state of normalcy. He extended his hand to Lanka in a friendly and comforting gesture and smiled softly; Lanka took it. "I know what you must be feeling right now," he said to her. One thing he had learned this week was that Czechs do not trust the police, and he knew that it would be more than just difficult for the girls to completely open up to him. Even though time was of the essence, and not particularly on his side, he had to be patient if he had any hopes of finding Suzanna and Vladimir through the two girls. "I promise I will protect you. Nothing bad will happen to you, you have my word. But you have to trust me."

Lanka looked at Hank and studied his eyes. She was still conscious of her betrayal. After a few minutes of soul searching and convincing herself that it was ok to trust the man sitting in front of her, she looked at Petra for a sign of encouragement. Petra had calmed down to a quiet sob; she had no more energy left to fight the situation. She looked back at her friend and whispered, "Go ahead. Tell them."

Lanka stared at her friend and said, "I think you should tell them,

Petra." And then everyone knew that Petra's inability to speak English had been a lie.

Making a point not to look at anyone in particular, Petra rested her head on Judith's shoulder and stared directly at the floor. She started from day one, when Mirek and Yuraslav had shown up at her office on Orange Beach to give her instructions from Vladimir on what to do with the office. She told them about the cutting of her beautiful blonde hair, the burning of their bloody clothes behind the trailer, the drive to Charlotte, the rapes and the escape. Everyone sat in sheer horror as they listened to Petra's story unfold. When she admitted to Hank that she had been the person who had faxed him the information, he silently nodded and smiled at her, encouraging her to go on. Finally, she ended her story with the words that nearly crushed Hank with disappointment. She spoke slowly and deliberately. "I don't know where Suzanna is. I thought she was in Atlanta with him at his house, but I know now that she isn't because I saw it on the news. They must be here. It only makes sense. I have all the documents with me, so Vladimir must be here to get some more. He probably has someone here that has a stash of unused identities that he can use to disappear. Either that or he knows I am here, and he wants the bag." She pointed to the duffel bag that Peter had carried in for her. "Everything I sent you is in that bag over there, plus the stuff that I was going to use for myself to escape." She knew that escaping was not an option for her anymore. It only added to her perpetual sadness and depression.

Hank allowed the silence for a moment, and then asked, "Petra, do you have any idea where they could be hiding in Myrtle Beach?"

She shook her head slowly, then said, "Probably at a Czech person's house, or a Russian's house." She began to cry again. "I hope that Suzanna is still alive. But if she is, she probably wishes that she was already dead. I know Vladimir. He is the devil."

218

Suddenly, the doorbell rang and Lanka and Petra jumped in fear. Judith's arm was squeezed so tightly by Petra's death grip that she thought it would break under the pressure. Hank stood up quickly to control the situation. "Shhh, everybody, its ok! It's just my friend who is helping me. It's ok." He looked at Judith and said, "It's Dell. Hold on, I will be right back." After a few minutes, Hank ushered Dell into the room, introduced him to everyone, and then repeated everything that Petra had told them. Dell listened with rapt attention, amazed at the way all of their paths had crossed. Then his cell phone rang. The caller was another officer who requested their presence at a suspicious Russian house on the other side of town. Hank called the Myrtle Beach police station and asked for a female officer to come to the Esther house and watch over the girls until he could get back to the house. They waited until she arrived, and then set out to join the other officers who had just phoned them.

CHAPTER FIFTY-SIX

Of all the Russians and Czechs that the Myrtle Beach police department had spoken to and interrogated since the previous afternoon, Ivan had been the most suspicious. The officers had initially come to his house to question his roommate who had popped up in the system for a bar fight a couple of months ago. While the officers were sitting in the living room talking with him, they noticed Ivan grow more and more uncomfortable as the hour passed. Something about his behavior had been more than strange. Finally, the officer had called into the station and reported the nervous man to another officer who was talking to a federal agent. Within minutes the FBI had arrived at the Russian house, separated the two roommates, and begun questioning them about everything; their lives, families, friends, and jobs. At one point, one of the officers asked Ivan for his identification. Nervously, he had told them that he lost his wallet several weeks ago. In another room, however, his roommate had given them an American driver's license and produced a legitimate visa. They had drilled him on what he knew about his roommate, Ivan. He had shrugged arrogantly at their questions. "I don't know anything about him. What he does is his business. I just sleep here."

"Where does he work?" was the next question.

"I don't know," he answered.

"Who does he hang around with?" the officer patiently asked.

"I don't know," he answered again. Throughout the questioning, the Russian had adopted it as his favorite answer, giving the agents little to go on. Not that the Russian was lying; he really didn't know anything about Ivan, nor did he want to know. All he knew was that his roommate had been privately talking on his cell phone a lot in the past week. Ivan had moved in no more than a month ago after his other roommate went back to Russia. When he had told his friends that he was looking for someone else to move in, he learned through friends that Ivan was also looking for a place to live. They had met in a bar, had a few drinks, and decided that they could get along. The only time that their paths ever crossed was in the hallway or the driveway. He had so far been pleased with Ivan's secrecy and independence because he wasn't interested in friendship. He only wanted to make sure his rent was paid.

Not satisfied with the way the questioning was going, but definitely suspicious of something, the police officers who accompanied the feds had ultimately decided to call Officer Myers and Detective Hank Jordan to join them. Myers had answered the phone, agreed that they should meet and informed them that he and Hank had some important information to share as well.

Fifteen minutes later, Hank and Dell rang the doorbell and walked into the house. First, they saw Ivan, who fidgeted uncomfortably in his seat while question after question was fired at him. Then, they walked into the next room to see the roommate, who sat smugly in his chair, rolling his eyes every time a question was asked. Hank looked at Dell and said, "You mind if I look around the house while you help them?"

Dell shook his head, "No, not at all. I am going back into the living room where the first guy is. He is definitely scared shitless about something."

Hank nodded and began to walk around the house, inspecting each room with a quick glance over until he arrived in the kitchen. Everything was neat except for the small breakfast table pushed up against the wall beside the kitchen phone. It wasn't dirty, but unlike the rest of the house, it was cluttered with scribbled papers and bills waiting to be paid. Hank walked over to the table and sat down in a chair to study the papers that littered its surface. He saw a phone bill, a cable bill, an envelope that had been mailed from someone in Russia, and various other papers with Russian words scribbled all over it. He was just getting ready to stand up and move on when he noticed a piece of paper sticking out of the pile. In no particular order it had numerous different Russian writings that listed the make and models of different cars, Russian names and accompanying phone numbers. As he picked up the piece of paper, he noticed, out of the corner of his eye, that Ivan had a clear eye shot at him from where he was sitting in the living room. Ivan was nervously staring at him, and Hank pretended not to see him. The longer he held the paper, the more Ivan fidgeted nervously and stared at him with serious interest. He heard the agent who was interviewing him repeat a question, and knew that whatever he was looking at was a source of serious concern for Ivan. Tuning him out totally, Hank concentrated on the paper and tried to figure out what was so important about it. At first glance, it appeared that someone in the house had been shopping for cars, especially since he couldn't read the notes that were scribbled beside each listing. Hank searched in vain, but couldn't find anything that stood out as suspicious. Making sure that Ivan could see every move he made, he decided to fold the piece of paper in half and place it in his pocket. Just as he slipped it in, Ivan, unable to control himself, shouted from the other room, "You cannot take that! Put it back where you found it! You cannot steal from me, I haven't done anything wrong! You must have warrant!" Hank slowly turned to Ivan and walked into the living room where the federal agent was sitting. Hank handed the folded paper to the agent and asked, "Do you by chance, know anyone who can read Russian?"

Ivan jumped up from his chair and his arm came crashing down on Hanks hand. He grabbed the paper and began ripping it into pieces before Hank or the agent could stop him. Then he began stuffing them into his mouth as quickly as he could. Hank pounced on him while the agents grabbed both of his fists. Together, they wrestled him to the floor and beat his back until he coughed up the pieces of paper onto the floor. The commotion was loud and Dell, along with another officer ran into the room to find out what was going on. Hank, still pinning Ivan to the floor, yelled at Dell, "Get the pieces of paper up, get all of them!" The agent and Dell got on all fours and hurriedly began picking up the soggy wet pieces of paper that Ivan had attempted to eat. Ivan struggled against Hank but couldn't free himself before handcuffs were slapped around his wrists. He fought Hank's restraints until he realized that he didn't have a chance in hell of going anywhere. Finally, out of breath and wincing in pain from Hank shoving his knee into his back, Ivan sat down with his back against the foot of the same chair that he had been sitting in before.

Hank yelled at him, "Tell me what that paper is! Deportation because of your lack of a visa is the last thing you should be worried about if you know anything about Vladimir! You talk to me now! What did that paper say? Why is it so important? " Ivan remained silent. Hank looked at the federal agent who was already on the phone requesting someone who could read Russian to be driven immediately to the house. Hank nodded at him, then turned back to Ivan. "It's just a matter of time before we get someone here that will tell us what that paper says. You might as well tell us now."

Ivan laughed bitterly and spat at Hank. "You dumb motherfucker! I don't have to tell you shit. And besides, you have already killed me!"

Hank, Dell, the fed, and another officer were desperately trying to piece the soggy paper back together before the translator arrived. They removed the wet pieces from the dry ones and spread them out onto the kitchen table where they attempted to work a puzzle that held some clue that they couldn't understand yet. While they worked on it, Hank ran over to the small table beside the phone and began to study every single thing he could read and understand. Finding nothing, he returned to the kitchen table to watch the progress of the paper puzzle and wait on the translator. That's when he spotted a small piece of paper that had fallen unnoticed on the floor behind Ivan's chair. He picked it up, unfolded it, and almost choked from his own excitement. On the paper were the last four digits of a phone number that ended with a dash and a V. He looked down at Ivan, who was all but frothing at the mouth with anger, and asked, "Does this V stand for Vladimir?"

Everyone at the kitchen table stopped their task and turned around to look at Ivan. His nervous silence and wild darting eyes spoke a million words, and they knew that it was Vladimir's phone number. For ten minutes, they looked through the chewed up bits of paper until they found the matching piece. They now had what they suspected to be Vladimir's phone number; and if it was, in fact, his number, then they also had proof that Ivan had been in contact with him. Hank suddenly wondered if the cars that were listed were possible escape cars. He turned to Dell quickly, "He was helping him, Dell. He knows where they are! He has been calling around looking for a car for Vladimir! He can't drive the SUV anymore after someone called into 911 yesterday!"

Dell nodded quickly and said, "Use the other guy in there to get information! Threaten him! Tell him anything you can to get him to translate this stuff! We can't wait for the translator. We need to know now!"

While the roommate was handcuffed and brought into the kitchen, Ivan, kicking and screaming, was removed from the living room and placed in a patrol car outside. The arrogant attitude that the Russian had displayed earlier was now lost, as he watched his roommate being dragged outside to the police car. Ivan had shouted at him in Russian, "Keep your mouth shut! Don't tell them anything! I will kill you!"

He glanced around the room at each one of the faces that peered down at him, especially at Hank who seemed angrier than everyone else. Hank leaned in closely to the man's face. "My name is Hank Jordan, and I am the lead detective on the Morrison murders in Alabama. Are you familiar with what has been going on lately?"

Oh, shit! the Russian thought. *My roommate is hooked up with all of that?* He wanted absolutely nothing to do with any of that mess, so he nodded quickly at Hank. "I have seen the news."

"Good, then we won't run into any problems with you not helping us anymore, now that you realize how serious this is. I am looking for a Russian named Vladimir Bereovsky and an American woman named Suzanna Novacek that we believe was kidnapped by him. I believe you can help us find them by translating what has been written on these pieces of paper." He paused to let this sink in as the man looked at the reconstructed piece of paper. "If you don't help us, I will personally see to it that you are sent to prison for obstructing justice and aiding a child rapist, kidnapper and murderer. Do you know what prisoners in this country do to child rapists?"

The Russian nodded his head and let it drop to his chest as he let a long breath out. He knew exactly what happened to those kinds of people in this country.

"And may I remind you that you are in the South. South Carolina to be exact and I don't think I have to tell you how Southerners react to those sorts of things, because even if you don't know, I am sure that you don't want to find out. You have, I am sure, been in this country long enough to know what a redneck is, hmmm?" Hank leaned closer to the man's face and slowly said, "Now, look down at the table and tell me what that piece of paper says. Now."

The Russian studied the pieces of paper and began to translate what had been scribbled all over the page. Some of the writing was smudged from Ivan's spit, making it difficult to translate in whole. Basically, it listed several different phone numbers for different cars, with a description of what Vladimir was looking for to escape in. There was a separate number for someone whose initial was D and an address with an asterisk that appeared to be unconnected to any of the cars;

there were seven addresses in total, and only six different cars listed. Dell flipped his phone open and started to call the address into the station when a cell phone began ringing somewhere inside the house. Dell flipped his phone off and everyone grew silent to listen to the ring. Hank followed the sound of the phone until he arrived at the chair where Ivan had been sitting. The phone stopped ringing. Hank searched all around the chair until he finally found it stuffed underneath the cushion of the chair. The number of the missed call read 404-763-2537, which was an Atlanta number. Hank held the phone up to the other officers and said, "It's Vladimir! It's the same number that I found on the piece of paper!" He quickly walked over to the table and placed the phone down in front of the Russian. If someone didn't call Vladimir back, it might signal to him that something was wrong, and they might lose him. Dell phoned the station and rattled off the address that wasn't connected with a vehicle, and then read off the other ones. Federal agents and officers all over the city were dispatched to each one of the residences and instructed to be extremely careful and quiet, so as not to disturb anyone inside the houses. Dell spoke carefully, "Have them surround the house that was not connected with the cars on that sheet of paper, but tell them not to make a single move until we get there!"

Hank looked at the Russian and asked, "Do you think you can sound and act like Ivan on the phone?" The Russian's eyes grew wide with raw fear, and he gave no answer. Hank and Dell waited until they had confirmation that the house was surrounded, and then turned back to the Russian at the table. Hank said a silent prayer that he was doing the right thing, and then said to the Russian, "Call him. Listen to what he says, and try to act like you know what you are talking about." Hank gave him the phone and pressed the callback button on the last missed call. "Remember what I said about the prison, and try your best to keep him on the phone as long as possible."

CHAPTER FIFTY-SEVEN

The young Czech man who had been brave enough to drug Vladimir had lost his nerve shortly after Vladimir passed out from the effects of the Rohypnol. Soon after he had given him the wine, he remembered that the driver was still in the other bedroom with Mirek. After several attempts to get the driver to drink the wine, he had finally given up after the driver threatened to shoot him if he asked again. Sorrowful and apologetic, the Czech man had tied Suzanna to the bed as Vladimir requested, and cried himself to sleep.

Suffering from a terrible hangover, Vladimir had woken up on the couch the next morning and cursed himself for getting drunk and falling asleep. His thoughts were still sluggish from the Rohypnol. In his attempt to stumble through the house to make sure everyone was still there, the thought never occurred to him that he had been drugged. The Czech guy who had been in the room with him last night was still asleep on the floor. When he had stumbled into one of the bedrooms, he found his driver asleep beside Mirek who was awake but unable to speak or move from being beaten so badly. Then he had walked into the other bedroom and found Suzanna tied just as he had requested to the bed, asleep. He had also found the Czech man who had tied her up, asleep as well on the floor beside the bed. Satisfied that no one had escaped while he slept, Vladimir had eventually made his way back to the kitchen to his cell phone and dialed Ivan's number. When he hadn't answered, Vladimir sat at the table rubbing his pounding head and waited for Ivan to call him back. Ivan should have answered, he thought. That car should have been ready for him in the driveway when he woke up. But nothing was ready. Ivan wasn't answering his phone calls, and he was still stuck in this hell hole of a house. He cursed loudly and woke up the Czech who was sleeping on the floor beside the television. He had been dozing on and off throughout the night, careful not move or make a sound; he had hoped, like a child, that if he was unheard and unnoticed, that he would be unseen as well.

He cowered on the floor and pretended to be asleep. Continuously shaking his leg while he pondered his next move Vladimir sat nervously at the table. Suddenly, his cell phone rang. He looked at the number and sighed in relief. Ivan was calling him back; nothing bad had happened and things were back on schedule. He picked up the phone without even saying hello. He shouted in Russian, "Where the hell have you been? I just tried to call you! Why the fuck didn't you answer the goddamned phone? I need that car, and I need it now!"

Hank and everyone else was listening to the conversation, and they smiled when they heard him ask about the car; they knew they were on the right track. After Vladimir cursed who he thought was Ivan for several minutes, he finally asked him again where the car was. The Russian roommate swallowed hard and tried his best to sound like Ivan. "Sorry. I was asleep when you phoned. It isn't ready yet."

There was a pause on the phone and Vladimir said, "Why are you talking like that? What the fuck is going on?"

Everyone in the room bit their lip and held their breath. The Russian took a deep breath and said, "Sorry, you just woke me up. The car is almost ready. I am waiting on a phone call now. I must have dozed off."

Vladimir was fuming with so much anger that he didn't even notice the white utility van pull up to the curb across the street. He started shouting again at Ivan, furious with his nonchalant attitude. "I am hanging up! You fucking call that person now, get my car and you call me back!"

Simultaneously, Hank and everyone around the table let out a huge breath of relief. Not only did Vladimir fall hook line and sinker for their Ivan substitute, but they also had complete surveillance of the house that they believed he was in. The house in question was owned by a local slumlord who was currently being detained and questioned at his home across town. He told officials that he was renting the house to two Czech men, and immediately handed over the lease to authorities so they could run background checks on the names listed on the lease.

Meanwhile, after he hung up on who he thought was Ivan, Vladimir pushed the kitchen table away from him with such force that it slammed against the wall on the other side of the room. The crash made such a loud noise that not only was everyone in the house immediately awakened, but the members of the SWAT team who were hiding outside heard it too. Just like they were instructed they kept their places and waited for Hank and Dell to arrive.

Vladimir ripped his way through the house like an angry lion about to maul everyone in his path. He threw the bedroom door open that held Suzanna and kicked the Czech man in the stomach, ordering him to leave immediately. Too much valuable time had passed since Suzanna had been in his possession, and he was ready to take advantage of her before his time ran out completely.

After her bath the night before, the man had failed to put the gag back on her properly and during the night she had managed to loosen the gag and spit it out. Now, as she watched Vladimir move towards her and the man who had been so kind to her run out of the room, she screamed as loudly as she could, in one final effort to elicit help from anyone who might hear her. He shut her up with his fist when he broke her jaw in mid scream. The blow alone should have been enough to knock her out; but the surge of adrenaline brought on by the ultimate fear of being raped raced though Suzanna's body and kept her conscious. He hit her again to make sure she knew that screaming wouldn't help her, and then violently began ripping her clothes off to expose her bruised and naked body. He jerked her bare legs wide open and retied them to the bed so that he could see everything that Suzanna had to offer. To most men, the bruises alone would have been an immediate turn off, not to mention the shape of her swollen face, but to Vladimir, it was an aphrodisiac. He stood up to admire her battered body, and then began to undress himself in front of her. She tried to turn her head away, but he just reached down and gripped fistfuls of her hair and forced her head back toward him. He wanted her to watch every single thing he did to her, and if she didn't, then he would make her. She surrendered and watched in revulsion as he began to stroke himself to a full erection. It triggered her gag reflex and spun her into a series a dry heaves, which momentarily blinded her with tears. Just when he achieved a full erection and began making his way onto the bed, the doorbell rang.

Struggling to pick up his clothes from the floor, he realized that his gun and cell phone were still in the kitchen. Naked and on his stomach, he crawled quickly to the kitchen table, grabbed them both and returned to the bedroom. Pointing the gun at Suzanna's head, he hurriedly replaced her gag. No one in the house made a move or a sound. The doorbell rang again. This time, Vladimir crawled to the window and craned his neck at the front entrance. He saw two men standing at the door. One man was a police officer and the other one was in plain civilian clothes. Their backs were to him, so he couldn't see their faces; not that it mattered, a cop is a cop. Vladimir crawled from room to room, looking for the two Czechs. Finally, he found them hiding together behind the shower curtain in the bathroom. He pointed the gun at them and whispered, "Go to the door and answer their questions but do not let them in this house! If I go down, I will shoot you on my way out, and if you run, I will shoot you through the window. Tell them that no one is here." Vladimir then backed out on all fours and crawled into the other bedroom where his driver was standing with his back to the wall beside the window, gun in hand, cocked and ready to shoot. "Put Mirek in the closet and come with me." Mirek was still heavily bound to a chair and gagged. The driver just picked him up, chair and all, quietly placed him in the closet, and followed Vladimir on all fours to the other bedroom. They quickly untied Suzanna from the bed and threw her naked body on the floor in the closet as well. Before they closed the closet doors, Vladimir tied her ankles together and hoisted her legs up in the air, wrenched them back towards her face, and tied them to her neck. The binding wasn't enough to choke her, but it was tight enough to stop any movement, especially with her hands tied behind her back. Suzanna violently struggled to draw in breaths of air threw her nose while she acclimated to her new darkness and hell. Then the doors of the closet were shut, sealing her in from the outside world.

The two Czechs answered the door and nervously stared at the two men on the front porch. As he held his hand out to one of the Czechs, Hank spoke first. "Hi, my name is Hank Jordan. Sorry to bother you but umm, we are looking for someone. A Russian guy, named Vladimir Bereovsky. We are going from house to house asking everyone if they know anything about him or where he could be hiding. I am sure you have seen it on the news." The Czech guys both nodded a little too vigorously for Hank and Dell not to take notice, and the fact that neither of them spoke also sent out waves of alarm. Hank tried to look inside the house, but one of the Czechs made a lame effort to block his view. He tried once more, "Can we come in for a second and talk with you about this person? It's important that we find him. He may have kidnapped a woman from Alabama."

The Czech who had been kind to Suzanna shook his head, and finally said in a shaky voice, "No, there is no one here but us." Then he looked at Hank, widened his eyes, and darted them back and forth from him to the back of the house to his right, never moving his head. Hank and Dell caught the silent cry for help, and Dell said loudly, so that whoever else was in the house could hear, "Ok, well, thanks you so much for your help. Sorry to disturb you. If you see anyone suspicious or hear anything, give us a call. You were the last one in this neighborhood, so I guess this area is safe." Dell handed him a card and quickly pointed to the van across the street to let him know that they were watching the house. The Czech man nodded quickly and shut the door.

The driver watched through the window and whispered to Vladimir when they were leaving. Hank and Dell got into their car and drove away. Unknown to the driver, they hurriedly parked on the next street over and walked through the yards of the neighbors' houses until they were back at the house again. They crouched low with members of the SWAT team who had chosen a thick group of tall privacy bushes lining the back of the lot of the house for cover.

After a couple of minutes, Vladimir's heart rate slowed down a bit, and he allowed himself to breathe normally again. He forgot entirely about Suzanna, hit redial on his cell phone and tried to call Ivan back, but, again, no one answered the phone. He wondered if Ivan was getting a friendly visit from the local police as well.

CHAPTER FIFTY-EIGHT

In the living room of the Esther's residence, Judith and Peter sat with Lanka and Petra. They talked with the police officers and a couple of FBI agents who had arrived at the house after Hank and Dell had received the call to help with the surveillance of the little green house. When the officers had arrived, Judith had been concerned about the treatment that Petra would receive; she had hoped that whoever had been sent to question her would be compassionate and sympathetic. After everything that Petra had endured in the time she had spent in the United States, she did not have the energy to go through an extensive interview by some young uncaring officer who just wanted to get in on the bust of the year. Fortunately, the first officer who had arrived on the scene with the paramedics was a woman in her forties named Gabby. Gabby had extensive experience with rape and abuse victims, and was wonderful with Petra. The whole time Gabby was in the room with her, Judith couldn't help but think of the character Olivia from her favorite television show Law and Order Special Victims Unit. She was very gentle with Petra and made sure that the male officers kept their distances until Petra felt safe and comfortable with everyone in the room. Marie Esther had stayed in the room until Petra had begun her story again. When she heard the gory details of what the men had done to her, she left the room in a hurry to make lunch; it had been more than she could take. Peter had also excused himself to help his mother, leaving Lanka alone to hold her friend's hand while she recounted, yet again, her many horrors.

During the questioning, Judith's cell phone rang in the kitchen. Even though she didn't particularly want to leave the room, she politely and quietly stood up and walked quickly to her purse, hoping that it was Hank on the other line. She snatched it up just in time before her voice mail took the call. "Hello?"

"Hey Judith, it's me Hank."

"Hey, what's going on over there? You think he's in there?"

"Yeah, we do think he is in there. Dell and I just went to the front door and asked if anyone knew the whereabouts of a Russian named Vladimir; we told them we were asking everyone in the neighborhood. They were nervous as hell, and denied our request to come in, but when I mentioned Suzanna, one of the men's eyes got really wide and he used them to signal us to the inside of the house. He never spoke, other than to tell us that no one else was in there, but the silent signal was enough to get our attention. I gotta get her out of there, alive and unhurt. What I am going to say next is probably our best option, but you're not going to like it very much."

Judith cringed and looked down at the floor. She knew exactly what he was going to say. They wanted to use Petra as bait. "Hank, is there any other way? She has been through enough already."

Hank sighed heavily into the phone, already regretting that this was the best and only option that any of them could come up with at the time; and time was definitely not something that any of them could spare. "I knew you would say that. We need her. Of course, we can't make her to do it, and I wouldn't blame her one bit if she says no, but it's really the best way to do this. I came up with a plan, and everyone here agrees it's the best way, and I hate to ask you this, but I need you to help."

Judith almost choked on her own breath. "What? Hank? You want me to go in that house? Are you insane?"

"No, Judith, absolutely not! Sorry, I didn't mean to scare you. All I need you to do is help talk her into it, you know? Stress to her how important it is to get Suzanna out of there alive, without a fight or a gun show. Look, I know she doesn't necessarily trust cops, and you are not a cop. If anyone has any influence over her right now, it would be you or Peter, and I am thinking you because you are a woman."

Judith let her breath out and closed her eyes. She could hear Petra crying her story in the background and wanted nothing less than to approach her with this plan. How could she possibly ask her to help by going up to the one man responsible for all of her pain and sadness? "Alright, Hank, tell me the plan. I don't know if it will work, but I will try my best. All I can say is that if she says yes, y'all better do everything in your power to help and protect her, during and after!"

"I have already talked with the FBI agents present, and protection for her afterward is already in progress. Ok?"

"Ok, I am listening."

"Alright, according to her story, she escaped from the house in Charlotte before Vladimir got there, and to his knowledge, she didn't even really know for sure that he was coming. So that means that Vladimir doesn't know for sure that she was trying to get away from him. For all he knows, she was running from the Russians who had raped her the night before. She has all of the documents and paper work that he wanted from the Orange Beach office, so right now would be a good time for him if he ran into her. I mean, he is trying his damnest to escape from Myrtle Beach. So, what I am thinking is.... to get Ivan's roommate back on the phone and tell Vladimir that Petra contacted him to help Vladimir escape; he will tell Vladimir that the only reason she fled in the first place was because she was afraid that the Russians and that other Czech guy, Mirek, would kill her and steal the documents for themselves. We can find a nondescript car that she can drive to his house, have the "Ivan substitute" vouch for it over the phone, and Vladimir, hopefully, will accept her help, thinking that it is his only way out of the Myrtle Beach. Plus, he gets the documents and new identification. Petra's face hasn't made the news yet, and we didn't leak to the press that we had anything faxed to us either. It's perfect. He will think that Petra was trying to help him all along, especially when she tells him that she watched Mirek hide the duffel bag at the tire repair shop."

Judith thought about it for a second before she spoke. "Are you sure that Petra knows Ivan? I mean, what if she doesn't? Wouldn't Vladimir suspect something if she doesn't know him?"

Hank fell silent. He hadn't thought about the possibility of Petra not knowing Ivan. "Good point. Hmmm, well, I guess this is a good time to ask her. You're right. If she doesn't know who Ivan is, then how would she get in touch with him to find Vladimir?"

"Alright," she sighed into the phone. "Let me call you back. I am going in there to talk to her right now."

"Ok, hey, actually, is an officer named Gabby still there? Dell wants to brief her about all of this. She can help you, according to him."

"Yeah, I think you are right. Gabby has been really good with Petra from the minute she walked in. Hold on and I will get her for you."

Judith walked back into the living room and handed the phone to Gabby who listened intently for several minutes. Then she snapped the phone shut, glanced at Judith and smiled down at Petra. She placed her hand on the shoulder of the agent who was questioning her, interrupting him in mid sentence, and said. "Ok, that's enough for a couple of minutes. I am sure Petra would like a break. Petra, would you like to walk into the backyard with me, get some fresh air maybe? It's safe back there, no one can see you. Maybe have a glass of water? Lanka, Judith and I will come with you, and we will leave these nice men in here to watch the front door."

Relieved, Petra nodded, happily accepting the offer of a break. The agent turned around and looked at Gabby questioningly for interrupting him. Gabby did not look at the agent, but she did give him a small but firm poke and squeeze on his shoulder to signal to him that it was not up for discussion. He backed off immediately and began to jot down notes on his pad of paper. The women helped Petra up and proceeded through the house to the back yard. On the way outside, Judith stopped and asked her mother for some refreshments. Without delay, Marie opened the refrigerator and brought out lemons for some fresh lemonade. She was happy for the chance to help in any way, and thankful that she had something to do other than listen to the poor girl's heartbreaking story. At first she started to grab some sugar, but thought better of it and opened a bag of Splenda instead; sugar would take too long to dissolve, and she wanted to get the lemonade outside as quickly as possible.

At first, Petra was scared to leave the confinements of the kitchen, but Judith, Lanka and Gabby gently coaxed her along until she finally gave up and ventured into the warm air. The woman walked together in the sunshine and out of the other officers' hearing distance. Since there was no breeze, the girls decided to sit on the front porch of the guest house that Hank had spent the night in; it offered just enough shade to keep most of the heat away. Marie came right behind them, set a pitcher of lemonade and four glasses down on a small wicker table and left them to talk in private.

Smiling reassuringly at Petra, Judith cleared her throat and asked her, "There is a reason why Gabby and I wanted you to come outside Petra. We needed to talk to you about something very important and then ask you a question, ok?"

234

"That's fine, what do you want to talk about? I told you everything already." Petra was absolutely drained.

"Yes, I know. Well, there is no easy way to say this, and I am certainly not going to sugar coat it, but I just got off the phone with Hank. He and the police believe that Vladimir and Suzanna are definitely hiding in that house that they are watching right now. They got some kind of a secret signal from one of the residents inside, and they are trying to figure out a way to get in the house or make Vladimir come out without harming anyone in the process. I know that you want to help Suzanna, you said it already earlier. Here is your chance. Before you say no, hear me all the way." Judith paused to let her calm down; the very mentioning of Vladimir caused her to panic slightly in protest. Judith took a deep breath and looked at Gabby and Lanka. "Petra, listen, you don't have to do this, ok? But I do want you to listen to me. Hank and everyone else thinks it is a good idea. You know how you escaped from that house in North Carolina?" Petra nodded. "Well, you didn't know that Vladimir was coming to that house, did you?"

She thought about the question for a moment before she answered, wondering what it would eventually lead to. "I suspected, but I didn't know for sure."

"Ok, well, then is it safe to say that Vladimir could possibly believe that you were running away because you were afraid of the Russians who had raped you, and also because you wanted to help Vladimir by going and getting the duffel bag? I mean, you could always say that you didn't trust the Russians or the guy that hid the bag, right? So you just planned to sneak off, retrieve the bag, and find a way to get to him so you could help him?"

With a very confused expression on her face, Petra thought about everything Judith was saying. She tried to comprehend it, but failed. She opened her mouth to ask Judith to repeat everything, but at the same time, Lanka gasped; she knew exactly where this was going. She took Petra by the hand and rapidly explained the plan to her in Czech language. Petra's facial expression changed from confusion to understanding and then to fear. She put her hands up in the air and said, "No! I am not going into that house! I want to help her, but I cannot go to Vladimir! They will kill me!"

Judith let out a sigh and looked at Gabby. They exchanged glances, and Gabby then took the lead. She bent down to where Petra sat panting in the wicker chair and stared into her frightened eyes. "Petra, honey, they will not kill you. I promise you that. You have my word, you can trust me. You haven't heard the rest of the plan yet. Do you know a Russian man named Ivan? Maybe a friend of Vladimir's?"

"Of course I know him. He is Vladimir's number one guy. He watches over all the offices."

"Ok, well, Ivan has been helping him all along to form a plan to escape. We have him in custody right now. We also have his roommate in custody, who we have been using to pose as Ivan on the phone to Vladimir. As far as we know, Vladimir doesn't suspect anything. The Russian roommate has contacted him using Ivan's' cell phone, and spoken with him about a car. Apparently, Ivan was trying to find him a get away car to leave Myrtle Beach, and we busted him right before he found one. That is where you come into the plan. If we can find a suitable car, we can place tracking devices on it, give it to you, and have the roommate call Vladimir with the good news. He will tell Vladimir that you came to Myrtle Beach with the duffel bag, and contacted him to tell him how you escaped because you didn't trust the men who were holding you. It's perfect. You take the car and the duffel bag to Vladimir, and he thinks that he can escape clean and free. New car, new identities, new everything. Once you are there, you can offer him advice about Suzanna; maybe talk him into leaving her. Either way, we have the house surrounded. If anything and I mean anything happens, we will be there to protect you. Our main objective is to get Suzanna out of the house safely, of course, as long as she isn't dead already."

Petra sat silently on the porch, staring as far away in the distance as she could. The plan made perfect sense, and she marveled out how smart the officers were. The police in her home town could never have come up with an idea as good as this on such short notice; nor would they be inclined to protect her or be as reassuring and comforting as Gabby and Judith had been. She thought to herself that maybe this is why Americans used the police so often, because the police really were caring and trustworthy. She thought about Suzanna and tried to picture her face. There was a chance she was still alive, but after everything that had probably been done to her, she might not even want to live. That is exactly how she felt only hours ago. Still, she remembered the promise that she had made to herself, and knew in her heart that she would be coming face to face with Vladimir soon. She would suck up her fear, swallow it, try to rescue Suzanna, and hope that she came out alive. Everyone sat in silence watching her think about the plan. Finally, she spoke, but didn't look at anyone directly.

"Ok, I will help her. But promise me one thing." Gabby nodded in response. "I have saved some money for my family, and I have no way of sending it to them. Promise me that if he kills me, you will send my family the money. I have all the papers on the account hidden in my apartment in Orange Beach."

Gabby nodded and said, "Absolutely, sweetheart, and thank you." She squeezed her hand and gave her a hug. Judith was already speed dialing Hank's phone number. Time was of the essence, and they had to find out what to do next. All of a sudden, Lanka spoke up. "Hey, I have a good idea! Ivan was probably looking for a car that belonged to a Czech person so it wouldn't be reported stolen. I have a car! You can use my car! I want to help in any way that I can."

Judith was waiting for Hank to pick up. She looked at Lanka and asked, "What kind of car do you have?"

"A 1995 blue Dodge Neon."

Hank answered the phone and Judith gave him the news. "It's a go. She is ready. What are we supposed to do now?"

Hank gave the thumbs up to Dell and the other officers crouching near; he carefully backed out of the trees and then quickly walked to the next street over. "Great! Thank you so much. Ok, here is the plan. First, we have to find a car."

"Nope, we have one. It's Lanka's, a 95' Dodge Neon. She came up with a good point. She said that Ivan was most likely looking for a car that was registered to a Czech person, so that there were no chances of it being reported stolen. It's perfect."

"Are you serious?" Hank's excitement grew. "Are the windows tinted?"

"Oh, uh, hold on a sec." She asked Lanka and the response was no. "No, sorry, they aren't."

"Ok, that's fine; we can tint them quickly with film, not a problem. Ok, now that that's taken care of, all we need to do is have the roommate call him back with the news that Petra has contacted him and they have a car ready. Put Gabby on the phone. I am going to let her talk to Dell.

Judith handed the phone to her and Gabby said, "Yeah."

Dell took the phone from Hank and said, "Alright, Gabby, we need you to get Petra over to the house that we are holding Ivan's roommate in. I also need you to have an officer follow Lanka to her house, tint her windows and bring the car to Petra."

"Gotcha. What's Ivan's address?"

Dell gave her the address, confirmed the details and hung up. Hank nodded his head at him and smiled. "I think this is going to work." He looked in the direction of the ugly green house. "Ok, Suzanna here we come, and God help you, Vladimir!" They called the officers who were holding the roommate and relayed the plan. Twenty minutes later, after the Russian was prepped and ready, and Petra was seated next to him at the kitchen table, Vladimir's cell phone began to ring.

CHAPTER FIFTY-NINE

Almost an hour had passed since the two officers had shown up at the front door asking if anyone had seen Vladimir. For thirty minutes, the house had been dead silent. Vladimir and his driver had crouched silently beside the window, watching for any strange movements in the neighborhood. The two Czech men had returned to their safety net in the bathroom shower, and Mirek and Suzanna were still locked up inside their separate closets, wondering when their last breath would finally arrive. Vladimir suspected something, especially when Ivan didn't answer his cell phone. Everything around him felt bad, wrong, like some terrible pressure of air was building up around him, weighing him down and robbing him of his sanity. Finally, after what seemed like an eternity, his cell phone rang, causing him and his driver to jump nearly out of their skin. He looked at the phone's screen and saw Ivan's number. Usually, he would have answered the phone with a string of curses and promises to kill him, but this time the number pictured on his screen flooded him with relief. He flipped it open and whispered into the receiver in Russian, "Ivan, tell me you have my car. Get me the fuck out of this place! Two policemen came to the door about an hour ago, asking about me! What the fuck? And then you don't answer your phone!"

The FBI agent who spoke Russian had arrived earlier and now sat next to the Roommate, listening to his every word to make sure that he didn't say anything to alert Vladimir. The roommate answered back in Russian, "Sorry, I was busy fixing everything. Yes, the car is ready, and this is your lucky day, my friend! You are not going to believe who showed up in Myrtle Beach to help you!" He paused to allow Vladimir to respond but received nothing but dead silence. He and everyone else in the room flinched with anxiety at the pause.

Finally, Vladimir whispered harshly into the phone, trying to keep his voice down, in case there were people watching the house. "Well? You idiot! Are you going to tell me or what?"

A sigh of relief broke out in waves across the room, and the roommate never missed a beat. "Yes, of course. It's Petra. She came to help. Petra is here. She says that she ran away from the house because she didn't trust them. She says that she watched Mirek hide the duffel bag and was afraid that they were all attempting to conspire against you. She called me, trying to find out how to get in touch with you. She brought the bag and its contents here so you can escape. Everything is here. I checked it already."

Vladimir's face lit up in a devilish grin. He sighed in satisfaction and nodded at the driver. He couldn't believe that Petra had actually escaped on his behalf, not to mention the fact that she came looking to help him. Ivan's words were true; his luck was unbelievable. If he wasn't so desperate, he would have immediately questioned it with doubt and suspicion. But the only thing on his mind was escaping Myrtle Beach and starting over. Now, he had a car, a new identity, and a chance to start over. "I always knew that she was a loyal one. That is why I hired her to watch the Orange Beach office. Send her to me now and make sure that she brings the documents! And hurry!"

Vladimir stood half way up, out of the crouching position, and then sat on the floor to flex his legs. He repeated everything to the driver, and then leaned back against the wall to contemplate his next moves. Should he kill Mirek now? Or leave and have someone else do it? Should he take Suzanna with him or leave her here to die with Mirek? He wanted to take her with him and rape and kill her, just so he could have the pleasure of slapping the police in the face, and punishing her for her husband's stupidity. But the more he thought about her being in the car with him, he realized that she would be too much of a liability. He also knew that she was in the closet listening to every word that he said to his driver. Even though she couldn't understand Russian, he wanted to make sure that she didn't have the capability to tell the police anything about him. He crawled on all fours to the closet door and slowly opened them. Naked and bound, Suzanna stared back at him with the eyes of a lost soul waiting to be taken to the next life. Even if the rope that tied her ankles to her neck was removed, she couldn't run away. The muscles in her legs were so cramped that they were numb from the lack of blood circulation. She just lay there in total submission. After Vladimir was sure that she was still tied up and helpless, he closed the closet doors again. There were more important things to do at the moment, besides feeding his evil desires. He had to get ready to go. His time had come, and Petra would be here any minute. He would have Ivan send someone else here to do his dirty work minutes after he was gone. Everyone who he would leave behind, including his own driver, would be bleeding from fresh bullet holes in their heads before he was out of the city limits.

CHAPTER SIXTY

Vladimir walked to the bathroom and ordered the two Czech men to go to the bedroom with his driver. Then he set out to change his appearance. First, he shaved his head. Then he rubbed bleach that he found underneath the sink into his eyebrows to turn them blonde. Since he hadn't shaved in several days, he now had a growth of hair on his face. He shaved it into a stylish goatee and bleached it to match his eyebrows. Satisfied with his new appearance, he returned to the bedroom and found new clean clothes and a pair of reading glasses that belonged to one of the Czech men. He put them on, along with a dress shirt and a pair of blue jeans, and stared at himself in the dresser mirror. For kicks, he reopened the doors of the closet to reveal himself to Suzanna. He kicked at her and laughed. "What do you think of me now bitch? You think I look sexy?" The driver laughed at his humor while the Czech guys sat nervously in the path of his loaded gun. They didn't say a word, but looked on in horror at the naked and bleeding girl tied up on the floor of their closet. The way her legs were tied to her neck left nothing sacred hidden, and it was the most grotesque display that either one of them had ever witnessed. Both of them turned their heads, looked down at the floor and closed their eyes so they wouldn't have to look at her anymore. She wasn't even aware that they were in the room. All she saw was Vladimir's evil face. There was nothing he could do to change or hide that; no amount of bleach or shaving could erase the evil from his smile.

Suddenly, the doorbell rang and the driver abruptly stopped laughing; he quickly returned to the window with his gun. Then he turned his head toward Vladimir and smiled. "She's here."

"Good. Let her stand there for a minute. Look around, does everything look ok? Does she look nervous? Did anyone follow her?"

The driver surveyed the situation quickly and said, "No, no one else is out there, and she is just staring at the door. Let's get the fuck out of here!"

242

Vladimir nodded and let him exit the room first. "You answer the door and make sure everything is ok. Then let her in, only if you think she is by herself, and make sure she has my stuff!"

"Ok." He walked to the door and opened it slowly. Petra stood in front of him, smiling back. On her shoulder was the duffel bag stuffed with its contents. He nodded at her, glanced both ways down the street and then nodded to Vladimir in the hallway. "Come in." On her way in, he grabbed the bag and roughly removed it from her shoulder, looked inside, closed it back and took it to Vladimir. Petra, for the most part was ignored. Doing exactly what Hank and Dell had told her to do, she took a couple of steps into the living room so that the officers hiding in the utility van across the street could plainly see her through the holes in the blinds. Standing there she gave them the sign that everything was ok by placing both hands on her hips; she wondered how stupid Vladimir had to be not to be suspicious of the van. When he came out of the hallway and stood in front of her, she knew instantly that it wasn't stupidity that deterred his judgment. One look at his face told her that Vladimir was going insane with fear, and that his judgment was clouded only because he was like a rat backed into a corner. His eyes were wild, and she watched in amazement at the transformation that had occurred; not the bleach job or his shaved head, but at the complete change in personality. Anytime she had been around Vladimir, he had always been totally calm, smooth and confident, in total control of himself and those around him. Now, he stood in the kitchen ignoring her and the open window, haphazardly plucking things out of the duffel bag like a child on Christmas morning searching through the contents of his stuffed stocking.

When he finally found a driver's license that suited him, he threw the contents back into the bag. Only then did he acknowledge Petra standing in the living room. When he looked at her, it sent chills up her spine, and she fought with everything she had within her to not vomit on his feet with fear.

He came to her and placed her face roughly in his hands, squeezing her cheeks a little too harshly to be considered nice. "Ah, Petra. I doubted you, you know? I thought surely when you escaped out of the utility shed that you're loyalty to me had failed. Pretty clever if I do say so myself. Hmmm? But Ivan tells me that you were running away from those men. Did they hurt you badly?" He slowly slid his hands from her face to her breasts, cupping them slowly, feeling her chest rise and fall rapidly from the blood that coursed quickly through her veins. He stood there admiring all of her bruises and cuts.

She stammered, unable to speak, and looked away. He removed one hand from her breast and squeezed her face again, bringing it back up to meet his stare. Still fondling her, a little more harshly this time, he continued to question her. "What did they do to you? Hmmm? Tell me how they hurt you so I can punish them." His hand left her face and wondered across her chest and slowly down to the waistline of her pants. She couldn't speak. Her tongue stuck to the roof of her mouth and fear welled up inside of her. Vladimir lost his patience and pushed her back onto the couch. He and the driver laughed at her as she struggled to get back on her feet. Finally, anger took over and allowed her tongue to move. She answered him. "Vladimir, you know I have always been loyal to you! How many years have I worked for you? Have I not done everything you ever asked of me? Yes, they hurt me, and for what? I knew that you were in trouble so I let them hurt me. I knew it was important to get back to where Mirek hid your things. I waited until it was all over, and I escaped. I didn't trust them. And so, here I am, ready to help you. But you must go now. The police are looking everywhere for you. It's all over the news."

Her words jerked Vladimir back to reality, and he turned around to say something to his driver. She stood up in front of the window again with both hands on her hips so the officers in the van could clearly see her. It was just in time, too. The officers had seen Vladimir fondle her and push her down onto the couch. They were forming a plan to bust into the house when she had stood up again, giving them the signal that everything was ok.

Vladimir spoke briefly to his driver in Russian, and then motioned Petra to follow him to the back of the house. Hank had told her that there was a possibility that this would happen, and that if she willingly left the window, they would wait; but if they saw him force her, they would raid the house immediately. Ultimately, they had left the decision up to her. Now, she stood, wondering what she should do. Leave the safety net of the window, or follow him down the hallway to some unknown fate. Finally, she walked, hoping that she would see Suzanna alive. Vladimir walked into a bedroom at the end of a hallway and told her to come in. There she saw two very frightened men on the floor beside the bed and blood smeared on the sheets, but no Suzanna. The blood, although it wasn't a lot, immediately made her suspect that Suzanna had been raped and disposed of already.

"Get on the floor." Vladimir pointed to a space beside the two Czech men.

Petra swallowed hard and struggled to think of something to say. "Umm, I am not going with you?"

He laughed and pointed his gun at her. "What, do you think I am crazy? Get on the fucking floor."

She fought the tears back and sat beside one of the Czech men. Vladimir turned his attention to his driver and told him to watch them. Then he dialed Ivan's cell phone. Across town, the agents and officers exchanged glances and gave the go ahead nod to the roommate to answer the phone. "Hello."

"Petra is here. I have everything. I am leaving now. Five minutes from now, send someone to clean up. There are five people, two in closets, and three on the bedroom floor. I want them disposed of immediately and the house wiped down. I will call you when I get to New York." Petra started crying in relief when she heard that he wasn't going to shoot her before he left. Vladimir knew she could understand a little Russian and thought she was crying in despair. It made him happy to hear her sobs. He grabbed a jacket that he had laid out before on the bed, made sure his gun was fully loaded, grabbed the duffel bag and walked towards the door with his driver. He instructed his driver to cover for him until he got to the car, then to go back into the house and wait for someone to join him so they could "clean up".

From inside the van, members of the SWAT team watched Vladimir as he walked through the house. They radioed the other members surrounding the house. Their fear all along had been that he would leave with a hostage, making it difficult to bring him down before he left in the car. They couldn't believe their luck when he exited alone with another man who was leading the way with a gun at his side. As soon as they had opened the front door the officers had given a signal, and Hank and Dell ran around the side of the house towards the front door while others moved to block the Russians from the car. Unfortunately, the signal had been given a second too early and all hell broke loose.

The driver spotted Hank first and spun around to fire off a shot. Hank returned fire and hit the driver in the leg, causing him to fall backwards up the front steps. His huge body formed a barrier wall for Vladimir to hide behind, and the confusion and gunfire gave them just enough time to duck and swing the front door back open. Dell opened fire at the front door, splintering the casing, and missing Vladimir by a millimeter. The door slammed shut and the Russians were back in the house.

"Hold your fire!" screamed Dell. Everyone concentrated on the living room window, but the two Russians had already fled towards the back of the house.

CHAPTER SIXTY-ONE

He ran through the bedroom door like a wild animal being hunted, tore open the closet door and grabbed at Suzanna. In the few minutes that Vladimir was gone, no one in the room had yet spoken, and Petra didn't know that Suzanna was in the closet. When the doors were jerked open and she saw the naked woman lying on the floor, her stomach lurched and she vomited all over herself and the two Czechs who were crouched on the floor beside her. Cursing herself for trusting the police, Petra covered her eyes and face with her hands and began to sob loudly. Ripping and cutting away at the rope that bound Suzanna, Vladimir was screamed in Russian, cursing everyone and everything. He flung her to her feet, but she couldn't stand on her own. The driver, who had taken a bullet in the leg and was now bleeding freely through his pants, picked her up and threw her over his shoulder, popping her collarbone in the process. Even though she was gagged and her jaw was broken, everyone in the room heard her scream out in pain through the tightly twisted fabric. Vladimir's mouth was covered with spit and sweat which gave him the appearance of a rabid dog. He pistol whipped one of the Czech guys, and then shot him in the head. The one Czech guy remaining on the floor was the one who had tipped off the police. He begged for mercy and got a swift hard kick to the mouth instead; he lay unconscious on the floor. Vladimir yelled at Petra to stand up and then looked at the driver. "You take Petra, and I will take Suzanna! They will not shoot us if we have them!" He cursed himself for being so stupid and grabbed Suzanna down from his driver's shoulders.

They dragged the women to the front door, and kicked it open. Hank and Dell were across the street behind the van with guns pointed at the door, and the rest of the officers were scattered around the property, ready to shoot at any minute. When they saw the driver first come out with Petra, the tension rose. They all knew that there was a possibility that it would come down to this, even though they had all assured her of her safety. But when Vladimir walked out with what was left of Suzanna Novacek, Hank's heart sank. The sight of her instantly brought tears to his eyes. She had been beaten almost beyond recognition, and stripped of any clothing. He pressed his lips together and watched helplessly as she was dragged through the dirt towards Lanka's car. Someone from the police force tried to talk calmly to the Russians through a megaphone, but it was of no use. The men ignored him and made their way slowly across the small yard towards their get away car.

 "Hold your fire!" was heard several times. The last thing that the Myrtle Beach police department wanted was a huge shootout in a residential neighborhood. Knowing that he was unable to help, Hank shook his head at the scene and watched. He steadily kept his gun pointed at the head of Vladimir and waited, hoping for something to happen that would stop them from leaving. As if on cue, the Russian driver lost control of the leg that had been shot, stumbled, and fell hard to the ground. As he fell, he lost his grip on Petra and his gun; since they were all walking close together toward the car, Vladimir tripped on him and fell as well. He landed hard, let go of Suzanna and immediately raised his gun back up. He pointed it at Petra who was reaching for the driver's gun that had fallen at her feet. Everyone was screaming, "No! Stop! Don't shoot!" But the actions had already fallen into place. Petra bent over to grab the gun and just as Vladimir pressed his finger to the trigger, Hank focused, aimed and shot Vladimir. The bullet raced through the air and made its new home in his left temple. Upon impact, Vladimir's finger found the trigger of his own gun and pressed, sending one bullet into Petra. Everyone rushed the Russians and the women. Sirens went off, radios screeched, and the paramedics who had parked down the street screeched to a halt in front of the little green house.

 Hank got to the women first. He knelt down beside Petra and saw where the bullet had entered. She nodded weakly up at him as a paramedic applied some pressure to the bullet wound. She had been shot in the shoulder, the bullet missing her heart by several inches. Hank turned his attention to Suzanna, who lay crying in the dirt. She couldn't speak, and even if she could there would be no words for her to say. The look in her eyes spoke volumes, and Hank wept as another team of paramedics placed her onto a stretcher and rushed her to the emergency room across town.

Vladimir was as dead as dead could be. Hank had delivered a perfect shot to the temple, and he lay on the ground in a puddle of his own brains.

The Russian driver was still alive, shouting and yelling in Russian as the officers placed handcuffs around his wrists. The scene was a nightmare. Television crews had arrived by car and by helicopter, and officers were now entering the house to check if anyone was still alive. There they found Mirek still tied to a chair in the closet, holding on to life by a string. They also found the dead Czech man and his friend, still lying unconscious in a coma from the blow to his head. Petra was lying on a stretcher when they pulled Mirek out of the house. As Hank watched everything unfold, he noticed Petra wildly waving at him from her stretcher and pointing to Mirek. He ran over to her so he could hear what she was trying to say.

"That is him! That is Yuraslav's partner! He helped kill dat family! Don't let him go! Don't let him go!" Petra pleaded through sobs.

Hank quickly shouted the information to the other officers, and Mirek was promptly handcuffed to his stretcher. It took about thirty minutes to remove everyone from the house and secure the scene, and by that time, Hank had had enough drama for one day. Exhausted, he sat in the surveillance van and dialed Hillary's number in Orange Beach. She answered on the first ring.

"Hey, we are watching the news! I was just getting ready to call you."

Hank sighed into the phone and said, "It's over, Hill. We got them. Call Ed Morrison and Suzanna's parents and tell them the news."

"Hank, are you ok?"

There was a silence for a minute and he choked up. A full minute passed before he could answer her. "No, Hill, I am not ok. You should see what they did to her." Hank shook his head and fought his tears from falling.

"But she is alive, right?"

"Barely."

"Well, that's good enough for me. Hank, she will be ok. Bruises go away. You saved her!"

Hank scratched the top of his head and let out a long breath. He had escaped crying for now, but knew it would come later when he was all alone. "Yeah, I know. I will call you later."

He pressed the end button and immediately dialed Judith's number. She answered on the first ring. "My God, Hank, are you ok? We are watching the television right now. Is everybody ok?"

"Yes, Petra was shot in the shoulder and Suzanna, well, she is still alive, but to what extent, I don't know. She looks bad…she looks real bad."

"Oh my God, I was so worried! Are you going to the station now?" Judith was worried sick. Hank was pitiful.

"Nope, I am coming to see you. I am done with this case. I need to lie down for a while, and then I guess I am going to the hospital."

"Ok, Hank. I will be right here waiting for you."

Dell was standing near the van waiting for Hank to emerge. He offered his hand to him and smiled. Hank took his hand and they shook,

exchanging thanks and wrapping up the ordeal. Finally, they let go of each other's hands, and Hank walked down the street towards his car. He would give his statement later, but for right now, he needed to get away and see Judith. On the way to her parent's house, he thought about Suzanna, Petra, and little Anna who was still recovering from her assault. He thought about her family, and all of the Czech people who had found themselves trapped in Vladimir's web, and wondered how some people could be so cruel and evil in this world. He had always known it was out there, but it had never landed on his front porch before. When he pulled into the Esther's driveway, Judith was waiting outside for him. She saw the sad look on his face and opened her arms to him, hugging him tightly until he felt like letting go.

CHAPTER SIXTY-TWO

Judith walked Hank to the guest house and ran him a bath. He was silent and thoughtful. It was unlike Hank not to talk to her, so she guessed that what he had seen at the little green house had just been too much for him to put into words at the moment. Judith did not press him. She could only imagine what the scene had actually been like, and totally respected his need for silence. He sat on the edge of the guest bed with his head in his hands, saying nothing.

After she finished running his water, she tiptoed to where he was sitting, kissed his forehead and said, "Take your bath. It will make you feel so much better. I will be back in a little while, and then maybe when you feel like it, I will drive you over to the hospital. It's only about five minutes from here." Hank nodded at her and rose to take his bath. Judith watched as he rounded the corner, and then slipped out the front door to go back to her mother's kitchen where she was waiting for her.

Marie was waiting by the window, lips pressed together in a worried frown. "Well, honey, how is he? Did he tell you what happened? Is he hungry?"

Judith slumped down in a chair at the kitchen table with a soft thump and placed her chin on top of her folded hands. She looked at her mother and gave her a worried smile. "No. I can tell you that I am sure that he is not hungry. Whatever he saw go down at that house has him pretty shaken up."

Marie looked disapprovingly at her daughter. "Well, if he is that upset, then why in the hell are you sitting in here? When a man is openly upset, that means he needs to be comforted...by a woman."

Judith stared outside the window at the guest house. "Well, Mom, we aren't exactly at that stage yet."

Marie rolled her eyes and sat down at the kitchen table. "Well, just exactly what stage do you think you're at with him? You've already slept with him. The least you could do is go over there and comfort him!"

Judy jerked her eyes at her mother in disbelief. "Mom! I can't believe you just said that! How do you know if we have slept together or not?"

Marie stood up from the table and gave her daughter a wink. "Oh, for heaven's sake, Judy Booty, it's not as if I was born yesterday, nor did I fall off the turnip truck. I have seen the way you two look at each other, and that look only comes from knowing each other's holy places. So get up and go over there and console your man!"

Judith, still in disbelief at her mother's candor and brutal honesty, slowly rose from the table and made her way back to the guest house. She found Hank sitting on the edge of the bed again, crying into his hands. He looked up at her, wiped the tears from his face and said, "Thank you for coming back. I haven't taken that bath yet."

Judith sat next to him and guided him down to the bed, and they lay there in each other's arms for a long time. Finally, Hank calmed down and looked at her. "Alright, I am fine now. I really needed to get that out of my system. Oh my God, she looked horrible. And she was totally naked." He paused for a moment before going on. "I don't know what all they did to her, but it was all my fault. I should have never left her at that hotel in Gulf Shores by herself."

Judith shushed him. "Hank, honey, it's not all your fault. It's not your fault at all! And, it's over. Thanks to you, she got out of there alive and is in safe hands. Let's go to the hospital and find out about her condition, ok? You alright with that? I think it would help you if you found out what her injuries are. I used to work there before I moved to Gulf Shores, and I still know people. C'mon, let's go."

When they arrived at the hospital, they had to fight their way through the mass of people in the lobby who had shown up to get details about the girls. Fortunately, once they made their way through the largest group of people, one of the nurses running by recognized Judith, waved at her, and pulled her through the doors that led into the belly of the hospital. Security guards had been posted there and the nurse had to assure them that they were ok. Hank flipped out his badge, and they were finally let through. Once inside the interior of the hospital, Judith asked the nurse about Suzanna and Petra.

The nurse, who was still walking quickly through the halls said, "Oh my God! It's been so long since I have seen you. I am on my way to surgery now, and I am in kind of a hurry, but the official word is that they will both be fine. One girl was shot in the shoulder. She lost a lot of blood, but she will be fine. The other girl was beat up pretty bad, though." Hank cringed and waited to hear more. "At first they were scared of internal bleeding. They found none. Basically, she has a bad concussion that has affected her hearing; that will go away with time. Her collar bone is broken in two places, and her jaw is broken; they'll have to wire that shut. As for the rest of her injuries, its mostly just bad bruises and cuts, that will heal pretty quickly. She stopped walking when they got to the doors that led to surgery, and turned quickly to hug Judith. "Sorry, I gotta go. It was really great to see you!" She was just getting ready to disappear through the door when Hank reached out to stop her.

"I have one quick question. Umm, was she raped?"

The nurse shook her head at him and as she walked through the doors she called back to him, "Rape test came back negative!" Then she was gone.

Hank let out a sigh of relief and looked down at Judith. "That's what I really wanted to know."

Judith nodded slowly at him, wrapped her arms around his waist and buried her face in her chest. "I know." It had been weighing on her mind as well. It was finally over.

CHAPTER SIXTY-THREE

The next day, Hank and Judith said goodbye to her family, and Lanka, whom the Esther's now regarded as a daughter of their own. They stopped by the station so Hank could give his statement, said goodbye to Dell, and then made their way to the hospital where Suzanna and Petra both lay in recovery from their operations. The bullet had successfully been removed from her shoulder, and Suzanna's jaw, collarbone, and other various injuries had been addressed. The girls had been placed in the same room, and even though Suzanna couldn't talk or move much, she was very much aware of everything that was going on around her. Hank and Judith entered the room and talked with the girls for about an hour. Suzanna wrote "Thank You" on a piece of paper and pushed it towards them, and then wrote another one for Petra. With her mouth wired shut, it was all she could do at the moment to express her gratitude. Hank hugged her, folded the piece of paper up and placed it into his wallet. He never threw it away.

Then, they called Sammy Perdue, who was waiting patiently at the airport, to make sure he was ready to fly them home. He gave them a big "Hell yeah!" over the phone, and slapped Hank hard on the back when they arrived.

"Well, Hank, you got them son of a bitches, didn't ya? I tell you one thing, damn it, if it was left up to me, there ain't no limits to the sufferin' that I would put on them boys. That dammed Russian and Czech. If you ask me, that Vladimir piece a shit got what was comin to him, but he got it too soon. He should have been put through some real ringers before eatin' that bullet. But, I guess, on the flip side o' that, he's got all of eternity to answer for what he's done. I don't expect the Devil's gonna give too much room to do anything but sit there and fry like a piece o' bacon. I'm proud of you, son! Real proud!"

Hank rolled his eyes at Judith who was already cracking up at the Sammy's evaluation of the situation and what should be done to the thugs. When they entered the jet, Sammy was still telling them exactly what he would do if he was in charge of their punishments while he walked around the plane doing his last minute checks before they took off. Hank shut the door and fell into the seat beside Judith. They kissed, on and off, throughout the whole flight. He knew that once he landed in Gulf Shores, he was going to have to deal with the war that had been brewing between the police force and Suzanna's parents; he, of course, would be front and center taking the heat. But, for right now, he pushed it from his mind and concentrated on the best thing that had ever happened to him in his life, Dr. Judith Esther.

When they landed, Hillary and the rest of the department were waiting for them on the tarmac, clapping and whistling. Hank stood up in the open door of the jet and waved back. On the way down the stairs, he looked back at Judith who was flushed with embarrassment from all of the people cheering them. "Hey, I have an idea. You wanna go fishing?"

Judith smiled at him and took his outstretched hand.

Please turn the page for a preview of Ryan Anderson's next novel,

The Artist

…….coming soon

CHAPTER ONE

In the early morning hours of August 29, 2005, one of the worst known natural disasters in the history of the United States made landfall. She hit the Gulf Coast with so much crippling, devastating vengeance that the world sat watching with their mouths open in horror, speechless at what Mother Nature had deemed necessary to do. Hurricane Katrina blew into New Orleans from the Gulf of Mexico with such an awesome force of winds and water that some of the levees holding in the contents of Lake Ponchatrain broke, drowning houses, cars, buildings and people who either couldn't or wouldn't heed the warnings and flee to higher ground or evacuate. This unforgiving fury of wind and water left behind an endless stream of debris and damage that would take years to clean and repair. Its impact on the current American way of life affected everyone, in all states. Human suffering reached phenomenal records. The Superdome was designated as the number one hurricane shelter. For those people who were not fortunate enough to make it there or find a way out of town in the days before Katrina made landfall, death by flooding or life by clutching the remnants of rooftops became their only options.

The Big Easy would no longer be the same, in more ways than one. Not only did it destroy lives, property, and historical buildings, but it also unleashed a human evil that the Gulf Coast wasn't totally aware of or prepared for. Katrina flushed this evil out of his hiding hole, the one he had relied on for two decades to feed his wicked hunger and desire. He couldn't swim. He never tried to learn. He knew the consequences of staying in his small house east of Bourbon Street, but didn't care. He knew he would survive. All of the years that he had spent in New Orleans had been a hell of a lot more dangerous to his life than a hurricane could ever propose, so he had made his mind up to hunker down and take all of the ripping abuse that Katrina could give him. By the time the hurricane had passed, seventy five percent of his beloved city was under water, including his own house. When it had become too much for him to handle, he had calmly climbed out of the upstairs window and pulled himself and a red waterproof duffle bag onto his roof. There, for quite some time, he hugged the roof and dug his fingernails into the shingles that were blowing off by the minute.

After the winds calmed down just enough for him to look around and let go of the roof with one hand, he quickly reached into the red bag, and retrieved a plastic bag. The bag contained an assortment of severed decomposed fingers, credit cards and driver's licenses, locks of hair, and several undergarments. These things were very dear to him; they were his collection of favorites, the ones that had really made a difference in his life. Gazing upon each item one last time, he remembered every detail of his collection, and how he had obtained them. Then, he threw them one by one, into the wind and rising water. He chose to treat this as a sacrificial ceremony. Hurricane Katrina had washed him completely clean, giving him a brand new life, and he was extremely thankful.

During the hours that he had spent on the roof top, he had plenty of time to think about his next move. He made up his mind about something that had been a pressing issue for sometime, decided to leave town as soon as the storm was over. His darling New Orleans would not be the same for a long time, maybe ever; and besides, with all of the damage and debris, police and security would be everywhere, imposing curfews, rules and regulations. He wouldn't be able to get done what he needed to do, so he decided to leave and make a new home for himself.

For several months the need to flee town had weighed heavily upon him. Years ago, he had exhausted the whores and prostitutes of Bourbon Street, and had carefully and methodically turned to the young, established but lonely young women of the Big Easy to feed his hunger, finely tuning the art of what he did. Although these women had been a more fulfilling prey than the prostitutes in his early years had been, they brought along a far worse liability than he had first imagined. People missed them and searched for them. They were loved; the prostitutes were not. Over the years, the police caught on to similar patterns of several of the murders, formed a profile with the help of the

FBI, and hunted him desperately. So far, he had been able to evade their grasp easily, simply by being the private man he had always been and also by killing in different ways and patterns. No one really knew him, liked him, disliked him, or thought about him. However, the media coverage of his work had become, in the last year, too public for his comfort. Months before Hurricane Katrina hit, he had researched many small towns and cities across the South East, looking for a new place to live, and one place in particular kept perfectly popping up in his plans.

There on his ruined rooftop, in the midst of one of the worst hurricanes to ever hit the United States, he watched dead bodies and debris float by as he made his final decision. He would wait until his rescue, and move to Orange Beach, Alabama. Not too far away, not too close, not too small, and not too big. It was perfect. Hours later, rescue teams arrived by boat and helicopter. Ignoring the stares and questions of the rescue team, he laughed out loud maniacally as they harnessed his body and lowered him into the safety boat. The rescuers figured that his close encounter with death, while witnessing the drowned bodies that were floating down the flooded street of the poverty ridden residential area, was probably enough to make this lone man laugh with hysteria. They never gave him, or his large red waterproof bag a single thought as they whisked the boat away in the direction of another rooftop that housed another family of five in need.

CHAPTER TWO

Almost one year after Hurricane Katrina massacred the Gulf Coast, Detective Hank Jordan found himself miserably fishing on the bay down Fort Morgan instead of his beloved pier in Gulf Shores. The pier had been completely destroyed by Hurricane Ivan in 2004, and the politics of the state of Alabama had so far made it impossible to build back. He could always fish the Perdido Pass in Orange Beach, but it was usually too crowded for his comfort. He was daydreaming of the days when he used to hook some live bait, and cast it out into the calm waters circling the end of the Alabama State pier, when, suddenly, he realized he had just hooked a Redfish. While he was reeling it in, his cell phone rang. The ring tone let him know that his partner, Hillary, was calling him with urgent news. Unable to reel in the fish and answer the phone call at the same time, he quickly cut the line, let the fish go, and opened his cell phone.

He sighed in disgust as Hillary told him the bad news. "Hank, this is pretty ugly down here. A couple of teenage kids found her in the dunes behind the Pelican Perch condominium complex. She is around 30 years old, wearing a wedding band on the only finger she has left, and ligature marks all the way around her neck."

Hank put his hand up to his forehead to wipe off the beads of sweat and gazed at the horizon. "Is the one finger left printable?"

"What do you think? Of course not. The pad was sliced off."

"Is she wearing any clothes?"

"Well, she is wearing a white sheet now, but, no, she was found naked."

"Alright. I will be there in about twenty minutes, Hill. I'm way down Fort Morgan fishing, but I am packing up right now."

Hank sat down on the grassy bank and began to gather up his fishing equipment. Taped to the inside of his tackle box was a picture of a child named Anna Morrison, and Hank took a moment to look at the child's face before he closed the lid. Anna was the sole survivor of her family, who had been brutally murdered in Orange Beach. Hank had been close to the family, and still visited with Anna as often as he could. Although several years had passed since the murders had taken place, the investigation was still fresh in Hank's mind; he was not looking forward to another one. Since then, Orange Beach had been at peace, except for the occasional bar fight between a drunken tourist and an even drunker local. A couple of illegal Mexican migrant workers had died on one of the oil rigs off the coast, but other than that, the sleepy little fishing village had been just that, sleepy and content.

Now, Hank Jordan had the dead body of an unidentified naked woman in the dunes of a condominium complex packed with tourists. Whoever the killer was, he wasn't stupid. He had made the effort to stall the identification of his victim by removing all but one finger, then slicing off the pad of the remaining one. They would have to rely on dental records to identify her, and that would take longer.

Hank loaded up his fishing rods and tackle box, threw out the rest of his live bait, and headed toward Orange Beach. On the way, he called the manager of the Pelican Perch Condominiums to let him know that he was on his way, and to ask him if he or anyone at the complex had reported anything or anyone unusual in the past twenty four hours. The manager had no information to give him, but he was desperate for the body to be removed. His vacationers were calling his office every second, demanding to be moved to Pelican Perch 2 in Gulf Shores, about ten minutes away, which was already packed. The local media was swarming the lobby of the office, and people were packing the beach, rubbernecking through the sea oats of the dunes and the police tape as much as they could for a glimpse of the dead woman.

When Hank arrived at the scene, the teenagers who had the misfortune of finding the body were still being questioned by the police. There were four of them, a brother and sister and two guys whom they had made friends with while on vacation. They had been throwing a Frisbee on the beach when the wind caught it and blew it into the dunes. The girl had run after it. While searching for the lost Frisbee, she had tripped on the dead woman's left arm. She now sat in the sand, shaking and crying hysterically while her parents and Hillary tried to console her. Her brother and his two friends were trying to appear unaffected and tough, but everyone knew they were all horrified as well.

Hank elbowed his way through the gawking tourists, stepped over the police tape and knelt down beside the dead woman. Blocking the view with his own body to make sure no one could see in, he removed the white sheet to see what she looked like. She was beautiful, even in death. There was dried blood caked around the stubs of what used to be her fingers, around what appeared to be stab wounds, and also between her thighs. He wouldn't know for sure until after her autopsy, but it looked like she had been stabbed, raped, and strangled to death. He shook his head in disgust at what a human could do to another human, and thought about Judith, his fiancée. Shuddering slightly at the morbid vision of something like this happening to her, he blocked her from his mind, finished examining the body, and walked away.

He was heading out of the dunes when something caught his eye a couple of feet away from the body. It looked like a leather strap, maybe from a belt or a purse sticking out of the sand. Hank tugged on the strap and pulled out a purse that had been buried only three or four inches in the sand. On closer glance, it turned out to be a satchel rather than a purse, made of soft suede. He opened the flap and peered inside. The satchel contained nothing but a single sheet of paper labeled picnic, and a list of items. All of the items but three had been circled. Hank stared at the sheet of paper for a couple of minutes, and finally waved over some officers to show them what he had found. It was no coincidence; the satchel had to be either the dead woman's or the killer's.

Hank walked down to the beach as the coroner took pictures and loaded her body into an ambulance that was backed up to the dunes. The sun had already begun to set, and a nice breeze began to blow in from the Gulf waters. He watched two dolphins play in the distance, and thought about Judith again. He pressed her number into the cell phone, and she answered on the second ring.

"Hey, Hank! I was just getting ready to call you. A nurse from the ER just came in to the cafeteria and said that an unidentified body of a woman had been found on the beach. What in the world is going on down there?"

Hank sighed heavily. "Well, you heard right. I am here right now, just finished looking at her. It's pretty bad, not real sure what to make of it yet. They are loading her in the wagon right now." Hank paused for a second to watch the waves ripple and to think of Judith's face. "I just wanted to call you and tell you that I love you."

"You are thinking about the Morrisons, aren't you?"

Hank sighed into the cell phone. "No, not really, I was just thinking of you. This woman is wearing a wedding band, so I guess she is married. It makes me shudder to think about how her husband will feel when he finds out, that is, if he isn't the one who killed her. I just can't imagine what I would do if it were you lying there."

Judith smiled on the other line at the tenderness in her fiancée's voice. "Baby, don't worry about me. Nobody is going to get me. Go find the killer. And, I love you, too."

Hank smiled and flipped the phone shut. Tearing himself from the sun's burnt orange reflection in the ripples of the Gulf of Mexico, he slowly headed back to the crime scene to help disperse the on looking crowd.